NOTHING TO SEE HERE

Susan Lewis is the internationally bestselling author of over fifty sensational novels across the genres of family drama, thriller, suspense, crime and romance – including the Richard and Judy picks *One Minute Later* and *I Have Something to Tell You*. She is also the author of *Just One More Day* and *One Day at a Time*, the moving memoirs of her childhood in Bristol during the 1960s. Following periods of living in Los Angeles and the South of France, she currently lives in Gloucestershire with her husband, James, and their beloved, naughty little dog, Mimi.

To find out more about Susan Lewis visit:

www.susanlewis.com
 /SusanLewisBooks
 @susanlewisbooks
 @susanlewisbooks
 @susanlewisbooks

Also by Susan Lewis

SUSAN
LEWIS

NOTHING
TO SEE HERE

HarperCollins*Publishers*

HarperCollins*Publishers* Ltd
1 London Bridge Street,
London SE1 9GF

www.harpercollins.co.uk

HarperCollins*Publishers*
Macken House, 39/40 Mayor Street Upper
Dublin 1, D01 C9W8
Ireland

First published by HarperCollins*Publishers* Ltd 2024
1

A catalogue record for this book is available from the British Library

ISBN: 978-0-00-847201-6 (HB)
ISBN: 978-0-00-847202-3 (TPB)

This book is set in Sabon Lt Pro by HarperCollins*Publishers* India

Printed and Bound in the UK using 100% Renewable
Electricity at CPI Group (UK) Ltd

This book contains FSC™ certified paper and other controlled
sources to ensure responsible forest management.

For more information visit: www.harpercollins.co.uk/green

To my long-suffering and wonderfully supportive husband, James Garrett.

SIXTEEN YEARS EARLIER

It was a glorious sunny June day, just after four in the afternoon, when Flora Gibson turned her truck and trailer off a leafy lane in the Berkeley Vale into the driveway of Kellon Manse. The wooden gates were open, so nothing unusual there, and the gravelled patch just off to the right, under a giant horse chestnut, was empty, so plenty of room for her to park and unload. She was only here to do the lawns today, front and back, maybe a bit of weeding, so it shouldn't be more than an hour before she was off to her last call of the day.

What a joy it was being a gardener in this sort of weather, warm, a little breezy and full of sublime countryside sounds and smells. And so peaceful. She was already picking up a tan, and the escaped strands of her knotted flame hair were lightening by the day. She might not be a beauty – actually, with her large nose, close-set eyes and slightly jutting jaw, she was a long way short – but the goodness in her soul radiated through her gentle nature, making her a favourite with most. She was going to be twenty-five next week and Jack, her live-in partner whose dad owned the landscaping company they both worked for, had some sort of barbecue party planned. She was looking forward to it. Jack was good at parties.

It took only a few minutes to unhitch the ride-on mower, to turn it around, clamp on her earphones and get started on the Manse's left side front lawn. It was identical to the right side, with a gravelled drive surging through the centre, sloping up to the main house where Flora could see Lexie Gaudion's white Volvo in the

1

wisteria-covered carport. A blue Audi was also there, suggesting Lexie had a visitor. No doubt they were around the back enjoying a cold drink on the terrace while taking in the spectacular view. This meant Flora and her roaring engine and flying grass probably wouldn't be welcome beyond the long row of beech hedges that separated the front and back gardens. However, she hadn't received a text asking her not to come today, so she ploughed on for the time being – Lexie would pop out and let her know if she'd rather the lawns waited for another day.

Half an hour later, she'd completed both lawns and emptied the grass catcher a couple of times, and as no one had appeared to stop her, she chugged the mower through a gap in the beech hedge to go on round to the back.

No sign of anyone on the terrace, although the kitchen and sunroom doors were open so if the noise was going to be a bother she'd soon find out.

She could only dream of one day living in a house as lovely as this with its red-brick walls, black slate roof and white framed windows. It was Edwardian in style, she thought, but wasn't sure, and like many of the properties around these parts, it belonged to the Kellon Estate. Now that was an amazing house if ever there was one, Kellon Hall. Jack and his father took care of the grounds there; there was such a lot of acreage that it was a full-time job for four of their gardeners. Flora helped out from time to time, mostly with weeding and mowing and strimming. The house itself, in spite of being seriously grand and massive, was, in her humble opinion, the kind of place that appeared out of the mist in horror films. All those medieval turrets and pointy-topped window frames, not to mention the clinging ivy and poky-looking attics. Inside wasn't much better from the occasional glimpses she'd managed to sneak. All dark wood panels, towering fireplaces and scary portraits. From where she was now, behind the Manse, she could see a couple of the Hall's tallest chimneys soaring up through the treetops – unsurprising when the properties adjoined one another. Although the Hall had to be at least a quarter of a mile away.

The weird, maybe sad, part of the Hall today was that Lexie's mother, Mean Margaret, lived there all on her own. She didn't even have a Mrs Danvers to take care of her, just a few cleaners from an agency who did their stuff once a week, and the locals who came each day to muck out the stables and exercise the horses.

Finally, Flora was ready to pack up and leave.

She glanced over at the open doors, surprised and, weirdly, a little bit bothered that no one had come out. She probably ought just to mind her own business and be on her way, but for some reason she found herself going across the terrace, not sure if she thought something wasn't right, maybe just wanting to be sure nothing was wrong.

'Hello!' she called, stepping into the empty kitchen. It was seriously grand, all black granite and white wood cupboards, with a huge centre island housing a bowl of china fruit and loads of letters and colouring books, some weigh scales and some table mats with the family's names on. David, Lexie, Rosaria, Amelia. 'Anyone at home?' she shouted.

No reply.

She listened, peering down the hall towards the half-open front door. No sound of anyone chatting.

Venturing a few more steps in, she called out again. 'Lexie! Are you in here?'

Still nothing.

It occurred to her that the Audi might belong to a bloke who could be, right this minute, upstairs giving Lexie one.

Best not get involved in that, she reflected, although it would be funny to hear them at it, wouldn't it?

She moved into the hall quietly, gingerly, and looked up the stairs. No sign of anyone and no rhythmic thumping or grunting or orgasmic shrieking.

She turned back and glanced into the sitting room. That was when her heart stopped beating.

'Oh fuck! Oh God!' she choked, clapping a hand to her mouth.

For a moment she wasn't sure she was actually seeing right. It was like some sort of massacre had happened.

She began to shake uncontrollably, almost sinking to her knees, but somehow she forced herself to run before anyone realized she was there. She had to get out of here, *now*. She needed to summon help. Just please, God, don't let anyone catch her first.

PART ONE

CHAPTER ONE

TODAY (SIXTEEN YEARS LATER)

Cristy Ward was engrossed in her task and not giving a moment's thought to how she looked or was being perceived. As far as she was concerned, the fact that she was a tall, slender woman (twenty pounds lighter than she'd been prior to her ex-husband's betrayal a few years ago – at least something good had come from all that humiliation and misery) couldn't matter less. And who with more than a couple of brain cells to rub together would even care how she looked now, in her late forties? In fact, with a thick blonde-highlighted curly bob and sharp but friendly caramel-coloured eyes, she had the kind of smile that could light up a room or chill someone to the bone, depending on how she used it.

She wasn't smiling now and nothing mattered more in this moment than the case in front of her.

'It became known as the Kellon Manse Murders,' she said, glancing up from her laptop to check her audience of three was paying attention. Of course they were – they were as fascinated by this unsolved mystery as she was. How successful they were going to be in finding answers, or unearthing material, evidence even, that the police might have missed, only time would tell, but they were going to give it a damned good go.

'Three women, shot in the head from close range,' she continued, going back to her notes. 'Thirty-four-year-old Alexandra – Lexie – Gaudion; her seventy-eight-year-old mother, Margaret Sallis; and Serena Sutton, Lexie's psychotherapist and presumably friend, given she was at the house. She was forty-four at the time of the killings. I guess you remember the case?'

She was looking at Meena and Harry Quinn, technically her bosses, although as co-creator and executive producer of *Hindsight,* she, Cristy, was fully in charge of the podcast's content and direction, along with Connor Church, her partner. He might be almost twenty years her junior, but he was as invaluable to her now as he'd been during their previous lives in TV news.

'Doesn't everyone?' Harry replied, with a quick glance at his wife. They too had backgrounds in television, Harry as an editor, Meena as a researcher, same programme as Cristy and Connor – and Cristy's ex, who was actually still there. The Quinns had left their positions long before Cristy and Connor had abandoned theirs to convert the glorious old building they were now in, close to Bristol's Harbourside, into three small recording studios and various sized suites of offices. They were dear friends of Cristy's, who had helped her through some seriously difficult times over recent years – not just the break-up of her marriage, but also the loss of her beloved mother.

Flicking back her mane of luxuriant dark hair, Meena said, 'Am I right in thinking that no one was ever convicted of these murders?'

Cristy nodded. 'You are,' she confirmed. 'Connor's already put together a detailed background of the case for you to go through, but essentially Lexie's husband, David Gaudion, was set to stand trial until the case mysteriously fell apart just before it was due to be heard in court.'

'That's right,' Harry murmured as more details began coming back to him. 'One day they believed they had enough to secure a conviction, the next they didn't. There was a bit of an outcry about that, as I recall.'

Pushing his thick-framed glasses higher up his nose, Connor said, 'There's a lot that doesn't add up about this case. In fact, it's pretty damned strange, if you ask me. In spite of all the media coverage it got at the time, something was clearly going on behind the scenes that was never revealed.'

If Meena and Harry hadn't been in India for their annual visit to her family these past four weeks, they'd already be up to speed on everything. As it was, they'd been happy to green-light from afar, with a meeting scheduled to discuss in detail right after their return.

Cristy continued, 'It's highly possible that new evidence came to light, or existing evidence was no longer deemed safe, but if that's correct, we have no idea what that evidence was.'

'If we're going to be objective about this,' Connor put in, 'and we are, one of the most important questions we need to answer is who might have carried out the killings, if it wasn't Gaudion? Our police source has confirmed that no one else was ever in the frame, and analysis of the scene, and the bodies, ruled out the possibility of a murder/suicide.'

'Plus,' Cristy added, 'there has never been another investigation.'

Frowning, Meena said, 'That's odd in itself. And what about Gaudion, didn't he try to clear his name after he was released?'

Cristy shook her head. 'Not as far as we know,' she replied. 'Or let's say, nothing has come to light yet.' She went back to her notes and pressed on. 'It could have been a contract killing,' she declared, 'especially given how the crime was executed – pardon the pun. You'll find details of that in the package Connor has prepared, but in brief, the type of gun that was used apparently confused the experts.'

'We've already interviewed the firearms guy who carried out the original analysis,' Connor told them, 'but essentially he told us what's already on file, that the pistol used – a Sig Sauer P230 semi-automatic handgun, chambered in .380 ACP – is of German make dating from the late Seventies, early Eighties, and, more interestingly, doesn't conform to a hitman's usual weapon of choice.'

'There is such a thing?' Meena interrupted in astonishment.

'Apparently,' Connor responded. 'I don't think they all go for the same model; it's just that this particular weapon doesn't show up on anyone's organized crime radar.'

Taking this in, Meena said, 'So this is why they think Gaudion did it? It wasn't a *professional* enough shooting?'

'I guess that's one way of putting it,' Cristy replied, making a note to find out the actual age of the gun. She thought it had been classed as vintage even back then, but it would be good to be sure, just in case it belonged to a collector. Was Gaudion a collector?

'Who else have you interviewed?' Harry asked, glancing out of the meeting room's open door as another podcast team came into the hallway and disappeared through to their office at the back of the ground floor – a generous space which had been a scullery during the building's original incarnation. The room Cristy and the others were currently in formed part of the east wing of the grand old merchant's house and was quite likely to have been a cosy and stylish dining room, with a huge marble fireplace, original cornices and two large sash windows overlooking what had probably once been a garden but was now a small car park.

Consulting her notes, Cristy said, 'So far we've interviewed the pathologist; a blood-spatter analyst who reported at the time; a footprint expert, also used back then; two of the original forensic team and one of the lead detectives. All, to a man and woman, remain baffled as to why the case never made it to court. As far as they're concerned it was cut and dried, no chance of an acquittal.'

'And yet Gaudion still walks free,' Connor stated.

'Where is he these days?' Harry asked.

'Good question,' Cristy responded. 'We haven't had much luck with that yet, but obviously we're on it. What we'd really like to know, though, is what happened to his youngest daughter who disappeared at the time of the killings.'

Meena almost gasped. 'Of course,' she cried. 'How the hell could I have forgotten that? Is there anything new about her?'

Cristy shook her head. 'I'm afraid not. Police records still show her as missing . . .'

'But not dead?'

'I think most presume that she is; it's just that a body has never been found. So her case remains open and is reviewed from time to time, but no new leads have ever turned up anything substantial.'

'Remind me how old she was when it happened,' Meena said.

'Ten. Her sister, Rosaria, was fifteen. She, too, is proving difficult to trace, but she was seen after the killings so it's not thought she was abducted and/or murdered along with Amelia.'

'What about the rest of the family? Do we know where they are?'

'Olivia, Lexie's sister, is still living a few miles from Stroud with her husband and children. Gaudion's brother, Richard, has a home in Kew with his wife, Astrid and their two kids. The extended family all still seem to be around in various parts of the country, but Gaudion's mother, Cynthia, is also proving difficult to contact, so no idea where she is and Richard Gaudion isn't prepared to tell us.'

'So could she be with David Gaudion?'

Cristy shrugged. 'Of course it's possible, but the general consensus seems to be that Cynthia Gaudion took her eldest granddaughter into hiding right after Gaudion was released.'

Meena's eyes widened. 'To keep the girl safe from him?'

'I presume so.'

'And they haven't been seen since?'

'Well, they must have been by someone,' Connor said, 'or the police would have been on it; it's just that we haven't found anyone yet.'

'What are the police saying?' Harry wanted to know.

'Very little, actually, but we're working on increasing our sources. However, we have had sight of some crime scene photos – way too horrific to go onto the website when it's up and running – it's up to you if you want to see them.'

'I wouldn't advise it,' Cristy put in, still sickened by the graphic images of Lexie slumped over a fallen parlour chair, arms and legs akimbo, most of her face missing, her mother crumpled across the fender, head in the hearth, and Serena sprawled beneath a half-open window, showing she'd had a few moments to break away from the others. How unimaginably terrified she must have been in those final moments.

Neither Meena nor Harry looked keen to take up Connor's offer.

'We have copies of some of the police files,' Connor continued, 'but gaining access to the entire case isn't happening right now. Obvs we're on it. Something of interest to note is that Richard Gaudion has made it clear he wants nothing to do with us and is talking to his lawyer about shutting us down.'

Harry gave a laugh. 'Good luck with that, matey,' he commented, 'and thanks for the publicity you'll give us if you try.'

Apparently needing to straighten it all out in her head, Meena said, 'So what we have is a triple murder, most probably committed by David Gaudion – do we have any reasons as to why he might have done it?'

'Various,' Cristy said. 'Marital disharmony, financial issues, the usual sort of thing, but nothing concrete.'

'OK, and we also have a missing child, thought to be dead at the hand of her own father?'

'Unless there was a hitman,' Connor put in pedantically.

'And if there was,' Meena continued, 'he was very probably hired by said father?'

Connor nodded. 'Although our police source who worked the case back in 2008 isn't convinced by the hitman theory and says not many of his colleagues were either.'

Absorbing this, Harry said, 'So, as I see it, based on what you've told us so far, you need to find out more about the evidence that got the trial stopped—'

'We're not actually sure such evidence exists,' Cristy put in. 'It's just an assumption we've made. You'll see the prosecutor's statement in Connor's background package, but it goes along the lines of: after careful consideration of all the material presented in this case it's been decided that its evidentiary value is insufficient to establish a case of murder. No detail on why the material was deemed insufficient, just that it was.'

Harry nodded thoughtfully. 'And the prosecutor isn't up for being interviewed?'

'Yet,' Connor replied.

'So now what I'm asking myself,' Harry said, 'is who did Gaudion know, or who did he have something on, to be able to get the case thrown out and, apparently, never reopened?'

'Good questions that we're working on,' Connor told him.

Meena sat back in her comfy leather chair and looked from one to other of them as she said, 'This is going to be one hell of an undertaking for you guys. Are you absolutely sure you want to carry on with it?'

'Of course we do,' Cristy responded, 'and you know us, we never give up until we get answers.'

Meena smiled. Cristy and Connor were terriers, ruthless in pursuit of the truth, and hadn't yet come up against an investigation they couldn't solve, or at least throw a whole new light on. 'So what next?' she asked, shaking her head at her PA who'd just appeared in the doorway.

'So much I hardly know where to start,' Cristy answered dryly, 'but moving away from all the tech and legal stuff, I recorded a Zoom chat yesterday with Flora Gibson, the gardener who found the bodies. She talked me through her day up to that point – a truly horrific moment in anyone's life, that's for sure – and she just emailed a few minutes ago to say the current owners of the Manse have agreed to her showing us around. They're South African and not currently in residence. While we're there, Flora's going to tell us what happened after she fled the scene.'

'We've also got our only existing police source lined up,' Connor added. 'As I said, we're working on increasing the number, but basically, Kevin Break – he's left the force now – was a detective constable at the heart of the original investigation and there's a lot about it that bothers him to this day. The statements and photos we have so far have come from the files he kept.'

'Is he willing to be named?' Harry asked.

'He is,' Connor confirmed.

'And what about Gaudion's family members and lawyers?' Meena asked. 'We know his brother's not playing ball, and you can't find his mother, but is there anyone else?'

'No one who's adding anything particularly interesting at this stage,' Cristy said, 'and not much luck with Olivia Caldwell either, Lexie Gaudion's sister. Apparently, Olivia had a really difficult time after losing her mother and sister – and her niece, of course – in such a horrible way, and doesn't want to open it all up again. However, it's possible she'll reconsider once a couple of episodes have aired, because she must surely want justice for what happened to her family.'

'We're guessing,' Connor added, 'that she's fully convinced it was Gaudion and already knows, or believes, that it can never be proved, so why put herself through the trauma of it all again?'

'What about the therapist, Serena Sutton?' Harry asked. 'She seems to be getting forgotten in the grand scheme of it all.'

'Actually, there's some interesting detail about her that we'll get into along the way,' Cristy told him, 'but for now, I want to play you the rough cut of an intro for episode one that we recorded yesterday using the material we already have.'

As Connor lined up the link on his laptop, Harry and Meena's assistant, Wendy, returned with a large jug of iced water. It was a welcome refreshment given the heat of the day with virtually no breeze finding its way in through the open sash windows, and the fan wasn't especially helpful. However, plenty of seagull whoopings and construction drillings were having no problem getting through to them, their own little dockland symphony.

Once everyone was ready – Harry with his feet up on the centre coffee table, Meena with her legs tucked under her in the cosy love seat, and Cristy poised to make notes – Connor pressed play.

The first voice came over clearly, with a slight West Country burr and a few hesitations:

'I swear I have never seen anything so horrific in my life. I still have nightmares about it. There was blood everywhere. Up the walls, all over the fireplace, covering the mirror . . . That's what I saw first, the blood, then I realized there were bodies everywhere . . . I didn't know how many at the time . . . I didn't stop to look. I was too terrified whoever had done it might still be in the house, so I turned around and ran.'

Cristy's voice was next.

'You've just been listening to Flora Gibson, the young gardener who, back in 2008, had the horrendous experience of discovering the victims in what came to be known as the Kellon Manse Murders. It's likely many of you will remember the case; for those who don't, it was the cold-blooded killing of three women, a mother, daughter and the daughter's psychotherapist, that was carried out at the Berkeley Vale home of David and Lexie Gaudion. It caused an absolute sensation at the time, not least because the Gaudions' youngest daughter, Amelia, aged ten, disappeared that day and has never been seen since.'

Meena's hand went up and Connor hit pause.
'How old would Amelia be by now?' Meena asked.
'Twenty-six,' Cristy replied.
'What about the eldest daughter?'

14

'Rosaria was fifteen when it happened,' Cristy said, 'so she'd be thirty or thirty-one today. She was at her grandmother's that day, apparently.'

'The grandmother being David Gaudion's mother, obvs,' Connor put in, 'given Lexie's mother was a victim herself.'

Nodding, Meena circled a finger for the playback to continue.

CRISTY: 'Somebody else who disappeared around that time – a matter of days after David Gaudion escaped trial and was released from custody – is his mother along with his eldest daughter. Apparently, the police are not concerned for their safety, but they won't say where they are – if indeed they know. We'll be looking into that further.

'As far as David Gaudion himself is concerned, we've been informed by several of his old neighbours that he left the area some months – possibly as long as a year – after his trial was cancelled. Apparently he was living at Kellon Manse, the scene of the crime, during that time, but no one from the locality has seen him since the house was sold at the beginning of 2010 and he moved away. It's worth bearing in mind here that Gaudion and his brother were born in the Berkeley Vale, as were Lexie and Olivia, and the four were well known to have a strong bond as children. You might think it odd that Gaudion should choose not to be in touch with anyone at all from his past – we know we do. Here's what his lawyer, Edmond Crouch, had to say when we contacted him.'

CROUCH: 'No, David isn't in hiding, and nor is he a recluse. He's simply a very private man who has no wish to revisit the terrible time he and his family went through back then, so I'm afraid I won't be passing on any messages.'

CRISTY: 'But you do know where he is?'

CROUCH: 'All I can tell you is that he will not welcome your enquiries.'

CRISTY: 'Even if they lead us to finding his daughter?'

There was a pause on the tape before Cristy continued:

CRISTY: 'Mr Crouch declined to answer that question, which is interesting in itself. Now, here's the voice of Sandy Trevelyan, an Oxford-based artist, who knew Serena Sutton, the third victim of the Kellon Manse Murders, for many years.'

SANDY TREVELYAN: 'Serena was devastated when her home and office – they were in the same place – were destroyed in a fire that happened a few days before she was murdered. I don't know if they've ever found a link between the two events, but the coincidence . . . Well, it's hard to think there wasn't a connection considering the timing, isn't it? I can only presume detectives weren't able to get a real picture of her relationship with Lexie Gaudion, or any of her other clients after that. Everything was gone. Was I surprised Serena ended up the way she did? Of course I was, and shocked, and extremely upset. You never expect something like that to happen to anyone, do you? Especially not someone you know and hold in esteem and affection.'

Meena piped up, 'Is it possible Serena Sutton was the real target in the killings? What does your ex-detective say about her?'

As Connor hit pause again, Cristy said, 'They were always pretty certain that Lexie was the target along with her mother, and Serena was – hateful term – collateral damage.'

'There's an interesting police report with some detail on why Serena was at the house that day,' Connor added. 'However, to avoid information overload, we aren't revealing it yet.'

'She was having an affair with Gaudion, and had come to tell Lexie all about it?' Meena suggested.

'Good theory,' Connor smiled, showing his boyish dimples, 'but no evidence of an affair to date, and the report throws a very different, although no less intriguing, light on the visit.'

'You can't stop there,' Meena protested.

'Sorry,' Connor laughed, 'you'll just have to stay tuned if you want to find out more.'

Scowling at him, Meena turned to Harry as he asked, 'Where does Gaudion claim he was when the murders happened?'

Cristy arched an eyebrow. 'Apparently he was out for a run. He says he left the house around two in the afternoon, at which point only his wife was there, and it was after five when he returned. By then the place was crawling with police. Flora Gibson, the gardener, was still being interviewed, so she saw him come back and has promised to tell us more about it.'

'Did anyone see him while he was out on this run?' Harry wanted to know. 'Surely he must have some sort of an alibi?'

'No one has ever come forward,' Cristy replied, 'but there are some pretty remote spots around that way, so maybe it's possible to go out for that long and not be seen.'

Harry looked sceptical. 'Three hours is a long time to be running on a hot day. Actually, I remember that being said at the time.'

'It was, but apparently it's not unusual for those who enjoy it to go out in the heat of the day, especially if they're training for an event in a hot climate.'

'Was he?'

'Not that we know of, but apparently he took part in several marathons in the years prior to the killings.'

They were all quiet for a moment, until Meena said, 'Well, it goes without saying that we won't have a problem getting backing for this, and the advertisers will be lining up. So, time to submit a budget – I'm sure you've already prepared one – then we can get you properly underway.'

After everyone had left the room – Harry off to one of the edit suites, Meena to her exec office on the first floor and Connor to his desk in the main production area, Cristy remained where she was, staring at the screen of her laptop. It was showing the head shot of David Gaudion that had been used a lot at the time of the killings. It showed a thirty-five-year-old man with thick, light brown hair swept back from his handsome face, the smile lines fanning his pale blue eyes making him seem relaxed, content, someone with not too much on his mind. Maybe that had been the case when the photo was taken, but appearing unconcerned hadn't done him too many favours during the height of the investigation.

A deliberate police tactic to turn public opinion against him?

For no explicable reason she found herself thinking of Matthew, her ex, and what he'd been like at thirty-five. Good-looking, certainly, over-confident, quite probably, charming, fun, attentive, great company . . .

She wondered if she hated him now and decided that she did. However, she wasn't an angry woman, never had been – although she had to admit to being pretty feisty at times – and she wasn't vengeful, or bitter, or sad. Actually, she was probably all of them if the truth were told, or had been in the first year or two of their break-up, but she no longer allowed the worst of her emotions to drive her. She was living a new life now, was completely happy with it, even if it did consist mainly of work with little time for anything else. Yes, she missed the fun she'd had with Matthew, and how *secure* she'd felt with him without even knowing it. Not that she felt insecure now – she was perfectly able to deal with life on her own – but she did feel a little lonely at times, and uncertain about what the future might hold for her.

Since nothing good ever came from self-reflection, or not of this sort, she quickly pushed it from her mind and refocused on David Gaudion. Not for the first time, she gave careful scrutiny to each of his features, from his deep-set, almost unsettling eyes, down the length of his slightly crooked nose and across the wide, full mouth that could have been feminine, and yet somehow wasn't. There was, in fact, an inherent masculinity about his strong jaw and the shadow beard darkening his naturally olive skin.

He was, without question, a striking-looking man, someone who was very probably used to doors opening for him that remained closed for others, who had people wanting to know him just to be in his sphere. It was often like that for beautiful people, men and women. They became used to getting what they wanted, almost expected it, and not necessarily out of selfishness or some sort of narcissism, or because they wanted to steal from someone less blessed; simply because it was the way life was for them. She'd been married to Matthew for long enough to recognize the type, although she hadn't realized how deeply her ex's sense of entitlement and invincibility had run until it was too late.

What did she actually know about David Gaudion?

Not much, was the answer, in spite of some pretty extensive initial enquiries. Back in 2008 he'd been a fourteen-year graduate of the London School of Economics, the father of two young girls, husband of an independently wealthy woman, a successful Westminster lobbyist who split his time between London and West Gloucestershire. Apparently he'd also been a long-distance runner.

They also knew that he'd grown up in the Berkeley Vale, along with his brother, and they'd been such fast friends with Lexie and Olivia Sallis from Kellon Hall that they were like family. The closeness had continued into their teens and early adulthood; in fact, there was nothing to say that they'd ever drifted away from one another in any meaningful sense. After all, David had married Lexie and they'd continued to live in the Vale. It didn't come much closer than that.

She wondered about Gaudion's darker side – didn't everyone have one? – and who, if anyone, might be prepared to discuss it? Certainly not his brother; Richard Gaudion couldn't have made that plainer, and clearly his lawyer wasn't going to be helpful either. However, there had to be old friends and colleagues from over the years who were willing to talk. It was just a question of finding them.

And what about his mother? Where the heck was she now? Still hiding from her son? Or was she with him and his eldest daughter, Rosaria? Was she even still alive given how old she must surely be if she was?

Cristy made a note to look into that; a near impossible task if it turned out the family had changed their names.

She clicked to the next image on her laptop.

Alexandra – Lexie – Gaudion, an understated yet undeniable beauty with dark, curly hair, lichen-green eyes, kittenish features and a pretty mouth. She was probably around thirty in this shot. Though she was laughing, there didn't appear to be the right sort of spark in her eyes, and no real engagement with the photographer was evident. Had David been behind the camera?

Of course, it was foolish to draw conclusions from a single moment that had been captured, probably randomly, on a day that could have just been off; or during a passing moment that bore no relation to the next. Lexie's family, the Sallises, had been landowners in the Vale for centuries – in fact, 'landed gentry' was an expression Cristy had heard often to describe them, and Lexie had a look of breeding and privilege about her, an inherent quality that seemed to set her slightly apart from more general folk.

It was the same with her older sister, Olivia, who'd be around fifty by now – people with that sort of money and background often wore well, so Cristy suspected Olivia was a striking older woman. It shouldn't be too difficult to find out, so she added it to her notes. It always helped to have the correct image of someone in mind when trying to approach them.

The next photo was of Margaret Sallis, a jowly, haughty-looking woman in her seventies who apparently had no living siblings. However, there had to be some extended family somewhere, and the neighbours could probably reveal quite a lot about the proprietor of most of their homes and businesses if they were of a mind to.

Next was Serena Sutton, acclaimed psychotherapist with all the right letters after her name, forty-four at the time of her murder, divorced and childless. Her hair was neat and silvery, her eyes deep brown and gentle, and her smile seemed to exude – in this shot anyway, which might have been taken by a professional given the soft focus and lighting – an air of compassion and calm. It was a good look for someone who dealt in other people's misery and secrets, suggesting she would be easy to trust. She must have had a whole slew of clients who'd have been willing to talk about her, but as far as Cristy was aware none had ever come forward or been found. More than a little odd, that, but stranger and more suspicious still was her office and all her records going up in flames only days before the murders.

Days before she'd driven her blue Audi to the Manse to see Lexie and her mother.

The biggest mystery of all, of course, was what could have happened to ten-year-old Amelia Gaudion? In the photos used

20

during the early days of her disappearance, she came over as a sparkly eyed, mischievous child with her father's thick fair hair and blue eyes and her mother's heart-shaped face. Apparently she'd loved animals, especially horses, dressing up, painting, water skiing and playing with her big sister. She'd been doing well at school, was in full health, and clearly had an active life and, to all outward appearances, a loving family.

Very much like Cristy's family had been before it suddenly wasn't that way any more. Why did thinking about it still make her feel so wretched inside when she'd moved on now? She had a different life – with her children still in it, obviously, but everything she'd held precious, the togetherness, the security, the unshakable belief in her marriage was long gone.

But this wasn't about her.

Oddly, there were no photos of Rosaria Gaudion, the elder sister, that Cristy had been able to find, though naturally the family and police would have kept her out of the public eye as much as possible when it was all going on.

Returning to the shot of David Gaudion, she sat with her eyes fixed on his, and because he'd looked right into the lens when the picture had been taken, it felt as if he was staring right back at her. It wasn't altogether an unpleasant feeling – he didn't come over as menacing, however it was slightly unsettling. She knew it was pointless to try to detect any signs of evil or psychopathy in him. Most murderers looked like everyone else, a regular father, brother, son, friend. Some were even as attractive as this one, which bizarrely, could make them seem more sinister than if they'd been downright ugly.

'Where are you now, David Gaudion?' she murmured. 'Who are you? How are you staying below the radar? And how am I going to find you? Because I will, I hope you know that.'

CHAPTER TWO

Cristy was in the passenger seat of Connor's VW Golf, laptop open in front of her, mic loosely in hand, ready to begin recording when the time was right. She glanced over at him as he slowed the car down, an odd response to the satnav's instruction to continue straight for one mile. 'Are you OK?' she asked as he stifled a yawn.

'Bad night,' he confessed, poking at his glasses and speeding up a little. 'Jodi woke up around two and wanted to talk about giving up work until after the baby's here.'

Knowing how excited and apprehensive his lovely young wife was with this, her first pregnancy, Cristy said, 'But she's already stepped back from her podcast, hasn't she? Didn't Lynette take over last week?'

'Yes, but only for the next two months; after that, the whole thing is parked until Jodi's ready to start searching the nation for good deeds again.'

Cristy smiled. Jodi's pod was a favourite with many simply for being so funny and upbeat and cognizant of the best rather than the worst in people. 'Well, isn't that the upside of being your own boss?' she said. 'You get to choose when you work. Anyway, how is she in herself? I mean physically. Scans still all good and everything?'

'Hundred percent, and most of the time she's cool with it all. It's just the middle of the night thing that gets her sometimes.'

Cristy checked her mobile as it started to vibrate. Seeing who it was she immediately rejected the call.

Connor glanced at her curiously.

'My ex-husband's wife,' she explained.

22

He pulled a face. 'Why's she calling *you?*' he demanded.

Cristy shrugged, trying and failing to breeze past the sudden jolt of memory that continued to sicken her every time it came to life. It was the moment Matthew had told her their marriage was over, the utter shock of realizing he meant it, that he really was going to break up their family for a girl less than half his age. A girl who'd come to Bath to appear at the Theatre Royal following her starring role in a hit TV series that Matthew hadn't watched, but Cristy had loved. It was only because Cristy had arranged for the starlet with huge eyes, full lips and exquisite body to come into the studios that Matthew had finally agreed to interview her. And that was where it had all begun.

What insidious trickery had been at work that day? Why had the fates decided to smash her world apart so brutally and irreversibly and to make such a damned fool of her – of them all really, given the media attention? Thank God that had died down, eventually, but the affair hadn't burned itself out; Matthew's obsession had grown ever deeper until finally he'd initiated a divorce so he could marry his true love. 'Because,' she said, bringing herself back to Connor's question about why Marley Dukes would call her, 'she's as big a dick, to quote my son, as he is.' With a sigh she added, 'She wants us to be friends. For the children's sake. Makes her sound almost mature, doesn't it? And there she is, not yet twenty-five.'

Connor nodded slowly. 'Well, I guess she can fuck right off,' he declared as if there could be no other response.

With a choke of laughter, Cristy switched on the mic as the satnav told them to take a left in one hundred yards. 'No script, making this up as we go along,' she informed him, and began to speak.

'Connor and I are just turning into the heart of the Berkeley Vale, scene of the Kellon Manse Murders, on our way to meet with Flora Gibson, the gardener who found the bodies. For those of you not familiar with this part of the world, it's in Gloucestershire, a huge swathe of rural beauty nestled between the western edge of the Cotswolds and the mighty River Severn. The weather today is glorious, blue skies all the way, and a world of green as far as the eye can see, which actually isn't that far at the moment as we're heading along a narrow, winding road hedged in by dense hawthorns. Nevertheless, there's a lovely feel about the area. It exudes peacefulness, making it the kind of place you'd want to spend a relaxing summer's day, or a holiday. Some of you might be familiar with the medieval castle as it's quite a popular wedding venue. It's also home to the Berkeley family and has been since the twelfth century. Its other dubious claim to fame is that it might be where King Edward II was murdered.

'That's going back a little too far for *Hindsight*. Our destination today is Kellon Manse, which was renamed Hillvale House when its new owners took over a few years after the killings. They're a South African couple, not in residence at the moment, but they've agreed to let Flora Gibson show us around. OK, we're stuck behind a tractor now . . .'

Switching off the mic, she sighed as she mulled over her own words, knowing there was plenty of scope for edits and drop-ins, but that was for later. For now she simply gazed out at the passing landscape, so tranquil and verdant and seeming to be its own small world of early summer beauty. The grassy banks were full of buttercups, purple bellflowers, sweet mock orange, bloody cranesbill, and all of them reminded her of her mother who'd had a passion for wildflowers. Even the pungent scent of wild garlic drifting in through the open windows was taking her back in time.

'It's hard to imagine anything violent ever happening somewhere like this, isn't it?' she commented to Connor as they entered the village of Rockhampton and meandered past the empty cricket pitch.

'Can anywhere claim to have no darkness in its past?' he responded bleakly.

Her eyebrows arched. 'You really are sleep deprived, aren't you?'

He was saved from answering as his phone rang. Seeing the name on the car screen, he said, 'Great! Kevin Break, our ex-detective. I just hope he's not cancelling on us. Hey, Kevin,' he barked out as he clicked on. 'How's tricks?'

'Fair, fair,' came the gruff reply. 'I got your email this morning but thought I'd ring to say all's good my end. Happy to chat – I just have to move it to the day after tomorrow if that's OK. Wife's got a hospital appointment I'd forgotten about.'

'No problem. I hope she's OK.'

'Yeah, yeah, nothing serious.'

'That's good. So, same time, same place?'

'Sure. She's offered to bake scones, so bring an appetite – and book a dental visit for after.'

Connor laughed. 'Noted. We're just about to interview Flora Gibson. Have you guys been in touch at all since the murders?'

'Flora? The gardener? She was a good witness, as I recall. Horribly shook up, obviously, after what she'd seen, but I remember us all being pretty impressed by how responsive she was on the day, once she'd managed to calm down a bit. Is she claiming to know who did it? That'd be a turnaround if she is.'

Connor smiled. 'No, this is just background stuff, first-hand account of discovery and all that.'

'Unless she surprises us,' Cristy put in.

'Is that you, Cristy?' Break called cheerily.

'It's me. Looking forward to seeing you in a couple of days. And thanks again for working with us.'

'I've been waiting a long time for someone to ask me about it,' he told her. 'I just hope you stay on it, because the last person to get in touch never called me back after I said I'd be happy to help.'

Frowning as she glanced at Connor, Cristy said, 'Who was that?'

'Can't remember her name now. I decided in the end she was one of those amateurs who fancy themselves as a true-crime podcaster. There are so many of them at it these days, setting up in their kitchens and blathering on about hangovers and babies and holidays, before they even get started on the meat of it all. At least you guys don't do that. It's why I follow you. Cut to the chase, proper professionals – only to be expected given your backgrounds and everything. Anyway, I'll see you Thursday. Good luck with . . . Iris.'

'Flora.'

'No, Iris is the name of the girl who contacted me before. Just came to me. Anyway, give my regards to Flora.'

Just as he rang off, a deer suddenly sprang out in front of them and Connor hit the brakes so hard that they swerved across the road, only just avoiding ending up in a ditch.

Shaken, he gripped the wheel and stared straight ahead in horror. 'Tell me I didn't hit it,' he implored. 'Please tell me I didn't hit it, or Jodi will never forgive me.'

Watching the graceful creature leap over a low stone wall and disappear into a shady copse, Cristy said, 'She's fine. Just make sure there are no fawns about to follow her. It's that time of year.'

'Are you serious?' He turned to glare at her. 'Are you saying I might have killed Bambi's mother, or Bambi himself?' He seemed genuinely appalled. 'Jesus Christ, how would I ever have explained that to Aurora when she's old enough to understand?'

Cristy laughed. 'No harm done, so man up and put it out of your mind.'

Grumbling under his breath, he straightened the car and drove gingerly on. 'How come you know so much about deer?' he challenged, as if she'd somehow colluded with the beast he'd nearly annihilated.

She shrugged. 'I don't really, only that they give birth around May and June – and I happen to think that Bambi is a totally traumatizing story for a small child, so maybe you want to rethink little Aurora's introduction to it.'

He threw her a look.

'Just saying,' she grinned. 'OK. Now, according to maps we're about to arrive at the destination, so keep a look out for Flora.'

A few minutes later, as they emerged from a sun-dappled tunnel of trees, they spotted a red-headed woman in denim dungarees and bright blue Doc Martens, waving them down.

'Hey!' Cristy cried as she got out of the car and Flora crossed the sun-baked road to greet them. She already knew that the ex-gardener was forty-one years old now, mother of three boys and part-time bookkeeper for her father-in-law's landscaping business. ('I did a course, about ten years ago,' she'd told Cristy during their initial chat. 'It was just after our eldest one was born.

No, I don't do much gardening now, apart from at home. Jack still hasn't made an honest woman of me, but I suppose there's always time.')

'Hope you haven't been waiting long,' Cristy said warmly as she clasped hands with the smiley, frizzy-haired younger woman.

'Just got here,' Flora assured her, and turned to Connor as he joined them, raising her sunglasses to see him more clearly. 'Nice to meet you,' she said, shaking his hand. 'I clocked you were a bit of a looker on the website, all those dark curls and sexy glasses. Not really my type, I have to say, but I can see why the girls would go for you.'

Cristy sniggered at his discomfort, and Flora turned to lead them a few yards further along the lane. 'Hot today, innit?' she commented over her shoulder. 'Don't worry, I should be able to offer you some refreshment when we get inside. The Venters said it would be OK.' Pressing a remote control, she paused a moment for the towering gates to slide apart like a pair of stage curtains. 'These were installed about a year after the Venters bought the place,' she informed them as they walked through. 'In David and Lexie's day there was only an old five-bar that was always open to the world, but obviously, after what happened . . .' She took a moment to make sure the gates were closing behind them. 'We had a lot of rubberneckers in the first couple of years,' she continued, 'crawled all over the place, they did . . . God only knew what they were hoping to see.' She pocketed the remote and gazed up at the splendid red-brick Manse, an impressively elegant three-storey house atop the gentle rise of a hillock. 'Well, there she is,' she declared, almost as if Cristy and Connor had been waiting years for this very moment.

It was certainly a beautiful place, Cristy reflected, and appeared extremely well cared for. No signs of its tragic history – as if there would be – but really, there was no sense of bleakness or horror at all. It came over as quietly benign at the centre of its sleepy, colourful gardens, and was partly shaded on one side by a giant horse chestnut. All that appeared different from the photos she'd seen were the shutters behind the windows and an ornate stone porch around the front door that blended so well with the period of the house it might have always been there.

Flora said, 'I used to think I'd never be able to come here again after what happened, but then, well, things change, don't they? Time moves on, and when the new owners needed someone to take care of it while they're not around, Jack put my name forward. He does the gardens now. They're pretty much the same as before, but the house is different. I don't mean structurally – it's a listed building so they have to "honour the integrity" – but obviously the Venters put in their own furniture and redid a few things. The kitchen's new and the sitting room fireplace was torn out and boarded up. I'd have put another in if it was up to me, but there we are . . . What's really changed, I'd say, is the atmosphere of the place.'

'In what way?' Cristy asked curiously.

Flora shrugged. 'It just seems . . . calmer in there now. Like all the craziness has been put to bed, never to return. Well, that's my take on it, but then not everyone has the same memories of it that I do, and let me tell you, it was crazy here the day it all happened.'

Glancing at Connor, Cristy said to Flora, 'If it's OK with you we'll start recording and talk as we walk, but any time you want us to stop . . .'

'Oh, I'm cool with it,' Flora assured her. 'I can't imagine I'm going to tell you anything you don't already know. Well, maybe I will. We'll see how it goes. Where do you want me to start? When I found the bodies or—'

'We already have that from the first time you and I spoke,' Cristy reminded her, 'so maybe you can show us where you ran to when you left the house?'

'Ah yeah, that's up over the back, behind the greenhouses. They're still there, actually. So's the gate I chucked myself over to get into the next field.'

As they started to stroll Connor said, 'Am I right in thinking Kellon Hall adjoins this property?'

Flora followed his gaze towards the dense treetops beyond a high bank of hawthorn hedges. 'Yeah, it's right over there. You used to be able to see the chimneys from here, but the oaks have grown so tall, they're blocked out completely now.'

'Who lives there?' he asked.

'No one. It was all shut up after Mean Margaret died, and the

28

only ones who go in there these days are my Jack and his team to take care of the gardens closest to the Hall. Tennis court's gone to rack and ruin, and the pool's in a terrible state. God only knows what the house is like inside. As far as I know, no one ever got murdered there, but let me tell you, it's a hell of a lot spookier than here. That'll be why they can't sell it, I'm sure. They don't even have any viewings as far as I know. One look at the outside and no one wants to go in. Even Olivia hates it there.'

'Does she ever visit?' Cristy asked.

'Rarely, and who can blame her? They were never happy there as children, her and Lexie, so Jack's dad says. He remembers more about them when they were young, being older and all that.'

'Why did you say Mean Margaret?' Connor wanted to know.

'Oh, right. It's what we called her, mainly because she could be a right cow when she wanted to be, which was most of the time. She hardly ever spoke nicely to anyone, we were all afraid to go there, so God knows what it was like for her girls. Maybe she was better with them, who knows, but I can tell you she was drunk more often than not. I've heard her husband was just as bad when he was alive. It's no wonder his horse bucked and threw him to his death – it sounds like he was a cruel bastard.' She sighed and shook her head. 'All that money and land . . . Didn't do 'em much good in the end, did it? I'm not sure they even had any friends to speak of, but as I said, I didn't actually know them. He died long before my time and . . . oh yeah, she was mean because she never gave anything to anyone, not for jumble sales or fundraisers, or the WI's efforts to help people overseas. Jack's dad threatened her with the law a couple of times if she didn't pay his bill. It was the only way to make her cough up. Everyone had the same trouble, and I don't think she was ever short, just . . . *mean*.

'Course, we all went to her funeral – you have to, don't you? Love her or hate her, she was part of the community, never mind that half the people who turned up wouldn't have minded being the one who pulled the trigger.'

Startled by Flora's bluntness, Cristy noticed that Connor's eyebrows had also shot up.

'So do you ever see Olivia these days?' he wondered as they drew closer to the Manse.

Flora shook her head. 'No call for her to come here, really, unless Jack's dad needs to talk to her about something to do with the garden, but she usually just tells him to carry on if something needs doing. Other than that, I send her bills by email and, unlike her mother, she's always a prompt payer.'

'Do you think there's a chance your father-in-law will talk to us?' Cristy asked as they rounded the side of the house to the back garden where a large stone terrace overlooked more immaculate lawns and well-tended borders.

'I'll ask,' Flora said, sounding doubtful, 'but he's already told me he doesn't want to get involved in any tittle-tattle, as he calls it. It's not that he's being difficult,' she insisted, 'it's just that he wasn't *here* when it happened, the way I was, and he's got a lot of customers around the Vale. If they thought he was going around talking about them . . . Well, you can see how it might look.'

Cristy said, 'But he must have known David Gaudion . . .'

'Oh yeah, everyone did. No doubt about that . . . So, here we are.' Flora pointed across the lawns to a sturdy five-bar gate in the hedgerow next to the greenhouses, then turned back to the Manse. 'I came out of there faster than Usain Bolt,' she recalled with a grimace. 'Honest to God, I thought I was about to get shot too. I've never been so scared in me life. I mean, you see the sort of thing I did and you think, holy fuck, I need to get out of here. I came this way because I remembered there was a car I didn't recognize at the front of the house – I guess in my panic I thought it belonged to the killer. I found out later that it was Serena Sutton's, but I didn't know that then. Or her. I only knew I could be next if only to keep me quiet . . . It wasn't till I hurtled over the gate that it occurred to me someone back at the house might still be alive and in need of help. It couldn't be me, though. No way was I going back in there, but at least I managed to dial 999. Bit of a miracle given how hard I was shaking.'

Certain she'd have been in an equally panicked state if something like it had happened to her, Cristy went to peer over the gate, picturing a trembling young woman cowering in a ditch the other side. 'What happened then?' she asked, gazing out across an empty field of long grass and buttercups.

'Well, it's a bit of a jumble now,' Flora admitted, 'but I

remember the operator telling me to stay where I was. No, first she asked if I was safe . . . Of course, I didn't know the answer to that, but I crossed my fingers and said I thought I was . . . She told me to stay on the line, and that someone was on the way. I can't remember how long it took for anyone to arrive, but oh my God, when they did . . . I had to explain to the operator where I was on the property, I suppose to make sure the police didn't shoot me . . .'

'So an armed response team turned up?' Connor asked, looking around as if a SWAT team with serious weaponry might even now be lurking in the undergrowth, ready to start advancing onto the lawns.

Flora nodded. 'They definitely came with guns, eventually, but before that I could hear all the sirens down in the lane . . . I found out after that no one was allowed onto the property until the armed officers turned up, and the operator just carried on telling me to stay where I was. Looking back, it was like being in a video game, but it was bloody terrifying, I can tell you that. Someone started shouting through a loud hailer for anyone inside to come out . . . Then suddenly this policewoman appeared over the gate and plopped down next to me. She got hold of me like I was a little kid, pulled me right up against her, and I didn't mind a bit. I needed someone to make me feel safe. She said I was, but we should stay quiet until we got instructions to move. Then she took my phone and told the operator who she was and that it was OK to ring off now.'

'Do you remember the policewoman's name?' Cristy asked, ready to note it down.

'Not off the top of me head, but I expect I can find it somewhere if I have a look.'

They started slowly back towards the house, the grass lush and springy underfoot, making Cristy wish she could take off her shoes to feel it between her toes.

'It seemed like ages before someone came to get us,' Flora continued. 'I might have had myself under better control by then, but once we came out of hiding and I saw what was going on out here, it shook me up all over again. Ambulances, police cars, vans, dogs, people everywhere. Lights flashing, radios going off, tents

31

going up . . . I ended up being taken to one of the ambulances, but I didn't want to get in. There was nothing wrong with me apart from shock, I guess. Anyway, they didn't argue, just sat me down on the tailgate and gave me water, put a blanket round me and stuff, while I sat watching the pandemonium, almost like none of it was real. I remember dreading them carrying the bodies out in front of me. I still had no idea who it was, or how many there were; I only knew I didn't want to see any of it ever again. Then a detective came to talk to me. He asked if I'd seen anyone coming or going from the house while I was cutting the grass, but I hadn't, so I told him no. He wanted to know why I'd gone inside so I said it was to check everything was all right, given the doors were wide open but no one had come out. He asked if I'd touched anything while I was in there, or did I see anything unusual – as if a bunch of dead bodies wasn't unusual enough! It was about then that I heard someone shouting and when I looked round I saw it was David Gaudion. A couple of policemen were holding him back but he tore free, pushed one of them over, even, and as he ran into the house he was shouting for Amelia. It hadn't occurred to me until then that either of the girls might have been in there. Honest to God, it was like a nightmare that just kept getting worse . . .'

In spite of knowing that the child hadn't been in there, Cristy couldn't help feeling the horror Flora must have experienced in the moments she'd feared it.

'I don't know what happened inside the house,' Flora went on, 'but David was out again in minutes and vomiting into a flower bed next to the front door.' Turning to Cristy she said, 'It's hard to act chucking up, isn't it?'

Agreeing that it was, Cristy said, 'Was he actually sick, or just retching?'

'From where I was sitting it seemed real enough. I assumed it meant Amelia was in there, but then all hell started breaking loose as they realized they now had a missing child on their hands.'

'Out of interest,' Connor said, 'can you remember what David was wearing? It was said he'd been out for a run . . .'

'Yeah, he was in all the gear and his hair was all sweaty. He looked terrible, like he'd . . . Well, I suppose a bit like I did after I saw what was in the sitting room. He was totally white, and kept shouting, "You need to find her! She has to be here somewhere." Obviously he meant Amelia.

'Everyone was already fanning out around the garden, climbing over into next door and the neighbouring fields. I was asked if I'd seen her, but I hadn't so I couldn't help. Except I told them to try the stables over at the Hall. She was mad about horses, spent a lot of time there, and I thought if she'd seen something and got frightened, she might have run there to hide.' She shrugged sadly. 'Of course we know now that she didn't, and I found out later she hadn't managed to get to her other grandma's either.' Her expression was bleak as she turned to Cristy. 'I suppose whoever killed her mother and the others took her and probably did away with her too.'

Knowing it was what the police had come to believe, Cristy said, 'You knew David, so do you think he could have done it?'

Flora's eyes widened. 'To his own daughter? No. No way. To his wife . . . Well, who knows what goes on behind closed doors, eh? I never saw anything bad going on between them, I have to say that, but I was just the junior gardener, so it's not like I knew them. As for Mean Margaret, well, I don't expect he had any more love for her than the rest of us, but who knows?'

'What about Serena Sutton?'

Flora shrugged. 'I'd never even heard of her until it all happened, so I can't answer that.' With a grim smile she waved a hand in the direction of the back door, 'Shall we go inside and get a drink? They've got one of those fridges that pumps out ice.'

A while later, after Flora had plied them with lemon squash and shown them the 'crime scene' that was now no more than an ordinary sitting room with no fireplace or much in the way of atmosphere, the three of them walked slowly back down the drive together. Cristy was struck once again by the tranquillity of the day with no more than a chorus of bleating and birdsong to break the gentle silence. She imagined it had been just like this during the minutes before the killings, nothing but stillness and sunshine, countryside scents and summery promise. Then, quite suddenly: *Boom! Boom! Boom!* Three women dead, a child taken . . .

Chaos and terror.

It had all happened sixteen years ago this very week.

She turned to look back at the Manse. 'I know I've asked you this before, Flora, but do you have any idea where David might be now?'

Flora shook her head slowly. 'Not a clue, I'm afraid.'

'Would you tell us if you did know?' Cristy pressed.

Startled Flora turned to look at her. 'No one's ever asked me to keep any secrets if that's what you're thinking. So the answer's yes, if I knew, I'd tell you.'

Deciding to believe her, Cristy said, 'What about his mother and eldest daughter? Did they leave the area at the same time he did?'

Flora thought about it. 'No, it was right after he came out of prison, or maybe it was before. Gordon, Jack's dad, would probably know better than me.'

'We heard that David came back here, to this house, after his release,' Connor said.

'Yeah, he did. Everyone was surprised, hadn't expected it at all, and of course the whole world had an opinion on whether or not he should have, or whether or not he'd done it.'

'What did you think?' Connor prompted.

'I've always found it hard to imagine him harming Amelia. I mean, he was her dad, wasn't he? On the other hand, I didn't know him that well, so it's hard to know what he might have been capable of.'

'How long did he stay here after his release?' Cristy asked.

'I guess it was about a year. He mostly kept himself to himself. His brother used to come quite a lot, and I saw Olivia, Lexie's sister, driving out of here once. She might have come more often than that, but it wasn't long after the time I saw her that he called my father-in-law to say he was leaving, and care of the house was reverting back to the Kellon Estate. In other words, we needed to deal with Olivia from now on.'

Cristy nodded pensively as they continued on out to the road. Once the gates had closed behind them, she said, 'I'm guessing your father-in-law might have known David quite well?'

Flora grimaced. 'Well, they weren't close or anything, and Gordon's older, obviously, but they both grew up around here, and they both played on the local cricket team.'

34

'I know you said Gordon wouldn't want to talk to us, but do you think he might consider it if we were to send him a list of questions beforehand?' Connor asked.

Flora shrugged. 'I don't know. He might, if he knows what you're going to ask. I'll put it to him if you like, and let you know.'

Cristy smiled. 'Thanks. And thanks very much for showing us around today. The material we've got is going to form most of the first episode.'

Flora looked down at the recorder. 'I'd forgotten it was on. I hope I didn't babble on too much.'

'You were terrific,' Connor assured her. 'I wish everyone was as easy to talk to as you.'

Flora beamed. 'Well, if there's anything else, just let me know. You've got my number.'

'Actually, there is one thing,' Connor said. 'Has anyone called Iris ever been in touch with you about doing a podcast?'

Flora frowned. 'No. You're the only ones I've heard from wanting to do something like this.'

'Thanks again,' Cristy said with a warm smile. 'I'll be in touch in the next couple of days, and I'm sure we'll be back soon – if only to indulge in one of those.'

Flora turned and laughed to see a sign draped over a nearby hedge. *Michelle's cream teas, first Sunday in the month from three to five. Everyone welcome.* 'Cynthia, David's mum, used to do them, back in the day,' she said, 'and more often than not, Lexie helped out. Olivia too, if she was around.'

Liking the scene this conjured, Cristy said, 'We're planning to drive past David's childhood home while we're over this way.'

Flora shrugged. 'It's easy enough to find, hardly a mile from here, but the old farm has long gone. A family from London bought the place years ago, tore it down and built a bit of a monstrosity, if you ask me. Amazed they got planning for it, but some people like the more modern look, don't they?'

A few minutes later Cristy and Connor were back in the car following Flora's directions to Gaudion's former home and mulling over the past half-hour. 'What made you ask about Iris?' Cristy asked.

He sighed as a tractor pulled out in front of them. 'I was just interested to know if she'd contacted anyone else. We don't want to be doubling up on this, do we?'

'No, we don't, but if she hasn't been in touch with Flora she's either not very good, or she's lost interest in the case. Now, do you think it's actually worth going to see where David grew up? If it's so completely different we can always do it the next time we're here, hopefully to talk to Gordon.'

'We need to work on a list of what we want to ask him,' Connor responded. 'I reckon he knows more than he might be willing to tell right now. In fact, I wouldn't be surprised if a lot of people around here do.'

'Me neither,' Cristy murmured, gazing out at the sleepy, sunny landscape and the quiet, rose-covered cottages. 'There's something about the place, isn't there? Beautiful though it is, it feels, I don't know, a bit closed off to outsiders?'

Connor nodded. 'So does that lead us to think David Gaudion might actually be here somewhere, hiding in plain sight, as it were?'

Cristy waited for an instinct to kick in. 'I'm not feeling it,' she replied, 'but there again, it's too early to dismiss it. If he is, Flora doesn't seem to know about it, and surely she would.'

'If you believe her.'

'Does that mean you don't?'

'Let's say I think she's on the level about what happened when she found the bodies and everything, but I reckon there's a chance she knows more than she's admitting to about what's happened since.'

'Hmm. What do you reckon about Amelia Gaudion? Do you think she's dead?'

Connor glanced at her curiously. 'Don't you?' he countered.

She pondered it for a while. 'I know this might sound crazy, but bear with me for a moment. What if her kidnap was behind it all? Someone who wanted a child, who'd maybe seen her and fallen in love with her decided to take her?'

'What, and they kill three people in the process? Definitely not seeing it. But even if you've got a point, wouldn't that make the killer more likely to be a woman?'

36

'Maybe two people were involved? Although there's never been any mention of that. Or of a woman.'

'We'll check it with Kevin Break,' he decided, and signalled to turn onto the A38.

After a while Cristy said, 'There's so much about this that isn't adding up, isn't there? Sure, it's the reason we decided to look into it, but we've hardly got started and we're already swamped with more questions than answers. Oh God,' she groaned as her phone rang.

'Don't tell me, Mrs Dickhead again?'

Cristy's smile was thin. 'No, it's the dickhead himself this time.'

'So let him fuck right off too. It's like they can't get over you and they're the ones who did the cheating.'

With the truth of those words still able to sting more than it should – *goddammit* – Cristy clicked on the phone and said snappishly, 'What do you want?'

'Nice,' came the response. 'I'm good and hoping you are too.'

'Come to the point.'

'OK, is Aiden with you?'

'No, why should he be?'

'I just don't know where he is.'

'Are you serious? *You* have custody of my fifteen-year-old son and *you* don't know where he is.'

'Our son, and I'm sure it's only temporary—'

'Well, it damned well better be. When did you last see him?'

'Saturday morning.'

'Jesus Christ, Matthew, and you're only calling me now!'

'You don't answer your phone,' he reminded her.

'What's wrong with texting, or leaving a message? Has he been to school?'

'I'm not sure. Still waiting to hear back from them.'

Wishing she could slap him, she said, 'Have you tried Hayley?'

'Of course, but she hasn't spoken to him and he's not there.'

It was a long shot – Aiden was unlikely to bother getting himself all the way to Edinburgh where his sister was at uni. 'What about his mates?'

'They won't admit to knowing where he is. I just can't be sure if they're telling the truth.'

'Did you have a falling-out with him?'

'I tried not to, but you know your son.'

'Oh, so he's mine now. Well, I have no doubt he's just being who he is and doing something radical somewhere. I'm on my way back to Bristol, should be there in about half an hour. Let me know if you hear anything.' She rang off and tried Aiden's number herself. Straight to voicemail. 'Call me if you get this,' she told him. 'Dad's worried and so am I now. We need to know you're all right.'

CHAPTER THREE

Forty-five minutes later Cristy was digging into her bag for her keys as she got out of Connor's car, while promising to call him as soon as she'd located her missing son. She wasn't unduly worried – he'd gone off radar before and usually turned out to be with a friend, or at some concert he'd forgotten to mention. There was also the inglorious occasion when he'd spent the night at a homeless shelter after 'getting chatting with some great blokes' who'd invited him for a sleepover.

Aiden was nothing if not his own person, a free spirit as Hayley often called him, or a bloody pain in the ass, to quote his father. Bright, musical, adventurous, selfish, kind-to-a-fault, unambitious, curious . . . There were so many ways she could describe him, but the one that generally came first to mind these days, and that hurt deeply, was unhappy. She could sense it in him, spiralling up into a little ball, in spite of his refusal to admit it.

'Just chill, Mum,' he'd say if she tried to probe. 'I'm cool, OK. You don't need to worry about me, I know what I'm doing.'

Sighing to herself, she crossed the maple-shaded courtyard outside her low-rise apartment block and reflected, not for the first time, on how lucky she was to have this flat at the Redcliffe end of the Harbourside, a mere stone's throw from the water. She'd bought it ten years ago with the money she'd inherited from her beloved mother. It had been an investment then, somewhere she'd carefully furnished and rented out on a weekly basis to barristers who came to Bristol for trials at the crown court. Since the ignominy and pain of her marriage break-up, it had been her home and she couldn't love it more – probably because it felt as though it was her mother who'd provided a refuge at one of the lowest points of her life.

After checking her mailbox she tossed the junk into a recycling bag set there for just that purpose, and carried on along the brightly lit hall to her front door. She knew, even before she'd unlocked it, that Aiden was inside. Firstly, the deadlock wasn't engaged, and secondly, the smell as she stepped over the threshold almost made her gag. Sour male sweat mixed with some sort of takeout food and the sickly sweet drift of weed.

Leaving her keys and bills on a windowsill, she dropped her bag and laptop beside the coat-stand outside her bedroom door and picked her way through an obstacle course of abandoned backpacks, boots and assorted clothing leading past the bathroom to the sitting room-cum-kitchen. If it turned out he'd offered her flat as a shelter for his new street-mates he was going to be in serious trouble.

'What the hell, Aiden?' she exclaimed, finding him slumped on the sofa wearing only boxers and a T-shirt and something weirdly frilly on his head. Next to him the coffee table and floor were littered with food cartons, drink cans and at least three half-full ashtrays, while sprawled across the rug in front of the open French doors to her garden was another male body, thankfully face-down as he was wearing nothing at all.

'Oh, hey, Mum,' Aiden responded, removing an earbud and craning his neck to see her over the sofa arm. His lovely thick, fair hair was lank and greasy and his navy-blue eyes bloodshot and bleary. 'Didn't hear you come in,' he said, abandoning the struggle to sit up. He was managing to sound both sleepy and cheery, and was clearly so stoned it was doubtful he knew which day of the week it was.

'Who's that?' she demanded, pointing to the naked man on the floor. 'Actually, I don't care who he is, just get him out of here. And what the hell have you got on your head?'

Aiden raised a hand to pull it off and started to laugh as if it were the most hilarious thing he'd ever seen. 'I think it's knickers,' he managed to guffaw. 'We found them at the festival. Look at all the little cows.' He clamped them over his face and mooed.

'For God's sake,' she muttered, and taking out her phone she quickly texted Matthew. *He's here, with me.* She wasn't going to tell him anything else at this point. If she did, he'd ring, or worse, he'd come here, and she really didn't want to have to deal with him as well.

'Aiden!' she shouted angrily as he started to light a joint. 'Put that out *now*! And get yourself in the shower. You stink.'

'Cool, cool,' he mumbled, staying right where he was.

She was about to go and prod the naked boy awake when the bathroom door opened behind her and a female probably twice Aiden's age appeared in what looked like some sort of body suit until Cristy realized she was actually naked and covered in tattoos.

'Oh! Hello,' the woman said, in heavily accented English. 'I'm Erika, pleased to meet you.'

Ignoring the outstretched hand, Cristy pointed at the bathroom and said, 'Go back in there, put something on and then leave.' To Aiden she said, 'I'm going into my bedroom now. You have ten minutes, by which time I expect to find you properly dressed, sobered up and ready with some sort of explanation for this . . . whatever it is.'

'Oh, Mum, chill,' he moaned. 'We've had a heavy couple of days . . .'

'Do it!' she growled, and kicking the backpacks and debris out of the way, she returned to the coat-stand, snatched up her bag and laptop and shut herself in her room, which, thankfully, didn't have anyone or anything in it that shouldn't be there.

'Bloody child,' she seethed down the line to Connor when she got through to him. 'He might be in one piece now, but I can't vouch for how long it'll remain the case.'

'Where's he been?' Connor asked, sounding as though he was getting out of his car.

'To some festival, apparently. And he's brought at least two strays back with him – I've no idea who else might be here, and I don't want to know. I just want them out of here so I can try to deal with him. And good luck with that, given the state he's in. Honestly, I sometimes think he inhabits another planet to the rest of us. Hayley was never like this, and as far as I know Matthew wasn't at his age in spite of being a total prick now.' She took a breath and suddenly gulped as a stranger's face loomed up at her window. 'What the f . . .?' she cried, leaping up from the bed. 'Who the hell are you? Get out of my garden.'

The face tilted in curiosity, as if not quite hearing.

'*Get out!*' she shouted, pointing in the direction of the French doors since the only way to exit her patio with its pots and borders was through the flat, unless he wanted to climb an eight-foot wall.

'Jesus, it sounds like bedlam over there,' Connor commented. 'Want me to come back to lend a hand?'

'Yes! No, I'll manage, and I know you've got antenatal tonight. I only rang because you asked me to, and to remind you to email over your notes about Kevin Break.'

'Will do, but let me know if things get out of hand, as if they're not already.'

With a grim smile, she said, 'I might just do that if they're not gone soon.'

In the end it was over an hour before the front door slammed behind her uninvited guests, and another two before Aiden finally emerged from his room, groggy, tousle-haired and still not smelling too fresh, but at least he seemed reasonably sober.

'When did you last shower?' she asked, snatching up a pile of his stinking clothes and going into the small laundry area to shove them into the machine.

'Uh,' he replied, yawning and scratching his head. Behind the grunge and half-sprung beard, he was growing into an attractive young man, although of course she was biased. Not that his looks ever seemed to interest him. Thankfully, he hadn't learned how to use them to his advantage yet, the way his father had mastered over the years, but she guessed it would come. If only he didn't resemble Matthew quite so much – it was like living with a constant reminder.

'What the hell were you thinking, bringing complete strangers into my home?' she demanded, watching him taking a fresh Coke from the fridge and popping the tab. 'This isn't your place to treat just as you like, you know.'

'Don't worry, don't worry, I know I'm not really welcome here.'

Stung, she cried, 'That's not what I'm saying. Of course this is your home too, but there are boundaries, Aiden, and such a thing as respect. God knows how long it's going to take me to get the smell out of here . . .'

'What smell?'

'The one you and your unwashed friends have created. It's foul.'

'Just a bit of weed . . .'

'And more body odours than I'd care to name, plus the junk food – and did someone vomit? No, don't tell me, just make sure it's properly cleaned up.'

'No one chucked up. You're exaggerating, as usual, and look around you – we tidied everything away before they left—'

'And I dread to think where half of it is now. Aiden, this isn't good enough. You should've been at school today . . . When did you last go?'

He shrugged and carried his drink outside to slump down at her mosaic-topped bistro table.

'I'm speaking to you?' she shouted as he took out his phone.

'And I'm checking dates,' he shouted back. 'OK, I was there last Friday . . .'

'Today's Tuesday.'

'No shit, Sherlock.'

'Don't do that,' she seethed through her teeth. 'You're fifteen. You have to go to school, it's the law. And you can't just disappear without telling anyone where you're going . . .'

Stifling a yawn, he said, 'If I'd told you I was off to the Isle of Wight you'd have tried to stop me.'

'Of course I would, and so would Dad. You can't just go running off like that.'

'Seems I did, and we had a seriously cool time. Great acts this year . . .'

'I don't care who was playing. As far as I'm aware it finished on Sunday, so where have you been since?'

'Getting back. We ran out of cash so we had to thumb it.'

'You hitch-hiked,' she groaned in despair. 'You know how dangerous that can be.'

'But I'm here, aren't I, and if you don't mind me saying, you don't seem very pleased to see me.'

Dropping her head into her hands, she took a breath and tried to work out the best way to continue with this. Nothing useful was coming to mind; everything was being swallowed by an overwhelming sense of exasperation and despair.

'I can go back to Dad's if you like,' he said with a shrug. 'That's what you want me to do, isn't it?'

She looked up, and spoke before registering the uncertainty in his eyes. 'It's where you should be, and you know it. It's your home, Aiden—'

'And this is yours.'

'Yes. It's also yours whenever you want to come and stay, but not like this.'

'So it doesn't really matter to you that I can't stand being in the same house as that ridiculous stick insect with her pathetic attempts to try and bond with me, to strike up a special stepmum/stepson relationship before the *baby* comes. She makes me want to puke. And so does he, fawning all over her like some geriatric goat.'

Cristy could only stare at him. This was the first she'd heard of a baby, and though she couldn't care less if Matthew started a second family, apparently she did, because Aiden's words had felt like a punch to the gut. It was making her want to scream and strike out in some sort of farcical rage. *She* was the mother of his children, not some 'ridiculous stick-insect' her son couldn't stand.

What the hell was the matter with her? How had some warped and deluded part of her mind tricked her into believing they might not actually be having sex, that their intimacy wasn't real when *obviously it was*?

She couldn't stand this, she really couldn't.

Except she had to. There was no alternative and anyway, she'd moved on, was no longer a victim of his deceit and betrayal. She wasn't going to let herself be sucked back into the incubus of it all as if it still had power over her. It was behind her, in the past, and she was looking forward, getting on with her life, making a great success of things without him.

Somehow she managed to pick up seamlessly as she said to Aiden, 'Is this your way of asking if you can come and live here?'

He shook his head. 'Nah, it's not my thing to go where I'm not wanted.'

'That is a stupid thing to say. You know you can come here—'

'What, to have you walk out on me again? The way you did when I was a kid of thirteen . . . No, twelve—'

'I didn't leave *you*, I left your father because he was having an affair. You know that—'

'But you didn't find somewhere close to my school so I could go with you—'

'I already had this place—'

'And you've never fought him for custody—'

'Because of the school—'

'Or for the house. Any sane woman would have made him sell up and taken half. It's your right. That place is worth millions—'

'It's also your grandmother's home. Do you want me to uproot her now, at her age, when she's lived there practically all her life?'

'You don't care about her.'

'Well, apparently I do, or maybe I was thinking of you . . .'

'You should make him get you somewhere in Clifton. He owes you, Mum, big time.'

'I don't want to live in Clifton. I like it here, and if you want to make it your home too, I'll speak to your father—'

'But it's not big enough for the two of us, not full-time! I'd have to do my homework on the dining table because I don't have a desk—'

'We can get you one—'

'And who's going to take me to school when you're not around?'

'I thought you didn't want to go to school.'

'Yeah, very funny.'

Still inwardly reeling over the baby news, she went outside to join him, wishing she had a glass of wine.

Focus, Cristy. Focus. It's a beautiful, balmy evening, one we should be enjoying in this beloved little haven of a garden. 'Look, I know I didn't do everything right when I found out about Dad and Marley,' she said softly, 'and I realize now I should have considered you more. But it was such a difficult time for me. I could hardly think straight. You remember how the press were camped outside the house trying to get shots of me coming and going, wanting to show how "broken" I was. Or of Dad and how "torn up or stressed" he looked.'

'Or what a bastard he was,' Aiden grunted, 'and old. They kept going on about his age and he bloody hated it.'

'His fault for cheating with a woman not that much older than his own daughter.'

Aiden nodded gloomily. 'Some of those female journos totally savaged him . . .'

'I didn't know you'd read it.'

'Course we did. It was our parents they were writing about, totally weird and fucking horrible. Just because you presented the local news—'

'Dad presents, I was a reporter.'

'Anyone would have thought you were major celebs . . .'

'Marley kind of is,' she reminded him.

'What, because she comes from acting royalty and she starred in some stupid series no one ever watched when she was sixteen?'

'She was eighteen, and though it sticks in my throat to speak up for her, she's done other work since and it's been very well reviewed.'

'Whatever! I fucking hate him for going off with her – and then *making me live with her.*'

Certain that this was why he was so unhappy, Cristy reached for his hands and was relieved when he didn't snatch them away. She loved and treasured her children more than anything else in the world, would do anything for them including giving up the pleasure she now derived from living alone. 'If you want to come here,' she said softly, 'we'll make it work.'

Staring at their hands, he said, 'Or you could tell him you want the house and he needs to fuck off?'

With a tired smile she said, 'The settlement's done. The house is his . . .'

'You know what,' he said, getting up, 'trying to discuss stuff with you guys does my head in. I need a joint.'

'Sorry,' she said, following him inside, 'not allowed.'

'I'll only go and smoke it on the street,' he warned.

Sighing, she put a hand to her head just as the front door buzzer sounded, announcing someone's arrival. Looking up, she murmured, 'I have a horrible feeling this is going to be Dad.'

Aiden groaned. 'Did you tell him I was here?'

'I had to. He was worried.'

'And so Matt-man comes to get me. Why? He doesn't want me there any more than you want me here.'

'Aiden, neither of those things is true . . .' She winced as the buzzer sounded more impatiently. She didn't want to let Matthew in, would rather actually never see him again, but the sharing of two children meant it couldn't be avoided.

Going to the entryphone, she checked she was right and pressed to release the door. By the time she returned to the sitting room Aiden had disappeared into his room, the door firmly closed and something by the Clash turned up to a volume that she hoped wouldn't bother the neighbours.

'Whoa! What the hell's been going on in here?' Matthew demanded, waving a hand in front of his face as he came in. 'It smells worse than a rugger locker room. Has he been smoking dope?'

Unable to look at her ex-husband for long, mostly because she loathed him, she went to pour herself a drink and pointedly didn't offer him one.

He raised an eyebrow at the snub.

God! How could he still make her treacherous heart flip after all he'd done? What was wrong with her? Why didn't she just focus on the extra weight he seemed to be carrying? Weren't men supposed to take better care of themselves when they had a shining new wife to impress? Wasn't the new wife supposed to be on the case?

Maybe things weren't going as well for them as they'd like everyone to think.

Then she remembered.

'I hear congratulations are in order,' she said, somehow wrenching out the words that didn't actually need to be spoken, so why had she bothered?

His eyes narrowed slightly as if he wasn't sure what she was talking about.

'The baby,' she stated.

At least he had the grace to look awkward. 'Ah yes, sorry, I was meaning to tell you, but things have been pretty hectic—'

'You don't need to tell me anything,' she interrupted. 'I just hope you're up for starting a new family at your age.'

He rolled his eyes at the jibe, and she added, 'Aiden doesn't want to come back with you.'

'And you've told him he doesn't have to?'

'No. He has no school clothes here, or books, or sports gear, so he needs to go with you. Just know that he's not happy at home and I'd rather he didn't make a habit of disappearing—'

'He's fifteen, doing what fifteen-year-olds do. Where did he go?'

'To the Isle of Wight Festival. I'm sure he'll tell you all about it if you ask. And, for the record, most boys of his age don't just bunk off without a word, nor are they smoking dope, or detesting their new stepmum, or wishing their mother had tried to take what was rightfully hers when their dad decided to trade her in for a younger model.'

He regarded her steadily, sadly. 'Are you really still so bitter?' he asked, sounding surprised – or was it faintly sorry?

'Everything about you makes me bitter,' she informed him tartly.

'And yet it wasn't so very long ago that you were begging me to try again.'

'In your dreams,' she raged, hating herself more deeply than ever for that hideous moment of weakness *more than a year ago*. 'There was no begging involved, and I suggested it for the children's sake, mostly Aiden's. I had no idea you were about to get married, or I'd have spared myself the effort.' And humiliation.

Why the f*** didn't feelings just curl up and die when they were supposed to, and make room for whole new branches of dignity to grow?

'Where is he?' he asked, looking around the still untidy room and seeming, as he always did in here, too big for the place.

She gestured to the bedroom door. 'Knock yourself out,' she invited and turned to start clearing up the kitchen mess that had apparently been overlooked in the pre-eviction blitz.

To her surprise Aiden didn't stop his father from entering, and as the door closed behind Matthew, she put on the radio rather

48

than try to hear what they were saying. It just about broke her heart to think of how hard her son was struggling beneath all his attitude and faux-chilled bravado, but it wasn't as if Matthew didn't care. She knew very well that he did. He'd never been a bad father, just, in the end, a totally lousy husband who she could never forgive for his treachery or, goddammit, get over.

CHAPTER FOUR

'I've been writing stuff down for you,' ex-Detective Constable Kevin Break announced as he led Cristy and Connor around the side of his wisteria-covered bungalow in Portishead to a neat back garden terrace with a panoramic view of the Severn Estuary. 'And I have a little bit of news you're going to want to hear. To do with the case, obviously. You wouldn't be interested in anything else.'

Intrigued, and appreciating the way this burly, bald-headed man with bowling ball muscles and lively dark eyes had dispensed with small talk, Cristy took the chair he waved her to, at a table in the shade of a magnificently flowering magnolia tree. Connor, looking a little crumpled and hot and as if he'd had another bad night, sat down heavily and lifted his laptop onto the table.

They'd spent all of yesterday at the podcast studios collating everything they already had on the Kellon Manse Murders while structuring, as best they could, a running order for the upcoming series. Today's interview with a police officer who'd actually been at the scene back in 2008 was very definitely an early bonus. The plan was to intercut his recollections with Flora Gibson's, and hopefully their combined accounts would ramp up the mystery of the case in a way little else could at this stage. Apart from an interview with Lexie Gaudion's sister, Olivia, of course, or David Gaudion's brother, Richard, or best of all, David Gaudion himself. Still no response from either of them, although nothing had been expected from David given that they still had no idea where he was.

'OK, let's hear the news,' Connor encouraged, rubbing his hands together and seeming to come to life.

Kevin's smile showed a gap in his front teeth and a dimple in both cheeks. 'Yeah, you're going to like it,' he promised. 'See, I've been in touch with someone on the force who was involved in the case with me, and she's still there. She's a way further up the ladder now, but like me, she has a bug in her bonnet about what went on back then. For obvious reasons, she doesn't want to go on the record with anything she might uncover for us, but she's agreed to use her privileged access to files we'd never get to see without having someone on the inside.' He grinned. 'So there you go, we already have our deep throat. That's an undercover agent for those not familiar with Watergate.'

Cristy and Connor exchanged glances; this definitely was good news, even better than they could have hoped for when they'd first contacted Kevin Break.

'I'll ask again if she's willing to meet you,' Kevin continued. 'It's likely to remain a flat no, but if she does say yes at any point, it might be best to do it here, out of the public eye and all that.'

'Of course,' Cristy agreed. 'Please assure her that we fully respect her need for anonymity . . .'

Kevin hadn't finished. 'She always had an instinct, same as me, that something's not right about what happened back then, and it stands to reason that someone knows a lot more than they're telling. Question is, who's the someone? Could be more than one person, of course, I expect you've thought of that. Anyway, whoever it is, I don't expect they're going to like your investigation much, so we best take care because we don't want to be thrown off course just as things start to get interesting, do we? I'm not saying we will, but let's keep our wits about us, especially once this starts airing. Any plans for that yet?'

Impressed, and pleased by the way he was throwing himself into the case, Cristy said, 'We're planning to drop the first episode next Tuesday at six and hope to do the same for each episode going forward. Much will depend on what we unearth, or who might make contact once the podcast is underway. People often get in touch after listening to an episode and sometimes their information can be quite valuable.'

'Even turn things on their head,' Connor added. 'We've had that happen before. Public engagement is a key element to most investigations, but obviously, as an ex-cop you already know that.'

Kevin grinned happily and waved an arm as a buxom woman with short platinum hair and several piercings emerged from the house carrying a loaded tray of refreshments. 'Just in time, B,' he declared. 'We were starting to gag out here.'

Smiling all over her pretty, plump face, his wife set the tray down, and said, 'I'm Bianca. Pleased to meet you guys. Obvs, I know you from the telly, Cristy, I was always a fan. Programme's gone downhill since you left, IMO. And you must be Connor. My Kev, here, was pretty taken with you after you met. Reckons you're the real deal. Anyway, tea in the pot, sugar, milk and lemon in the bowls, and some of my special scones. Cream's fresh from the farm down the road, and we grow the strawbs ourselves in our allotment, don't we, babe?'

'We do,' he confirmed, 'and we've got a great crop this year.'

'OK, so I'll be inside if you need anything,' she assured them. 'Facilities first on the right as you go in, phone charger in the kitchen if you need one.'

As she left, Cristy noticed Connor eyeing the perfectly scrumptious-looking scones. Kevin was grinning, clearly eager to see if they'd heed his warning. In the end, deciding it would be rude not to at least try one, Cristy lifted the smallest one onto a side plate and added a scoop of cream and jam.

Connor did the same while Kevin filled three dainty cups with tea and started to laugh as Cristy bit into her scone and widened her eyes in amazement. It was probably the best she'd ever tasted, crumbly and buttery and just the right amount of currants.

'Gotcha!' Kevin chuckled. 'She was a runner-up on *Bake Off*, my missus, a few years back. How lucky does that make me?'

'Very,' Connor murmured, using his fingers to make sure not a single delicious crumb escaped. 'Just as well you're not her publicist the way you sold them to us.'

Clearly finding that hilarious, Kevin dropped a slice of lemon into his tea and then opened up his notebook. 'So, now, I expect you guys are keen to get started. I've never done anything like this before, but I expect I'll catch on soon enough. I usually do.'

Helping himself to another scone, Connor set the laptop to record and nodded to Cristy to begin.

'Just forget the computer's there,' she advised Kevin. 'Use your own words, at your own pace, and don't worry about getting things in the wrong order – we can always sort that later.'

'I thought it was an interview,' he said, puzzled. 'Aren't you going to be asking me questions?'

'I am, but we'll treat it more like a chat. Let's begin with you introducing yourself so the listeners will hear, in your words, who you are and how you're connected to the case.'

Kevin nodded, quickly scanned his notes, then cleared his throat to begin.

'I'm ex-Detective Constable Kevin Break. I left the force about ten years ago. I've got a body-building gym now, not far from my home, that's doing all right, and we're looking to expand sometime in the next year or two. It suits me a lot better than being a cop, but that's not to say I didn't enjoy serving the public back when I did. I worked some pretty big cases before I decided to make a change, and I probably could have gone up the ranks, but, to be honest, after the Kellon Manse Murders, I started to lose a bit of faith in the job. We had our man, everyone knew that, but then something happened and next thing we knew he was walking before he even got to trial – and all our hard work was kicked out like yesterday's trash.'

CRISTY: 'Why were you so certain it was David Gaudion?'

KEVIN: 'Everything pointed to him, didn't it? I mean, if you were looking at it from our point of view, and there wasn't really another. Or not that we knew of. OK, maybe he wasn't suspect number one at the get-go, but it was crazy the day the bodies were found. First we've got a triple homicide on our hands, then we find out a child is missing, probably abducted . . . David Gaudion turns up like a hurricane, pushing at officers, punching one, shouting at others to do their jobs . . . We all thought he was in shock – bloke comes back from a run to find police and forensics all over his house, who wouldn't go into shock? Especially once he finds out his daughter is missing.'

CRISTY: 'How did he know his daughter was missing at that point?'

KEVIN: 'I'm not sure he did for certain then. Of course, later, we all thought it was an act, and a pretty good one, I have to hand him that. But on the day he said he'd called into his mother's, and his youngest daughter wasn't there, so they'd assumed she'd made her way home. We had no reason – yet – to suspect him of taking the child himself. There was nothing to suggest it. Or to say he'd committed the murders, come to that, but obviously it was early days. A couple of senior officers took him aside to try and calm him down, but whatever he told them then, he didn't give a full statement concerning his whereabouts at the time of the offence until the next day.'

CONNOR: 'Do you know where he spent that first night?'

KEVIN: 'As I recall, he was out searching for the girl. They do that, you know? Killers, kidnappers, rapists . . . They join in with the search like butter wouldn't melt. Makes me sick to my stomach.'

CONNOR: 'Were you part of the search?'

KEVIN: 'No, they have special units for that. My job, over the next couple of days, was to corroborate Gaudion's claim he'd been out for a run.'

CRISTY: 'And did you?'

KEVIN: 'I tried, believe me, but I couldn't find any witnesses, no one to say they'd spotted him running past, even at a distance, and that was when we first scented that things weren't adding up. How can someone as well-known as he was in the area be out in full of view of the world for over three hours and not be seen by anyone? Obviously, we did all the house-to-house calls, most particularly along the route he said he'd taken, but he'd either made himself invisible, or his neighbours had got a fit of the blinds. Not one of 'em recalled seeing him that day.'

CRISTY: 'What about his car? I guess you checked to see if anyone had noticed it coming or going from the house at the crucial time?'

KEVIN: 'We did, and no one had. It was in the garage at the Manse when we found it and, according to the techies who examined it, it hadn't been used since the previous weekend.'

CRISTY: 'He could have used another vehicle?'

KEVIN: 'If he did, it didn't belong to any of the family, but yeah, you're right, he could have hired one, or borrowed it, even stolen it, but we never found anything to say that he did. No one saw him, or his daughter. The whole community turned out to help search for her. I don't think a blade of grass was left unturned, or building unchecked, or ditch uncovered, but there was never any sign of her.'

CRISTY: 'At what point did you discover that a rifle was missing from Gaudion's home?'

KEVIN: 'It was the day after the killings. He couldn't account for where it was. He kept saying it was always kept in a locked case in the basement, and I daresay it was until suddenly it wasn't.'

CRISTY: 'Was it ever found?'

KEVIN: 'Yes, in Seedown Woods, just behind the nearby village, which happens to be on the route Gaudion claimed to have taken for his run. One of the search team came across it about a week after the murders. It was hidden in some undergrowth, no ammunition anywhere, and it hadn't been fired either. However, Gaudion's fingerprints turned out to be all over it – you'd expect that given it was his, but a couple of Amelia's were found on the butt.'

CRISTY: 'So what did you make of that?'

KEVIN: 'Lots of theories. She struggled with her abductor; her father had been teaching her to shoot . . .'

CRISTY: 'At the age of ten?'

KEVIN: 'They're country folk.'

CRISTY: 'Were there any other prints?'

KEVIN: 'Not that I was ever told about.'

CONNOR: 'Meaning you thought something was being kept from you?'

KEVIN: 'Not then, but later it crossed my mind.'

CONNOR: 'None of this was made public at the time? The rifle, the woods, the fingerprints?'

KEVIN: 'It was decided to withhold it until it could be established that Amelia had actually been in the woods that day. It turned out she probably had, and in that spot . . . More footprints, DNA from urine found in the soil. Gaudion's Nike prints were there too, clear as day, same as the ones he'd been wearing while "out for a run".'

CRISTY: 'How did he explain that?'

KEVIN: 'He claimed he and Amelia often searched the woods for rare bits of nature, or whatever, for her to take into school. The footprints around where the rifle was discovered could have been made at any time during the preceding days, or weeks – there hadn't been much rain, it wasn't a common place for anyone to walk in – and it turned out, once forensics did their thing, that both father's and daughter's footprints were, indeed, all over the place.'

CONNOR: 'Had Gaudion been arrested by the time you made these discoveries?'

KEVIN: 'I don't think so. He'd have been interviewed under caution by then, that's for sure, but as far as I remember we arrested and charged him after the results of another footprint analysis came back. Same Nikes, his size, made by someone who'd stepped in his mother-in-law's blood and trodden it into the carpet on the way out of the house.'

CONNOR: 'You must have had his trainers analysed?'

KEVIN: 'Of course, and they came back with not a trace of blood on either one of them, but he'd had plenty of time to wash it off, hadn't he? Or to swap them for another identical pair. Who can say?'

CRISTY: 'How did he explain this footprint?'

KEVIN: 'By saying he wasn't the only bloke in the world with a pair of size eleven Nike P-6000 running shoes. I think that was the brand, something like it anyway.'

CONNOR: 'He was right, he wouldn't have been the only one who had them.'

KEVIN: 'Bit of a coincidence, though, don't you think?'

CRISTY: 'Was any other evidence used at this point to support a charge?'

KEVIN: 'You mean apart from him not having an alibi? It was starting to stack up pretty well by then, and as we went forward all kinds of stuff started coming out of the woodwork. What's stuck with me all these years though . . . Not that it weighed so much against Gaudion, but there was a small box found at the murder scene, velvet, like the ones you get from a jeweller. Inside they found a small gold butterfly necklace. Lexie Gaudion and Serena Sutton were wearing identical ones. Both women also had a tattoo of the same thing on their pubis – well, we thought it was a tattoo until the pathologist told us it had been branded on.'

CRISTY: 'Ouch! I guess that's why rumours of a cult started flying around?'

KEVIN: 'For sure. And then there was Serena Sutton's offices being burned to the ground, presumably, possibly, to stop anyone finding out about things they'd rather stayed hidden.'

CONNOR: 'Meaning the arsonist and the killer are probably one and the same?'

KEVIN: 'Definitely a possible, but nothing was ever proved. Nor could we put Gaudion in Oxford at the time of the fire, but his alibi that day was his brother. Apparently they were both at the flat they shared in London all that day and through the night. Convenient, that, wouldn't you say?'

CRISTY: 'So are you saying Serena's home and office were destroyed to cover up a cult that she was a part of? Maybe even running?'

KEVIN: 'It was a theory, but we didn't get very far with it.'

CONNOR: 'And you thought David and his brother might also be involved?'

KEVIN: 'Let's just say something very strange was going on: branding, butterflies, burning down of buildings, murder of three women, disappearance of a child. It was certain Lexie was a client of Serena's, her sister Olivia told us that, but with no records of their meetings we could never find anything else to tell us what was really going on.'

CRISTY: 'But if there was a cult, there must have been other members, surely?'

KEVIN: 'I point you back to the fire – no records, no names – although we had a few anonymous calls claiming to know things they were afraid to talk about.'

CONNOR: 'Were they taken seriously?'

KEVIN: 'They might have been if they'd actually come forward. As it was, it never amounted to more than a few calls.'

CRISTY: 'So what's your take on the theory of a cult now?'

KEVIN: 'I reckon it exists, or it did back then. Maybe it's still out there. All I can tell you is we might have got somewhere with it if the whole case hadn't suddenly been shut down.'

CONNOR: 'Why did that happen?'

KEVIN: 'Who knows, but it was odd, that's for sure. What I can tell you though is that no one who knew Serena was prepared to believe she'd get herself involved in anything out of the norm. They all said she was a professional to her core, only cared about other people's well-being and would never use or abuse her position for some sort of personal gain, especially not in a cultish way.'

CRISTY: 'The butterfly branding notwithstanding?'

KEVIN: 'Most of them didn't know about it. Those who did said they thought it was a tattoo, and if it wasn't they couldn't explain it.'

A few moments of silence passed before Connor finally turned off the tape.

Without prompting, Kevin said, 'There are a lot of secrets buried in that family – I'm talking about David and Lexie Gaudion now, and the mother, over at the Hall. For my money that's where the heart of this lies. So, I'd say, the person you really need to talk to is Olivia Caldwell.'

'We're trying,' Connor assured him, 'but she's not answering our messages.'

'Mm, can't say I'm surprised. She definitely won't want all this dredged up again. From what I hear she had some kind of breakdown after losing her mother and sister that way. Her niece too, of course. It was hard for her and I don't suppose it's got much easier over the years. That sort of thing never does, does it?'

Cristy could hardly imagine how she'd react if she lost family members in such a horrific way. 'You must have interviewed her,' she said. 'Did she have any thoughts on who might have done it?'

'I wasn't there when she gave her statements, but I never saw anything in the files to say that she suspected anyone other than her brother-in-law.'

Sitting forward, Connor said, 'Here's what's intriguing me. When the case was let go, the trial abandoned, was it because something had come to light to prove that Gaudion hadn't done it?'

Kevin shook his head. 'If it was, then it was nothing I ever knew about,' he replied gravely. 'We were told that the evidence we had come up with wasn't strong enough for the prosecution to take into court and win.'

'Did you agree with that decision?'

Kevin shrugged. 'I'm not a lawyer, but I wasn't the only one who thought there was a case to answer, and we all believed there was a reasonable chance of winning.'

'Did you carry on with the investigation after that?' Cristy asked.

Kevin nodded. 'A couple of detectives stayed on it, yes. I was reassigned myself, but nothing new ever came up. Obviously, the search continued for Amelia, but as you know she was never found, and I don't reckon she ever will be. Poor kid. If you ask me, she saw what happened to her mother and grandmother – who'd done it – so he killed her too. And then the murdering bastard got away with it.'

CHAPTER FIVE

A few hours later Cristy was sitting at a table outside the popular waterside café waiting for Meena to take the ferry across from the office to join her. Thanks to the weather, hundreds of people, mainly tourists, were milling about, feeding ducks, taking in the sun or in some noisome cases getting horribly drunk. She shuddered at the idea of Aiden being amongst them, although she'd heard from him today, a brief text saying *At school, Be Happy,* a little riff on Bob Marley's classic.

She'd also heard from Matthew: *Felt things didn't go too well with us last night. Sorry if it was my fault.*

As far as she was concerned, there was no *if* about it.

She hadn't responded: she had nothing to say and no desire to give him reason to be in touch again.

Shielding her eyes, she peered across the water, swimming in sunlight, towards the SS *Great Britain*, searching for a sign of Meena, and yet distracted, as always, by Brunel's magnificent creation, sitting proudly, gleamingly in its custom-built dry dock. Her parents, as a courting couple back in 1970, had watched the great vessel's miraculous return to its birthplace, waving their flags, cheering and bursting with pride to see its tired old rusted hulk being towed under the celebrated engineer's other spectacular landmark, the Clifton Suspension Bridge. Her dad used to love reliving the memory of that day and had taken her on so many tours of the ship since its splendid restoration that she felt she could find her way around in the dark.

Hayley and Aiden probably could too, for Matthew had taken them on regular tours during their younger years, and as a very special treat, only a few months ago, he and Marley had hired it out for Hayley's eighteenth birthday party. How harshly that had stung for Cristy, having her own plans for her daughter's big day seized from her grasp, and how wretched she'd felt about her own meagre suggestion that they – she, Hayley, Aiden, Connor and Jodi – celebrate with a dinner at the waterside café, Hayley's favourite restaurant. They'd done that, and she knew Hayley had enjoyed every minute, but it was never going to feature as one of the standout experiences of her life, the way a party on the SS *Great Britain* would.

Since there was no sign of Meena boarding the ferry yet, Cristy turned her attention back to her glass of wine, and the notes she was making about this afternoon's interview with Kevin Break. The man had been as frank and forthright as they'd hoped, and there was no doubt his account of the investigation had managed to paint an extremely interesting picture of early events. And, extremely usefully, the concerns he and some of his colleagues had been left with were going to prove perfect for a repeat tease throughout the series.

She and Connor had, of course, found several suggestions of a cult during their initial research, but they hadn't come up with anyone to talk about it yet. However, Kevin's comment today was certainly going to grab listeners: 'Let's just say something very strange was going on: branding, butterflies, burning down of buildings, murder of three women, disappearance of a child . . .'

There was a lot to follow up on, that was for sure, but for her the two standout questions remained: (1) Why had no one continued to seek justice for their murdered loved ones following Gaudion's release? and (2) Why had Gaudion himself not, as far as they were aware, tried to clear his name, if, as he'd claimed, he didn't do it?

She checked her mobile as a text arrived: *Sorry, should be there in 10. Mx*

There was also one from Aiden: *Pyramid Stage here I come. Dad got tickets for my 16th.*

With a horrible wrench in her heart, she put the phone aside and picked up her wine. Aiden had been on Matthew's case for at least the past four years to use his contacts to get them into the 'only place in the world I ever want to be' and clearly he'd now done it. Presumably this was how Matthew had got Aiden to go home with him so easily on Tuesday night. He'd never been above a spot of bribery, and he'd obviously know that this dream come true for Aiden would put her at a miserable disadvantage.

Why, she wondered, would he want to do that? She never played a one-upmanship game with him (not that she could pull it off if she tried), and she'd never done anything to hurt him, or to try to make him feel small. What did he get out of doing it to her when he was the one who'd cheated, broken up their home, humiliated her privately and publicly, and brought about a fast divorce so he could marry 'the big love of his life'? That was what he'd called Marley when the affair had first come out into the open, and Cristy, who'd loved Matthew with all her heart and had truly believed he felt the same, couldn't imagine ever forgiving or forgetting those callous words.

She wondered if he and Marley were also going to Glastonbury with Aiden. It was a festival she and Matthew had been to many times over the years. They'd done so much together, as a couple, as a foursome with the children, as a big family when her parents, and both of his, were still alive. Aunts, uncles, cousins, old friends and new used to come to the house in Leigh Woods for Christmas and birthdays, summer parties and the end of dry January. They'd loved to entertain, and she'd been so happy in her marriage, had felt blessed and so certain that nothing could ever come between them that when it had, she'd been completely unprepared, and utterly devastated.

Still, she was pulling things back together now, mostly thanks to Meena and Harry, who'd talked her into setting up the podcast, and to Connor who'd resigned his assistant producer's job on their old programme to come and work with her. They'd been a great team, the two of them, when they'd been covering stories for the local news and various documentaries. He'd howled in protest when she'd decided to walk away from her thriving career, had begged her not to, had insisted, furiously, that she was braver than that, but she wasn't. She simply hadn't been able to go on facing Matthew every day knowing he'd spent the night before with Marley, and knowing, too, that everyone was watching them, gossiping, pitying and in some cases probably gloating.

'Hey, sorry I kept you,' Meena cried, sweeping in, all beautiful black hair and exquisite features. 'Issues with the BBC over something you don't even need to think about,' she explained, bracelets jangling as she blew Cristy a kiss while sinking into an empty chair. 'I left Harry dealing with it, but I expect we'll have to call in the lawyers. Are you going to have another of those?'

Seeing it was indeed time for a top-up, Cristy turned to summon a server to order two white wines and a plate of antipasti. 'So whose podcast is in trouble?' she asked as Meena turned off her phone.

'Frances and Jean's,' Meena sighed. 'They've gone over the top with their "lifestyle choices" again and the sponsors are refusing to sign off without certain changes. That's what happens when you've got backing, of course – they reserve the right to have a say in things you'd rather they just butted out of. However, no problems so far with *Hindsight*. Not that I'm expecting any. Annie Grayson at the Beeb just about bit my hand off when I told her about your new series . . .'

'You went to the Beeb first?' Cristy said, surprised.

'I promised Annie I would, you know how much she loves what you do. You pull in the listeners and your subscriptions are off the scale in comparison to most true-crimers. But don't worry, I'm also talking to Sky, Audible and Global, so we could end up with a really decent budget to supplement what we've already put your way, and I don't anticipate any problems at all with the advertisers.'

Cristy was smiling. 'You're amazing,' she declared.

'As are you,' Meena smiled back as their drinks arrived. 'Harry and I are always saying we're lucky to have you. People really want to listen to you . . . Sure, in the early days, they were hoping to hear all sorts of crap about your private life, but it's not about that any more.' She clinked her glass against Cristy's, took a sip and then grimaced in a way that told Cristy something not quite so good was coming up next.

'Do I need to brace?' Cristy asked.

'Probably,' Meena admitted. 'Apparently, Matthew and *herself* are hosting a dinner for the cast of a play about to open at the Old Vic, and Harry and I have been invited.'

Cristy's throat turned dry. It was hard to smile. 'That's very kind of them,' she commented lightly.

'Effing insensitive if you ask me,' Meena argued. 'They know you mean the world to us and we don't appreciate being put in a position where we feel we have to choose sides. It'll always be yours, of course, but you know Harry and Matthew go way back, and they—'

'You must go and not even think about me,' Cristy told her.

'As if,' Meena cried in protest. 'I've already told Harry we have to turn it down, because no way am I going to be dragged into a cosy foursome with *that child* as a part of it, and I reckon that's what she, or Matthew, or both are trying to pull off.'

Suspecting it might be, Cristy said, 'Let's try not to make things awkward for Harry, though. I honestly don't mind if you go . . .'

'Yes, you do. I can see how upset you are and now I wish I hadn't told you. We should have just replied saying we're not free that night and been done with it. And that's actually what we will do. I'll call Harry right now.'

'No, really,' Cristy protested as Meena turned her phone back on. 'I'm OK with it, honestly.'

Meena started as her phone vibrated. 'Harry,' she announced. 'I'm going to speak to him over there, where you won't have to listen. Just don't eat all the olives before I get back.'

As she weaved through the tourists towards the boats, holding her phone to one ear and a finger to the other, Cristy picked up her drink and, rather than try to deal with the last couple of minutes, made herself focus on what she and Connor had planned next for the podcast.

Still no reply from Flora Gibson about whether or not her father-in-law had actually read the questions they'd sent over, which was a shame given how long he'd known the Gaudion and Sallis families. However, he couldn't be the only one who'd grown up in the Vale at the same time as David and Lexie; there had to be plenty of others, it was just a question of finding them. Door-to-door, shops, pubs, village halls, churches . . . There surely had to be someone willing to give them some background on the victims and the perpetrator; someone who didn't only have memories of the early years, but opinions, theories, even knowledge, of what had happened that day in June 2008.

Unconsciously, she slipped into wondering what she and Matthew had been doing during that time. She'd have been heavily pregnant with Aiden, of course, and Hayley would have not long turned three. They'd had a holiday planned for late August, a villa in the South of France with a pool, a tennis court, a terrace overlooking the distant Mediterranean, and with enough bedrooms for friends and family to join them. It had turned into a wonderful two weeks in spite of the sleepless nights and breast-feeding. Matthew had been so proud of his new son, and was so besotted with his little girl that Hayley already had him wrapped around her finger. Cristy remembered her lovely tanned limbs, inflatables and bouncy balls, lots of rosé, succulent cantaloupes, Provençal olives, and delicious barbecued fish. They'd loved their time there so much that they'd even investigated buying the villa, but the owner hadn't wanted to sell.

It was just after their return that she'd been appointed producer/reporter of a new current affairs programme due to go into production around the time her maternity leave was over. Matthew had been so thrilled when she'd received the news and had sworn that he, as news anchor and head of programmes, had not used his influence to strong-arm the board. 'You got it because you're good,' he'd assured her, and she'd believed him, because she'd had no reason not to back then. They'd always trusted one another to be truthful. They were each other's best friend, harshest critic and soul mate, she'd thought, until they weren't any more.

Gathering her thoughts back from the brink, she decided to wonder about the Gaudions' marriage rather than her own. What had gone wrong for it to have ended the way it did? Had they once been just as happy as she and Matthew with their beautiful home and two lovely young daughters? Were they still in love when their world had suddenly imploded? What kind of secrets had been buried with Lexie, Mean Margaret and Serena Sutton? What had Serena been doing at the Manse that day? Had David really been out for a run?

How could he have been without anyone seeing him?

Calling up a photo of him on her phone, she studied his face again, the pale blue eyes that seemed to be teasing whoever was behind the camera; the start of a smile that had no doubt burst into life the second after the shot was taken. He appeared a confident, maybe even slightly arrogant man, someone who enjoyed privilege and standing in his world. She knew he'd been a successful finance lobbyist for a major firm in the City while Lexie was a stay-at-home mum. He'd have been in and out of Whitehall, as well as some of the world's biggest banks, while Lexie had been doing what exactly?

Getting Gaudion's ex-colleagues to speak about him probably wasn't going to be easy, although Connor had already put in several calls and not everyone had come back to them yet, so no reason to give up hope. Finding someone to talk about Lexie should be easier, and yet they didn't have anyone in the frame for it yet.

Speaking to Gaudion in her mind, she said, 'You must have moved in some pretty murky, even dangerous circles given the world you were in, so is that why you've gone into hiding since the murders? Did Lexie find out about something she shouldn't have? Was she going to report you? Is that why she lost her life?' After a pause she added, 'Some would describe your elite world as a cult; I think I would. All that exclusivity and ritual, nepotism and political manipulation. So what sort of Pandora's box are we about to open with this case? Will it be one filled with evil and corruption, or is there something else entirely lying in wait? Speak to me, David Gaudion, I want to hear whatever you have to say.'

CHAPTER SIX

'I've been wondering if David Gaudion was involved in some sort of cult,' Cristy remarked to Connor the next morning, 'but actually what's making more sense, given the matching butterfly necklaces and brandings, is that Lexie and Serena were involved in something, and maybe Serena was at the Manse that day to try and recruit Mean Margaret?'

They were recording their musings, and as Connor tucked one of his headphones behind an ear he said, 'Because of the butterfly in a jewellery box? A kind of new member token?'

Cristy nodded slowly and picked up her coffee. They were perched on a wall outside the podcast studios, taking a break from patching together Flora's and Colin's interviews ready for next Tuesday's opening episode. 'It could be,' she continued, still thinking aloud, 'that David came back earlier than expected that day, realized what was going on and . . . lost it?'

Connor grimaced. 'And just happened to have a semi-automatic handgun about his person to sort things out once and for all?'

Cristy wrinkled her nose. 'Maybe he was lying in wait, knowing Serena was due to visit.' She wasn't even slightly convinced by this and could tell that Connor wasn't either.

'I keep asking myself,' he said, 'would he really have shot dead three women, one of them his wife and the child's own mother, while the child was in the house?'

'Maybe he didn't know she was there. The records tell us that she and her sister were taken to their grandmother Gaudion's that day, before everything kicked off, and according to said

68

grandmother's statement it wasn't unusual for Amelia to sneak back to Kellon Hall's stables to be with her horse.'

'That puts her at the Hall, not the Manse.'

'True, but she was close by, so maybe she decided to go over to the Manse for something and no one saw or heard her come in?'

'OK, so suddenly realizing Amelia had witnessed the killings, Gaudion then – what? Grabbed her . . .'

'And a rifle from downstairs . . .'

'. . . spirited her out of the house – he couldn't have shot her there or there would have been blood in the house – so he takes her to Seedown Woods which are, what, a mile away, all uphill?'

'About that.'

'How did they get there, given we know his car wasn't used that day?'

'He could have carried her across country. There's access to the fields at the back of the Manse.'

'Mm, hard to imagine, especially if she was struggling, but let's go with it for now. So they get to the woods and what happens then? No blood was found to suggest he shot or even injured her, nor do we know for certain that he took her there that day, only that they had been there at some point.'

'But the rifle was found there. That has to mean something.'

'True, but what? It doesn't seem to have much significance to anything insofar as it wasn't the murder weapon, and nor had it been fired. Also, the record states that there was no blood on Gaudion when he got back to the house after his run. Only sweat, and a lot of it.'

'He could have gone somewhere to change into sweaty gear that he'd stowed ahead of time and then returned later to get rid of all the bloody stuff.'

'So what did he do with Amelia while he was changing clothes?'

Stumped, Cristy could only shake her head. 'It's not adding up, is it?'

'Not the way we're looking at it right now. Unless he wasn't acting alone.'

'There's never been mention of anyone else, apart from a

possible hitman that the detectives more or less ruled out.' She paused with that, and said, 'Murder is almost always about love or money. So now I'm asking myself, was he having an affair with someone who assisted him that day? He could even be with her now, wherever he is.'

Connor looked at her askance. 'Offing the wife, her mother and friend is a bit of a drastic alternative to divorce,' he pointed out.

Cristy smiled. 'Unless he stood to get the money. With Mean Margaret and Lexie out of the way, who stood to inherit the Sallis fortune?'

'Most likely the sister, Olivia, whose husband, we know already, is rich as fuck, so we have to ask ourselves, why would she? Gaudion, or his daughters, were most probably the main beneficiary to his wife's share of the estate, but we don't know what that amounted to, and I don't get the impression he was short of a few himself, so I can't see this as a motive for him. However, we ought to go back to Kevin about it, find out if he knows how much checking was done into Gaudion's finances. Still a weird way to get out of debt or secure your future, if you ask me, but desperate times and all that . . .'

Letting the silence run for a while as she tried to hook onto some logic, or an idea that might propel them in another direction to cast another, clearer light on events, Cristy finished her coffee and said, 'It beggars belief that no one saw him out running that day. Or anyone coming and going from the house.'

'Mm, I get that it's pretty remote, but all the same . . .' Connor agreed. 'What was it, some kind of ghost town that day?' His mobile rang and he quickly stopped the recording as he clicked on the call. 'Hey. Are you OK?' *Jodi*, he mouthed to Cristy.

Jodi's excited voice rang out. 'I think she just burped,' she gushed, loud enough for Cristy to hear.

'That's amazing,' Connor cried as if it were the world's greatest baby-feat.

'It could have been a fart,' Cristy put in.

Jodi laughed and said, 'I heard that, and I guess it could have, but that's cool. Either way, it proves she's going to take after her father . . .'

'Hey!' Connor protested.

Still laughing, Jodi said, 'Sorry if I'm interrupting something.'

'You're not,' Cristy assured her, even though she was. She was a dear, generous soul of whom Cristy was extremely fond.

'So what are you guys up to?' Jodi asked.

'We're sitting outside in the fresh air, taking a break,' Connor told her. 'How about you?'

As Jodi answered, Cristy checked her own phone and saw to her surprise that she'd received two missed calls from the same London number, and a message on the family WhatsApp from Hayley.

Hey Mum, Just to let you know Hugo and I still coming as planned, but will be later. Dad's only got us tickets to Glasto. GOAT. If OK with you we'll come to yours after. And before we go to Oslo. Love you, Hx

As Cristy fought down her emotions, she couldn't help wondering what had happened to 'I'll never speak to him again; I hate him; she's a bitch; they're sick.' All things Hayley had raged repeatedly during the first year of the break-up. In fact, she really hadn't spoken to her father for at least nine months, refusing all contact with him, wouldn't even eat at the same table as him, in spite of still living, mostly, under the same roof. She'd had to finish school and sit her A levels, so moving out at that time would have been too disruptive, and Marley hadn't moved in properly until Hayley had decamped to Cristy's. She'd stayed with Cristy throughout that summer until finally taking off for a gap year, by which time Cristy had secretly been relieved to have the flat to herself again. She loved her daughter more than life itself, but Hayley's insistence on dishing out advice and offering comfort when Cristy had only wanted to be left alone had been an ordeal she'd dearly wanted to end.

Of course, Matthew and Marley had flown out to Australia for a visit while Hayley was there, and had taken her to Bali for a holiday. They'd also promised that when she came back they'd help her find an apartment in Edinburgh.

Such a generous Daddy. And such a helpful stepmum who'd

offered to help Hayley furnish the new place when the time came. Apparently, Marley had an eye for interior design.

'Are you OK?' Connor asked, ringing off from Jodi.

Cristy forced a smile. 'All good,' she replied. She held out her phone. 'I've had a call from a London number. Do you recognize it?'

He took a moment to search his laptop for contacts relating to the Kellon case. 'Not on the list,' he replied. 'Give it a try.'

Cristy did and a moment later was listening to an automated voicemail with no subscriber ID. 'Hi, Cristy Ward here,' she said, 'you rang me a few minutes ago. My phone's on now if you want to try again.' Ringing off, she said, 'It'll no doubt be some telemarketer, but you never know, it could be someone with something to say about David Gaudion.'

'Or Lexie, or Serena,' Connor added, consulting his emails. 'Oh, great, there's a message here from Flora Gibson. She's sent it to you too.' He read it swiftly and fist-pumped a *yes*! 'Her father-in-law has read the questions and is willing to talk to us. He'll be around tomorrow after three.'

'Excellent! Where do we meet him?'

'At his place. The address is here. I'll confirm we can make it. We can, can't we?'

'Of course.'

'OK, so why are you looking like that?'

She raised her eyebrows. 'I was just wondering,' she said, 'if he consulted someone before he agreed, needing to get the go-ahead.'

Connor's eyes rounded. 'You mean like David Gaudion?'

Cristy shrugged. 'Or Richard Gaudion. Or Olivia Caldwell. Or anyone. I could be wrong, but it'll be interesting to hear what Gordon What's-his-name has to say. Ah, here's the London number again. Hello, Cristy Ward speaking,' she said into her phone.

There was a pause before a young-sounding female voice came down the line, quiet, a little hesitant and plummy. 'I've heard the promos for your podcast,' she said, 'so you're looking into the murders.'

'That's right,' Cristy confirmed, putting the call on speaker so Connor could hear. 'Is there something—'

'I didn't talk to anyone before, I thought it best to stay out of it.'

Immediately intrigued, Cristy said, 'Does that mean you know something? Would you like to share . . .?'

'I don't want to go on the record, I just want . . . I think you should know that once your podcast is out there . . . It might have happened already now it's known what you're doing. If it hasn't, people are going to claim that Amelia Gaudion is still alive, they might even say they've seen her, or can give you information about where she is. I can save you a lot of time and wasted energy by telling you now that you won't find her. No one will, because she's dead.'

Cristy's eyes widened as she and Connor stared at one another. 'How do you know that?' Cristy asked carefully.

'Because I know – *knew* – her father.'

Cristy waited, hardly breathing. 'Who are you?' she asked softly.

Ignoring the question, the caller said, 'He's a fake . . . Charming, of course, and very good looking – or he was. I don't know what he's doing now, or where he is, but he's a cruel man, ruthless . . . He's an abuser. Why else do you think his mother took the eldest daughter away?'

Cristy looked at Connor again, having no idea how to answer that.

'I thought you should be warned,' the woman said. 'Whatever anyone tells you, Amelia is gone, and he was – is – a monster.'

Cristy started to speak, but the woman had already rung off.

Clicking off at her end Cristy fixed Connor with intense, unfocused eyes, taking her time to assimilate what had just happened. 'Are you thinking what I'm thinking?' she asked.

'Help me out,' he replied.

'Is it possible,' she said, still thinking it through, 'that the woman who just rang could have been Amelia Gaudion herself, trying to tell us that she doesn't want to be found?'

Connor's eyes dilated in shock, until he realized that bizarre as it might seem, Cristy could actually have a point. 'Try calling back,' he said.

Cristy did, but a recorded message told them that the number was no longer in service.

'That was fast,' he commented incredulously.

Cristy nodded. 'We have to try to get hold of her again,' she said, 'and there's only one way to do it.'

CHAPTER SEVEN

CRISTY: 'We're back in the Berkeley Vale today on our way to talk to Gordon Bryce, father-in-law of Flora Gibson the gardener who discovered the bodies at Kellon Manse. I'll tell you a little more about Gordon and why he's important in a minute; first I want to share something pretty extraordinary with you. We've received a call from a woman who wouldn't identify herself, but she gave us some extremely interesting information concerning the case that we're really keen to discuss further. We've no idea if she was a hoaxer; we just want to say to her, if she's listening, please get in touch again. If you'd rather not call, you can message in complete confidence through the *Hindsight* website which is now up and running again.'

'OK, back to today, and we've just turned from a leafy lane into the Bryce Landscaping driveway travelling along a gorgeous sun dappled trail with huge lime trees either side of us and buttercup fields spreading out almost as far as the eye can see. I wonder, is there anything as uplifting as the sweet, earthy smell of the countryside at this time of year? Or as pleasing as the birdsong and babble of streams? Am I making it sound idyllic, that's because it is. A beautiful, sleepy haven here at the western edge of the Cotswolds and must be, surely, a wonderful place to grow up.'

Connor came to a stop at a fork in the drive and she spotted what he had: two handwritten signs springing out of the long grass, one offering 'nurseries' to the left, the other 'machinery' to the right. 'Nurseries,' she declared. 'I can't imagine they live amongst the tractors and combine harvesters.'

Following instructions, Connor took it slowly along the potholed trail. 'Do you think we should ask him about the anonymous call?' he said. 'You know, get his thoughts on it?'

Cristy had been considering this. 'If it seems appropriate, we will,' she replied, 'but we'll have to stay on script at first or he might shut us down, given how coy he's been about talking to us at all. Crikey, how many greenhouses are here?' She half-laughed as they began passing through a small village of them. 'All this horticulture can't just be for the good folk of the Berkeley Vale – he must be supplying garden centres and the like all over. Ah, there's Flora, and I guess that's our man with her. I'll describe him for the recording later and try to be a little more complimentary than stout, blunt and bald.'

With a laugh, Connor brought them to a stop between a muddy Land Rover and a saggy trampoline, and in front of a house that had clearly been added to many times over the years given its several roofs, chimneys and various façades. Not somewhere likely to feature in *Architectural Digest* or *Country Living* any time soon, although it exuded its own sort of character.

'Hi, welcome,' Flora cried cheerfully, skipping to greet them as they got out of the car. 'I see you found us OK. Well done. This is Gordon, or Grandpa, depending on who you are.' She tugged him forward by the arm. 'Don't be scared,' she advised them, 'he's not as fierce as he looks.'

'Worse,' Gordon Bryce grunted, and held out a soil-encrusted hand to shake.

Suspecting he was more used to dealing with plants than people, Cristy smiled warmly as she said, 'Pleased to meet you, Gordon.'

'Mm, likewise,' he growled, barely meeting her eyes, although she sensed that behind the grumpy exterior, which was indeed fierce given the bristling eyebrows and deep scowl, there was the glimmer of friendliness.

'Thanks for agreeing to talk to us,' she said. 'This is Connor, my co-producer.'

As the two men shook hands, Flora said, 'I've set us up over here, under the cedar in the shade, if that's OK. Cold drinks in the jugs – lemon squash in one, elderflower in the other, but I'm happy to make tea or coffee if you prefer.'

'What you have here is perfect,' Cristy assured her, sitting down at an old picnic table surrounded by discarded toys and a few flowering pots. 'Thanks for thinking of it.'

As the men joined them, they exchanged a few pleasantries about the weather and how long it had taken to get there while Cristy opened her notebook and Connor set up to record. Finally, drinks poured and levels checked, Cristy noticed that Bryce was now looking as though he was about to have his teeth pulled. She wondered if his reluctance meant he had something to hide. Perhaps he was afraid of saying too much and offending someone? Or he could just be suspicious of the media; after all, plenty were.

Hoping he wasn't suddenly about to back out on them, she affected her best calming tone as she said, 'OK, we'll start recording now, but we can stop at any time if you're not comfortable.'

Bryce nodded, his eyes now fixed on Connor's laptop as if it were about to transform into something hostile and hungry.

Flora said, 'We had a chat last night about what he wants to say, so should he begin with that?'

'Of course,' Cristy agreed, pleased to hear he'd been giving some thought to this. 'If you just tell us your name first, who you are, what you do, that sort of thing, and then we can get into—'

He blurted over her:

'I'm Gordon Bryce of Bryce Landscapers. I'm sixty-two, widowed last year, and I've lived in this house all my life. I knew David and Richard Gaudion when they was growing up, Lexie and Olivia too. We weren't at school together or anything, I'm older than them, and anyway they didn't go locally after the juniors. They always hung out together, the four of them, mostly at Cynthia and Don's farm – that's David and Richard's parents. Cynthia used to have all the kids over, she was like that, loved everyone and everyone loved her. She knew how to make life fun. Don was a good bloke too, hardworking, sensible sort unless he'd had a few, but I suppose you can say that about us all. Anyway, he was a top batsman. He played on the local team for years, was captain for a while until the job fell to me. He was still knocking over the stumps when David joined from the under fifteens. He was a mean bowler, that lad. Richard, his brother, was never into the game, he was keener on rugger. He'd generally come to watch when we were playing at home, though, cheering his dad and brother on, and the girls came too. A regular little clique they were, those four. The stuff they used to get up to, the pranks they played . . . My missus often used to say we was lucky they all went away to school for months on end and we only had to put up with their mischief during the holidays. Not that she minded them. No one did. They never meant any harm, even if they did keep getting into trouble. I don't mean with the police or anything like that, just with Cynthia and Don who tried to keep an eye on them the best they could, but you know what kids are like. Especially them what go to boarding school. The freedom goes to their head when they come home again.'

He stopped, seeming unsure how to continue, so Cristy, staying with the questions she'd emailed over, said,

CRISTY: 'You've mentioned the Gaudions, Cynthia and Don, a couple of times, but what can you tell us about the Sallises, Lexie and Olivia's parents?'

Bryce sucked in his lips as he considered this, and gazed down the drive almost as if expecting one of his old neighbours to suddenly show up.

BRYCE: 'The Sallises was, how do you say? A cut above. I think there was proper aristocracy in his family, back in the day, although he didn't have a title as far as I ever knew. Nor her, but she was from good stock too, somewhere in Somerset, I think. They was all about horses, the pair of them, big on the hunt, never missed one. We used to say they'd trade their kids for a new thoroughbred if it ever came to it. The kids theirselves was mad about horses too, all four of 'em. Off they'd gallop up over the meadows like they'd been born in a saddle, and as often as not you wouldn't see 'em for the rest of the day. Heaven knows where they used to go, but Cynthia would send them off with picnics and maps, and if they wasn't back by an hour before dark Don would set off to find them. There was no mobile phones then or it might have been easier.'

CRISTY: 'Would you say that David and Lexie were childhood sweethearts?'

BRYCE: 'Mm, I've been thinking about that since I saw your questions, and the answer is I honestly don't know if they were. You've got to remember, I wasn't one of their set, so to speak – too old for one thing, and the wife and I never mixed socially with the Sallises or the Gaudions. So all I can tell you is that the kids was close all the time they was growing up. Those girls didn't have it easy living at the Hall, their parents wasn't . . . Well, they wasn't always the most attentive or caring of people. I never saw them show any proper kindness to anyone, to be honest, not even each other. If the girls needed a bit of tenderness, you know, maternal stuff, it was Cynthia they went to.

'Come to think of it, going back to your question, my missus always used to say Lexie was sweet on David, but she'd have known more about that sort of thing than me. All I can tell you is any discos or parties where you needed a partner, the four of them would always turn up together. It used to drive a lot of the local girls wild because those lads, David in particular, could have had his pick, but he never showed any interest in any of 'em. They was stuck fast to each other, those four.'

After taking a hearty sip of his lemon squash, he wiped his mouth with the back of one hand and continued.

BRYCE: 'I'm not sure what happened when they started

uni, except they went in their different directions, London, Exeter . . . I forget where else. Richard and Olivia was the first to go, being the eldest, David was next and Lexie was last. She went to Oxford, bright young thing she was, always top of her class, getting awards for her projects and the like – it was all in the local paper, Cynthia used to make sure of it. Come to think of it, she might not have finished her degree, but best not to quote me on that, because I don't know for sure. I can't tell you either how much contact they was having with one another during those uni years, with them all being in different cities and pursuing different paths. What I do remember though is that they always came back for the holidays . . . I remember 'em at the carol services with Cynthia and Don, and midnight mass. The Sallises were big churchgoers, although they never dug in their pockets for the collection. Nor did they ever invite any of us to the Hall for Christmas drinks, the way others in the big houses around here do. Anyway, I don't want to end up talking ill of the dead, so you can take that last bit out . . .'

He was glaring so menacingly at Connor that Cristy almost laughed at Connor's hasty promise to do so.

Seeming to think it was a good time to refresh their drinks, Flora filled the glasses and told her father-in-law he was doing brilliantly. Whether or not he was pleased to hear it only he knew.

After checking they were still recording, Cristy said:

CRISTY: 'When they came home from uni, did they ever bring any friends with them?'

BRYCE: 'Oh, I don't know. I was never looking that closely. I was a father with small children of me own by then, had me hands full with other things, especially after I took the business over from my dad.'

CRISTY: 'Do you recall David and Lexie getting married when they were still at uni?'

BRYCE: 'Mm, I think they might of, yeah. I can't be too

80

sure, but they was young, I know that, and if it happened locally . . . Well, I don't remember it, no.'

Aware she was venturing onto thin ice now, as she hadn't mentioned anything about the marriage in her questions, Cristy made it sound vaguely offhand as she said,

CRISTY: 'I guess they moved into the Manse after they got married.'

BRYCE: 'No, they didn't do that right off, as I recall. It was in bad need of fixing up, so after the wedding – that must have happened in London, I think, because I'm sure it didn't happen here. Anyway, they stayed at the farm with Cynthia and Don for quite a while when they moved back. Well, she did, David was up and down to London a lot, finishing his degree, starting a job . . . I don't know exactly what he was up to. He might already have graduated, I can't rightly recall.'

CRISTY: 'She didn't stay with her own parents? Even though she must have been pregnant by then?'

BRYCE: 'No, it's Cynthia a girl wants at a time like that, not old Mean Margaret, but the wife said she saw her going over to the Manse most days to check on the building works. I'd see her meself, sometimes, when I was at the Hall. Always friendly, nice girl. Not overly chatty or anything, but she had a good way with her. My missus always got on really well with her. I'm not sure you'd describe them as friends, exactly, but they'd have long chats about kids and stuff, especially after little Rosaria was born. Sweet thing she was, always with a smile, right from the get-go. As sunny as a summer day all year round. Shame about her, you know . . . Well, I guess you're not supposed to mention it these days so better take that out as well.'

Wondering what he was talking about, Cristy glanced at Flora, hoping she might explain, but Flora seemed not to be listening. Instead, she was watching the computer, apparently fascinated by the graph of sound levels flickering up and down on the screen.

Deciding to ask her about Rosaria later rather than put Gordon off his stride now, Cristy batted away a fly and returned them to the interview.

CRISTY: 'Did you take care of the gardens at the Manse after David and Lexie moved in?'

BRYCE: 'I did. She was busy with the kiddie and the horses at the Hall, but David asked me to work with him on the landscaping. He didn't want anything fussy or grand, he said. Just the long line of beach hedges you see there today, separating front from back, a level playing area close to the house for Rosaria's swings and the like, and nice lawns . . . A lot of roses, I guess because of the child, and solid boundaries to make sure she couldn't wander off. The gates was always shut when she was younger, but not so much after she started to understand that she mustn't go out into the road. She was a good girl, always did as she was told. I often think about her and wonder how she coped after all that happened.'

CRISTY: 'Is she still with her grandmother?'

Bryce's eyes came warily to hers.
She tried again.

CRISTY: 'It's where she was the day it happened, isn't it?'

BRYCE: 'That's right. She was like her mother in that respect, spent more time with Cynthia than in her own home.'

CRISTY: 'Would you happen to know where they are now?'

BRYCE: 'No.'

CRISTY: 'How about David? Do you know where he is?'

BRYCE: 'That wasn't on your list, but no, I haven't seen any of them since Cynthia took Rosaria and moved away.'

CRISTY: 'But didn't David stay in the Manse for a while after he was released? You surely saw him then?'

BRYCE: 'Yes, but we didn't speak much and then he moved away too.'

Sensing it would be a good idea to stop recording for the moment, Cristy gave Connor the signal and turned back to Bryce. 'Were you in touch with either of them before agreeing to do this recording?' she asked bluntly.

His eyebrows shot up and his cheeks burned as he said, 'I told you, I haven't seen hide nor hair of them since they left.'

'Seeing isn't the same as speaking.'

His colour deepened. 'You can play with words as much as you like, but I'm telling you I don't know where they are.'

Certain if she pushed it any further he'd walk away, she gave Connor a nod to continue and took a different risk as she said:

CRISTY: 'How would you describe David Gaudion? I don't mean in looks, I mean in character.'

Bryce paused, looking uncomfortable, but after a moment or two he answered the question.

BRYCE: 'Well, he was a clever young bloke; out of my league, that's for sure with all his knowledge and stuff, but he was always friendly to me, enjoyed a good laugh if the occasion was right. I guess you could say I liked him.'

CRISTY: 'Would you consider him to be a good father and husband?'

BRYCE: 'I haven't agreed to any of this, but OK, he was away a lot during the week, for his job, but whenever I saw him with his family . . . Yeah, I'd say he was a good father and husband, until . . . Well, we don't really know what happened, do we?'

CRISTY: 'Does that mean you do, or don't, think he committed the murders?'

BRYCE: 'I didn't want you dragging me into this, it's not right when I don't have any first-hand knowledge.'

CRISTY: 'But you do have an opinion?'

BRYCE: 'That's as maybe, but I don't have to share it.'

CRISTY: 'That's sounding as though you think he was behind it.'

BRYCE: 'You can tell yourself what you like, but if you want the truth I find it very hard to believe he did it, but who knows what goes on behind closed doors. I'll tell you this, though, he'd never have hurt his own daughter. Amelia. Feisty little thing she was, spirited, you know, but there was no harm in her. Just a bit too used to getting her own way if you ask me, like most kids these days.'

Flora's hands flew up defensively as he directed the last comment at her.

Still treading carefully, Cristy said:

CRISTY: 'We've heard he could be violent, abusive even. What would you say to that?'

BRYCE: 'Load of fucking rubbish, is what I'd say to that. He was no more violent than my dead wife, and she was an angel, take it from me. So whoever told you that either didn't know him, or they was making mischief.'

But none of us know what goes on behind closed doors.

Deciding not to remind him of this, Cristy smiled and said, 'OK, unless there's anything you'd like to add, I think we're done.'

Seeming both surprised and even a little put out not to be asked more, he gave a surly nod and started to get up.

'Actually, there's one other thing I'd like to clear up,' Connor said, stopping him. 'I'm not recording any more, so this can remain between us unless you'd like to go on the record with it.'

Bryce waited, seeming tense, but for the moment willing to listen.

'Is there anything you can tell us about why David might have wanted to kill his wife . . .'

'Oh no, I'm not getting into that,' Gordon interrupted irritably. 'Everyone around here had an opinion on it back then, and I daresay they still do now. Me, all I can tell you is, it's none of my business what goes on in other people's lives and I've never been someone who approves of gossip.'

Connor pressed on, undeterred. 'Do you have a theory on why the case was dropped so abruptly, before even getting to trial?' he asked.

'Well, I'd say it was a lack of evidence, wouldn't you? That's what they said at the time, or something like it, and if there wasn't any evidence, then in my book he probably didn't do it.'

'And if he didn't, who do you think did?'

Bryce fixed him with fearsome eyes. 'Well now, that's the sixty-four-thousand-dollar question, isn't it?' he growled. 'So let's hope *you* can answer it.'

CHAPTER EIGHT

'So what did you make of that?' Cristy asked as she and Connor headed out of the Vale back towards Bristol.

He grimaced thoughtfully. 'I'd say cagey, ambiguous. He didn't actually tell us much that was useful, it was more his . . . manner that got me thinking.'

Nodding agreement, she waited for an ambulance to pass, lights flashing, siren blaring, and said, 'He either doesn't believe Gaudion did it, or he doesn't *want* to believe it, but he's obviously not keen to say who he thinks could have.'

'If he even has anyone in mind for it, and I didn't get a sense that he did.'

'No, me neither. He wasn't actually all that easy to read.'

'Unless he wanted to be, so I'd say he had a good measure of us. Anyway, where does this leave us with our anonymous caller who claimed Gaudion was a monster? Still thinking it might have been Amelia?'

'No idea what to think, but it was only a theory, definitely not something to run with until she gives us more. If she ever does. Let's talk about Rosaria, the eldest daughter. He made it sound as though she had some sort of disorder or disability. Have you come across any mention of that?'

He shook his head. 'There's not much about her at all, apart from the fact that she was fifteen when the murders happened and was taken into hiding somewhere by her grandmother just after Gaudion's release.'

'She must have been interviewed at the time, but we haven't seen any statements, so let's ask Kevin Break what he knows—'

'Speak of the devil,' Connor interrupted as Break's name came

86

up on the call screen. 'I was hoping we might hear from him today . . . Kevin! You got my email?'

'Sure did,' came the hearty reply, 'and I've got a couple of things that might help you. Thought I'd ring rather than try typing it into my phone.'

'No problem. We're all ears.'

'OK, first, my mole has confirmed what I thought, that there's no record of David Gaudion experiencing any sort of financial problems at the time of the killings. The reverse, in fact – he had a few tucked away, big numbers, played the markets a lot, derivatives, commodities, you name it, and was pretty good at it. No anomalies uncovered, no debts or dodgy loans. So, unlikely he was after his wife's inheritance, which would have been bad news for him if he was, because it turns out there wasn't much left in the pot once probate was over. By now it's probably more of a burden than an asset if you ask me.'

'Is he joint owner with Olivia, presuming she inherited from her mother?' Cristy asked.

'I don't know, you'll have to go to the land registry for that.'

'OK, good info anyway,' she said, making a note. 'Not sure where it gets us, but it seems we can rule out money as a motive, at least for now. Was another woman ever mentioned back in the day?'

Before Break could answer, Connor said, 'Have you managed to get hold of Gaudion's witness statements yet?'

'Still drawing a blank there,' Break confessed, 'which is strange, but not necessarily unheard of. Things go missing all the time, then turn up again out of the blue. Or when someone's ready for you to see them.'

'Do you reckon they've been pulled?' Cristy asked.

'It's possible, but for your purposes right now, I can tell you that I watched Gaudion's interrogators at work myself and they were pretty good. He was cool, co-operative, a bit strung out at times, impatient, kept worrying about his daughter, didn't say much about his wife, until eventually, on the advice of his lawyer, he gave a prepared statement and resorted to no comment. No sign of that statement yet. Anyway, while he was still talking he admitted to having a few female friends, but no romantic involvements as such, and none were found. Obviously we spoke to his colleagues in London, but they all sang from the same hymn sheet when it came to affairs of that sort. So, if he did mess around, it wasn't in the office.'

'He had a flat in London,' Cristy pointed out. 'Were his neighbours interviewed?'

'They were, and no one saw anyone coming or going, apart from the brothers or their wives. None of his mates outside of work even hinted at another woman either, and plenty were questioned. I can try to get hold of those statements if you're interested in seeing them.'

'They could be worth a read,' Cristy replied, noting it down.

'Anything else come up about Serena Sutton that we don't already know?' Connor asked.

'Yeah, actually, that's why I'm ringing rather than typing. Turns out they had more on her back then than I'd realized. Remember, I wasn't part of the team investigating her. Anyway, apparently alongside, or maybe extra to her psychotherapy business, she offered some sort of life-coaching service. There's no paper trail for this, thanks to the fire, and nothing on the internet or in her phone records to establish much, but apparently a couple of women did come forward during the weeks after the killings to say they'd been clients of hers and had been invited to join a group called . . . Hang on, I've got it written down . . . Here is it – Papilio.'

Connor screwed up his nose as he turned to Cristy. 'What sort of name is that?'

Cristy said, '*Papillon* is French for butterfly, so I'm going to guess Papilio is Latin.'

'Correct,' Kevin told her. 'I looked it up and indeed it is Latin for butterfly.'

Thinking of the butterfly necklaces at the murder scene, Cristy said, 'What else does it say about this group?'

'No online profile that I can find, and there's no mention of any investigations into it before or since the murders. What's more, there's nothing in the police files that my mole has unearthed to confirm Lexie Gaudion as a member of the group, but I point you once again to the fire.'

'OK,' Cristy said thoughtfully. 'We know that many cults present themselves as life-coaching groups, so that's sort of tying in. There are dozens of podcasts about those that have been uncovered . . .'

'You're right about that,' Kevin confirmed. 'I've listened to a few and it's been proven over and over to be a successful way of extorting big bucks from the gormless and gullible. I never understand why they can't see what's going on, poor buggers, but I guess it takes all sorts. Anyway, the fact that Lexie and Serena both had butterfly necklaces and brandings surely tells us they were in quite deep with this Papilio sect.'

Agreeing with that, Cristy said, 'Do you think Serena was running it?'

'Me, I've got no idea, but the detectives focusing on her had her down as more of a recruiter, and obviously her psychotherapy client list was full of the mentally vulnerable. Aka, easy prey in that they would be people desperate to change their lives, or make sense of them, or to feel valued. It says here in the investigation notes: "If there was a cult, or scam, Serena Sutton unlikely to have been working alone. Ex-husband, Paul O'Malley, remains person of interest." That was dated end of July 2008. Nothing since. It's like the investigation just got dropped after that.'

Cristy inhaled deeply. 'OK, we need to process this before we speak again, so let's move on to Rosaria Gaudion, the eldest daughter. Gordon Bryce intimated that there was some sort of problem with her.'

'Really? News to me, but as I'm sure you know, kids are handled by specialist officers, so I never actually got to meet her.'

'Is it possible to find out if she was interviewed?' Cristy asked.

'Could be tricky, they're very protective when it comes to children, but I'll get onto it and let you know.'

'Thanks, we'd appreciate it. Now, here's something else for you. We received an anonymous call yesterday from a woman telling us categorically that David Gaudion killed Amelia.'

'Is that right?' Kevin sounded more amused than concerned.

Cristy pressed on. 'She claimed she knew him and said he was cruel, abusive, a monster. Did you ever hear that about him?'

Kevin sighed. 'More times than I can count. People come out of the woodwork when things like this happen, you know that. There was a frenzy of fury against him, everything from the sort of name-calling you just mentioned right through to long-slow-death threats. They were all nutters, trolls or whatever you want to call them. On the other side of the coin, he received actual fan mail during the time he was in custody, like he was some sort of rock star, for God's sake, and a few of the letters were pretty explicit. I saw a couple – yeah, they got passed around – and there were offers the like of which took perverted to a whole new level. The saner ones – if you could term them that way – requested visits, or proposed marriage, or offered psychic readings to help find his missing daughter.'

Shaking her head, Cristy said, 'Sounds like we can forget our caller then.'

'I wouldn't be putting any store by her myself. It'd be different if she gave you a name or agreed to meet. I guess you tried ringing her back?'

'We did, and got nowhere.'

'About the psychics offering help with Amelia,' Connor said, accelerating around the Aztec West roundabout onto the Gloucester Road. 'Were any of them followed up?'

'Yeah, some, but by the time I left the force there must have been over a thousand different sightings, from Scotland to Florence, Croatia, Weymouth, you name it. None of them ever led to anything. Unfortunately, there are a lot of time-wasters out there trying to get their fifteen minutes. Anyway, my next client's just turned up so I'll leave you to mull over our little chat. If you need anything else, drop me another email, or I'll be in touch after I've met with my mole, which should be in the next couple of days.'

'Any chance we can meet her too?' Cristy jumped in.

'I'll ask.'

After he'd rung off Cristy sat quietly for a while, staring absently at the shops and cafés and wondering, as they passed the side streets that led to Bristol Prison, how it had been for David Gaudion during the time he was held there on remand. Would his insane level of fame have singled him out for 'special treatment' inside? Had he been grieving for his wife, fearing for his daughter, or simply focusing on himself and how he was going to get away with what he'd done?

'Do you reckon Gaudion might have been running the cult?' Connor ventured as they approached the Bear Pit Roundabout.

Cristy turned to look at him. 'What makes you say that?' she asked, wondering why it hadn't occurred to her to think the same.

He shrugged. 'Just trying to piece it together. I guess we don't know for certain that it was a cult, apart from the brandings . . . What sort of person allows themselves to be burned like that? And why?'

'If anyone understood the minds of cult victims, a lot of fortunes and lives might have been saved by now.' She pointed at the screen as Jodi's name came up.

'Hey, babe,' he said, clicking on. 'All good?'

'Yeah, fine. Can you talk?'

'Sure. I'm driving and Cristy's with me . . .'

'Good, she'll probably want to hear this too. I just had a call from Matthew.'

Cristy's insides jolted. 'You mean my ex, Matthew?'

'The very one. He wants to turn *All Good Things* into a regular spot on the evening news.'

'You're kidding,' Connor muttered.

Cristy was blindsided. It had been her idea to use Jodi's highly successful podcasts about people who selflessly carried out good deeds as a light news item. She'd put it to Matthew about a year ago and he'd never got back to her. Now, it seemed, he was trying to present it as his own ray of amazing inspiration, while at the same time casting his net wider around her friends, trying to reel them into his nefarious sphere.

'Cristy?' Jodi said. 'Are you still there?'

Shaking herself, Cristy said, 'I'm surprised no one from his office has been in touch sooner. Did you accept?'

'No!' Jodi cried indignantly. 'I mean, it is a great idea – obviously I would think so – and it would definitely reach more people and boost my listener numbers, but, I'm sorry, I just don't trust him.'

'Me neither,' Connor growled.

Knowing that trusting Matthew would never have been an issue pre-Marley, and loving them for their loyalty, Cristy said, 'He wouldn't have offered unless he was serious. I think you should at least discuss it with him. When are you planning to start up again?'

'Not until Aurora's at least six months old. But I just don't feel right about it, Cristy. After what he did to you . . .'

'You need to put that out of your mind. It's wonderful of you to consider my feelings, but you can't let it stand in your way. How did you leave it with him?'

'He said he was going to give me some time to think it over and he'll call again next week. I told him not to bother, but he'd rung off by then.'

With a grim smile, Cristy said, 'You know how determined he can be when he's set his mind to something, so, like I said, talk to him and get a fuller picture of how he sees this working. And please, please, don't hold back out of loyalty to me.' She wanted Jodi to, desperately, but how selfish would that be? Not to mention childish.

'I don't care for the position he's put me in,' Jodi said, 'I need you to know that, but OK, I'll take his call next time he rings and let's see where we end up. Where are you guys now?'

'Just coming into the city centre,' Connor replied. 'I should be home soon.'

'OK, great. Are you up for some supper with us this evening, Cristy?'

Cristy smiled. 'Thanks, that would be lovely, but I've got a lot to do before we go back into the edit tomorrow. Maybe one day next week?'

Jumping in, Connor said, 'Tuesday, when the first episode drops, Meena and Harry have arranged their usual drinks, so maybe we can do something after that?'

'Sounds like a plan,' Cristy said. 'Will you be joining us for the drinks?' she asked Jodi.

'Don't I always?' Jodi replied. 'Oh, here's my mum trying to get through, so I'll love you and leave you.'

After she'd rung off, Cristy and Connor sat quietly until they reached the leafy courtyard of her apartment complex. As they came to a stop next to her car, she said, 'I'm fine with Matthew's offer, honestly. Like I said, it's a good idea, and you know it is.'

He nodded for her to look at her front porch.

Following his eyes, her heart wrenched as she spotted Matthew perched on the small brick wall surrounding the raised flower bed.

'Want me to come in with you?' Connor offered.

She was tempted, if only to throw Matthew off his game, whatever it might be, but she said, 'No, it's fine. I can deal with him.'

"K, call if you need to. Otherwise I'll see you in the morning.'

Moments later, as Connor reversed back to the road, Cristy fought down the conflicting emotions battling inside her and went to confront her ex. He was looking, as usual, unspeakably pleased with himself, and way more attractive than any man of deceit had a right to.

'I come in peace,' he assured her, holding up his hands to show no weapons, no malice. His eyes sought hers; his expression was droll, expectant, and maybe a little wary.

'Why have you come at all?' she asked, wanting to push past him and go inside. Instead she kept back, deliberately putting a distance between them. 'We have nothing to say.'

'I just want to talk,' he said. 'Things aren't the way they should be between us—'

'Oh, for God's sake!' She started to turn away. She'd go to the Co-op to get some food, anything rather than stand here exchanging nonsense with him.

'Come to Glasto with me and the kids,' he said quickly.

She turned back in disbelief.

'There's an extra ticket. I got it in the hope you'd join us.'

'What the hell is wrong with you?' she raged. 'You're married to someone else now or have you somehow forgotten—'

'I want us to be friends. So does Marley. It would be good for the kids too.'

'Just go, Matthew. I've got nothing to say to you.'

'Don't just dismiss it. Think about it. Who will it serve for us to go forward with all this animosity still eating away at us? It's not good for the children, or for me, and certainly not for you.'

Feeling she might actually hit him if he stayed a moment longer, she turned on her heel and marched away.

'Cristy, for God's sake,' he called after her. 'I thought you'd be a grown-up about this, put Hayley and Aiden first . . .'

She forced herself to keep going, to ignore what he was saying. She needed to get away from him before she said or did something one or both of them would bitterly regret.

She stayed inside the Co-op on Redcliffe Street for the next ten minutes, giving herself time to calm down and him the chance to fuck off and die. Absurdly and really annoyingly, she was struggling to hold back tears, but they were more of anger than any ongoing idiocy connected to heartache. She detested him, she really did, as much for what he'd done as for thinking he could show up whenever he liked to torment her. *Bastard!*

To her relief he didn't come into the shop after her, and when she eventually returned to the courtyard with a small bag of groceries there was no sign of him, or his car.

She was already inside with the door firmly closed behind her and a glass of wine in her hand when she received a text from him.

This isn't over.

Howling with frustration, she managed not to throw the phone at the wall and went to open the French doors instead. This was the trouble with Matthew up-himself Jennings, and always had been – he wanted everything, truly everything, and everyone. He seemed to think he had some God-given right to whatever he set his mind to, and apparently he couldn't conceive of the fact that someone, anyone at all, could resist him, not even the wife he'd betrayed.

Sitting down because she had to, she closed her eyes for a moment and breathed slowly, deeply, absorbing her small garden's sweet, familiar scent of gardenias and jasmine and roses. It made her think of her mother and how much she had loved these very flowers. It was why Cristy had planted them, to evoke memories of beautiful, happy times, to make her mother feel close.

'What would you advise?' she murmured softly as if her mother could hear and was aware of everything that was going on. 'And please don't tell me I should do as he asks, because I can't, not even for the children. I'm not even sure it's what they'd want.'

Shrinking from the thought of asking them in case they considered it a great idea, she sipped her wine and checked her phone. No more messages from him, thank God, but she found a lengthy exchange between Aiden and Hayley on their WhatsApp group. Mercifully there was nothing about their father's ridiculous plan to make them all a happy family at Glasto, or about Marley's new baby. The very thought of that caused Cristy's heart and stomach to churn with all the old pain and anguish she'd thought had finally gone away.

What the hell was going on with him? First he reaches out to Meena and Harry, then to Connor and Jodi, now to her? Did he think he was the Dalai bloody Lama for God's sake, put on this earth to spread peace and harmony to all? Maybe he was undergoing some sort of Damascene conversion on the road to becoming a father for the third time. Whatever was driving him, surely he realized how offensive and insensitive she found his attempts to win over her friends? She'd thought at first it was to wrap them up and shut her out, but now she had no idea what he was up to. She wondered if Marley was behind it in some way, with all her Gwyneth Paltrow Gloopiness and interpersonal bubble-head stuff. But surely to God no sane woman, no matter how spiritually cleansed or noble, wanted the ex-wife hanging about on the fringes of her idyllic new world?

An hour later she was well into her second glass of Sauvignon and still failing to focus on the work she'd intended to do this evening, when she began to wonder if she was being too harsh. Too intractable. Wouldn't it do her good to open up her heart a little, to stop being so hurt and judgemental, so victimized and self-protective? What was wrong with learning to forgive, with making life easier for her children, with accepting that sometimes things just didn't work out the way you expected them to?

She was on her own now and Matthew was with someone else. Hard as that still was even to think about, it was a truth, and the only one really suffering here was her. It had been almost three years, and yes, they'd been awful, worse than she could possibly have imagined, but wasn't it time now to let go of the pain and move on? She was the bigger person here, or at least she could be if she tried.

She glanced at her phone as a text arrived and her heart turned over when she saw it was from Matthew.

Thinking of you. Hope you're OK.

Grabbing the phone, she tapped a quick message back that consisted of only two words and the second was *off*.

CHAPTER NINE

The following Tuesday, with the first episode of *Hindsight* successfully edited and uploaded to all major platforms, Meena filled four glasses with champagne – juice for Jodi – and prepared to announce her good news.

'OK, guys,' she declared, smiling happily from behind her desk. 'We've landed more sponsorship for the rest of the series – still to be signed on the dotted line, but it means we can now double the size of your team.'

'Wow! Bring 'em on,' Connor cheered, knocking his glass to Cristy's. 'We've still got half the Berkeley Vale to interview, not to mention Gaudion's London connections, Serena's clients if we can find them, plus her ex-husband, and we could definitely do with some help trying to track down Lexie's old friends.'

'Still nothing from Richard Gaudion or Olivia Caldwell?' Harry queried, needing to be sure.

Cristy shook her head. 'But we're hoping that now the first episode is out there we might hear from at least one of them over the coming days, or, better still, from David Gaudion himself, although we're not holding out too much hope on that front.'

'But don't let's rule it out,' Jodi put in, stretching out her supermodel legs and resting her drink on her tiny bump. Her whole demeanour was one of radiance and calm, her green eyes reflecting quiet excitement and happiness.

Cristy smiled. 'Thanks for the optimism,' she said. 'You never know what can happen once people start listening, so anything's possible, including, maybe, another call from the woman who claimed Amelia was dead.'

'Is there any chance Olivia Caldwell could have been behind that?' Meena wondered.

Having considered this herself, Cristy said, 'If there's bad blood between the two families, and I think we can assume there is, then I guess it's possible they'll try to use us to get to one another. However, as far as Olivia's concerned, I'm sure she could cause more harm to the Gaudions if she gave an interview, and she's still ghosting us, so we have to read into that what we will.'

'Do you think she knows where David Gaudion is?' Harry asked. 'Or his mother, come to that?'

'Only she can answer that,' Connor said, sliding an arm around Jodi's shoulders, 'but from what we've heard so far, the sisters were quite close, so Olivia's got to have some sort of insight into Lexie's marriage, her mental health – remember the therapy – and the reasons why David might have wanted such a brutal end to it all. Presuming it was David, and as we know, the jury never got to debate that so we, the new jury, are still out on that.'

'Any useful insights into him so far?' Harry asked.

'Everything we have is in the pod,' Cristy assured him, 'so there's nothing to label him a monster, or to say he isn't.'

'Kevin Break, our ex-detective, who you've heard in the podcast, has more or less convinced us to forget about our mystery caller,' Connor added. 'Apparently, the police were inundated with similar calls at the time of the killings and we're bracing ourselves for more in the coming days and weeks.'

'Gaudion has, or had, a fan club,' Jodi announced. 'No accounting for some people, is there?'

'I think it was a good move to speak to the anonymous caller through the pod,' Meena declared, 'although it might turn into an invitation for other whackos to air their views.'

'True,' Cristy agreed, 'but what sets this one apart, for now at least, is that she got in touch before we dropped the first episode. Obviously, she'd heard the promos, but she also called my mobile number, which isn't on the website. So I'd like to know how she got hold of it.'

'Does Olivia Caldwell have it?' Meena asked.

Cristy nodded.

Meena shrugged, as if to say, I rest my case, then turned to Connor. 'You mentioned something yesterday about your ex-detective getting hold of Rosaria Gaudion's police interview.'

He nodded. 'He hasn't got back to me about that yet. It could be her statement is harder to source given she was a minor at the time, so specialist officers would have been involved. What's a little odd, though, is that Flora Gibson hasn't answered Cristy's email asking about Rosaria and what sort of "problems" she might have had.'

'She's been pretty fast off the mark until now,' Cristy explained, 'but this time not so much. If I don't hear from her in the next couple of days, I'll give her a nudge.'

'Why do you think Rosaria's statement could be of interest?' Harry asked. 'She wasn't there that day, was she?'

Cristy shook her head. 'No, but as David Gaudion's eldest daughter there could be some dynamite stuff about her dad in whatever she told the police.'

After they'd sat with that for a moment, Jodi said, 'Someone who's not getting much of a mention is Mean Margaret. Are you still thinking she was an incidental victim – you know, wrong place, wrong time?'

'It seems most likely,' Cristy replied, 'but, of course, we're keeping open minds. One thing we do know about her, or let's say no one has contradicted it yet, is that she was more or less friendless, a disengaged mother and a drunk.'

'I agree with you,' Meena said, 'that they were probably trying to recruit her into the life-coaching group – what's it called again?'

'Papilio,' Cristy provided. 'It's apparently what the police thought at the time, still do as far as we're aware. We're hoping to talk to Serena Sutton's ex-husband in the next week or so, if we can track him down. They seem to think he was involved in the group, maybe as a member, or even a founder, but nothing was ever pursued so we don't really know.'

Jodi said, 'I've been reading up about butterflies – thank you, Jodi, you're very welcome – and I found some pretty interesting stuff.' She was already scrolling through her phone. 'Any idea if the brandings or the necklaces were of a particular colour?'

Intrigued, Cristy said, 'Not yet, but I've emailed Kevin Break about it, because I think I've read what you have. Off the top of my head, yellow butterflies represent honour and loyalty?'

Jodi nodded.

'Blue denotes emotional depth and insight?'

Jodi nodded again.

'Take it away,' Cristy invited.

Reading from the link, Jodi said, 'Green equals fertility, love and health. Red is passion, surprise, surprise. And purple "reflects those who have the power to manifest miracles or guide others".'

'Who doubts there was a cult now?' Meena said, obviously fascinated.

'It certainly looks that way,' Cristy replied. 'We just don't know how malevolent, or not, it was.'

'Brandings,' Jodi pointed out.

'Yes, but nothing to say, yet, that the exchange of money or sexual favours or any sort of brainwashing occurred to achieve your butterfly colours. However, they certainly have all the symbolism of change and transformation any cultist could wish for. And, apparently, that's what life-coaching is all about, breaking free of your doubts and insecurities and opening your heart to your full potential.'

'A kind of logical next step after psychotherapy,' Connor added. 'At least for some.'

'Do we know yet why Lexie Gaudion was having therapy?' Jodi asked.

Cristy shook her head. 'We still know frustratingly little about her – even news reports at the time are pretty vague – but hopefully that'll change when we speak to more people from the Vale, given she lived there for most of her life.'

'And now we're getting more hands on deck,' Connor said, 'we're standing a good chance of achieving that sooner rather than later. So who are you assigning to us?' he asked Harry.

Harry twinkled. 'Clover and Jackson,' he replied, raising his glass.

'Fantastic,' Cristy cheered.

'You're lucky they're free,' Meena told them. 'They've only just come off a twelve-parter about serial killers, and you know how in demand they are around here. However, I've had them in mind ever since you floated this idea and I'm sure you have too.'

Cristy grinned. 'As committed investigators they have no equals.'

'You can take over the front office,' Harry informed them, reaching for his phone as it rang. 'There are enough desks in there, and all the other paraphernalia you'll need. Move in tomorrow, if you're around. Or we can get Clover and Jackson to sort it.'

'We're back to Berkeley Vale in the morning,' Connor informed them, 'retracing as much as we can of David Gaudion's run.'

'I'll get out your trainers,' Jodi smiled sweetly.

He laughed and tilted his head to hers.

Meena looked curiously at Harry. 'Why don't you just answer the call?' she asked as his phone rang for a second time.

His eyes came worriedly to Cristy's. 'Because it's bloody Matthew,' he confessed. 'He'll want to know if we're going to make this dinner.'

'Tell him yes,' Cristy said. 'Presuming you want to go.'

'He does, I don't,' Meena replied, 'but if you're sure you don't have a problem with it . . .'

'I don't. In fact, I wouldn't be surprised if he invites me as well.'

Meena blinked uncomprehendingly.

'I'm on his guest list for Glastonbury,' Cristy told her, perversely enjoying this.

Jodi choked on her drink. 'Are you serious?'

'He wants us to be one big happy family.'

Meena was clearly astounded. 'With or without Marley?' she wanted to know.

'With.'

'Shit, the man is deluded. Is that honestly what he said?'

'More or less.'

'So what did you say?' Jodi asked.

'I'm afraid it's not repeatable, but I think he got the message. So, on second thoughts, he probably won't invite me for the dinner. Harry, honestly, take the call.'

With a sigh, Harry clicked on the phone and said, 'Sorry, mate,

I'm in a meeting. Can I call you back? Great. About . . .' His eyes returned to Cristy as he said, 'You're listening to the podcast . . . OK, hang on . . .' He put a hand over the phone and said to Cristy, 'He wants to know if you're here.'

'Tell him I am, but I'm busy.'

Harry repeated it, listened again and said, 'He has some information regarding your case that you might want to hear.'

Cristy's eyes widened. She wanted to ask what sort of information, but this was getting childish so she reached for Harry's phone.

'What is it?' she said shortly.

'Good, I've got you at last—'

'For Christ's sake, Matthew, did you just lie to Harry about having information?'

'No, because I do know something that might help you, but—'

'If you're about to try and blackmail me into agreeing to your ridiculous urge to expand your family . . .'

He laughed. 'I was going to say that I don't know how up to date my intel is, but if you're up for a quid pro quo . . .'

'I'm not. Please just give me the information.'

'OK, but tell me first, have you spoken to Olivia Caldwell yet?'

'If you're listening to the podcast, you'll know that we haven't.'

'I have a number for her.'

'As do I, but she isn't answering her calls, or returning my messages. How do you know her?'

'I interviewed her about six years ago. Not to do with the case – as far as I know, she never talks to anyone about that – but she was keen to get some publicity for a fundraiser she was involved in, so we gave her some air time.'

'How come I don't remember this?'

'I've no idea, maybe you weren't in that day. It was hardly a big deal. She was only there a few minutes, but she gave me her number in case I – or we – wanted to attend the event.'

'So what is it?'

As he read it out she quickly checked it against the one she had for Olivia. It was different, so presumably one of them was incorrect, and there was nothing to say it wasn't hers.

102

'Thanks,' she said. 'If you don't mind texting it to me . . .'

'I'll do it right away. Good start to the podcast, by the way, but if I were you, I'd—'

'No one's asking for your opinion,' she snapped.

'You always used to welcome my critiques.'

'Not any more. Goodbye, but don't forget to send that number.'

A moment later the text arrived accompanied by a short message that said, *Please don't tell me to f*** off again, it hurts my feelings.*

Tempted to do just that, right now, she put her phone away and refocused on the celebration which had, as these events usually did, turned into more of a production meeting.

It wasn't until later, as she, Jodi and Meena strolled along the Harbourside to the Olive Shed for dinner, with Harry and Connor following on behind, that Meena said, 'Correct me if I'm wrong, but Matthew seems to be contacting you quite a lot lately.'

With a roll of her eyes, even as her heart contracted, Cristy said, 'You're right, he is, but if you're asking me what's going on with him, your guess is as good as mine.'

'Do you think Marley knows?' Jodi asked.

'He kind of implies that she does, but whether or not that's true, once again I'm as in the dark as you are.' Standing aside for a young couple to steer a twin buggy past them, she said, 'Do you think I'm only hurting myself by not agreeing to be friends? That's what he says.'

Jodi huffed. 'I can see how it might suit him if you all chummed up, but how's that going to work for you? I couldn't do it myself, if I were in your shoes, I know that much.'

'Me neither,' Meena agreed. 'I think, if it keeps up you should confront him, ask outright what the f*** he really wants, because if it's you—'

'Or a threesome,' Jodi put in.

'Oh please,' Cristy choked and laughed. 'You're putting me off my dinner.'

Laughing too, Meena said, 'What matters is that he doesn't end up hurting you again, and to be honest with you, I think you're still vulnerable to that, so cosying up as friends can't be an option.'

Cristy didn't argue, because Meena was right. She still wasn't fully over the break-up; she just wished she knew when that day might come, and how she would know when it had.

'You need to meet someone else,' Jodi said as they approached the restaurant. 'And we, Meena, need to get on board with making it happen, whether that's internet, blind dates—'

'Hang on, hang on,' Cristy interrupted, 'before you get carried away, you are going to have enough to do when Aurora gets here without trying to sort out my love life. And you, Meena . . . Well, we all know how disastrous your few attempts have been at introducing me to someone "suitable" . . .'

'Because you won't engage!' Meena cried. 'The solicitor was a real catch, I thought. Handsome, minted, entertaining, divorced . . .'

'He was fine, nothing wrong with him at all that a gallon of breath freshener wouldn't have sorted out. OK, listen, I know you had my best interests at heart, but I wasn't ready, and frankly that hasn't changed. So please, let's drop the subject, shall we, because the last thing I want is Harry and Connor weighing in on the case.'

As she walked on ahead she didn't miss Jodi's whisper, 'I know just the person to help us with this. Leave it with me,' but it was a battle she'd have to continue another day.

CHAPTER TEN

CRISTY: It's just after ten-thirty in the morning and Connor and I are back in Berkeley Vale following the route that David Gaudion took for his run on the day of the murders. The stretch we've just joined is cross-country, so we're on foot now heading for Seedown Woods. This, you will remember, is where the missing rifle was found, along with Amelia's DNA and what were believed to be her father's footprints mingled with hers.

'We know the whole area was combed extensively and repeatedly after her disappearance and his arrest, and obviously we're not expecting to find anything this many years later. However, we're hoping for a sense of where David was during the final stages of his run.'

CONNOR: Before his world was blown apart, if we're going to believe he wasn't responsible for the killings.'

They walked on quietly, feeling the warm, grass-scented air embracing them as they followed a rugged trail past a terrace of rose-covered cottages and a derelict outbuilding of some sort, recording the melodic sibilance of the countryside and the crunch of their feet on the gravel. They passed no one and could hear no sounds of farm machinery or distant traffic. No planes overhead, only the chatter and piping of random birdsong.

CRISTY: 'I'd say that where we are is about a mile and a half from the Manse, as the crow flies, and it's all flat here, easy terrain for someone as fit as David Gaudion was said to be. We can see the woods at the top of a pretty steep hill, which we'll have to climb, but our woodland trail app has brought us to a five-barred gate that's chained and padlocked.'

CONNOR: 'There's a stile next to it, that's completely bound up in barbed wire. Weird, given it's supposed to be a public right of way. Still, there doesn't seem to be anyone around and as there's no livestock in the field – or none that we can see, we'll chance our luck . . .'

Cristy went first, a careful up and over the rusted bars of the iron gate before jumping down onto a dry, stony patch and turning to take the recorder from Connor as he followed. They stood side by side for a moment, two small figures at the foot of a precipitous meadow with the odd gnarled oak for shade and nothing much resembling a path. Had Gaudion seriously taken this *mountain* in a run? Cristy wasn't even sure she could make it on her hands and knees. Still, according to the app and their notes it seemed to be the route, so charging herself up with a deep breath, she gestured for Connor to go ahead and fell in beside him.

CRISTY: 'We're hiking up towards the woods now – great workout for the thighs, I can tell you. Oh! A fox! It's just darted between some trees about fifty feet away, and leapt a four-foot hedge as if it wasn't even there. Such agility, most of us can only dream of.

'OK. We're still going up. The buttercups . . . are on the wane now . . . just a few straggled . . . here and there, but . . . plenty of cowpats, and . . . flies! You can probably hear I'm sounding quite breathless now . . . Connor, on the other hand, in true fox-style, is making it seem almost effortless. Don't you just love him?

'Finally we're at the summit and surrounded by billowing countryside that stretches for miles and miles in all directions . . . Hardly any sign of life, apart from a couple of horses in a paddock, way in the distance, and some sheep studding a few of the nearby fields . . . Right in front of us, just a few metres away, is Seedown Woods. Now we're up close we can see that it's more of a copse, and would you believe, it's completely fenced with no apparent access. At least not this side. We'll just make our way round to the other side . . . It's very dense in there, dark, tangled, brambly – the trees are immense, a lot of pines, some have to be at least eighty feet high. It can't be an easy wood to move through, *if* you were able to get in.'

CONNOR: 'Someone's coming.'

Cristy spun round to find a short, ruddy-faced man in dark overalls and a threadbare cap approaching them in long strides, a broken shotgun over one arm, a lively Collie bounding along beside him.

CRISTY: 'Ah, it looks like the local farmer is coming for a chat – at least his gun isn't pointing at us, and the dog seems . . . friendly. Hello, sir, I wonder if you could—'

FARMER: 'You're trespassing on private land. You need to turn around and go back, or get yourselves into the next field. That's where the public footpath is.'

CRISTY: 'Sorry, we followed an app and it brought us this way.'

FARMER: 'Then you turned too soon. The gate down there is locked for a reason – lucky for you the herd's not grazing this part today. So if you could get yourselves to the stile over there . . .'

CRISTY: 'Of course, we'll go right away. But I wonder, could you tell us why the woods are fenced in?'

FARMER: 'It's to keep the cattle out, and the wildlife safe. We've had poachers around here trying to bag a trophy or two, and it's a popular site for nesting owls. So, it's off limits, like the rest of this land.'

CRISTY: 'Understood, we're on our way. Sorry again for our mistake, but just one more question . . . Did you happen to know David Gaudion when he lived around here?'

FARMER: 'Ah right, I thought that's what this might be about. You're doing that podcast thing, aren't you, digging it all up again. We don't want that, any of us . . .'

CRISTY: 'But have you never wanted to find out who committed the murders, given no one has ever been tried for the crime?'

FARMER: 'What difference does it make now? It's not going to bring any of them back, is it?'

CONNOR: 'But you did know David Gaudion?'

FARMER: 'Yeah, all right, I did, but am I going to talk to you about him? The answer's no. Now, once again, there's the stile into the next field. I don't think it's ready to collapse yet. You'll find the track once you're on the other side.'

Accepting they weren't going to get any further here, Cristy treated the grumpy man to a friendly smile, and turned to begin wading through the long grass in the direction they'd been pointed. 'Did you get all that?' she asked quietly as Connor fell into step beside her.

'I did,' he confirmed.

They continued in silence, feeling the farmer's beady eyes boring into their backs, and the gun still resting over his right arm.

The stile turned out to be a few rungs of rotten wood all snarled up in a nest of brambles, but apparently there was no other way off this private land unless they wanted to turn back, so bracing herself Cristy went first.

A few minutes later, after tearing her shirt and hair free from the thorns, she waited for Connor to join her and said, 'Are you still recording?'

He nodded.

CONNOR: 'Whoever that bloke was, he was pretty buttoned up about Gaudion, wasn't he?'

CRISTY: 'And something tells me we're going to run into quite a lot of that around here. I have to wonder why they'd want to protect him, if that's what's happening, after all this time.'

CONNOR: 'Maybe it's themselves they're protecting.'

CRISTY: 'From us? Could be. Or are you thinking Gaudion is still wielding some sort of influence around here?'

CONNOR: 'No idea, but what I do know is that we're clearly being watched, because our friend back there appeared out of nowhere right when we got to the woods. Frankly, I've had the feeling of eyes on our backs ever since we left the car, haven't you?'

Cristy had.

She turned to survey the way they'd just come. No sign of the farmer now, or of anyone else. There was, however, a truly spectacular view ahead of them, all the way over to the River Severn and the Forest of Dean beyond.

CONNOR: 'Jesus! What the hell's that?'

Starting, while already marking this moment as a great tease for the next episode, Cristy followed his gaze out to the hazy horizon.

CRISTY: 'You mean the great monstrosity of a building that looks like it belongs in a horror film? It's Berkeley Power Station, probably just a nuclear waste store now. However, much more interesting, and closer to home – isn't that the back of Kellon Hall down there, through the trees?'

Connor took a moment to locate it, and started to nod.

CONNOR: 'Sure looks like it. And next to it, about a quarter of a mile further on ... Is that the Manse? Yeah, it is. Do you reckon we could get to it from here?'

CRISTY: 'It's pretty steep, but at least it's downhill this time, so let's give it a try and hope we don't find ourselves accosted by someone else with a gun before we get there.'

The descent through knee-high grass and over stony, churned up ground was slow going and precarious in parts, although they seemed to be on some sort of path that led down to a buckled iron gate all bound up with orange twine. They climbed over and made their way across the next field. When they finally came to the flat, picking their way through deep and uneven wheel tracks, they reached the impenetrable hawthorn hedge marking the boundary of the Kellon Estate.

'Let's head for the Manse,' Cristy said quietly.

Following on behind, Connor said, 'Why are we whispering?'

With a laugh, she said, 'I don't know. Do you think anyone's around?'

'The feeling hasn't gone away,' he confessed.

Knowing what he meant, she kept going anyway, staying close to the hedgerow until they were confronted with yet another decayed wooden stile giving access into yet another field.

Ten minutes later, with the Manse's black-tiled rooftop and upper windows in clear view, Connor said, 'That gate over there? Isn't it the one Flora Gibson threw herself over after she found the bodies and fled the house?'

Recognizing it too, Cristy waited for him to start recording again and headed towards it.

CRISTY: 'Didn't Flora say that David Gaudion came up the front drive when he returned from his run?'

CONNOR: 'Kevin Break said the same.'

CRISTY: 'Well, if he really did follow the route he gave to the police, he must have been at the top of the hill at some point, so he'd have been able to see all the commotion going on at his house. So why didn't he run back this way and leap over the gate to find out what was happening? It's a far quicker route that he must surely have known about.'

CONNOR: 'And yet he apparently chose to go back to the

110

road, which must be a good half-mile in the other direction, and return that way.'

Cristy turned to stare back up the hill, trying to get a sense of the man who'd once run through the fields and lanes, who must surely have climbed and leapt stiles, heaved open gates, swerved ditches and thrust through woodland. What had he been thinking as he'd covered the miles? Who did he stop to call, if he'd called anyone? The records of the time showed nothing from his number, and the tracker had been off. He could have used a phone box, but wouldn't someone have seen him, and who would he call anyway?

Three hours was a long time to be out on such a hot day, so had he stopped somewhere, met someone?

Had the three women been alive when he'd left the house?

He'd said that only Lexie was at home when he'd set off. Did that mean he'd lain in wait somewhere and come back when all three were assembled?

The overarching question, of course, was: had he been out on a run at all?

CHAPTER ELEVEN

By the time Cristy and Connor returned to the studios, Clover and Jackson had already turned the front salon production office into something akin to a police incident room. There were whiteboards filling the back wall, one detailing the crime, its victims and the suspect, the other charting the progress of the *Hindsight* investigation. There was a list of who'd already been interviewed and whether a follow-up was needed or scheduled; another of who was still to be spoken to and what action had been taken to get hold of them. And a graph of some sort – Jackson always loved a graph, and he was usually the only one who understood it. There were also blown-up headshots of Lexie, Margaret and Serena across the top of the boards, three perfectly intact female faces, so unlike the most recent photographs Cristy had seen of them. The headshot of David Gaudion was the largest and situated below his wife's, holding centre stage. He might be an attractive man, Cristy thought to herself, but the way he looked almost as if he was enjoying the attention was making it hard to remain objective.

'Like it?' Clover asked, her sunny face beaming with pride at what she and Jackson had achieved so far.

Cristy held out her arms and laughed as Clover bounced into them, all bejewelled dreadlocks and gangly limbs. 'I love it, and it's wonderful to see you,' she said, squeezing her tight. She turned to Jackson, scrawny, shy, brilliant, droll, with hair like a spring-onion top and beard to match. Because he wasn't keen on the tactile thing, she simply waved and said, 'With you guys driving this, who knows where we'll end up?'

It was Connor's turn to greet Clover with another bruising

hug, followed by a fist bump with Jackson. 'Surprised you haven't got it solved already, mate.'

Jackson grinned. 'Got to admit, this one's a conundrum. If it wasn't him, where are the other suspects? There've got to be some, or one at least . . . Are you holding anything back?'

'Nothing at all,' Connor assured him. 'Do you think it wasn't him, then?'

Jackson shrugged. 'Not ready to commit on that yet.'

Connor's eyes fell on the newly installed coffee bar. 'Shit, will you look at that, Cristy. They've even rigged us up our own café.'

Clover laughed. 'Bit of an exaggeration, but glad you like it. Sandwiches on the way. Well, they will be when I go get them. Meantime, we need to organize a transcript of this morning's recording, ready to work it into the next episode . . .' Connor had emailed it over on the way back from the Vale and apparently Clover and Jackson had already listened to it. 'Good work, guys,' Clover continued, 'throwing up the question of why Gaudion didn't return to his house the back way. Have you asked Kevin Break the question yet? It must have come up at the time.'

'We've left a message,' Cristy replied, and went to dump her bag on what was clearly her desk given the half-collapsed clay pen jar made by Hayley aged twelve, wine-time coaster, gift from Aiden, and pile of old notebooks – all transported from her temporary stay in the main office. Four of the desks in this front office had been pushed together to form a square, with a large computer terminal, or two, on each, along with all the other technical paraphernalia they needed. There were other desks around the room's periphery, useful for table-top storage, and two worn leather sofas were facing one another in front of the huge sash window.

"K,' Clover began, bringing her screen to life, 'Jackson has networked us up so we can keep track of what everyone's doing, and I've made a list of all emails, phone numbers, addresses, anything to do with the case that we need to share. I know you have a new number for Olivia Caldwell, Cristy, so I'll add it now, unless you tell me it's a dud.'

Taking the coffee Connor was offering, Cristy said, 'I'll text it over, but no one's answered yet so I can't say for sure that it belongs to her.'

'Have you left messages?'

'Only one so far. I'm going to try again this afternoon, so I'll let you know how it goes.'

'Do I take it still nothing from the brother, Richard Gaudion?'

Cristy shook her head. 'He's bound to have a lot to tell, but I only have an email address for him at the moment. You've got that, I take it?'

Clover nodded as she typed.

'I know initial research showed him living in West Kensington,' Jackson said. 'Any confirmation of that yet?'

'No, but we know he's a senior partner at a major law firm in the City. We can't get past his secretary, surprise, surprise, but if it comes to it we'll try doorstepping him.'

'Second homes?' Clover asked.

'We need to get onto that,' Cristy told her.

Clover nodded, changed the screen, and the subject. 'I've scheduled you some editing time in the main suite on Thursday and Friday, but obvs Jacks and I can put something together if you need to be elsewhere. All for your approval later, of course.'

Cristy checked her phone as it rang. 'Well, well, it's Flora Gibson,' she announced. 'I'd almost given up on her.' She put the call on speaker so everyone could hear – it was a habit they'd fallen into during previous podcasts that saved an enormous amount of time in the long run. 'Hi, Flora. Good to hear from you.'

'Oh, hi, Cristy,' came the slightly breathless reply. 'Sorry I didn't get back to you before. I got your email, but it's been a bit chaotic here, three boys, not much peace, you know how it is. Anyway, you were asking about Rosaria Gaudion, and I . . . Well, Gordon said I shouldn't be telling you about her because she's just an innocent who needs protecting, but I'm sure you don't mean her any harm, if you ever find her, do you?'

Cristy's eyebrows shot up with amazement. 'Of course we don't, Flora. I'm surprised you'd think we—'

'No, I don't think that. I just . . . I'm not sure what I'm saying . . . It's just that Gordon's right, she does need protecting, and it's not for the likes of us to be talking about her behind her back.'

Perplexed and concerned, Cristy said, 'If she's vulnerable in some way, and it sounds as though she is—'

'Yeah, she is, and she won't be able to talk to you, so best not go there really. If you don't mind me saying. Anyway,' she ran on with a nervous laugh, 'you've made me quite famous around here after the podcast went live. People are saying I shouldn't have talked to you, but I don't have anything to hide, so why shouldn't I? My husband agrees with me, but Gordon's a bit upset about it all. I keep telling him he didn't say anything that wasn't true, and if the others would just open up a bit, we might actually get somewhere and find out who really did it.'

'Because you still think David didn't?' Connor said.

'Oh, hello, Connor. No, that's not what I'm saying, because I don't know if he did, but it would be far better to know for sure, wouldn't it?'

'Of course,' Cristy said, 'but going back to Rosaria . . .' She stopped at the sound of a loud thump at the other end. 'Flora? Are you OK?' she asked worriedly.

'Sorry,' Flora replied. 'I've got to go. I think one of the boys just fell down the stairs.'

The line went dead and for the next few moments they looked at one another, trying to puzzle out what the call had actually been about.

'Without knowing what's wrong with Rosaria,' Cristy said, 'we're not going to work out how it could play into what happened.'

'Or if it does in any way,' Connor added.

Clover was already logging the call. 'Big mystery,' she declared, 'but chances are Kevin Break will give us a heads up if/when he locates the police interviews.'

Cristy was impressed, although not surprised to realize Clover really had been doing her homework.

'OK, moving on,' Clover continued, 'responses are already coming in to the first episode and I expect they'll continue as everyone catches up with it. They're mostly email and social media, a couple of texts on the podcast phone – we've put the number on the website, by the way, and taken your two off. Anyway, I've sorted what we have so far into various categories: those who focus mainly on Gaudion—'

'Anything stand out there?' Cristy interrupted.

Clover checked. 'Actually, there are only three in that section at the moment – two want to be paid for their info and one who can't spell or put a proper sentence together, but apparently he saw "Henry Gordon" in Penzance last week.' She looked up and Cristy pulled a face.

Clover continued. 'We have a category each for the victims, obvs, and . . .' She looked up again. 'I'm afraid there are a lot wanting to know about your love life, deep concern, empathy and understanding – and a few with offers I hope you'd refuse given their nature.'

Cristy's eyes closed as she shook her head. 'You can just delete them,' she said.

Storing them in a specially designed folder, just in case, Clover ran on. 'Some of the messages about David Gaudion are quite explicit too – some real sickos out there, but we knew that already. On the upside, there's a lot of genuine support for you and Connor and the fact you're doing this.'

'Any more stand outs?' Connor prompted. 'Not about us, about the case.'

'Yeah, right.' A couple of clicks and, 'The first could be from the woman who rang you, Cristy. The one who claimed to know Gaudion and accused him of being a monster.'

Cristy's interest was instantly piqued. 'What does she say?'

Clover read aloud, '"I heard you talking to me on your podcast. I understand why you think I might be a hoaxer, but I can assure you I am not. David Gaudion's everything I said he is. I want to help you find him, but I'm afraid of what might happen if I do."'

Cristy waited.

Clover shrugged. 'That's it. No name and we haven't been able to trace the email yet, Jacks is still working on it.'

'So what's she afraid of?' Cristy murmured.

'Or *who* is she afraid of?' Connor corrected.

'Gaudion,' Jackson answered.

'It's the most likely answer,' Cristy said, 'but we won't know unless we can speak to her.'

'I've replied to the message as if I'm you,' Clover said, 'assuring her of total confidentiality and that you'll meet her wherever she feels safe.'

Cristy nodded. 'Good. Actually, at the end of her call she said something about his mother taking the eldest daughter away. Did she mention it again?'

Clover shook her head and moved on. 'Jacks and I are going to spend tomorrow doing a door-to-door around the Vale to see if we can get anyone to talk, unless you've got other plans for us.'

'No, sounds good to me,' Cristy replied.

'Great, because we've got a message here from someone called Hannah Gains. I'll read it out. "Hello, I knew Margaret Sallis quite well for a number of years, probably better than most, and I'm happy to chat if you'd like to get in touch. My number is below, or you can answer this email. Let me know when you're coming and I'll pop the kettle on. Toodle-pip. HG."'

'Toodle what?' Connor choked.

'That's what I said,' Jackson told him.

'If she's using phrases like that,' Cristy said, 'it's quite likely she was a contemporary of Margaret's. I don't recall her name coming up before, do you?' she asked Connor. 'I mean in any police or press interviews from the time.'

He shook his head.

'That's what I thought,' Clover said. 'I think it's worth following up, if only because we don't have anything on Mean Margaret really, other than the fact that she was Lexie's mother, a bit of a recluse and a drunk. Maybe this Hannah can shed more light on things. Shall we make a point of talking to her tomorrow?'

'Do it,' Cristy agreed. 'Now, I don't know about the rest of you, but I'm starving and I think we should have a little celebration of you two coming on board, Clover and Jacks. So shall we see if we can get into the Harbourside Kitchen?'

Finding herself with three eager takers, she quickly checked her phone for urgent calls or messages, found nothing that couldn't wait and started to leave.

'An email's just come in from Kevin Break,' Connor said, 'so I'll meet you there.'

Ten minutes later he joined them waterside, slipping into a vacant chair under a parasol and reaching for the cold beer they'd already ordered for him. 'Good news and bad news from Kevin,' he announced. 'Still no luck getting access to interviews with Rosaria Gaudion, but he's got another detective who worked the case back then to agree to meet with us.'

'You're kidding,' Cristy said. 'That's great. Is this person still on the force?'

'Apparently, yes. At quite a senior level now.'

'It keeps getting better. So when do we meet them?'

'Tomorrow. Eleven a.m. at the White Hart, Littleton-on-Severn.'

Much later in the day, after the others had gone home, Cristy remained at her desk browsing through the listener messages that Clover had streamlined into various categories. It was always worth a second look, just in case something with potential managed to slip through the net. Not likely with Clover, but even she couldn't know everything. For instance, no one had ever mentioned the name Iris to her, there hadn't seemed any reason to. However, there was an email in the junk list that read,

For your own sake you should let this go. You don't want to end up like Iris.

It was an unusual enough name for Cristy to feel slightly alarmed by the message, which could be a threat, or a warning.

She quickly typed in, *Who are you?* and hit return.

After a few moments her message bounced back, so she forwarded the original to Connor with a *what do you make of this,* and continued to scan the rest of the junk mail. Clover was right, there were some serious deviants out there, people who probably ought to be locked up, but there were also some truly kind women reaching out to her with moving accounts of their own betrayals. They'd messaged her a lot during the worst of the break-up so she knew already that she couldn't read them all; they were often too long and anyway too many. But the fact that anyone would take the time, and put themselves through the angst of writing about their awful experiences in order to try to make her feel less alone, touched her deeply.

It also, inevitably, made her think of Matthew.

She hadn't heard from him today – was it really only yesterday that he was last in touch? It felt longer, and it also felt wrong to be waiting for something she actually didn't want, except in a perversely self-destructive sort of way. It was habit, of course. She'd got so used to him being a part of her life, the mainstay of it actually, that even after all this time she still seemed unable to accept that there would never be any going back.

Of course the baby made it totally impossible now, and because she knew him so well she understood that being powerless to change anything was making him feel trapped. That was why he wanted her back in his world; it would allow him to think, in a convoluted and actually quite pathetic way, that he could have it all. But he couldn't, and nor could she. It was well and truly over between them and had been since the day she'd found out about Marley. Of course she'd tried to hang on, to convince herself, and him, that it was just a passing thing, he'd get over it, they could put it behind them, but giving Marley up wasn't what he'd wanted back then. She couldn't be sure it was what he wanted now, probably not, but whatever was in his mind, she knew now that they could never repair the damage he'd done, and even if he couldn't face the truth of that, she was going to make sure that she did.

Her phone rang, and as if to make a mockery of her fragile resolve, her first thought was of him, and she felt crushed when it wasn't. Then, realizing who it actually was, she quickly clicked on. 'Cristy Ward speaking.'

There was a brief hesitation before the woman at the other end said, 'I'd like to know how you got this number.'

Resisting the urge to obfuscate, or even outright lie, Cristy said, 'You gave it to my ex-husband a few years ago.'

'Ah yes, Matthew Jennings. And he passed it to you. I see. Well, I'd appreciate it if you left me alone—'

'Olivia! Please don't ring off. I'm aware that you don't like to discuss what happened to your mother and sister—'

'Then why do you keep bothering me?'

'Because I'm hoping that in your heart you're as keen as we are to find out what actually happened that day at the Manse.'

'And you think you can succeed where the police failed? That's quite . . . arrogant, if you don't mind me saying.'

'Maybe, but I think we both know that the investigation was . . . hampered, shut down . . . I'm not sure what happened to it, only that your brother-in-law was not forced to face justice—'

'And in your opinion he should have been?'

Cristy blinked. 'Isn't that what you think?'

Olivia sighed. 'There is so much you don't know and I doubt you ever will. Have you spoken to Richard Gaudion?'

'He's not responding to our messages.'

'No, I don't suppose he would.'

'Are you in touch with him?'

There was a mirthless laugh. 'No, I'm not in touch with any of that family.'

'Do you happen to know where David is? Or his mother?'

'No.'

'Would you tell me if you did?'

Another pause. 'You're very persistent, Ms Ward . . .'

'Cristy, please.'

'. . . but as I keep trying to tell you, that terrible time is a long way behind me now. I really don't want to resurrect it, so if you don't mind . . .'

'I understand, really I do, but before you go, I've had a call from someone – anonymous, but it was a woman – who claimed your niece, Amelia, is dead.'

'Ms Ward, Cristy, you surely know that has been the case for a great many years.'

'But it isn't official. A body has never been found and this caller is saying that David Gaudion is, or was, abusive. She called him a monster. Is that how you would characterize him?'

Another moment before Olivia said, 'I think this conversation is over now—'

'Please, just think about meeting me. We don't have to record anything you say, I'm happy to be guided by you . . .'

'If I change my mind about anything I'll call you, but please don't call me again.'

CHAPTER TWELVE

The following morning Cristy took the wheel as she and Connor set off to meet Kevin's ex-colleague, DSI Frances Rush. Apparently she'd been a DC, same as him, back at the time of the murders, and had worked the case, but she was now a much-elevated detective superintendent heading up the region's OCU – Organized Crime Unit. They weren't sure yet why she'd decided to meet them, but they'd find out soon enough. For the moment they were focusing on the mysterious Iris and the email that had come in yesterday.

'Without a surname she's virtually impossible to trace,' Connor grumbled as they circled the roundabout at Aust to begin winding through several miles of country lanes to Littleton-upon-Severn. The village and its pub was much further south in the Vale than the places they'd visited so far, so they were taking a different route today. 'I contacted Kevin asking if he could give us any more about her,' Connor continued, 'no word yet. Meantime, I've tried googling all sorts of name, date and location combinations, but I'm not getting anything that makes any sense.'

'I did the same after the call from Olivia,' Cristy responded. 'So Jacks is working on tracing the sender?'

'Yes, but if it's someone who doesn't want to be traced then the account has probably already been closed, so it's not going to be straightforward.'

Cristy wondered if now was the time to admit to how spooked she'd felt last night walking home from the studios, certain someone was following her along the waterfront past the M Shed and Mud Dock, over the Redcliffe Bridge and into the courtyard of her apartment complex. She hadn't spotted anyone, nor had she been approached, but instead of going straight into her flat she'd waited for one of her upstairs neighbours to park his car and had gone into the building with him.

In fact, it wasn't only the email that had unsettled her, she'd realized when she'd finally closed her front door, it was also what the anonymous caller had said about Gaudion in her follow-up message: 'I want to help you find him, but I'm afraid of what might happen if I do.'

Deciding not to hold back, she shared her unease with Connor and waited as he sat with it for a moment, apparently taking it seriously, which didn't actually help when she'd been trying to shrug it all off this morning as an overreaction due to tiredness.

In the end, he said, 'I've no idea if you were being followed, but I don't like that you felt you were, not when three women are dead, shot at point-blank range, with a small child possibly looking on. A child who hasn't been seen since. OK, sixteen years ago, but opening it all up again brings it right to our doorstep.'

'You're making me feel so much better,' Cristy said wryly.

He glanced at her. 'Sorry, thinking out loud and forgetting to filter.'

'So you're asking yourself, is the killer coming after me, or us, to try to stop us digging too deep?'

'*If* he shut this Iris down, which is what the email is basically saying, then it follows he'll try to do the same to us.'

They both glanced at the call screen as Cristy's phone rang.

'I don't believe it,' she muttered, her teeth gritting as Marley's name came up. 'What the hell does *she* want? This is the fourth time this morning.'

Connor leaned in to press reject, but she stopped him. 'I might as well take it,' she said. 'If I don't, she won't stop pestering me.' She clicked on and said shortly, 'Hello, Marley, what can I do for you?'

'Oh, you've answered, thank you, thank you,' Marley gushed in the warm, husky voice that never failed to make Cristy cringe. 'I hope I'm not interrupting anything. How are you?'

'I'm about to go into a meeting . . .' Cristy said.

'Don't worry, I'll be quick. I just wanted to say how much I enjoyed the podcast. I listened to it earlier, after my yoga class.

You do these things so well, Cristy. You have me completely hooked, longing to know what comes next, or what you might manage to uncover. You're so talented, really you are.'

Cristy watched Connor fake-vomit and had to smile. 'I'm glad it worked for you,' she responded coolly.

'Oh, it certainly did. And I've been thinking, maybe I should recommend it to a couple of directors I know. It could make a fabulous TV series, don't you think?'

Cristy was incredulous given how little of the story Marley could conceivably know at this stage, and besides, the very last thing she wanted was Marley trying to take over anything else that was hers, or even to become a part of it. 'I really haven't given it any thought,' she said truthfully. Then, because she couldn't stop herself, 'Presumably you see yourself playing the role of Lexie Gaudion?'

Marley's laugh was musically light. 'Busted,' she said, 'but I understand there's a way to go with her character development. We don't seem to know much about her yet, do we? Or is it part of next week's episode?'

Trying not to bite out the words, Cristy said, 'I guess you'll have to wait and find out. I'm sorry, but as I said, I'm about—'

'Yes, yes, of course. Just one last thing – will you reconsider coming to Glasto with us? It would mean so much to Hayley and Aiden to have you there, to me and Matthew too.'

Taking a bend too fast, Cristy said, 'I've already given Matthew my answer.'

'I know, you're too busy, but a girl's got to have some fun. It's obligatory. Actually, I'm sure you already know that Hayley and I are going shopping in London tomorrow to get a dress for some ball she's attending in Oslo. Why don't you come too? We're on the ten-thirty train out of Temple Meads . . . you there . . . some lunch . . . Hayley . . .'

'The line's breaking up,' Cristy told her, and before it could right itself she abruptly ended the call.

After a moment Connor turned to look at her.

'Don't say anything,' she said, keeping her eyes straight ahead, arms stiff, heart pounding.

He stayed obediently silent while she continued driving,

pulling into lay-bys and gateways to allow other cars or vans to pass, winding through the lanes to their destination. The worst part of the call, the one she was going to find extremely hard to get past, wasn't that she'd known nothing about a trip to London or a ball in Oslo, although both were bad enough; it was learning that Hayley was apparently already in Bristol and hadn't told her. They'd spent at least half an hour WhatsApping when Cristy had got home last night, mostly about the podcast as Hayley had just listened to it, but they'd had a back and forth about other things too and there had been no mention at all of Hayley being at her dad's. Cristy couldn't understand why she wouldn't have told her. Did it have to be a secret? Was she afraid it upset Cristy to think of her being in the home they'd always shared, that held so many precious memories for them, and now, like a big ugly cuckoo, had another woman squatting in the nest? It did upset her, a lot, but worse was having Hayley keeping things from her. Unless she was planning to surprise her later today. It wouldn't be unusual for her daughter to do that, and if it happened Cristy would go along with it, act delighted and amazed, because of course she would be overjoyed to see her girl. However, if Hayley set about trying to persuade her to go to London, or Glastonbury . . .

'Kevin,' Connor said, checking his phone as they drove past the White Hart and pulled into the car park behind. 'He's probably checking where we are.' Hitting speaker on his mobile he said, 'Hi, mate. We've just arrived—'

'That's great,' Kevin interrupted. 'Fran should be there by now, or soon will be, but I'm afraid I'm not going to be able to make it myself. B had a nasty fall last night, knocked herself senseless, had to be carted off to A&E and we're still there.'

'Oh, that's bad luck,' Connor exclaimed. 'Is she OK?'

'She's conscious now, and feeling daft, she says, but she can't put any weight on her right foot, so could be she's broken something. They're taking her to X-ray sometime in the next hour. I can't leave her . . .'

'No, you mustn't do that,' Cristy told him. 'Apart from anything else, she'll need you to take her home.'

'She will, and thanks for being cool with it. I've already called Fran to let her know, so she's not expecting me. Sorry to let you down, but you'll do great without me. Just let me know if you need anything after.'

'Don't worry about us,' Connor told him.

'Give B our love,' Cristy added, 'and wish her well.'

'Will do. Oh, I saw your email, Connor, about this Iris person who contacted me. Haven't had a chance to look into it yet, but I will when I get home.'

'Thanks,' Connor said, 'and take it easy. I'll be in touch later to find out how B's doing.'

As the call ended Cristy came to a stop in the shade of a silver birch tree and got out of the car. A keg delivery was clearly in progress at the back of the pub, but there was no sign of anyone else, and only two other cars in the car park. She looked up at the olde-worlde building, all white-washed walls and green timber window frames. At this time of day the place had probably only just opened, and sure enough, when they got inside and their eyes adjusted from bright sunshine to sudden gloom, it was clear they were amongst the first to arrive.

Going to the bar where a plump young girl with pink hair and black-rimmed eyes was removing towels from the taps, Connor said, 'We're meeting someone here—'

'You've spelled bream wrong,' the girl broke in shrilly. 'It's got an a, not two ee's.'

Connor and Cristy watched a young lad amend his mistake on the chalkboard, and turned back to the young woman as she said,

'Sorry about that. Kind of downgrades the food if we don't get it right, is what I always think. Anyway, you're meeting someone, you say. If it's a lady it could be she's already here.'

'It is,' Cristy confirmed.

'OK. You'll find her right through there, in the garden. Can I bring anything out for you? She's ordered coffee.'

'Same here. Two Americanos, no milk, thanks,' Connor replied.

Ducking under an archway, they crossed a cosy, low-beamed saloon bar with an enormous stone inglenook and ancient flagstone floor, and exited through a porch to find DSI Frances Rush already rising from a picnic bench to greet them. She was a slight, almost scrawny woman of around fifty with tousled mousy hair and a sallow complexion, and was casually dressed in a Springsteen T-shirt and faded grey jeans.

'Hi, you're Cristy Ward, I recognize you,' she said, shaking Cristy's hand more vigorously than Cristy had expected. Her deep brown eyes showed friendliness and warmth, though there was an edge to her that signalled it might not be a good idea to get on the wrong side of her. 'And you must be Connor. Good to meet you both. I hope this place is OK for you.'

'Absolutely,' Cristy assured her. 'Thanks very much for agreeing to see us.'

The DSI nodded, and gestured for them to sit down. 'I was concerned at first about how well it might sit with my superiors if I were to assist in your podcast,' she admitted, 'but then I reminded myself that I'm stepping down from the force at the end of the year, so what is there to lose?'

'I'm thinking pension?' Connor suggested.

She smiled. 'They wouldn't dare. Besides, a number of the top brass who were the decision makers at the time of the Kellon Manse Murders have moved on, or passed on, or forgotten all about it in a couple of sad cases.'

Realizing she was referring to dementia, Cristy said, 'So is anyone left who might try to shut us down?'

'You mean like they did with the trial?'

Cristy nodded, appreciating the frankness.

Rush fixed her with a contemplative stare. 'It wasn't the police who shut the case down,' she reminded them. 'It was the CPS – Crown Prosecution Service. They decided they didn't have enough evidence to secure a conviction.'

'But you didn't agree?'

'No, we didn't. And I don't believe the CPS lawyers we'd been working with agreed either. The instruction came from a much higher level, and so that was the end of it.' It was clear from her tone that it hadn't actually ended there for her, or many of her colleagues, and yet apparently they'd been powerless to contest it.

'The trial was one thing,' Connor said, 'but the police investigation . . . How come it didn't continue after Gaudion's release? That would surely have been the normal course of events, to get more evidence?'

'Actually, it did continue, and of course the search for Amelia Gaudion remained a priority for well over a year, but that was handled by another division. Naturally there was cross-over, there had to be, but the teams working the murder inquiry – there were three, one for each victim – we carried on for as long as we could, never really making any headway, until gradually we found ourselves being assigned to other cases.'

'And this one, in spite of how big it was at the time, and all the questions that were left unanswered, was never reopened,' Connor stated.

Rush inclined her head to confirm it.

Wishing they were recording this, Cristy said, 'So, would you be prepared to say on tape that there was a whitewash, or a cover-up?'

Instead of answering the question directly, Rush said, 'We've never been able to prove it.'

They paused as their coffee arrived along with a plate of chocolate bourbons.

Watching Rush help herself to a biscuit after the waiter had gone, Cristy said, 'Do you have any objection to us repeating what you've told us so far? We don't have to attribute it to you, if you'd prefer we didn't, but it's dynamite stuff that could unlock all sorts of things for someone else who might have been involved in the original investigation. Or indeed in the shutting down of it all.'

Connor added, 'I'm sure you know very well that over time, as people's lives change and priorities shift, certain loyalties can also take a different turn. There could be someone out there who's just waiting for someone like you to start the ball rolling on this.'

Rush sipped her latte as she thought. The quiet around them, the bees and songbirds, the muted kitchen clatter, was part of a perfect day, so far removed from the violence of the one they were discussing that there seemed a sense of unreality in the air. Cristy wondered how difficult DSI Rush was really finding it to be here. How deeply had the murders affected her at the time, and how often had they preyed on her mind since?

In the end, Rush put her cup down and said, 'Actually, you can mention my name.'

Both Cristy and Connor looked at her in surprise. Not what they'd been expecting.

'Something was very wrong with the way just about everything to do with that case was handled,' Rush continued. 'Three women died, a child disappeared, a man got away with murder and since the day of Gaudion's release no one's ever done anything meaningful about it. It's time for the corruption, or protection, or whatever was going on back then, to be exposed and justice allowed to proceed, unimpeded.'

Connor looked like it was his birthday. 'In which case,' he said, reaching for his backpack, 'would you be OK with us recording this interview?'

Rush nodded. 'Knock yourself out. If something comes up that I think might be better unsaid – I mean for all our sakes – I hope you'll respect my request for an edit?'

'Of course,' Cristy assured her, opening her notebook, 'but before we get started, can I ask if anyone else has ever contacted you about making a podcast?'

Rush frowned as she thought. 'Your approach to Kevin is the only one I know of, but I believe a documentary producer was in touch with the press office a few years ago. I guess nothing came of it because I haven't heard about it since.'

Intrigued, Cristy said, 'Do you think it could be because he/she was "asked" to give up on the project?'

Rush's eyebrows rose as if this had only just occurred to her. 'I'm afraid I can't answer that. It only came to me as rumour, but I do remember thinking that we were finally going to get an opportunity to start holding people to account for Gaudion's release. But then, as I say, it went away and we were all caught up in other things . . .'

'Would there be a way of finding out who the producer was?' Cristy asked.

'I guess I could go back to the press office and ask. They might have kept a record.'

Making a note to follow up on that, Cristy waited for Connor's thumbs up and said to Rush, 'I know you won't be a stranger to microphones, but here's my spiel anyway. We can do this any way you like. You give us the information you're happy to share, speaking straight into the mic, or we continue to chat the way we are now. Or we do a combination of both.'

Rush's eyes flitted about the garden as she considered this. All the other tables were empty, and only their parasol was raised to shield them from the sun. In the end, apparently reaching a decision, she said, 'Why don't we begin with Papilio? You're familiar with the name?'

Cristy nodded and Connor put on his headphones and hit record, while Rush drew a tablet from her bag. After opening whatever files or crib notes she'd decided to bring with her, she began.

RUSH: 'I was involved in the Papilio aspect of the case, which was viewed by some, including many of my colleagues, as a cult, and I wouldn't argue with that. But I can tell you that Paolo Morelli, the group leader and Serena Sutton's ex-husband, had a big problem with it. Incidentally, his real name is Paul O'Malley, and that's how we always referred to him. I believe his mother was from Dublin and his father from Liguria, and O'Malley changed his name either to make it sound less Gaelic or more Italian – who knows what he had in mind. Anyway, he was the brains behind the organization that he and Serena set up to offer "life-coaching and intrapersonal skills" for those who felt in need of this kind of support and . . . direction, I suppose. We believe that many who signed up, particularly in the early days, came directly from Serena's psychotherapy client list, a natural progression, O'Malley would say, to all the good work they'd already done on developing their inner power. Joining Papilio would help them to go even further towards reaching their "higher-selves" and "true human potential". I don't have transcripts of all his waffle – there was a lot of it, as you can probably imagine – but there were several mantras. The one I remember is "be more, have more, do more", and there was a lot about "personal workshops" and "goal-setting programmes". The way he spoke was . . . actually, it was quite compelling, this odd blend of Irish and Italian accents, soft and lyrical, and his manner, his eyes,

130

had a way of drawing you in, of mesmerizing you even. We used to joke about taking turns to question him to make sure no one fell under his spell.

'Anyway, we weren't able to trace any of his fledgling angels. The Papilio records were lost in a fire. You know about that . . . ?'

Cristy nodded.

RUSH: 'It was, obviously, highly suspicious that everything about the group was destroyed only days before the killings, but arson was never proved, and O'Malley, who was suspect number one for a while, was alibied at the time of the blaze, and of the murders. He was in Ireland giving a series of "exclusive motivational speeches", and we never found anything to say he'd given the instruction to burn his ex-wife's place to the ground. These speeches, incidentally, always happened at a secret venue, usually someone's home – mansion to you and me – where the host was an established and trusted member of Papilio and the attendees were all potential . . . "chrysalises". That's what he called them. And they only got to first base, i.e. these meetings, by private invitation from someone who "could vouch for them".'

Finding it interesting the way Rush was drawing quotes around certain words, signifying a direct reading from her tablet, as well as an undisguised scepticism, Cristy watched her check her phone as it vibrated. Whoever it was went unanswered.

RUSH: 'A couple of followers, for want of another word, rang in after we allowed the suggestion of a cult to go public, both female, and both wanting to correct the record. As far as they were concerned, it wasn't a cult, it was a wholesome and nourishing form of therapy and healing, and it wasn't long before O'Malley's lawyers were all over us threatening action if we "invaded their clients' privacy, or deliberately misrepresented him or his organization" again.

131

So we had to row back, at least publicly, but I have to say O'Malley wasn't, apart from over that, a difficult customer. He seemed at ease describing the purpose of Papilio to us, although he was always careful to guard the members' identities. The only one who actually gave us any real information insisted on remaining anonymous and would only talk to us by phone. At first what she told us comprised a lot of what I've just related to you, so she was obviously reading from an O'Malley script, but then she got into the sums of money involved.'

Cristy and Connor exchanged glances. Didn't it always come down to money in the end, especially where cults were concerned?

RUSH: 'Actually, I'll come back to the financial aspect of it all in a moment. For now I'll stay with how the group worked, because I guess you're interested in that?'

Cristy nodded and watched Rush scroll to what she was looking for.

RUSH: 'OK, so the progression to full and lasting "self-confidence and emotional ecstasy", was achieved in stages, and at the accomplishment of each stage a pendant was awarded. I know you've already asked Kevin about the butterflies Lexie and Serena were wearing at the time of the shooting, so here's more or less how it went: Someone on their first stage of enlightenment would be given a Brimstone pendant – this is a yellow butterfly, male, I believe – that was apparently relevant to the journey, but I'm not sure we ever found out how. Anyway, the necklace itself was generally gold with citrine stones at the wing tips. Its purpose was to signify the wearer's commitment to "honour and loyalty". By the way, you can find a lot about the symbolization of butterflies online. It's not rocket science, although the way O'Malley and Serena used the mystique and I guess religious allegories surrounding these tiny creatures . . . Well, maybe that was its own kind of rocket

132

science given the upward trajectory of the spiritual journey they were selling.'

Rush scrolled on down her screen and continued.

RUSH: 'In all there were five or six levels of achievement, each one celebrated with a ceremony, again usually held in someone's home or the private room of a fancy hotel. We never got to the bottom of what actually happened during these ceremonies, apart from the awarding of different coloured butterflies. Red, green, purple ... Garnets, peridots, amethysts. It would take four or five months of intense coaching to attain the necessary degree of enlightenment and understanding to go up a level, and during this period members were required to undertake a lot of self-improvement study as well as engage in various acts of self-denial. This could mean anything from fasting for a day, or wearing no make-up for a week, right through to no sexual relations for a month. O'Malley wasn't particularly forthcoming about the denial aspect of the "journey", but our informer insisted there was nothing sinister in the requests, it was all about commitment and cleansing.

'Now we come on to the money. You've probably already guessed how it worked ... Each level of attainment cost the participant upwards of twenty-five thousand pounds – in some cases it might take longer to reach the goal and so the sums involved increased.'

Stunned by the amounts, Cristy quickly noted them down and said:

CRISTY: 'Did you ever find out how many members there were?'

RUSH: 'According to O'Malley, there were several thousand all over the world. If that was true, as far as we ever knew they'd all signed up voluntarily, because no one ever came forward to say otherwise. We found no evidence of blackmail or any other sort of underhand means to elicit the astronomical sums that were paid. As you probably know, that sort of practice often features prominently in a cult.

'What was indisputable, however, was the fact that the members had to be wealthy, and fully invested in their journey to fulfilment, or whatever the final goal was supposed to be. As one of my colleagues put it at the time, they were women – and they were mostly women – who had nothing better to do with their time or money. And who'd never want to be exposed for being duped out of a small fortune if Papilio was ever revealed to be a cult.

'Remember, Paul O'Malley wasn't obliged to give us any more information than he wanted to. If he'd remained a suspect in the murders it would have been a different story, but with no evidence to link him to anything – it was all morally dubious, of course, and actually screamed of a scam – but we couldn't really do anything about it, and obviously it wasn't a priority.'

CRISTY: 'Did he, or the anonymous caller, talk about the brandings?'

Rush called up the relevant paragraphs.

RUSH: 'It was not undertaken by all members, but those who chose to make the commitment were "fully supported at all times and someone always remained with them as the butterflies entered the body to dissolve all forms of negativity and fear to bring about growth and renewal".'

Cristy blinked as she tried to get her head around that.

RUSH: 'I know, bizarre, bonkers even, but I guess it made sense to them. O'Malley, incidentally, didn't want to discuss the brandings, although he didn't deny they happened. It's quite possible they were organized by Serena and he banked the proceeds.'

CRISTY: 'So people actually paid to be branded?'

RUSH: 'Anything up to seventy-five thousand, we were told. I know, hard to comprehend, isn't it, but I guess to some that isn't a lot of money. We consulted another psychotherapist at the time and he explained a great deal about how a vulnerable person can be preyed upon and exploited when at their lowest ebb. They become desperate to belong, to find answers and an understanding of good versus evil, to discover a way to forgive themselves even, and an exclusive society such as Papilio, that offers support and comfort and a rarefied kind of healing, would be like finding the holy grail. There's no knowing how much Paul O'Malley has made from these vulnerable women to date, but our best estimates back then put it right up there in the millions.'

CRISTY: 'And Lexie Gaudion was one of these women.'

RUSH: 'Apparently. Her butterfly, incidentally, the one she was wearing when she died, was studded with peridots, which meant she'd completed her journey to becoming spiritually healthy and fertile. Serena's necklace was an amethyst, which I'm told denotes her qualification to counsel and guide others. There was something about miracles as well, but it's not noted here, and it's too long ago for me to remember the detail.

'The third butterfly at the scene, the one still in its box, was made from plain gold. O'Malley tells us that this was – or is – awarded at the time of introduction to the group. So, we deduced that Margaret Sallis was either being inducted, or perhaps simply persuaded to become a member at the time of the killings. Her daughter, Olivia, confirmed it when we spoke to her.'

Cristy sat back, needing a moment to absorb all this, and to give the hovering waitress a chance to clear the table. It was extraordinary trying to imagine the world within a world that was emerging, to think of those who'd been sucked into it in the hope of it enriching their lives in ways they'd been unable to find elsewhere. What was missing for them? Why did they believe this obscure sort of treatment with symbols and mantras, denials,

135

brandings, suffering and the paying of huge sums of money, could complete them?

Why would Lexie Gaudion need it?

After the waitress had gone, leaving them alone again, Cristy spoke first.

CRISTY: 'We know that Lexie Gaudion was undergoing psychotherapy, and obviously she belonged to this cult, but did anyone ever go into any detail as to why she felt she needed it?'

RUSH: 'Obviously we don't have a first-hand account of what it was like being married to David Gaudion, but I think we can presume it wasn't a bed of roses given the rumours of affairs and the lengths she went to to try and find an escape, or some meaning to her life – or whatever she was searching for.'

CRISTY: 'Did he have affairs?'

RUSH: 'I believe so, but the allegations were looked into by another team and as far as I'm aware they never opened up avenues it was felt worth exploring.'

CRISTY: 'Anything else about him?'

RUSH: 'It was said that he had a temper, that he didn't appreciate being questioned, would only co-operate if he felt his interrogator was of equal intellect. He liked mind games, apparently, could run rings around more junior detectives, but even the experienced guys were wary of him, knowing how skilful he could be when it came to tricking them into making fools of themselves.'

CRISTY: 'Is this something he did regularly?'

RUSH: 'Hard to say. I'm just repeating what I heard at the time. I had no dealings with him myself.'

CRISTY: 'OK. So let's go back to Lexie. What sort of things did people say about her?'

RUSH: 'She was described to us variously as fragile, insecure, sometimes fearful, lacking in self-worth, but also kind and generous, studious, a keen horsewoman. Some said she was a faithful wife, others accused her of being a serial adulterer. She was a great mother, or she was neglectful, much like her own . . . Several mentioned her gift for learning and the wasted opportunity at Oxford. She came down when she was pregnant with her eldest and never went back.'

CRISTY: 'Did she work after the child was born?'

RUSH: 'She did a lot for charities, fundraisers, sponsorship, that sort of thing, and she gave riding lessons at the Kellon Hall stables. But there's no record of her having a career of any sort, if that's what you mean.'

CRISTY: 'It's been intimated to us that all was not well with the eldest, Rosaria Gaudion. Do you know anything about that?'

RUSH: 'I know that she had – or has – Down's Syndrome, if that's what you're referring to.'

Cristy and Connor exchanged glances. Why on earth would Gordon Bryce and Flora Gibson feel so uncomfortable about mentioning it? There was no accounting for how some people viewed disabilities, and it made Cristy sad to think of how much work there was still to be done on that front.

RUSH: 'I'm sure you know this already, but the best person to talk to about Lexie and Rosaria Gaudion is Olivia Caldwell, Lexie's sister.'

CRISTY: 'We're trying, but right now she isn't being very forthcoming.'

Rush glanced at Connor and said, 'Perhaps what I'm about to say next shouldn't go into your podcast.'

Switching off, he gestured for her to continue.

Rush said, 'It's no secret that Oliva was very protective of her sister, I think that was the case through most of their lives, but I don't feel comfortable about discussing her breakdown following the murders as if it were merely incidental to the case. For her it couldn't have been worse – she lost her mother, her sister and her niece, so I believe it's for her to tell you about her grief, if she's willing, and you already seem to know that she isn't.'

Cristy nodded. 'But if it were you, and it was your family, wouldn't you want to find out who did it?'

'Of course, but don't you think Olivia's inaction tells us that she believes her brother-in-law was responsible? So she'd see no point in trying to find anyone else. And the fact that Gaudion has never done anything to try to clear his name, maybe that tells us the same thing.'

Because she had to, Cristy said, 'Would you mind if we got that last bit on tape? We don't have to mention the breakdown, but if we could take it from where I asked what you would do if it were your family?'

Seeming to have no problem with that, Rush waited for Cristy to repeat the question then gave the answer again, this time adding,

RUSH: 'Have you tried speaking to David Gaudion?'

CRISTY: 'Do you know where he is?'

RUSH: 'No, but his brother surely does.'

CRISTY: 'I'm afraid Richard Gaudion is someone else who doesn't want to engage with us.'

Rush didn't comment on that, although she didn't appear surprised.

CRISTY: 'Were you involved in David Gaudion's interrogation?'

RUSH: 'Not personally, but I observed some of the interviews.'

CRISTY: 'Can you tell us something about him?'

Rush fell silent as she smiled grimly and slowly shook her head. Not for the first time, Cristy wished they were interviewing on camera, for though Rush's words were unspoken, her manner was intriguingly expressive.

RUSH: 'Where does anyone begin about David Gaudion?'

Cristy waited; she could sense Connor's tension too.

RUSH: 'I'm afraid he isn't easily described, but I will say this, he was clever, personable, actually quite easy to like. He had us all taken in at one time or another, but we soon learned that he was a consummate actor. Or, put another way, he conformed very well to the profile of a psychopath.'

Rush checked her phone as it vibrated again, and Cristy could tell she was about to end the interview. It didn't matter; the last statement had given them the perfect cliff-hanger for the end of the next episode. They didn't need any more today.

'What you've told us,' she said as Rush turned off her tablet and packed it away, 'about the cult, the cover-up, the contradictions over Lexie's character, and that last comment about Gaudion, will make a podcast in itself. I can't thank you enough for speaking to us so frankly.'

Rush smiled and shrugged, as if it were nothing. 'It actually felt good to get some of it off my chest,' she admitted. 'It's been haunting me for years, so I hope you get somewhere with this.'

'You'll speak to us again? About Gaudion?' Cristy prompted.

'I will, but I won't be able to throw any new light on what happened. Or on where he is. You need to keep trying with Olivia Caldwell and Richard Gaudion for that.'

'What about Cynthia Gaudian and Rosaria? Do you have any idea where they are?'

'I'm afraid not, but I'll see if I can get Gaudion's police interviews to you; they should be helpful if you're after an insight into the man.'

Amazed and thrilled by the offer, Cristy said, 'I'm starting to wonder how we'd ever have done this without you.'

'Actually, going back to the cult for a moment,' Connor said, before Rush could shake hands with Cristy, 'was it generally thought that it was Lexie's involvement in it that led to the murders? If she was handing over large sums of money, was it Gaudion's way of stopping her?'

'It's certainly the motive the CPS favoured,' Rush replied. 'Her bank records showed withdrawals of over two hundred thousand in cash during the last few months of her life.'

Connor gave a low whistle.

'But there was more than just the cult,' Rush continued. 'We knew it was important, but we just couldn't ever put our fingers on what was missing.'

'Do you know where Paul O'Malley can be found now?' Cristy asked.

'The last I heard, he was running a healing centre in the Caribbean, but that was a few years ago. I expect he's changed his name again by now, but even if you manage to find him it's highly unlikely you'll get him to talk. He only opened up to us because he knew, if he didn't, it wouldn't end well for him. He's very secretive about his organization – no online presence that I've ever heard about, it's all word of mouth, and obviously the banking is well out of UK jurisdiction. Anyway, I'm afraid, I really do have to run.'

'Actually, can I just circle back to the documentary producer you mentioned?' Connor jumped in.

Rush nodded. 'I've made a note. I'll let you know if I can find out anything about him.'

'That's great, thank you, but there was a podcaster too. She was called Iris, no surname yet. She contacted Kevin Break about the murders, but then he never heard from her again. As far as we can tell, no one else to do with the case has heard from her either, but yesterday we received an email advising, or warning us to stop the series if we didn't want the same thing happening to us as happened to her.'

Rush's eyes widened.

'How seriously do you think we should take it?' Cristy asked cautiously.

140

'Well, given how much has been covered up or shut down in this case over the years, I'd be wanting to find out from this Iris why she stopped.'

'We're trying to locate her,' Connor replied. 'Meantime, would you care to venture a guess as to who might be behind the email?'

Rush thought. 'A couple of names spring to mind. Richard Gaudion, could even be Olivia Caldwell, but if pushed I think my money would be on David Gaudion himself. It's the kind of thing he might do to mess with you.'

CHAPTER THIRTEEN

Later in the afternoon the whole team was back at the office, Cristy making notes as she listened to a playback of DSI Rush's interview, while Clover and Jackson collated the recordings they'd made of their chats with various residents of the Berkeley Vale. Connor was surfing through emails on his phone when he suddenly cried,

'Newman!'

The others looked up, mystified.

'It's from Kevin,' he explained. 'Iris-the-podcaster's surname is Newman and . . . Hang on, he's done some digging and . . . Oh shit! No! *Seriously?*'

'What?' Cristy demanded.

Connor regarded her aghast. 'She got knocked off her bike – and killed.'

Cristy blanched.

'Who are we talking about?' Clover demanded.

Cristy told her to check the listener emails and said to Connor, 'When did it happen?'

He consulted the email again and read out the attached news extract. '"Twenty-eight-year-old Gloucester woman, Iris Newman, was tragically killed last Tuesday evening in a hit-and-run incident while cycling home from an evening out with friends . . ."' He looked up again. 'Kevin's saying it was about two weeks after she approached him, which would make it . . . about ten months ago.'

'WTF!' Clover exclaimed, having found the email Cristy had directed her to. 'How did I miss this?'

Cristy had the news article about Iris up on her screen now. 'They're not saying it was an accident,' she muttered, struggling to take in the enormity of it. 'Christ! She was left in a ditch . . . And they think she might have survived if someone had called it in right away.'

'We need to speak to Gloucester Police,' Connor declared, reaching for his phone.

As he made the call, Cristy scanned the rest of the article and felt her heart splitting between horror and pity for the poor girl who'd been struck by an unidentified vehicle around nine-thirty in the evening less than a mile from her home.

Iris was greatly loved by her friends and family and was engaged to be married to local car salesman, Joe Mead (30). Her parents, school teachers Jennifer and Robert Newman from Worcester, are said to be in a state of shock and are being comforted by other family and close friends. Gloucester Police are asking for anyone who might have been in the vicinity of Parsonage Lane at around nine-thirty last Tuesday evening to contact them on the number below.

Connor was through to someone at the station. 'No, we don't have any information regarding the incident as such . . . OK, can you give me an update . . . Sorry, yes, I'm a producer on the podcast *Hindsight* and we believe Iris was looking into the same case we are at the time of her death.' He waited, wrote quickly on his pad and said, 'Yes, we've received an email that might . . . OK, if you give me an address, I'll forward it. Right, will do, thanks very much. I'll be in touch.' As he rang off all eyes were on him.

'They still haven't traced the vehicle that hit her,' he told them.

Cristy hardly knew what to say. This wasn't the news any of them wanted to hear. It felt surreal, terrifying even, as they considered the chances of Iris's death being an accident.

'Would it be inappropriate to try and contact her parents or fiancé?' Connor asked.

'I think we should,' Cristy said, 'but first, to try and safeguard all of us . . .' She reached for her handheld recording device and switched on.

CRISTY: 'The following is a statement to be included in episode two of *Hindsight– the Kellon Manse Murders.*

'I want to share with you an email we received after the first episode was dropped. We have no idea who sent it, but by the time this episode airs we will have passed it to Gloucester Police. It says, *For your own sake you should let this go. You don't want to end up like Iris.*

'Iris, we now know, was Iris Newman, a young podcaster from Gloucestershire who was killed in a hit-and-run incident two weeks after approaching ex-DC Kevin Break about the Kellon Manse Murders. You will have heard Kevin interviewed during our first episode. It's highly likely Iris contacted others from the time of the killings. We don't yet know who they are, but obviously we'll be looking into it – and of course we can't say at this stage that her accident had anything to do with her podcast, but the *Hindsight* team will be on the lookout to make sure nothing similar happens to any of us.'

As she clicked off, she sat back in her chair, feeling slightly breathless and disoriented as she looked at the others. Had she really just recorded a message to someone who'd killed three women sixteen years ago, and perhaps another much more recently? Were they seriously going to air it? They couldn't without the permission of Iris's family . . . She was finding it hard to think straight. 'If any of you want to back out of this now . . .' she said.

'Not happening,' they chorused, almost as one.

She wasn't surprised by their loyalty and determination, but was nonetheless concerned. On the other hand, they – or she – could be guilty of a massive overreaction here, a connecting of dots that was forming another picture altogether; they just weren't seeing it yet. 'We're assuming the email was a threat,' she said, 'and I think we have to treat it as such, but let's keep in mind that it could as easily have been a warning from someone once – or twice – removed from the Kellon Manse Murders. Someone who, like us, is genuinely worried that Iris's death might not have been an accident.'

'Good point,' Connor said, 'but I need to send that opening link you just recorded to the police to get their take on whether or not to include it. If they give the go-ahead – and Iris's family are on board for it too – I'm of the opinion we should use it as a promo and upload it right away.'

'Gets my vote,' Jackson put in. 'The sooner it's out there the sooner our emailer will know we're not taking any shit from him – or her.'

Cristy didn't disagree. 'I'll get Meena or Harry in here,' she said, picking up her phone. 'They'll want to know about this.'

'He's at Lord's today,' Jackson told her, 'and we passed Meena on her way to the BBC when we came back.'

After sending Meena a text to get in touch when she could, Cristy waited for Connor to finish forwarding the email and link to the police and said, 'OK, let's move on from that for now. I'd like to hear what you guys, Clover and Jacks, managed to get today.'

Clover was already lined up with the highlights of her and Jackson's visit to Hannah Gains, self-proclaimed old friend of Mean Margaret Sallis. 'She has to be ninety, if a day,' Clover told them, 'sweet, mad as a box of frogs at times, amazingly cogent at others – and she was totally thrilled to have her very first "person of colour" in her picturesque little cottage.'

Connor almost spilled his drink. 'Did she actually say that?' he spluttered.

'She wasn't quite as "on trend" with her terminology,' Jackson informed them, 'but yes, she was a little bit smitten with our Clove who's welcome to visit anytime, and would she like to attend church with her on Sunday to give all the old "codgers and biddies something to tongue-wag" about. "We can pretend you're my long-lost daughter," is what she said.'

As the others burst out laughing, Clover rolled her eyes and continued, 'I don't think there's any doubt that she knew Margaret. She only lives a mile or so from the Hall and has been in the same house for most of her life. She retired about thirty years ago after a long career as the deputy head of an elite girls' school in Worcestershire, but she spent all her holidays and free time in the Vale, so she's definitely a local.'

'What did she tell you about Margaret?' Cristy prompted.

'Actually, quite a lot of what we've already heard about the drinking and general misanthropy, as Hannah called it, so I don't have that ready for playback. I've started with how she began barging her way into the Hall some time back in the mid-Eighties, insisting Margaret needed to be "prised from her shell", and "encouraged to engage with the world". Apparently, after a couple of years of being thrown straight back out the door, she was eventually allowed to stay a while and her visits became quite regular, at least once or twice a month. She didn't like the Hall, she said, thought it had a creepy feel to it, but she was concerned about Margaret being lonely and friendless with two small children, as the girls were back then. Here's what she said in her own words:

HANNAH GAINS: 'Everyone has to have someone, don't they, and I felt sure there was more to Margaret's reclusiveness and hostility than most of us knew. Sadly, I never really did get to the bottom of what ailed her, she didn't speak to me much while I sat there knitting or crocheting, sharing titbits of news, while she poured herself yet another gin and stared at nothing. I think, in a way, she was glad to have me there, it might have made her feel less abandoned, not that she ever said as much. It was just how she seemed, as if everyone had let her down somehow, or maybe she'd let herself down. She became especially melancholy after her husband died – that's when I really started forcing myself on her – although around the time of the funeral she kept saying he was lucky she hadn't broken his neck for him. She called him all sorts of names, probably best not to repeat them now.

'She never seemed to bother about being a single mother, never gave the impression that motherhood meant much to her at all, in fact, but who knows what was really in her stony old heart?'

CLOVER: 'Did you know her daughters?'

HANNAH GAINS: 'Oh yes, yes, they were little sweethearts

when they were young. Minxes, mind you, but what child isn't, especially when they don't get much discipline? I'd have been so proud if they were mine, even with the naughtiness, but Margaret, she seemed almost constantly irritated by them, particularly after their father died. They could only have been ten and eleven when he went, very young to lose a parent, but I'm not sure their loss was an issue Margaret ever addressed. She was always snapping at them to leave her alone, or go and find something to do that wasn't in her way. If they weren't there when I called round, and they often weren't, she never seemed to know where they might be and didn't give the impression of caring very much either. Looking back, I think she was in an awful state of depression, poor thing, but I didn't know much about those things then, still don't really, but I can't think why else she was so mean-spirited and unhappy. It was lucky for everyone that Cynthia Gaudion took the girls under her wing. They used to make a beeline for that farm every time they left the Hall, everyone knew that. All the kids loved going to Cynthia's, and Margaret's girls had a lovely, sibling sort of bond with the Gaudion boys.

'Margaret herself, though, she was a sad and bitter woman, and her husband, when he was alive, wasn't a pleasant man. I never really spoke to him, it was clear he didn't have time for me, and to be truthful, I was a little bit scared of him. I never heard him raise his voice or show any roughness towards anyone, but I never had a good feeling about him, only about the girls. They used to pop in to see me from time to time when they were young teenagers, the boys too . . . Usually they were playing Knock Out Ginger, or trying to steal my apples, and I'd go after them like the witch they thought I was. I wasn't a witch, of course, but I could see what a thrill it gave them to pretend I was.

'I don't think they saw me that way later, when they were older. They were always respectful then and even said they liked the sweaters I knitted for them. I never saw one of them wearing one, mind you, but at least they were polite to my face.'

Clover stopped the playback, and said, 'She goes on quite a lot more in that vein, lots of tangents, fond memories, that sort of thing, but eventually we got her onto the week before the killings.'

HANNAH GAINS: It was a Wednesday, as I recall, when I went round there and Margaret seemed in unusually good spirits. Margaret in good spirits could be quite alarming, you understand – so out of the ordinary, it was like watching an odd sort of metamorphosis, or the coming back to life of a zombie. Anyway, on this day, she actually invited me in, even offered me a drink, something she'd given up on a very long time ago. I declined, as usual. Never before six for me. She helped herself to her usual large gin and next-to-no tonic . . .

'Oh, I remember you wanted me to describe her. . . Well, by then she was looking pretty terrible if I'm being honest. Painfully thin, her face was sunken and very lined, and her eyes were quite yellow. I don't think she was a well woman, but that day she seemed almost . . . gay. Can I use that word in the old-fashioned sense? I asked what had put her in such a good mood and she said that Lexie was going to introduce her to a miracle worker.'

Cristy noted this down as the playback continued.

CLOVER: 'Did she say who the miracle worker was?'

HANNAH GAINS: 'I asked, but she put a finger over her lips to signify they were sealed. Well, I'm not one to pry so I left it there. I just felt glad that she was so pleased to be sharing something with Lexie. She really hadn't treated either of her children well over the years, did I already tell you that? She was a woeful mother, I'm sad to say, but I think Cynthia Gaudion had a very good influence on them, being the naturally maternal type. And of course going away to school and not having to live in the dreadful atmosphere of that house will have helped to straighten them out a bit too.'

Clover moved them on to the next highlight.

HANNAH GAINS: 'I was sorry when Lexie dropped out of university. She was such a bright young thing. Always top of the class when she was at junior's. She won prizes for some of her projects. Everyone thought she had a great future ahead of her; she was quite gifted in the sciences. Or was it . . . That's right, she wanted to become an anthropologist, Margaret once told me. Olivia's strengths had more of an artistic bent, literature, theatre, music, that sort of thing. She was quite a talented singer, even as a small child, and she was often the lead in school plays. Margaret didn't go to watch her performances, but Cynthia and Don Gaudion did. I'm sure the boys went too, and Lexie was very proud of her sister. I believe Olivia has a chain of flower shops now, and they're doing very well. Her husband, Winston Caldwell, or is it William? I'm not sure. Anyway, he's a very important man, just like his father. They're landowners over near Stroud, with all sorts of businesses, mostly agricultural, I think, but they do a lot of work with young people. There was a son who died from a drug overdose when he was eighteen. That's when his parents opened up a rehabilitation centre to help young people who ran into trouble, even those fresh out of prison, I believe. They're a good family. It pleases my heart no end to think of Olivia being a part of it after all she's been through.'

Clover said, 'I thought that was an interesting little insight into Olivia's world, and now we come on to David and Richard Gaudion.'

HANNAH GAINS: 'They weren't interested in farming, either of them, which I know was a big disappointment to their father. But Cynthia and Don were never the sort to stand in their sons' ways. David went into the City, I think, or was it politics? Whatever it was, I guess it all came to a stop after what happened. I don't know what he does now, but I believe Richard is still a lawyer, real estate . . . Or it might be something to do with tax. Whatever it was, Cynthia and Don had a lot of reason to feel proud of their boys . . .'

149

Clover said, 'She got quite gloomy at this point and didn't really want to continue, so we broke for another cup of tea – she loves tea – and after a while she started to perk up again. Eventually I got her back onto the subject of Lexie. She seemed happier talking about her than about David.'

HANNAH GAINS: ' . . . did I tell you she wanted to be an anthropologist? Yes, I believe I did. I think she'd have made a fine one, but sadly it wasn't meant to be. She was quite a different girl when she came back from university, you know. She'd always been the quieter of the two sisters, more introverted, I'd say, a little less flighty anyway, but she had a marvellous sense of humour, it was quite a joy to watch her laugh . . . That was before she came back from Oxford, not so much after.

'Margaret wasn't thrilled about the pregnancy, I can tell you that. Some of the things she said . . . May God forgive her for such anger and intolerance towards one of her own, and thank goodness for Cynthia who didn't think twice about taking dear Lexie in. David married her, of course, he had to with a baby on the way, but he carried on with his degree – he was at the London School of Economics, I believe, and came back most weekends. You'd often see them in a pub, or walking together, or driving about the countryside.

'When Rosaria was born . . . Pretty name, don't you think? That was when they moved into the Manse, or maybe it was after. It's hard to be clear about timings after all these years, but what I remember quite clearly is that Margaret had always refused it before. She wasn't known as Mean Margaret for nothing, I'm afraid. But then along came dear little Rosaria and, lo and behold, Margaret hands David and Lexie the keys. Whether it was because of the child's condition I never knew, Margaret never mentioned it nor was she the type to be much moved by it, but they got the place in the end. And Margaret carried on as if the child didn't exist, which was sad, because she was such an engaging little mite, sunny natured right out of the womb. Everyone loved her and David was a doting dad. I always said that about him, but it's possible others will tell you differently. I've heard some terrible stories about him since it all happened . . . I don't believe a word of them, myself, and nor will I until you can show me some proof. It all started because of that cult business, I'm sure of it. It never ceases to amaze me the things some people come out with when they know nothing about something. You have to wonder where their heads are, and their hearts?'

There was a lengthy pause, making Cristy think Clover had stopped the recording, until Hannah said:

'Over time, Margaret became quite good with the child, insofar as she was good with anyone. If she didn't want to engage with her she wouldn't, and if Rosaria cried she had to be taken home. But there were times when she held her, and even talked to her, which was something I'd never seen her do with her own, and I think she had Rosaria up on a horse and in a saddle before she could walk. It was the same with Amelia when she came along. Oh dear, Amelia, dear oh dear . . .'

The sadness in her voice seemed to linger in the room even after Clover stopped the recording, a trail of sadness that was almost a keen. 'She doesn't want to believe the little girl was murdered,' Clover told them. 'She tells herself that Amelia was taken to another family who continue to love and cherish her to this day. I think it's a fantasy that allows her to sleep at night.'

Deciding it would be a good idea to prepare the old lady before they aired anything about the anonymous call insisting Amelia was dead, Cristy said, 'What else did she say about David?'

'Actually, not much really. She didn't want to speak ill of him, that was for sure, but as for going any further about the murders, it was easy to see how much it upset her, so we didn't push it.'

'What about Cynthia?' Connor asked. 'Did she give any indication of where she – or David – might be?'

'I asked, but she said she has no idea. Although she remembers being surprised when David returned to the Manse after his release. She said everyone kept their distance during that time; no one knew what to say to him and he didn't try to force any sort of contact with them. He basically kept himself to himself, coming and going, Hannah had no idea where, but she recalls dropping him a note to let him know that if he needed a friend her door was always open.'

After allowing a moment for them to sit with that, Jackson said, 'There's something else about Margaret you'll want to hear. It's right at the end of the interview.'

Clearly knowing what he was referring to, Clover lined it up.

HANNAH GAINS: '. . . I'd been at the Hall about an hour that day – this is two or three days before it all happened. It was the last time I saw Margaret, in fact. I'd stopped at the stables on my way in for a little chat with Rosaria and Amelia, so I knew they were around, but they didn't come in with me. I found Margaret in a strange sort of mood, not upbeat the way she'd been during my last visit – this time she was jumpy, distracted, and hardly seemed to know I was there, until she suddenly registered it and gave me a peculiar stare. Then she told me it was time for me to "bugger off" because she had other things to do. It wasn't unusual for her to speak to me like that, I didn't take offence, I was used to it, but what was unusual was her seeing me to the door. She generally left me to find my own way out, but this time . . . Maybe she wanted to be sure I left the premises. I don't know. I was just about to set off down the drive when, out of the blue, she asked me if I ever wore jewellery. It seemed such a strange question coming from her who didn't even wear a wedding ring any more, and she certainly wasn't one for girl-talk. I told her I had a few pieces that came out for special occasions, and she said that the next time I saw her she'd be wearing a necklace like Lexie's. She seemed almost devilishly pleased about it, as if it might be something she was going to steal, but looking back in the light of what happened, I don't think

152

I was right about that. Anyway, I'd never noticed Lexie's necklace so I said something along the lines of "how lovely" and she said, "Olivia's going to be very cross with me, but who cares about her?"'

As the recording stopped they sat quietly with Hannah's closing words, taking time to picture Margaret Sallis getting excited about joining a scheme that her daughter – someone she'd shown little affection for, or interest in – belonged to. 'Sounds like she was the kind of mother who got a kick out of playing one sister off against the other,' Connor commented.

Cristy nodded agreement. 'I wonder if she knew at that point how much the necklace was going to cost her?' she asked dryly. 'I mean in a monetary sense.'

'If she did,' Jackson replied, 'I don't think she mentioned it to Hannah, because all she said was – play right to the end, Clove.'

HANNAH GAINS: It's such a shame what those butterfly pendants cost them. I wonder what the truth of it all is? Let's hope you find out, my dears, because I really would like to know. Oh, and if you do see David, please tell him my door is still open.'

An hour later they were still at their desks, enjoying the ice-creams one of the studio's assistants had popped out for, while listening to other snatches of interviews from that morning. Amongst them a retired postman who'd said, 'There was always all sorts of business going on at the Manse. I can't tell you what it was, but I definitely thought it was dodgy.' A farmer who'd grumbled, 'Shouldn't be digging your noses into other people's business, that's what I always say.' An old friend of Richard's who'd warned, 'You never wanted to be on the wrong side of those brothers, I can tell you that much, especially not David. He gave me a good hiding more than once when we were kids.' A junior school contemporary of Olivia and Lexie who sounded pleased to share the memory of calling them 'the sexy-Sallises. Always after the boys, they were. I wouldn't be surprised if all sorts of swapping went on between those four when they got older.'

'I heard they were into Satanism,' a pub landlord confided. 'That's what the cult was about, and that poor little girl got used as a sacrifice.'

'Cynthia had a brother on Exmoor, and another somewhere near the Lake District. I expect she went to one of them. No idea where she is these days.'

'We saw David a few years back, in London. I know he recognized us, but he didn't speak. To be fair, we didn't either. I mean, what do you say to someone who got away with murder?'

'Oh, he did it all right. No doubt about it, but he had friends in high places, didn't he? Friends who were a part of that cult and they didn't want it all coming out, which it would have if the case had gone to trial.'

'There's more,' Clover said, stopping the recordings, 'and opinion of him could hardly be more divided. For everyone who called him an abuser, or a pimp, or a cultist, there was someone else to say he was one of the nicest blokes they ever knew. A great husband, a loving father. So I'm not sure we're any further along with the kind of man he really was.'

'A proper Jekyll and Hyde,' Jackson commented, fixed on his screen.

'Or a psychopath,' Connor said, quoting DSI Rush.

As they all felt the chill of that, Jackson said, 'Well, here's something we can be certain about. Ownership of Kellon Hall and the surrounding estate was transferred to a trust following the death of Margaret Sallis. The trustee is Olivia Caldwell, and the beneficiaries are named as Marcus and Rebecca Caldwell, and Rosaria and Amelia Gaudion.'

Cristy's eyebrows rose.

'Interesting that Amelia's name is still there,' Connor commented.

'I guess it has to be, given no death has been registered,' Cristy pointed out. 'So no mention of David Gaudion being a trustee, or anything else to do with the estate?'

Jackson shook his head. 'If the place sells, I guess Rosaria will get Amelia's share, or maybe another trust will be set up. Anyway, doesn't seem that David stands to make anything out of it, at least not directly.'

They looked up at the sound of a commotion outside in the car park. For no reason that made sense, Cristy felt a sudden pang of unease and she could see that the others were feeling it too. It lasted no more than a moment, before a beautiful blonde-haired girl bobbed up from nowhere and stuck her head through the open window shouting, 'Surprise!'

Laughing, as her eyes filled with tears, Cristy got up from her chair.

'Sorry if I'm interrupting,' Hayley cried, 'but I can't wait any longer to see you.'

'Come here,' Cristy said, hauling her into the room.

'Don't leave me out here,' Aiden shouted. 'The monsters might get me.'

'You are the monster,' Hayley told him from inside Cristy's bruising embrace, and Aiden, all scrawny five foot ten of him, leapt over the ledge into the room.

'Hey, guys,' he grinned, going to fist-bump Connor, Jackson and Clover. 'Excuse our arrival, the sis has her way of doing things. Not hanging out for long, have places to be, plugs to sort.'

'Plugs?' Cristy queried.

'Don't ask,' Hayley cautioned.

'Glasto coming up at the weekend,' Aiden announced, 'got to have supplies.'

'I told you, there'll be plenty there,' Hayley scolded. 'Mum! It's so good to see you. I've missed you so much. Can we hang out, just us two, tonight? Or are you already booked?'

'I'm free,' Cristy smiled, 'and I think we're almost done here for the day?'

'Go!' Clover instructed. 'We'll text if anything comes up before we leave.'

'Hey, who's the dude?' Aiden broke in, peering at the 'crime scene' board.

They all turned to look at the dominant shot of David Gaudion at the centre of it all.

'Oh wow!' Hayley gasped. 'He's the one who did the killings, right? OMG, he looks just like . . . what's his name . . . That guy in *Fight Club*?'

'Ed Norton?' Aiden said, clearly not seeing it.

'No, the other one. I forget his name, but the one with spiky hair and blue eyes. You know who I mean, Mum.'

'Classic psycho combo, that,' Aiden commented knowingly.

Hayley pulled a face. 'Says who?'

He shrugged. 'I heard it somewhere. Anyway, I'm out of here. Mum, can I crash at yours later?'

'I'm staying there tonight,' Hayley reminded him.

'Cool. I'll take the sofa. See you high-key people in the not too distant,' and with an athletic vault he was back through the window and gone.

'He's such a jerk,' Hayley snorted.

'But we love him,' Cristy reminded her.

Hayley laughed. 'We do,' and checking her mobile, 'Oh great, it's Hugo. I'll see you outside, Mum. Love to all of you,' and blowing them a kiss, she wafted out through the door, all long, tanned legs and crinkly waist-length hair.

'I just love your kids,' Clover grinned as Cristy started to pack up her things.

'They're yours,' Cristy retorted, sardonically. 'OK, so do we all know what we're doing tomorrow?'

'Me, I'm chasing Gaudion's work colleagues,' Jackson answered, 'and digging up whatever I can find about Papilio and Paul O'Malley. It would be great to get him on tape if we can, or someone on the inside who can confirm it's still operating. I also want to start looking at music and sound effects for Ep. Two.'

'I'll be editing the Rush and Hannah Gains interviews,' Connor announced. 'I'd like to intercut some of the juicier neighbour comments, Clove, if you can set them up.'

'On it,' she responded. 'I'll sit with you for some of it, if that's OK, but my main task tomorrow is scanning the hundreds of messages we've got coming in. This is the only downside to podcasts – you've got no idea when someone's going to listen, and so the best, or most useful, responses can turn up at any time.'

'The interview we really need,' Cristy said, turning to assess the board, 'is still Olivia Caldwell. Just as good could be the anonymous caller who insisted Amelia was dead.' Her eyes came to rest on David Gaudion's, almost as if they'd been drawn there. His hair wasn't spiky, nor was he wearing one of the high-collar shirts Brad Pitt had favoured in *Fight Club,* but his eyes were certainly blue. She felt a fleeting sense of something she couldn't quite define as she regarded him more closely. Unease, yes, intrigue, naturally, but there was something else, something more . . . viscerally disturbing, as if he was actually looking right back at her and seeing . . . what? What could those ice-blue eyes see from where he was – and why was she asking herself such an absurd question when she was staring at a standard 2D photograph?

CHAPTER FOURTEEN

'She was quite pretty, wasn't she?' Hayley mused as Cristy brought two long-stemmed glasses and a dish of nibbles to the garden table.

Seeing she was connected to shots of Lexie Gaudion on the podcast's website, Cristy said, 'Yes, she was,' and felt thankful they hadn't posted any of the crime-scene photos; they weren't images she'd want her daughter to see, or anyone else come to that. Lexie should be remembered the way she'd been before that terrible day.

'The mother looks a bit of a dragon,' Hayley commented, 'and the other one . . . Serena the cultist, she's kind of like her name, don't you think? You know, serene, sophisticated . . .' She looked up and grinned, 'and gorgeous, just like you.'

Cristy laughed and tweaked her nose as she went back inside to open a bottle of wine. 'Can we leave that alone now?' she called over her shoulder. 'I've had enough of work for one day. I want to talk about you.'

'Oh! Hang on, just got to answer this,' Hayley called back, and her thumbs began speeding over the tiny screen.

After pulling the cork and checking her own phone, Cristy returned to the table and unfurled the awning to shade them from the early evening sun. While walking back from the studios, along the waterfront, they'd run into so many people Cristy knew, mostly from her TV days, that she was glad to be alone with Hayley now.

Well, she would be once Hayley had finished with her texting.

'Sorry, all yours,' Hayley declared, casting her mobile aside and picking up the glass Cristy had just filled. 'Love you,' she smiled, making a toast.

Cristy's heart melted. 'Love you too,' she said, 'but you look tired.'

Hayley rolled her eyes. 'Tell me about it,' she groaned. 'Flight got cancelled, next one delayed, waited an age for bags to come through in Bristol, then when we got to Dad's—' She broke off grimacing awkwardly. 'You know I got here last night, right?' she asked tentatively.

Cristy nodded.

'And I didn't tell you because I wanted to surprise you today. Well, actually, because Marley and Dad had arranged this family dinner,' she mock-gagged, 'and Aiden threatened to go mental if Hugo and I didn't show up for it. And I figured he has to deal with them on his own a lot, so it would be mean of me to let him down and come straight here. Which was what I'd intended to do—'

'It's OK, you don't have to keep explaining,' Cristy interrupted. 'I must admit, I wondered why you didn't mention it when we were WhatsApping last night . . .'

'Cos I'd decided by then to surprise you. Oh Mum, were you really hurt when you found out? I'm sorry, I didn't mean . . . Actually, how did you find out I got in last night?'

'Marley told me.'

Hayley blinked. 'Seriously? You've spoken to her?'

'She's taken to calling me quite a lot lately.'

'What about? God, she is such a piece of work, isn't she? And *so* controlling. I mean, she comes across as all sweet and lovely, Miss Generous trying for a best stepmum award, but underneath she's constantly working out how to make stuff all about her. Hugo can't stand her already. He doesn't let it show, obvs, but he much prefers you—'

'Where is Hugo?' Cristy interrupted. Much as she might like to hear negative reports of Matthew's new wife, and soon-to-be-mother of his third child, it wasn't a good idea to encourage Hayley's antipathy.

'Oh, he took off to Cornwall with some mates this morning,' Hayley said, helping herself to a pretzel. 'We're meeting up at Glasto on Saturday.' More guilt clouded her eyes as they edged to Cristy's. 'They invited you, didn't they?' she asked cautiously.

Cristy nodded.

'Well, I, for one, don't blame you for turning them down. I mean, why would you want to hang out with her, or Dad, after the way they treated you? I'm just glad I don't have to live in that house any more . . . Oh, by the way, did you know that Granny's moving into that posh retirement village in Failand?'

Cristy's stomach dipped. Her mother-in-law, the antagonistic old bat who was the main reason she'd moved out of the house instead of fighting for it, just so the old lady wouldn't be forced from the home that had been hers for decades, was leaving? And now the divorce settlement had been agreed there was nothing Cristy could do to get what some would consider was rightfully hers.

'I think even she can't stand being around them any more,' Hayley was saying, eating more pretzels. 'She actually said to me last night, when no one else was listening, "I don't know what your father sees in her. She might be easy on the eye, but she drives me nuts with all her airy-fairy nonsense and ridiculous name-dropping." I nearly shrieked. I mean, that's a change, isn't it, from when she was wondering what Marley saw in Dad, a man more than twice her age who was going to struggle to get it up before the decade was out. She's such a controversy, Granny. If you ask me—'

'Sweetheart, you don't have to do this,' Cristy said gently.

Hayley frowned. 'Do what?' she asked, confused.

'Malign Marley to try and make me feel better. I've told you before, it's OK if you like her—'

'I so don't! I hate what she's done to you and our family and I always will. And now I hate the way she keeps trying to push herself onto me, like we can be each other's best friends, ffs. Do you know what's happening tomorrow? I'll tell you. I'm meeting Tallulah and Kate in London to go shopping – I need to get something for a ball Hugo and I are going to in Oslo when we're there – and Marley's only gone and invited herself along. I so don't want her to come, but there's no putting her off, because apparently she's got a meeting with her agent anyway, and she wants to take us for lunch and help choose the dress and she'll even pay for it. I told her, I don't need her to pay for it, Dad's already given me some money, but once that woman's made up

160

her mind . . . She'll turn it into the Marley show, I know it, and typical Tallulah and Kate, they're really excited to meet her, just because she's famous. They're especially hoping she'll bring her dad along.' She gave a shudder.

Taking a sip of wine, Cristy said, wryly, 'She invited me to join you.'

Hayley was astonished into silence – but only for a moment. 'Will you come?' she asked doubtfully. 'I mean, I'd love you to, but do you really want to hang out all day with *her*?'

'I turned her down.'

Hayley pulled a face. 'What's she up to?' she asked suspiciously. 'First she wants you to come to Glasto, now a shopping trip, and she was talking last night about how "marvellous" it would be if she could star in a TV adaptation of your podcast. You know, I reckon she's got more of a thing about you than she does about Dad.'

Sighing, Cristy skipped over how Marley and Matthew had been reaching out to her friends, and said, 'I honestly don't know what's going on with her, but I do know that I have no desire to be in their world. I've done my best to put it all behind me, to start again and move on with my life . . .'

'And you're doing brilliantly, you really are. When I think of what a mess you were when it happened . . . Well, not mess, I didn't mean that exactly . . .'

'It's OK, because I was, but the worst of it is over now.'

Hayley's youthful blue eyes filled with worry. 'Are you sure?' she asked gently. 'I can't imagine it doesn't still hurt, because I know how much you loved Dad. I always thought it was the same for him . . .'

Cristy reached for the bottle to top up their glasses. 'Maybe it's time to change the subject,' she said. 'Shall we order in? Or we could pop round the corner to Pasture if we can get a table?'

Hayley reached across the table to squeeze her hand. 'I'm sorry,' she said. 'Have I upset you?'

'No,' Cristy lied, 'I just don't much like talking about it. I'd much rather hear about you and Hugo and how things are going in Edinburgh. When are you off to Oslo, by the way?'

'Next Tuesday week, and I was thinking, if it's OK with you, that Hugo and I could stay here with you when we get back from Glasto?'

'Of course you can. It'll be lovely to see more of you.'

'And we'll make some time like this, when it's just us, OK? There are things I need to talk to you about and we probably ought to be on our own for it.'

Intrigued and a tiny bit concerned, Cristy said, 'You're not going to tell me you're pregnant, are you?'

Hayley laughed. 'No way! One little brat in the foreseeable is plenty enough, thanks very much. Oh God, sorry,' she groaned, clapping a hand over her mouth. 'I'm talking about her again. That's what she's like, she manages to make everything about her even when she's not there.'

Unable to stop the memory of how tender and loving Matthew had been during her pregnancies – he was probably being the same with Marley now – she got up to check who was calling. *Talk of the devil.*

'Hi,' he said when she answered. 'How are you?'

'I'm fine, thanks.' She didn't bother returning the courtesy. Childish, she knew, but she didn't really care. 'What can I do for you?'

'Ah, right, yes. Is Hayley with you?'

'She is. If you want to speak to her, her phone's on.'

As if she hadn't spoken, he said, 'She's looking good, isn't she? I think Edinburgh's agreeing with her. And Hugo's a great guy. We really liked him.'

Remembering that last night would have been the first time Matthew had met Hayley's boyfriend, while she'd spent a weekend with them in York a couple of months ago to celebrate her birthday, she said, 'That'll please her.'

There was a pause that seemed to go on a little too long before he said, 'Actually, I was wondering if she's changed your mind about Glastonbury this weekend.'

Feeling a tight band closing around her head, Cristy glanced across to where Hayley was busy messaging again. 'Was she supposed to try?' she asked, more abruptly than she'd meant to.

'Let's say I hoped she would. We used to love it back in the day, you and me—'

'That was a long time ago,' she cut in sharply, 'and I have another call coming in so I'm afraid I have to ring off.' It wasn't a lie – DSI Rush's name had just flashed up on her screen and she'd far rather talk to her.

'Ah, Cristy. I hope this isn't a bad time . . .'

'No, not at all. Do you have some news for me?'

'I do, but I'm afraid you're not going to like it too much. I put in a request for David Gaudion's statements and I've just been informed that they can't be traced. Same goes for Richard and Cynthia Gaudion's, Olivia Caldwell's and Paul O'Malley's.'

Cristy felt it almost like a blow. The main suspect and four key witnesses. It beggared belief. It was also going to make their podcast a bit thin on the ground without any of them.

'It's not unheard of for files or evidence to go missing,' Rush said. 'The system's not as foolproof as some might think, and sometimes things turn up in places they're not supposed to be, or after some further digging. Whether or not these will, I can't say right now. I just wanted you to know that I can't send them to you at this time. What I can send is a bunch of statements given by Serena's friends and family, but they're mostly about her character and the break-up of her marriage to O'Malley. I don't think they'll move things on very far. Or they certainly didn't back then.'

Thinking fast, Cristy said, 'Would you be willing for me to include what you've just said about the most important statements in next week's podcast?'

'Do it,' Rush said. 'It'll be interesting to see if it brings them to light.'

CHAPTER FIFTEEN

The following Tuesday, against the background sound of heavy rain pounding the car park outside, the team, plus Meena, Harry and Jodi, were sitting around the production office listening to the final edit of episode two prior to upload.

As they'd received the go-ahead from Gloucester Police and Iris's family to include the 'Iris email' suggesting they abandon the series, it was right at the top of the podcast, as planned. Clover and Jacks were due to visit the fiancé tomorrow.

The main body of the episode began with DSI Rush's interview and what had been discovered about the life-coaching programme Papilio during the police investigation. At this stage, for their own legal protection, Cristy had been careful to point out that nothing criminal had been uncovered regarding the group.

Next came Hannah Gains's memories of David and Lexie Gaudion's early years, and her recollection of Margaret Sallis's perceived eagerness to receive the same necklace as Lexie. There was then a section with Cristy and Connor reacting to the comments made by friends and neighbours, including the pub landlord's mutterings about a satanic cult and sacrifices.

The closing minutes, designed to exert maximum pressure on whomever it might concern, were delivered by Cristy.

'At the time of bringing this episode to you, we can reveal that the statements given to police by David Gaudion and his brother Richard; his mother, Cynthia Gaudion, and Lexie Gaudion's sister, Olivia Caldwell, cannot be found. Nor can those of Serena Sutton's ex-husband Paulo Morelli, real name Paul O'Malley. This could be down to sloppy archiving, or, we have to ask ourselves, is something a little more malevolent at play? On that note, we'd like to invite Sir Victor Green, who was Chief Constable at the time of the murders, to comment on the missing statements – or anything else he can recall about the case.

'We're also still very keen to talk to Olivia Caldwell, who must surely want to know what really happened to three members of her family on that fateful day. Unless, of course, she already knows, and if she does, maybe she'd share it with us.

'Now I'm going to leave you with DSI Rush's words about David Gaudion.'

RUSH: 'He had us all taken in at one time or another, but we soon learned that he was a consummate actor. Or, put another way, he conformed to the profile of a psychopath.'

CRISTY: 'OK, that's it from *Hindsight* for this week. Thanks to everyone who's contacted us with some really encouraging messages of support following our first episode last week. And to our hundreds, yes hundreds, of new subscribers. If you have any leads you think we should follow, or memories of the Kellon Manse Murders you're prepared to share, our contact details are on the website and I can guarantee you your message will be read or listened to.

'Incidentally, we're particularly interested to hear from anyone who was – or is – a member of Papilio's life-coaching programme. And it'll be interesting to see if there's a follow up to the "Iris email" in the coming days. If there is, we'll be sure to let you know.'

Before she got into the regular sign-off that thanked the exec producers and sponsors, Connor stopped the recording and reached for his beer, ready for feedback.

Cristy was first. 'We need to take out the bit about being keen to talk to Olivia,' she declared.

'Why?' Meena protested. 'I think it's good to call her out the way you have.'

'When we spoke last week,' Cristy replied, 'she said she'd think about meeting me, so we need to give her more time. At least until this episode, and maybe the next, have aired.'

Agreeing, Connor set about making the edit right there on his desktop, while Harry topped up the wine glasses. 'Nice move on Victor Green,' he chuckled. 'If something dodgy did go on with this case, and we know it did, he has to have known about it.'

'How old would he be now?' Jodi asked. 'I'm thinking Alzheimer's.'

'Well, that would be convenient,' Clover scoffed.

Reading from his screen, Jackson said, 'He's going to be seventy-four next birthday and lives in the South of Spain with his much younger, by the look of her, third wife, and their two children. So he's not exactly next door.'

'We're a global operation,' Connor reminded him. 'It'll get to him sooner or later, and I'll bet on sooner, because anyone and everyone who had anything at all to do with that case is going to be glued to this series by now.'

'Including David Gaudion,' Meena commented gleefully. 'So, do we agree with DSI Rush that he could be behind the "Iris email"?'

The team glanced at each other to see who wanted to answer. 'The jury's still out,' Cristy said, 'but it seems the most likely at this stage.'

Jodi shifted to a more comfortable position on the sofa. 'Connor mentioned you're going to talk to Iris's family, so what are you hoping to get from them?'

'Anything they're prepared to give us,' Clover replied, 'from whether she might have received threats before the "accident", to access to her computer, to their thoughts on the police investigation into her death.'

'Gosh! Are you thinking there could have been another cover-up?'

Clover shrugged.

'OK,' Connor announced, 'edit complete, and it's two minutes to six, so we're good to upload?' He was looking at Cristy.

'Go for it,' she told him, raising her glass.

As he began hitting the right keys a rousing cheer erupted from the meeting room across the hall where another podcast team clearly had some reason to celebrate.

Dryly, Meena said, 'Sounds like Inge and Macy have got the Consumer Protection Association on board to provide regular inputs into their pods. They've been in there all afternoon discussing it, so if it's the good news it sounds like, Harry and I ought to pop over there. Everything OK here?'

'We're good,' Connor assured her.

'Another great episode from a cracking team,' Harry stated as they started to leave. 'Can hardly wait to hear what comes next.'

The door had barely closed behind them when Cristy said, 'So what does come next? Anything Clover can get from Iris's family is, for the moment at least, a side issue to the main story, and we don't have anything for that in the schedule right now.'

Jodi said, 'How much value did you put on the neighbour who said Cynthia Gaudion has brothers in the Lake District and on Exmoor?'

Cristy regarded Jodi with amused approval. 'You're smart,' she told her, turning to her computer. 'First stop is finding out Cynthia's maiden name, and there's a good chance Flora Gibson or her father-in-law will know that.'

'You send the email, I'll take it over from there,' Jackson told her, 'and if I do manage to track one of them down . . .?'

'Hand it back to me,' Cristy said. 'I'll contact them myself.'

'Are you looking for a job?' Connor asked his wife.

'Already got one,' she reminded him.

Remembering Matthew's offer, Cristy asked breezily, 'Have you met with my ex about joining his broadcast team yet?'

Jodi flushed as she shook her head. 'It's scheduled for next week . . .'

'Hey, you guys,' Harry interrupted, putting his head round the door. 'Why don't you come and join the party? The more the merrier.'

'Count me in,' Clover cried, 'just have to finish up here.'

'Right with you,' Jackson said. 'Mine's a double whatever it is.'

Harry's eyes were on Cristy. 'I'd love to,' she said, meaning it – she had a lot of time for Inge and Macy – 'but I've promised to meet Hayley and her boyfriend at the Olive Shed in . . .' she checked her watch, 'five minutes ago.'

'We're with her,' Connor apologized as Harry looked at him, 'but don't worry, we'll put our heads round on the way out.'

When eventually it was just Cristy, Connor and Jodi in the office, Jodi said quietly, 'Before we see Hayley, how did it go at Glastonbury last weekend?'

Although Cristy's insides reacted, she had no good reason to feel tense or upset. She was simply glad it was over and the children were back in Bristol, so she no longer had to worry about Aiden getting high, or Hayley starting to bond with Marley, or Matthew having a way better time at the festival than he'd had with her when they were young. 'If the WhatsApp calls and messages were anything to go by,' she said, starting to pack up her things, 'I'd say they had a great time.'

'Do you regret not going?' Jodi asked cautiously.

Cristy's eyes widened in surprise. 'God, no,' she replied honestly. 'I mean, if things were different, if we weren't where we are . . . But no, I'm not sorry I turned it down. Actually, I'm not sure how much Matthew saw of Hayley and Aiden. They never seemed to be with him when they contacted me – Aiden was with his friends, Hayley and Hugo with theirs, and I know they all slept in tents. I doubt Matthew and Marley did that. I can see them renting some fancy yurt or RV – and to think they might have expected me to share.' She shuddered and laughed and silently scolded herself for feeling ludicrously hurt and abandoned all over again.

'What about the shopping trip to London?' Jodi asked, allowing Connor to haul her to her feet.

'Marley didn't go in the end,' Cristy said. 'Apparently she had morning sickness.'

Jodi made no comment, in spite of being afflicted by the same unpleasant condition herself. 'Hayley sent me a picture of the dress she bought for the ball. It's gorgeous.'

Cristy smiled. 'Isn't it? She's going to look stunning on the night. I wouldn't mind being there to see her steal the show, although with all those Scandinavian goddesses to compete with . . .'

'She'll breeze it,' Connor insisted. 'She takes after her mother.'

Cristy laughed. 'I was never so beautiful nor so skinny. Anyway, looks like the rain's stopped, so we should make a move or she'll be ringing to find out where we are.'

As they started down to the waterfront, Jodi linked Cristy's arm and said, in a hesitant tone that instantly worried Cristy, 'There's something I should tell you.'

Cristy braced herself. 'Sounds ominous.'

Jodi grimaced. 'I'd call it weird, but anyway . . . I had a call from Marley yesterday. She wanted to know if I would consider being her "pregnancy pal".'

Cristy came to a stop and stared at Jodi.

'I know, revolting, isn't it,' Jodi grimaced, 'but it's what she said. "We're going to be new mums for the first time – me before her of course – but shall we do it together?" Whatever that's supposed to mean. I didn't ask. I just said it was very sweet of her, and I'd get back to her on it.'

Cristy's eyes closed in dismay and frustration. 'What is it with those two?' she growled. 'It's like they're turning into a couple of stalkers, and frankly, they're starting to spook me even more than the Iris emailer.'

Connor slid an arm round her shoulders. 'FYI, Jodi's not going to do it.'

'I just have to find a way of telling her,' Jodi added. 'I mean, really, why would I want to chum up with her when I don't even know her? She must think just because she's famous or something that I'll consider myself honoured to be chosen, and actually what I feel is a bit freaked out. She knows we're close, so does Matthew, so why are they coming on to me like this?'

'To get to Cristy,' Connor reminded her.

'But you must meet with him about featuring your podcasts on the nightly news,' Cristy said. 'I don't want you rejecting that on my account, because what you do deserves to get more coverage.'

'OK, I just wish it was someone else who'd come up with the idea rather than him.'

Connor shot a look at Cristy. 'I reckon someone else did,' he said, 'but apparently Matthew's happy to take the credit. Is that your phone or mine?' he asked Cristy.

'It's the podcast mobiles,' Cristy said, digging into her bag as

Connor patted his pockets. 'We should have turned them off after the upload so calls could go to messages. Dealing with random public is easier that way.'

Finding his phone first, Connor checked the screen and held it out for Cristy to see. *No Caller ID.*

'That's a deliberate choice,' she commented thoughtfully. 'Might be worth finding out who it is, just in case,' and taking the phone she clicked on, putting the call on speaker. 'Cristy Ward.'

'Ms Ward, thank you for taking . . . It's Ja . . . Br . . . from Hargr . . .s . . .'

'I'm sorry, the line is breaking up,' she told him.

'You are sailing very close to the wind . . . Defamation . . . or even libel if you continue in this vein.'

Getting the gist of what was being threatened, she said, 'I think you'll find we're covered by our disclaimers, but if you'd like to discuss it further . . .'

'. . . my client's privacy is being . . .'

'Who is your client?' Cristy interrupted.

'. . . so I must ask you to cease your unfounded allegations and character slurs or you will hear from me again.'

'I didn't catch your name,' Cristy said over him, but the line had already gone dead.

Groaning in frustration, she handed the phone back to Connor.

'Sounded like a lawyer,' Jodi stated.

Cristy nodded agreement.

'But for whom?' Connor queried. 'And for God's sake, the episode's only just dropped. Has there even been time to listen to the whole thing yet?'

Cristy checked her watch. 'Just about,' was the answer. She was thinking fast. 'To get onto us so quickly, via a lawyer, means someone was expecting to be mentioned today, so I'd say the "client" is either Paul O'Malley or Victor Green, although I think we can rule Green out given the speed of the contact, which isn't to say we won't hear from him in due course.'

'It could be David Gaudion's brief,' Connor broke in, already checking his contacts. 'What was his name?'

'Edmond Crouch,' Cristy provided, 'and that's not what this

guy's name sounded like. Didn't he say Ja . . . something? Could be, Jacob, Jake, Jason . . .'

'OK, here's Crouch's number and the firm is called . . . Hargreaves and Stratton.'

Cristy's eyes widened. 'Try connecting,' she said.

Connor did so and waited as an out-of-hours recording invited him to leave a message.

'We'll try again in the morning,' Cristy said, 'but it's sounding like it was Gaudion's lawyer, unless, of course, he and O'Malley are with the same firm?'

It was Connor's turn to look surprised, until he realized that there was no reason why this couldn't be possible, and if it was the case, what should they be reading into it?

A few minutes later, as they approached the waterside tables at the Olive Shed where Hayley, Hugo and Aiden were already tucking into wine and charcuterie, Cristy's personal mobile rang. Having a horrible feeling it might be Matthew, she left the phone in her bag and said to Aiden as he bounced up, 'I had no idea you were joining us.'

'Hey, Mum!' he cried. 'Looking bougie.'

'What?'

'It's a compliment,' Hayley assured her, getting up to embrace Connor and Jodi.

'We're not staying,' Aiden told them. 'Hugo and I are going to watch Harry Wilson at the Fleece?'

'Who?' Connor asked.

'He's a mate of mine,' Hugo explained. 'Great vocals. He's on open mic tonight. Hey, Cristy. Good to see you.'

'You too,' she smiled, embracing him. She liked the lad, a lot, and knew that Hayley was trying not to be nuts about him, but she was on a losing streak there given his looks, charm and irresistible Scandinavian accent. Cristy had been taken with his parents, too, on the one occasion she'd met them – one more occasion than Matthew had been granted if she was counting, which she wasn't, but actually was. They were, apparently, fantastically wealthy and well-connected in their homeland, in London too, by all accounts, although they'd come over as agreeably down to earth and unaffected during the short time she'd spent with them.

'OK, you guys can go now,' Hayley informed them. 'I just didn't want to wait on my own,' she explained to her mother, 'and I knew you'd be late, because it's Tuesday. Jodi, you look amazing and thanks so much for the link you sent for accessories. It's the best. I'll show you what I've ordered.'

As she started to scroll, the boys made good their departure while Connor and Jodi sat down and Cristy decided to check her mobile, given it had rung three times straight. The screen ID read An 1, the name she'd given to the anonymous caller. Intrigued and hopeful, she quickly showed Connor, clicked on and hit speaker. 'Cristy Ward,' she said.

'Hi,' came the response, 'I don't understand why you didn't mention Amelia in your podcast this evening. Do you think she doesn't matter?'

'Of course not,' Cristy replied, frowning as she looked at the others. 'I'm just not sure what you expected me to say.'

'I told you, she's dead.'

'But we only have your word for that and unless you tell me who you are—'

'She's buried in Seedown Woods.'

Warily, Cristy said, 'But it was thoroughly searched and dug up, at the time she disappeared.'

'You're assuming she was there then.'

'We know she wasn't.'

'But she is now. She was taken there long after the police had gone. Please check, then maybe you'll believe me that David Gaudion is a monster.'

As the line went dead Cristy looked at Connor. 'Her body was hidden *after* the search,' she said quietly. 'And the woods are fenced off now.'

He visibly shivered. 'I hope to God this doesn't turn out to be some satanic shit, because that sort of thing creeps the hell out of me.'

CHAPTER SIXTEEN

'It got mentioned a few times,' DSI Rush admitted when Cristy called the following morning about the possibility of a satanic cult, 'but nothing ever came of it. Did this anonymous person actually say it was that?'

'No, she didn't, but it was mentioned by a local landlord and those woods are fenced off now. No idea if it's related, it probably isn't after all this time, but we're trying to get to the bottom of why it's out of bounds. Meantime, I've tried texting the caller using the number she rang me on but I'm not sure the messages are being delivered, and needless to say she's not picking up.'

'OK, I'll pass on what you've told me to the missing persons unit, but I'd say there's zero chance of the woods being dug up again based on this sort of tip-off.'

This was exactly what Cristy had expected. 'OK, I'll let you know if I hear any more from her,' she said. 'Now tell me, have you had any feedback on your starring role in our podcast yet?'

Wryly, Rush said, 'I'm inundated with fan mail already. Joke. Silence from the upper echelons, not so much from the rabble I'm blessed to work with every day. Neat move on Victor Green, by the way. He's not going to like that one bit. Has he been in touch yet?'

'Still early, but we're expecting to hear something.'

'I'm sure you will. Oh, incidentally, the press office guys are searching for the documentary producer's details. It could take a while because the person I spoke to reckons it was at least seven or eight years ago that the request came in and they've done some shifting around over there since. I'll let you know as soon as I hear anything. Sorry, but I need to go now, another call coming in.'

'No problem. Thanks for everything, and if you need any help dealing with your newfound fame, you know where to find me.'

She could hear Rush laughing as she rang off, and was smiling herself as she swerved to avoid an overly determined cyclist pedalling furiously past the old cargo cranes outside the M Shed.

It was a typical morning rush along the Harbourside with a hectic two-way flow of commuters, joggers, scooter riders, dog walkers and early-rise tourists heading to their various destinations. On the water a V formation of rowers was speeding past the round-harbour ferry, and a lone sailboat began winding a path through the sluggish current. She wasn't worried about being followed at this time of day, not with so many people around, and nor, she realized, had she felt concerned last night when she and Hayley had strolled arm in arm back to the flat. In fact, she hadn't even thought about it until now, but it was only fleeting as she took in the fresh air and uplifting shot of caffeine. Her walk to work was twenty energizing minutes of exercise and freeform thinking, sometimes taken up by a podcast, but rather that than the sad state of her personal life as used to happen with swamping regularity during the height of it all.

By the time she turned off at Spike Island heading for the studio, she'd finished her coffee and was in the middle of voice-messaging Hayley on WhatsApp. '. . . I woke him up before I left, but I'm afraid he just rolled over and went back to sleep. He has school today so please make sure he gets there. Book him an Uber if you have to and I'll pay you back.'

Minutes after she'd entered the production office Connor came in behind her, finishing up a call on his mobile. 'OK, mate, thanks. I'll get back to you if there's any more.' He dropped his heavy bag on the floor next to his chair, went to heave up the window, and headed for the coffee machine. 'Good morning,' he said brightly, and immediately groaned at the cold, stale jug of yesterday's brew. 'That was Kevin Break on the phone. He recalls a few mentions of satanism coming up back then, but apparently no one took them seriously, and he reckons the chances of anyone digging up Seedown Woods at this time are nil. They need more to go on than an anonymous caller who could well be a nutter. Have you managed to speak to Rush yet?'

'I have,' Cristy confirmed, 'and she said more or less the same. So, unless this person calls again, I say we park the issue and come back to it when, if, we need to.'

'Good call. Any luck with the bloke who rang threatening defamation?'

'I'm about to email Edmond Crouch to find out if it was him, or someone from his firm. I'd call, but we know from past experience that I won't get past his secretary.'

As she fired up her desktop and entered the password, Connor made the coffee then groaned. Wading through emails, texts, social media and voice messages was not his favourite task, although he had to admit when one came good it was like Liverpool scoring the winning goal.

For the next hour or so they ploughed their way through the latest influx of messages, moving most to 'fanmail', some to 'second read', more than they'd like to 'abuse', and none to 'action'.

'"I can tell you exactly where to find Amelia,"' Connor read aloud at one point. '"She's changed her name and I can give you that as well. It'll cost five thousand big ones. Can send bank details." Honest to God,' he muttered, and in accordance with their policy not to engage with blackmail or bribery, he moved it to junk.

'I've had three of those so far,' Cristy said, 'one claiming to know where Gaudion is for ten grand; same for Amelia, twenty grand; and another claiming to know who the real killer is for forty grand. So your guy's selling himself short.'

With an ironic smile Connor plugged in his AirPods to make a start on the voicemails, while Cristy returned to the digital messages. As they worked silently and diligently, birdsong drifted in from outside, along with distant hammering and drilling from the nearby dry dock. After a while Cristy became strangely conscious of Lexie, Margaret and Serena on the wall behind her, the women at the heart of their investigation who could no longer speak for themselves, but who surely wanted their killer brought to justice once and for all. At one point she found herself glancing round at David, positioned at the centre of it all. So many questions raced through her mind, not only, *Where are you? Did you do it? Why are you hiding?* But *Have you listened to the podcast yet? Were you involved in the cult? Are you behind the Iris email? If so, what did you mean by it?*

At eleven Connor began setting up to record a chat between them, while Cristy made a quick check of recent emails. Seeing one had arrived from Flora Gibson, she immediately opened it. 'And here we have it,' she murmured.

'What?' Connor queried.

'Cynthia Gaudion's maiden name,' she replied. 'Apparently it was Phelps. Thank you, Flora, or Gordon Bryce, whoever answered the question. And here you are, Jacks,' she added, forwarding the message to him. 'See if you can find at least one of the brothers on Exmoor or in the Lake District, presuming they're still there, and still alive. Shouldn't take you long,' she added with no small irony.

Another email dropped into her inbox and she exclaimed in surprise. 'Well, look who we have here,' she said dryly. 'Edmond Crouch himself and – wait for it – turns out it *was* someone from his firm who called to, I quote, "request you to proceed with greater caution regarding our client's character".' She looked across at Connor. 'No threats there,' she noted. 'Altogether a milder tone than his colleague's last night.'

'Because they don't have a leg to stand on regarding defamation or libel,' Connor pointed out.

Opening a reply box, she spoke aloud as she typed, 'Dear Mr Crouch, thank you for the clarification and the call from your associate. You will be aware of our disclaimers, and I want to assure you that we always proceed with caution. We are still very keen to talk to your client and would greatly appreciate it if you could pass on our request. Please assure him of our utmost discretion if he wishes to speak off the record . . .'

'Don't say that,' Connor argued. 'We want him on tape.'

'True, but if we can actually meet with him, we'd surely stand a better chance of persuading him to talk than we can like this.'

Connor conceded the point and she continued, 'You already have my contact details, but you'll also find them at the bottom of this email. Our invitation also extends to you, should you be open to speaking on your client's behalf.' She looked at Connor again in case he wanted to add anything.

'Sounds good to me,' he told her.

After signing off she pressed send, and said, 'I can already tell you what his answer will be, the same as it's been all along: "My client is a very private man and has no wish to revisit this painful episode in his past." But I'm convinced the further into this we go, the more likely it'll become that he, or even Gaudion, will feel compelled to say something.'

'I'm with you on that,' Connor agreed. 'It'll be interesting to see what ends up triggering it.'

Cristy turned to look at David Gaudion again, taking in the pale blue, watchful eyes and partly smiling mouth. She knew now that he must have listened to the podcast and instructed his lawyer to be in touch. So he was out there somewhere charting it all, taking in what was being said, assessing the accuracies and inconsistencies, the suspicions of old friends and neighbours, the portrayal of his dead wife's cult membership, DSI Rush's damning character judgement of him. He'd be listening to her, Cristy, the tone of her voice, the degree of belief or scepticism in her words, the force of her determination, the indications of just how open her mind was to alternative scenarios. He'd probably be wondering how malleable she was, how easy to trick or wrongfoot or even bring down. He might even be studying the look of her if he'd accessed the website. The fact that he could be closing in on her like some kind of predator was as unnerving as the bizarre and unwelcome sense of connection she was suddenly feeling towards him. It was as though they were locking in as adversaries, him on one side, her on the other, and the real battle was only just beginning.

She turned away, trying to dismiss the nonsensical overreaction, but in spite of being ready to record with Connor now, she was still very much aware of Gaudion's eyes on her back.

It was an hour later, while she and Connor were in the middle of their recording, that Clover and Jackson FaceTimed with their news.

'I think we might have something,' Clover announced as soon as everyone was connected. 'Iris's laptop is still at the house she shared with her fiancé, Joe, and he let us have a surf of it.'

'The police didn't take it after the accident?' Connor asked.

'He says no one even asked for it. Anyway, he knew she was hoping to make a podcast about the Kellon Manse Murders, and apparently he told her it was too big a case for someone with her lack of experience. He didn't know until we got in touch that she'd actually made a start on it.'

'So right after getting our call,' Jackson continued, 'he went through the laptop himself. This means he was able to take us right to what he'd found.'

'Lots of internet research about the murders,' Clover ran on, 'but it was her emails that were most interesting. There was the one to Kevin Break, along with his reply, and another to Paolo Morelli—'

'Address defunct now,' Jackson put in. 'I've already tried and got a bounce back.'

'She was in touch with Paolo Morelli, right at the start of her research?' Connor said incredulously.

'What does she say in her message?' Cristy asked.

'Nothing about the murders,' Clover replied, 'only about the cult, except she didn't call it that, obvs. She asked if they could meet to talk about life-coaching as it was something she was interested in. There was no reply on the laptop, but he must have answered, possibly by phone, because a few days later she sent an email to someone called Miranda Ritchie. We've already uploaded it so you can see it.'

After getting it up on screen, Connor read it aloud:

'From Iris Newman; to Miranda Ritchie: Dear Ms Ritchie, I was given your name by Paolo Morelli who says you are willing to talk to me about being a member of Papilio. I believe you have been with the group for the past four years and that you have enjoyed much success with both your spiritual journey and in your personal confidence during that time. I am very keen to explore how the programme works and so would be extremely grateful if we could meet to discuss further. With my best wishes, Iris Newman.'

'What that tells us right away,' Clover pointed out, 'is that Papilio is still operating, or it was a year ago, and under the same name.'

'So how come he engaged with her and is apparently blocking us?' Cristy wanted to know.

'No idea. Anyway, Miranda Ritchie got back to her saying she'd be happy to meet and Iris should give her a call to set it up. We don't know if they did ever get together, because Iris was killed a week later.'

Cristy felt a bolt of alarm as she looked at Connor.

'Just to be clear,' Jackson put in, 'Joe Mead claims never to have heard of Miranda Ritchie until today and we believed him.'

'He's really keen to help in any way he can,' Clover told them. 'Anyway, we checked Iris's online calendar – no mention of Miranda Ritchie there, and nothing in her handwritten diary either.'

'So was she the victim of a hit-and-run before a meeting could happen?' Cristy wondered aloud. 'Or after they realized her interest was connected to the Kellon Manse Murders?'

'Only Miranda Ritchie can tell us that,' Clover pointed out, 'and would you believe, there's a number for her here. So, do we call her?'

Cristy didn't take long to think. 'Do it,' she said, 'but don't tell her who you are right away. Say . . . what can you say?'

'I've got my cover story,' Clover assured her. 'I'll make out I found her number while going through Iris's emails because I'm organizing a get-together of Iris's friends to mark the one-year anniversary of her death.'

Cristy was impressed. 'Elaborate, but good,' she smiled.

'Is Joe Mead OK with all this?' Connor asked.

'As I said, he's keen to help, and actually there is going to be a celebration of Iris a year on from the day she died.'

Feeling the sadness of that, the loss so many young people must have felt following the untimely death of a dear friend, Cristy said, 'Why don't you try this Miranda Ritchie now.'

Clover pressed the number into Jackson's phone and put the call on speaker.

The number you have dialled has not been recognized, please hang up and try again.

Clover did, twice, but the message was the same. 'OK, we're obviously getting nowhere there,' she sighed, handing the phone back, 'but I think you're going to be interested in this . . . Iris was also in touch with David Gaudion's lawyer, Edmond Crouch. It was just a request to talk to him about the case for a podcast and a short reply from Crouch with all his bollocks about client confidentiality. However, what's important is the fact that she made contact, so Crouch and presumably Gaudion, were aware of her intentions.'

Cristy and Connor stared at one another as they absorbed this. 'What are the dates on these emails?' Cristy asked.

'Both the one to Morelli/O'Malley, and the one to Crouch were sent three weeks before she died. Crouch's response came a week later.'

Drawing the inevitable conclusion, and feeling her head start to spin, Cristy said, 'OK, I think you need to pass this on to Gloucester Police. It'll be interesting to see what, if anything, they do with it. Meantime, you're going to see her parents now?'

'We are,' Jackson confirmed, 'but Joe has asked us not to mention any of this. He says they were upset enough about the police investigation, never felt enough was done. So he reckons best not to go there unless we're certain something's going to come of this.'

'OK, makes sense,' Cristy said. 'Good job so far, now get yourselves some lunch if you haven't already, and when you can, give us an idea what time you'll be back.'

After the call ended and everything was logged, Connor began an online search for Miranda Ritchie, while Cristy drafted another email to Edmond Crouch asking if he'd ever met Iris Newman. She didn't imagine he had, but seeing Iris's name in an email from her could suggest she was connecting dots he'd rather she didn't know existed. If nothing else, that would surely shake him up a bit.

'I'm coming up with dozens of hits for Miranda Ritchie,' Connor grumbled, 'there's even a coach with the same name, basketball, not life. I guess there are a few who could be promising, whatever that's supposed to look like – I'm going for wealthy, troubled, that kind of thing, but it's not exactly the sort of detail you'd put on your profile.'

Cristy sat back in her chair. 'Do we actually believe that a cult is at the heart of this?'

Surprised, he said, 'You're sounding as though you don't.'

'I'm definitely not dismissing it, but I'm worried we're letting this aspect of it distract us in a way that isn't going to end up proving useful.'

'So what are you saying? We give up on Miranda Ritchie?'

She turned to the board behind her again and searched the women's faces as though one of them, or even Gaudion himself, might provide some sort of insight or inspiration. 'All I can tell you right now,' she said, 'is that we need a strong interviewee for the next episode—'

'Ah! This is interesting,' Connor interrupted. 'Not about Miranda Ritchie. It's a direct message just popped up on Twitter.' Checking Cristy was listening, he read it out loud:

'I was a friend of Lexie's at Oxford. She was science, I was history and French. I don't know why she left when she did, but there were a lot of rumours, and I feel sure her sister, Olivia, will know the truth of them. I've no doubt David Gaudion does too. If you want to discuss further my number is below, but if you don't mind I'd rather not go on the record. Fiona Mooney.'

As they mulled this over, Cristy kept coming back to the hunch she'd had a few days ago that Lexie's early departure from uni might somehow be significant. 'I'll call her,' she decided. 'What's the number?'

Moments later they'd made the connection. 'This is Fiona. How can I help you?' The voice was firm, cultured, a little throaty, and conjured an image of a sophisticated woman in her late forties, which Fiona presumably was if she'd been at Oxford with Lexie.

'Fiona, it's Cristy Ward here—'

'Oh gosh!' Fiona Mooney broke in, sounding less sure of herself now. 'I wasn't expecting to hear so soon. If at all.' She laughed nervously. 'I probably shouldn't have sent that message, I could end up in all sorts of trouble . . .'

'But you did, and what you told us was extremely interesting. Incidentally, this call can be in the strictest confidence. We won't use anything you say if you don't want us to, and we aren't recording.' It was true, they weren't – there had to be some honour somewhere, even though there was a chance they'd end up regretting it. 'When you say there were rumours about why Lexie left Oxford, can you tell me the nature of them?'

'Actually, they were pretty awful and I honestly don't know how true they were, but I guess, given what happened after . . .'

'What happened after?' Cristy prompted, poised to note it down.

Fiona Mooney inhaled audibly and a long moment passed before she went on, 'I don't want to give you any names. You probably wouldn't know them anyway, but if you looked them up you'd soon realize who they are. What sort of families they're from.'

'OK, no names,' Cristy agreed.

Still sounding unsure about proceeding, Fiona Mooney said, 'You'll have heard, I'm sure, about the kind of things certain types get up to at uni, all the hideousness they inflict on one another, communities, innocent victims . . . Well, there was a group like that at Oxford when we were there – when is there ever not? They were all from privileged backgrounds, money, rank, nobility, landed gentry, that sort of thing. The sense of entitlement came off them in waves and was as repellent as the drunken binges and games they played . . .

'There was one, I can see him now, smooth, arrogant bastard

that he was . . . He developed a bit of a thing about Lexie, kept bugging her to go on a date with him, but she wasn't interested, not romantically, anyway. I guess she flirted a bit though, the attention was nice and he was good-looking, there was no doubt about that . . . I suspect he became a bit too persistent because I remember her telling me that she wished he'd leave her alone. I can't be sure how long that was before I went to her room one morning and found she'd gone. A few weeks, maybe, or perhaps not as long as that. I didn't connect it with him, not then, and I actually can't connect it to him now. It's just a feeling I had at the time, that he was in some way involved in why she'd left so suddenly.'

'Did you try calling her to find out if you were right?'

'Umpteen times. I even asked him if he knew why she'd disappeared, but he just scoffed as if I was a nobody, and in his eyes I guess I was. Anyway, I got a message from her eventually letting me know that she wouldn't be coming back.'

'Did she say why?'

'No, but there were all sorts of rumours flying around by then. Some said that she'd been sent down for selling drugs – she never touched them, I can tell you that – others said she'd accused a professor of rape so had to be got out of the way, then I heard she'd been assaulted, *used* in some sort of ritual . . .'

Cristy's eyes shot to Connor's.

'It was terrible, some of the things that were said,' Fiona Mooney continued, sounding as though it still upset her to think of it.

'Did she know about any of it?' Cristy asked.

'If she did, I didn't tell her. I mean, why would I repeat such awful things when I knew how much they'd hurt her, and when I had no idea if they were true? Actually, I'd almost forgotten this, I went to Kellon Hall once to try to see her, but she wasn't there, and her dreadful mother . . . God, the things that woman said to me . . . Lexie had told me how difficult and even cruel she could be, but I'd never imagined anyone like Margaret Sallis.

'Anyway, it was a few months after I'd fled for my life – that was how it felt leaving Kellon Hall – that I heard Lexie had had a baby. With the timing and everything . . .' She took a breath and let it go slowly. 'I haven't mentioned any of this for years, I've tried not to think about it . . . That poor girl. I supposed it meant at least one of the rumours was true, but I had no idea which one, nor did I try to find out.'

'Did you ever tell the police any of this?' Cristy asked. 'I mean, after she was murdered?'

'Oh yes. I was interviewed, twice, quite extensively, before and after David was arrested. Of course, that was many years later.'

'Did you know David?'

'Not well. I met him a couple of times when he came to Oxford for parties, but I doubt he'd even remember me.'

'Was he with Lexie when he visited?'

'I wouldn't say *with*, but they were definitely close. They grew up together . . . Of course you already know that. She talked about him quite a lot, and his brother . . . I asked her once if she was secretly in love with one of them, because sometimes it seemed that way to me, but she dismissed it saying something like they'd always be in her life and that was how it would stay.'

'Did Richard visit Oxford as well?'

'Yes, but I never met him. Both he and David knew some of the bad boys – I saw them hanging out together at parties, and they could have gone on to the orgies and such like after; I don't know because I never went to them myself. And nor did Lexie. She was a serious student, her research meant everything to her.'

Cristy looked at Connor as he drew a finger across his throat, a signal to end the call. She nodded and said to Fiona, 'Would you mind if I called you again later or tomorrow? You've given me a lot to think about and I'd like to get my questions into an order we'll both feel comfortable with.'

'OK,' Fiona responded, drawing out the word, 'just as long as you promise to keep my name out of it.'

'Of course, you have my assurance on that, but how would you feel about me quoting you as an anonymous source?'

Sounding increasingly anxious, Fiona said, 'You know, you're better off speaking to Olivia if you haven't already. She'll know much more than I do, and you'll be able to trust what she says.'

'We're trying to persuade her, but at the moment we're not getting very far.'

'Then she probably won't thank me for raking it all up again. Maybe I was wrong to get in touch . . .'

'No, really—'

'Listen, I want you to get to the bottom of what happened to Lexie and her mother, the other woman too, I really do, but frankly I don't want to end up with the same sort of thing happening to me, so maybe we should leave it here.'

CHAPTER SEVENTEEN

By the time Cristy clicked off from Fiona Mooney, Connor had already found the woman online. 'This has to be her,' he declared, scrolling through the second website that had come up on his search. 'Good optimization,' he commented. 'So, she's one half of Mooney and Mooney Translation and Interpreting Services, which apparently breaks down cultural barriers, creates universal understanding . . . and has an impressive client list: governments, corporations, banks, publishers . . .'

'How can you be sure it's her?' Cristy asked, coming to look over his shoulder.

'Because,' he said, clicking back to the 'Our Team' link, and opening the profile of co-founder Fiona Mooney. 'Here we are, graduated Oxford in 1995 with first class honours in French and History. I reckon this is her.'

Cristy studied the profile photo of a woman who was roughly her own age with crinkly dark hair, wide cheekbones and an engaging smile. She looked successful and confident, like someone at the top of her game.

Connor continued reading, 'She's married to the other co-founder, Alan Mooney, and is the proud mother of four sons.'

Still looking at the photo, Cristy balked at the thought of four Aidens, and then felt faintly deprived. 'Unfortunately, we can't use any of what she told us,' she said. 'Even without mentioning how we got it, the lawyers won't allow it.'

Connor sat back in his chair. 'I'm asking myself, could Paul O'Malley's name be amongst those she won't give us? I'm thinking about the ritual now. I mean, what the hell was that about?'

'I admit it set off alarm bells for me too, but if he was one of the so-called bad boys and there was an assault of some sort, why would Lexie have anything to do with him again?'

Connor pulled a face. 'Good point. Interesting that Gaudion knew them, though, and Olivia surely has to know who they are. If they're even relevant to any of this.'

'It's worth exploring,' Cristy replied, returning to her desk. 'I'm going to message Olivia with what we've just learned. I won't mention where or how we heard it, but if Fiona Mooney is on the level, or even if she isn't, Olivia will surely have to react one way or the other.'

Half an hour later Connor came across a message on the podcast voicemail-service asking for a senior member of the team to contact Sir Victor Green. The caller, female and who sounded English, repeated a Spanish number twice and added, 'He is looking forward to hearing from you.'

'When did it come in?' Cristy asked, glancing at the time.

Connor checked. 'About twenty minutes ago.'

'OK, so let's get him on the line. However, before you do that, you'll never guess what's just dropped into my inbox?'

'A response from Olivia?'

She shook her head. 'A reply, finally, from Gaudion's old boss, Anthony Anderson, chair of Quantrell Communications, who is apparently still in position.'

'Ah, the god of government ministers looking to get their pockets lined,' Connor quipped with not much irony. 'He's American, isn't he?'

'Canadian,' Cristy corrected, quickly scanning the email. 'So, he's sorry he hasn't got back to us sooner, been away on holiday, but has now caught up with our podcasts. He's happy to connect with us on Zoom,' her eyebrows raised in surprise at that, 'or he will forward a copy of the statement he gave to the police in 2008. Very accommodating,' she commented, already making space for him in the next episode if this actually went somewhere. Quoting directly now, she continued. '"I will state here that nothing has changed in my high opinion of David Gaudion. He was an extremely talented young man destined for a great future as a lobbyist, or any other profession he might have chosen, until the tragic events at his home derailed his life. I was disappointed when he didn't rejoin us following his release, but the decision, of course, had to be his. I no longer have any contact with him, so I am unable to say where he is, but I can put you in touch with someone who might be able to help. I've checked with her, and she assures me she is willing to discuss her friendship with David. Her name is Maria del Smet and she is currently based in our Brussels office. She is copied in here, so you will be able to contact her directly."'

'Maria del Smet?' Connor jumped in, already checking their files. 'We haven't heard that name before.'

'You're right, we haven't,' Cristy agreed. 'And here's why: "She was not interviewed by police at the time of their enquiries, and didn't voluntarily contact them as she was still married to another member of our team. That relationship has since been dissolved. She has no knowledge of what happened in Gloucestershire on that dreadful day, but she will talk about David and whether or not she still has contact with him. If, after reading this, you still feel it's worth talking to me I'll ask my assistant to set up a time that will suit. I wish you success with your investigation. Anthony Anderson."'

'Got her,' Connor stated, raising his hands from the keyboard with a flourish. 'Senior Director, European Relations. Been with the company twenty-four years, now aged fifty-three, and is, in my professional opinion, a bit of a stunner.'

Smiling, Cristy called up the website and found Maria del Smet for herself. She was indeed a beauty. There was a lengthy résumé of her achievements since her time at Princeton, where she'd earned herself a Masters in Finance before going on to join Merrill Lynch in 1992. A year later she moved to the New York office of Quantrell's and was transferred to London in 1994 (interestingly, about the same time as David Gaudion started his career with the company). She'd left Quantrell's in 2014 to take up a position with the European Parliament advising on fintech and securities, and rejoined in 2018. She married Colston Risburgh, head of financial services at JWP, in 2020. No children, stepmother of two.

'Are you going to contact her today?' Connor asked, checking his watch.

'I'll email to introduce myself and suggest we meet on Zoom sometime tomorrow, if she can make it. Let's hope she can, because she's sounding like a great addition to next week.'

'Presuming she was Gaudion's mistress, and it sounded very much like it.'

'And presuming Olivia doesn't come through by then, but even if she does, I have a horrible feeling she'll insist on speaking off the record.'

Connor was checking his watch. 'I need to leave,' he told her. 'Jodi's car is in for service and we're due to pick it up at five. Anything else here before I go?'

'Victor Green?' Cristy said wryly.

He slapped a hand to his head. 'So much activity today. How could that have slipped my mind? Are you going to call now?'

'I thought I would, but if you want to . . .'

'It won't make a difference if I'm a few minutes late, and I want to hear what this guy has to say.'

Scrolling to the Spanish number, Cristy pressed it into the computer phone while Connor activated the speaker and prepared to record.

'Hello, it's Cristy Ward here,' she told the woman who answered. 'I'm calling for Sir Victor Green.'

'Ah, *si, si,* he is here. I will pass you over.'

A moment later Sir Victor's gruff, Geordie accented tones came down the line. 'Mrs Ward,' he practically boomed. 'It's good of you to return my call. I hear the weather's behaving well with you over there at the moment.'

'It is,' she confirmed. 'Probably not as hot as it is with you, though. Thank you for responding to the invitation we issued in the podcast. I apologize for the unorthodox measure—'

'Doesn't matter,' he interrupted. 'You've got what you hoped for. Here I am—'

'Actually, before we continue, do you have any objection to this call being recorded, and possibly used in the next, or a future podcast?'

'Mm,' he grunted. 'I thought you'd ask that and the answer's no, I don't object, so do whatever you have to.'

'Thank you,' she replied as Connor hit record and gave the thumbs up.

'OK, we're rolling,' she told Green, 'and you probably know what I'm going to ask you first—'

'If I know what happened to the missing statements,' he cut in. 'The answer is, it's been a long time since I retired from policing, but I've always believed them to be where they're supposed to be – that only changed when I heard your podcast yesterday. Can I throw any light on their whereabouts now? I'm afraid not, but from my long experience with the force, these things usually turn up eventually.'

Deciding to come right out with it, she said, 'Is it possible they could have been *made* to disappear?'

Sounding unfazed, he said, 'You mean, as in some sort of . . . cover-up? If that happened, and I'm not saying it did, I knew nothing about it.'

Giving that a moment, in case he wanted to add anything, she pressed on in a slightly different vein. 'How did you feel when you heard that David Gaudion wasn't going to stand trial?'

With no hesitation, he said, 'Angry. Frustrated for the officers who'd worked so hard on the case. They were confident of a conviction and I supported them in that, but ultimately it was down to the CPS and they didn't feel they had enough evidence to go forward.'

'Why wasn't the investigation continued following Gaudion's release?'

'It was, but there wasn't much heart in it, I have to admit. As far as we were concerned, we'd already found everything we needed, and the CPS obviously agreed with us at the start, or they wouldn't have agreed to press charges. By the time it came to the trial there was even more to support a guilty verdict – I know you're talking to Frances Rush, she'll be able to give you details, and she'll be in touch with others who can help – but in a nutshell it didn't matter what we threw at them, the decision was made to pull the plug and there was nothing we could do to fight it.'

'Do you have any idea who, exactly, made the decision?'

'No, but I can tell you that Gaudion had a lot of friends in high places, and I mean very high.'

'Can you give us any names?'

'No.'

Accepting she was unlikely to change his mind on that now, she said, 'What did you make of the Papilio aspect of the case?'

He took a moment to consider it. 'It sounded whacky to me, worrisome in some ways, potentially influential, but we never found anything to tie it to the actual killings. True, the leader, I've forgotten his name now . . .'

'Paul O'Malley. Or Paolo Morelli.'

'Right. He had some labyrinthine financial strategies going on, but the forensic accountancy team weren't ever able to find any evidence of wrongdoing. You know about the fire at Serena Sutton's home? Yes, of course you do. Something else that was highly suspicious, but again the experts were unable to rule it as arson.'

'Did you ever think Gaudion might be involved in Papilio?'

'If he was, it never came to light, or not that I knew of, but to be honest with you, not much would surprise me about this case. Even now.'

Cristy glanced down as Connor slid a note across to her. Scanning it quickly, she nodded but didn't act on it – it wouldn't help at this stage. Instead, she said, 'What's your view on the fate of Amelia Gaudion?'

'You mean the child?' He sighed and took a moment to respond. 'The fact she's never been found . . . I know there are a lot of theories out there, and plenty of crackpots who'd lead the police a wild goose chase given half a chance, but if she'd survived it I think we'd know by now.'

'Does that mean, given you believe Gaudion committed the murders, that you think he also did away with his daughter?'

'That's always been a difficult one,' he confessed. 'There was never anything to suggest he'd harm his own child, no history of abuse or neglect, or none that we uncovered . . . Rumours, yes, but I direct you back to the attention seekers and crackpots. It's hard to see what else happened to her though.'

'So you decided she saw the killings and he had to make sure she couldn't tell?'

'Worse things have been done to try and cover up a crime.'

Unable to imagine what they might be, Cristy said, 'Why do you think Gaudion shot his wife, mother-in-law and Serena Sutton?'

'I can only tell you what you probably already know, that some very large sums of money had been taken from his wife's account in the months preceding the murders, and it looked highly likely that the mother was about to start doing the same. As for Serena Sutton? She was the conduit, the collector, recruiter, whatever she called herself. So that's why she was there.'

Cristy glanced over at Connor to see if there was anything he wanted to add. When he shook his head, she said, 'I really appreciate you speaking so candidly to us, Sir Victor. It's possible I'll have some follow up questions, so would it be OK to contact you again if I do?'

'You have my number,' he replied. 'It's been a pleasure talking to you.'

After he'd gone Cristy picked up Connor's note. *He's reciting lines, telling us exactly what he's supposed to.*

'I don't disagree with this,' she told him, 'but I do believe Gaudion had friends in high places. Hard not to, considering what he did for a living, the kind of circles he moved in.'

'Maybe time for a deeper dive into Quantrell's client list?' Connor suggested.

'We already know how generic it is on the website – banking institutions, international financiers, securities agencies: there's so much secrecy at play that it would take MI5 to get in the door.'

'OK, then the next question is, did Gaudion have something on one, or more, of the top clients? The head of a bank, a massive donor to a certain political party? Maybe there's a network of dodgy dealers that includes someone who was in government back then. Is that how he got out of going to trial?'

'If he did have something,' Cristy replied thoughtfully, 'then presumably he still has it. A kind of permanent get-out-of-jail card.'

They sat with that for a moment, until, remembering the time,

Connor said, 'We need to listen to the tape again, but not now, if that's OK.'

'Go,' she told him. 'I'll ring Clover and Jackson, find out where they are, and let you know if I hear anything from Olivia.'

'Great.' He glanced at his watch again. 'They should have been back by now, shouldn't they? Or at least rung in.'

Experiencing a pang of concern, she quickly picked up the phone.

'Aaaagh, we're stuck in traffic,' Clover growled. 'There's been an accident on the M5. But nothing to report from Iris's parents. We'll write everything up when we get back.'

'OK, good. There have been some developments here. I'll enter them into the system so you can update when you're ready. Connor and I will probably both be gone by the time you get back.'

'No probs. Have a good one.'

Connor was at the door. 'What are you doing this evening?' he asked, shouldering his bag.

Taking a moment to remember, she felt slightly anxious as she said, 'Hayley's been trying to have a chat with me for over a week and I promised that it could be tonight, with Hugo and Aiden at the cricket with Matthew.'

'OK, cool. Don't forget to call if anything comes up,' and a moment later he'd gone, leaving Cristy to work on a structure for next week's podcast, while trying to ignore the uneasy and inexplicable sensation that David Gaudion wasn't only watching her now, but had somehow been listening to the calls she'd just made, along with her and Connor's subsequent conversation.

It was crazy thinking, she knew that, but there was no denying how much the man was starting to get to her.

Two hours later she was in the back garden with Hayley and laughing so hard it was making her ribs ache. 'I don't believe it! That can't be for real,' she cried, dabbing at her eyes and having to turn from Hayley's laptop, unable to bear any more.

'He's totally gross,' Hayley protested, as if the man on the screen had set out deliberately to offend her. 'I mean, why would anyone do that?'

'Don't ask me!' Cristy sighed and started to laugh again. 'You're the one who thought internet dating was a good idea.'

'If I'd known this was the kind of thing your generation posts I'd never have mentioned it. This guy's arse is like a hairy melon, for God's sake. Does he seriously think someone's going to be attracted to it? Oh shit! Look at this one, he's only got *everything* on display and it's not even all that big. I think I'm going to throw up.'

'Stop! Stop!' Cristy begged, reaching for her wine. 'I told you it was a bad idea, and I don't *want* to meet anyone.'

'Oh, this one's cool,' Hayley declared admiringly. 'But he's only five foot eight, too short for you. Ah, how about this one? OMG no, he's only holding a whip and handcuffs . . .' She shrieked with laughter and just had to read some of his profile, '"I'm Tim, and I'd love you to beat me in any way you choose. I'm up for anything, just send me a pic of you as a dominatrix . . ." Have you got one of those?' she asked her mother.

With a choke of laughter, Cristy said, 'That's enough. They're all deviants and weirdos.'

'We're on the wrong site,' Hayley decided. 'Let's try another.'

'No! I'm not going for it, no matter who you find or what you say.'

'Why not? Oh, Mum. You don't want to be on your own for the rest of your life, do you? And you're a brilliant catch. It's just a case of sifting through all the crap to get to the right one.'

'Doing it this way . . . It's not for me.'

'But everyone does it these days.'

'How did you meet Hugo?'

'That's different.'

'Why?'

'We're at the same uni and have friends in common. That's a thought, you've got tons of friends, so why haven't any of them introduced you to someone?'

'They've offered,' Cristy admitted, and gently pushed down the lid of the laptop. 'The difference with them, is they know how to take no for an answer.'

Hayley pulled a sulky face and fixed Cristy with her lovely blue eyes as she assessed the moment. 'Tell me the truth,' she said in the end, 'are you still in love with Dad? I'm not judging if you are, I realize it takes forever to get over what you went through, but now, with the baby coming and everything . . . I just want to see you happy, happier than them, because it's what you deserve.'

Cristy smiled past the twist in her heart. 'The last thing you need to be worrying about is me,' she chided, 'especially when you have so much to look forward to – and when I'm perfectly happy with the way things are. I'm enjoying my freedom, believe it or not, and—'

'Why don't we find the right site and set up a real profile for you? You'll have so many hits, I swear it, and they're not all jerks out there. There'll be someone really special just waiting to sweep you off your feet.'

Cristy got up to check if the barbecue was ready to use. 'I'm really busy with the podcast at the moment, so maybe in a few months. Now, can you get the salmon? I think it should go on. What are we having with it?'

'I've made an avocado, asparagus and tomato salad and a fruity kind of coleslaw. They're in the fridge and we've got some wicked cannoli from Taste of Napoli to finish.'

Cristy's mouth watered; this was one of her favourite desserts and she so rarely treated herself these days. 'You spoil me,' she teased, 'and you're going to make me fat. How will I ever meet anyone then?'

Hayley rolled her eyes, and disappeared inside, returning moments later with the salmon on a plate and Cristy's mobile under an arm. 'I think you're going to love this marinade,' she said, 'so please don't call Dad back before we eat, or it might end up spoiling the meal.'

Cristy frowned. 'Did he ring?'

'Only about six times.'

Immediately worried, Cristy took the phone. 'I have to get back to him, it could be about Aiden.'

'They're at the cricket!' Hayley cried, throwing out her arms. 'What can happen to the idiot there?'

'Hopefully nothing, but I won't relax until I know for sure. Take over here and if it's nothing urgent I'll tell him—'

'To get lost?'

Cristy laughed. 'Something like that,' and opening recent calls she clicked on Matthew's name. 'Is everything OK?' she asked as soon as he answered.

'Yeah, it's fine. Nothing to worry about.'

'You rang six times,' she reminded him.

'Yeah, I was trying to reach you while the boys were getting drinks. They're on their way back, but I don't want to speak on the phone anyway. I was wondering if we could meet up? Maybe over the weekend?'

'Why?'

'I need to talk to you.'

'What about?'

'Like I said, I'd rather not do it on the phone. I could come to yours. If you let me know when is best for you—'

'I'll probably be working all weekend—'

'Twenty-four-seven? You have to go home at some point.'

'When I will want to relax and sleep. What is this really about, Matthew?'

'I'll tell you when I see you.'

'But I don't want to see you.'

'That was hurtful.'

She almost laughed. 'When compared to some of the things you've said to me in recent times . . .'

'I know, I know, I'm sorry.' He sighed. 'There's something I need to discuss with you—'

'About one of the children? Your mother and the fact she's moving to a retirement village?'

'Not exactly.'

'Are you intending to bring Marley?'

'No. She's away at some actory-reunion-thing this weekend, so it's easy for me to fit into your schedule. It might be good if neither Hayley nor Aiden were around—'

Snapping angrily, she said, 'I don't know what's going on with you, Matthew, but I can't say right now when will be convenient, and Hayley's just made supper—'

'So you have to go. Just call or text if you can make it. OK?'

Without promising anything, she abruptly rang off and put the phone on the table, already knowing it was going to take her a few minutes to calm down.

'What was it about?' Hayley asked, glancing up from the barbecue.

'I've no idea,' Cristy replied, reaching for her wine and draining the glass. He'd find a way to hurt her all over again, she felt sure of it, so the answer had to be no, she wouldn't damned well see him. And certainly not alone.

CHAPTER EIGHTEEN

By the following morning Cristy had heard back from Maria del Smet, Gaudion's ex-colleague at Quantrell's, to say that she was in Prague today, but could fit them into her schedule at eleven a.m. UK time. Cristy immediately confirmed the arrangement, following it up with a Zoom link and request to know if del Smet was willing to be recorded.

No reply on that yet, and, frustratingly, nothing from Olivia Caldwell either.

'I felt sure she'd respond to my last message about Lexie's reasons for abandoning her degree,' she said, shaking out her raincoat and hanging it on the back of the door.

'Still early days,' Jackson reminded her. 'Maybe she hasn't picked it up yet, or she needs time to decide how to handle it.'

Considering Olivia's rumoured breakdown following the killings, Cristy felt a pang of guilt over the way she was now almost harrying her into reliving it. And for what? It wasn't as if it was their job to try to solve the case; their purpose was simply to tell it from an insider's perspective and hopefully to throw new light on the original investigation. Maybe even get it reopened. They were succeeding in some respects, clearly ruffling feathers somewhere given the warning call from Gaudion's solicitor, plus Anthony Anderson's unswerving support of an ex-employee generally thought to be an unconvicted killer. Curious, that, when they'd expected the man to distance himself as far as possible from Gaudion. There was also Victor Green's swift, almost rote, response to their challenge, and the 'Iris email' (interestingly, nothing more from that source since they'd made it public). Viewed subjectively, it was starting to feel like a slow, inexorable breaking open of doors that had been locked shut for too long.

So, as far as Olivia was concerned, maybe it would be kinder to leave her alone for a while and put more pressure on Richard Gaudion. After all, he must know as much as anyone about Lexie's reasons for leaving uni, not to mention how his brother had managed to escape trial. He probably even knew whether or not said brother was guilty.

Would he really protect the cold-blooded killer of three women and possibly a child, even if the culprit was his own flesh and blood? How far did sibling loyalty really stretch?

Going to her desk, she said, 'If we don't get Olivia, or someone else from the family, I can see us having to post a short episode next week, because the statement from Anderson and interview with Victor Green aren't going to cover an hour on their own. However, if Maria del Smet comes up with something sensational . . . I'm remaining hopeful she will, especially as she hasn't spoken out before. If nothing else, it'll show that the original investigation was not as thorough as it should have been.'

'We were just discussing the idea of Clover and Jacks going back to the Vale to ask around about the woods being fenced off,' said Connor, 'and about a possible satanic cult. We could get quite a lot of good material out of that.'

Doing his best ghost impression, Jackson said, 'We can definitely whip up some spooky. Listeners always love that stuff, so leave it to us. Meantime, thought you'd want to know that an email's come in from the police press office giving details of the documentary producer who showed interest in the murders. Apparently, it was eight years ago, so whether anything's still current with his number and email we've yet to find out.'

'What's his name?' Connor asked, getting ready to google him.

'Will Casson, and I've already looked him up. Quite a few TV credits to his name, all before 2015, not so much since.'

'Is he still alive?' Clover asked worriedly.

Cristy shot her a look. 'He'd better be,' she responded, 'or we really might have to call a halt to this.' To Jacks she said, 'Try

199

emailing first. Tell him who we are and ask why he didn't pursue his initial enquiries into the Kellon Manse Murders.'

'On it.'

'OK. Anything else of interest come in overnight?'

'Still checking,' Clover said, 'but your agent rang just before you got here. She's been trying your mobile but can't get an answer.'

Cristy sighed. 'That's because I'm avoiding her.'

Clover was clearly perplexed. 'Why would you do that?'

'She'll have a whole slew of things she wants me to do, from radio shows to TV interviews, to chairing online debates, to appearances at book fairs, to a catwalk strut in Paris. Not serious about the last one, obviously, but I think a couple of women's magazines are keen to get some "glamorous" shots of me for some future issue.'

'And that's a problem because?' Clover prompted.

'Because I'm not into self-promotion, or being tricked into talking about surviving a broken marriage, and I know that's on most agendas now I'm sort of back in the limelight. So, I'll ring when this series is done and I have some more time on my hands to deal with other things.'

'Meantime you could be promoting us?' Connor pointed out.

Since there was no arguing with that, she slanted him a look and went to pour herself a coffee. 'We're doing OK,' she reminded him, 'and if you're so keen on getting the word out to a wider audience, you could always take up Global's offer to be a stand-in for Lewis Goodall.'

He laughed. 'It wasn't an offer, just a suggestion made by Meena, I believe, and no way am I as classy as that guy.'

'Don't undersell yourself, although if our current government knew even a fraction of what he does about compassion and politics, the country might be in a very different place right now.'

Apparently not listening, Clover said, 'I've popped messages to Kevin Break and Frances Rush to make sure they've never heard of Maria del Smet. We don't want to be putting it out there that they missed her the first time around if they didn't.'

'Good shout,' Cristy told her.

'Tracked down any of Quantrell's clients yet?' Connor asked Jackson.

'Still a way to go, but it seems one of the senior partners got caught up in the cash-for-questions scandal back in the Nineties. He's not with them any more, and I can't see it tying in to Gaudion. He'd have only just joined the company at the time so would have been far too junior to be mixing with government ministers yet. Anyway, staying on it. I'll let you know if I come up with anything, but I have to say, trawling their dealings is like going blindfold into an underground cave full of dead ends.'

'The world behind top politics and high finance could make the mafia look transparent,' Clover muttered as she continued sifting through their social media accounts. 'Oh, another message here from Bart Simpson, Cristy's number one fan,' she announced delightedly.

As they all laughed, Cristy said, 'Please don't tell Hayley or she might try to make me go on a date with him. She's on my case about meeting someone new, and as sweet as dear Bart seems, as a self-described pipe and slippers bloke with a "quite good pension" and passion for old Vespas, I don't think he's for me.'

'Nevertheless, Hayley does have a point,' Clover told her. 'You should be getting out there more. You're gorgeous—'

'OK, this conversation is over,' Cristy cut in quickly. 'I'm going to start compiling some thoughts on what it must have been like for those three women during the moments before the shootings. We haven't really put ourselves in their shoes yet and I think it's time we did. Obviously, we can't know anything for certain, but we can pose some theories in a chat, Connor, such as what they might have seen or heard in the moments before they were murdered. Was there time to be afraid before the first shot was fired? How terrified were the other two after seeing what had happened to the first? Did the killer check all three were dead before he left? What sort of interaction did he have with the child? It's grisly, I know, and probably gratuitous given there's virtually no evidence to provide an accurate picture, but I'll sketch something out and we can take it from there.'

The rest of the morning passed swiftly as they used forensic, pathology and coroner's reports to guide them, along with expert analysis on bullet trajectories and residue; statements explaining blood spatters and what could be read into them, and various other police and scientific hypotheses until it was time to connect with Maria del Smet.

It was evident, as soon as she appeared on the screen, that she was outdoors, probably in a park given the leafy background and twittering of birds. She was a lot like her profile photo, beautiful, composed, with dark, almond-shaped eyes and a full-lipped mouth. Her hair, also dark, was tied back from her face and her jewellery, what little there was of it, looked tasteful and expensive. 'Hello,' she said in a faintly accented voice. Although her company profile described her as Belgian, she was clearly of Asian descent, and her English, based on the single word she'd uttered, sounded American.

'Thank you for agreeing to talk to us,' Cristy said, smiling warmly while thinking that for all her outward charm and easy insouciance, this wasn't a woman she'd care to cross.

'I hope you don't mind,' del Smet said, holding up a take-out coffee. 'Got to take the opportunities where we can, yes? Oh, and sorry I didn't reply to your email about recording this chat. I've been quite tied up this morning, but I'm happy for you to do so. I have nothing to hide. Not any more.'

Her smile, seeming sincere, was captivating. Thanking her and checking that Connor was recording, Cristy began by asking the woman to tell them her full name, who she worked for and how well she knew David Gaudion.

With formalities out of the way, del Smet continued.

DEL SMET: 'I'm afraid I haven't seen him for a long time. We were close once, and for quite some time, but we were much younger then. When we first "found each other", you could say we were two insecure and eager newbies in an office of scary high-fliers. Everyone was so switched on and powerful, made us recent recruits feel as though we'd never stand a chance of catching up. I was older than David by about three years, and my marriage was . . . difficult,

202

while his was . . . Well, there were issues, that's for sure, but I never got the impression he was intending, or hoping to end it. If anything, he seemed to greatly value his family life.'

And yet he embarked on an affair, Cristy thought but didn't say.

CRISTY: 'Did you ever meet Lexie Gaudion?'

DEL SMET: 'No, I didn't. She rarely came to London and there would have been no reason for us to get together even if she did, unless we were at the same function or social event, of course. But it never happened.'

CRISTY: 'The issues in his marriage – can you tell us what they were?'

DEL SMET: 'He was concerned about her mental health. She suffered with severe bouts of depression and she had a very difficult relationship with her mother – I'm sure you already know that – and he worried about the effect it was all having on their daughter. They only had one when David and I were first together. He wanted to help his wife; I was never in any doubt about that. She was a priority for him. What we had was secondary, for us both. We fulfilled a role for one another that was never meant to impinge on the rest of our lives, and didn't.'

CRISTY: 'Do you know if Lexie was receiving any treatment for her depression back then?'

DEL SMET: 'I know that David regularly consulted doctors, specialists in the field of psychology and psychiatry, but there were no real breakthroughs for her until much later. Actually, until after someone put him onto Serena Sutton. Their second daughter had been born by then. I remember how happy it made him to see Lexie's moods improving thanks to Serena's guidance, and hopeful that it might be a turning point of some sort. I think it was for a while, but then things started to go downhill again and I know the frustration of it, his sense of helplessness and even despair, used to drive him out of his mind at times.'

CRISTY: 'Do you know who put him touch with Serena Sutton in the first place?'

DEL SMET: 'I think it might have been a client, someone whose wife had suffered similar issues, but I don't recall him ever saying who it was.'

CRISTY: 'Did he ever describe the improvements he was seeing in Lexie?'

DEL SMET: 'He said she seemed calmer, less reticent with the girls, more willing to engage . . . I fully expected him to bring our *arrangement* to an end at that point, but he didn't – it can be quite difficult to let go of an emotional support until you're absolutely sure you don't need it any more. And it turned out he did still need me, because his concerns about Lexie returned and so I remained his escape and *confidante*. Please know that this was reciprocal; he spent a lot of time listening to me agonizing over my own situation and I was extremely grateful to him for it. I think it was being able to talk to him, to express my self-doubt and fears of failure, that finally gave me the strength to leave my marriage.'

CRISTY: 'When his concerns returned, were they the same as before?'

DEL SMET: 'No, actually, it was about money then. She'd begun withdrawing large sums of cash from their account. I think also from her own, but I can't be certain of that. Apparently, she'd joined a life-coaching programme as an adjunct to, or maybe it was a progression from, the psychotherapy that had been doing her so much good.'

CRISTY: 'Do you know if he tried to stop her making these payments?'

DEL SMET: 'I'm sure he did, but what actual steps he took . . .'

She stopped and turned her face away from the camera for a moment, making Cristy wonder if someone else was there, just out of shot. If there was she didn't speak to them, and there was no sound of another voice before she turned back.

DEL SMET: 'If you're trying to lead me into saying that I think he killed his wife and the others in order to stop the haemorrhaging of funds, then you're out of luck, because that's not what I think.'

CRISTY: 'Can you share with us what you do think?'

DEL SMET: 'Just that it wasn't him. And as for the nonsense about him harming his little girl . . . I will never believe that. He wasn't a cruel or abusive man, he was decent and caring . . . Ambitious, of course, and fiercely competitive, but he'd never have been employed by Quantrell's if he wasn't. He had a brilliant mind, and a great sense of humour. People listened to him, and it was hard not to be drawn to him, but he certainly wasn't a psychopath, no matter what the police are trying to tell you.'

CRISTY: 'He worked a lot with people in high office?'

DEL SMET: 'Of course.'

CRISTY: 'Anyone we know? Names we've heard of?'

DEL SMET 'I'm sure you're aware that we're subject to a high degree of confidentiality, so I'm afraid I can't answer that question.'

Cristy glanced at her phone as a message arrived. Seeing who it was from, she was momentarily thrown.

It didn't matter, it could wait. Time to shake things up a bit.

CRISTY: 'Can I ask where you were on the day of the killings?'

DEL SMET: 'Of course. I mean . . . Sorry, I wasn't expecting . . . Actually, it happened on my birthday, which I always spend

205

with my cousin at a spa, either in Monaco or Baden Baden. That year we were in Monaco.'

CRISTY: 'It's possible, once this podcast goes out, that someone from the police will contact you . . .'

DEL SMET: 'I thought the case had been closed.'

CRISTY: 'It's a multiple murder and missing child. Those cases never close, even if they aren't being actively pursued.'

DEL SMET: 'No, no, of course not. I just . . . Sorry . . .'

She moved her phone, seeming to check the time or maybe she was talking to someone. Perhaps she'd been recording this interview too. She came back into shot.

DEL SMET: 'If we're done here, I have a meeting I can't be late for.'

CRISTY: 'We're good. Thanks very much for taking time out of your day to talk to me.'

DEL SMET: 'You're very welcome. I hope my contribution will help lead to the real killer.'

As the screen darkened and the call ended, Cristy told Connor to keep recording. 'Let's get our thoughts about this on tape,' she said. 'To begin with, I wonder what she thinks she said to help lead us to the "real killer".'

He shook his head. 'We'll have to listen to it again, but I'll say this for her, she was very . . . polished. Always ready with an answer, apart from the zinger you landed on her about where she was that day. She didn't seem to like that too much.'

'Or the fact that the police might contact her,' Clover added.

'Are you thinking she might have been involved?' Jackson wanted to know.

Cristy shrugged. 'I wouldn't bet the house on it at this stage, but something was off about her. Did anyone else get the impression she wasn't alone on that park bench, or wherever she was?'

'It definitely looked like it to me,' Connor replied. 'So what do you reckon, someone from Quantrell's making sure she stuck to a script, or could it have been Gaudion?'

Cristy regarded him thoughtfully, disturbed by the idea of Gaudion manipulating from the periphery. 'At this point we've got no way of finding out,' she replied. 'So let's park it, but keep it in mind and move on to what she said about Lexie's mental health. That's the most we've heard about it to date, and the fact that Gaudion discussed it with his mistress . . . What do we think about that?'

'Actually,' Clover put in, 'I'm wondering if they really were lovers. I mean, is it credible that no one else knew about the affair when it apparently went on for years? These things always get out eventually, and the fact that the police never got wind of it—'

'Unless they did, and whatever happened about it has gone the way of Gaudion's statements,' Connor put in.

'If you're right about that, then it's making Quantrell's look shadier than ever,' Jackson stated. 'Pressure from somewhere to get Anderson and his cohorts expunged from enquiries?'

'Both she and Anderson were quite categoric about Gaudion not being guilty,' Cristy said, 'so what I'm asking myself now is, are they using *us* to get some sort of message to Gaudion?'

'Like letting him know they still have his back?' Connor ventured.

'In the hope their secrets remain safe with him,' Clover added.

Cristy said, 'The fact that she's not alibiing him makes me more inclined to believe that she was at a spa that day. Which doesn't mean she's off the hook over some sort of a cover-up.' She turned to the message she'd received during the interview. 'Let's leave it for now,' she said, 'because I have some good news. I've just heard from Olivia Caldwell, and she's finally agreed to meet.'

'Wow!' Clover exclaimed, wide-eyed. 'Where? When?'

Cristy read out loud, '"If you can come to Kellon Hall on Saturday around three we can talk there without interruption. I will give some thought to your request to record our interview and let you know when I see you. Olivia Caldwell.'" She looked at Connor. 'Are you up for it?' she asked.

'Count me in,' he assured her. 'We always knew we'd be working this weekend, so Jodi's sister's coming tonight.'

Cristy smiled. 'Then I'll message back to say how much we're looking forward to meeting her.'

CHAPTER NINETEEN

CRISTY: 'Connor and I are, once again, back in the Berkeley Vale. This time, on our way to Kellon Hall, which you'll remember was the home of Margaret Sallis and her daughters, Lexie and Olivia. It's Olivia, the older sister, we're meeting today, who hasn't been keen to talk to us until now. We don't know yet what's changed her mind, but I can tell you we're mightily intrigued to find out more.

'Unlike the last time we drove along this leafy country road that snakes past the main entrance to both the Hall and the Manse, it's raining today and a chill wind is rattling the trees, much like the prospect of meeting the Hall's ghosts is rattling Connor.'

CONNOR: 'You can mock, but tell me you'd be happy to come here alone.'

CRISTY: (LAUGHING) 'Fair point. I know we've mentioned before how spooky the place looked from afar and we've no reason to believe it'll be any better up close. However, what's changed this time around is access to the property. Whereas the gates were firmly chained and padlocked before, they're now standing wide open and the driveway beyond looks almost welcoming. The grounds, as we've been told, are well taken care of.

'OK, we're passing along an avenue of balsam poplars now and the lawns – actually they're fields – either side are richly green with a smattering of buttercups holding their own in amongst the spear thistles and curly docks. A dozen or more crows are pecking into the long grass . . .'

CONNOR: 'It's called a murder of crows.'

CRISTY: 'Of course, yes, I'd forgotten that was the collective noun. How inauspicious is that, even though the actual murders took place next door. Still . . . We can't actually see Kellon Hall yet . . . Ah, there it is, just coming into view and, oh my goodness, I'm sure a shiver just ran down my spine. How about you, Connor?'

CONNOR: 'There's still time to hightail it out of here.'

Laughing, Cristy killed the recording and continued to take in their surroundings as they drew closer to the bleak, grey stone mansion that was more like a castle than a hall. Its towering façade and crenellated roofs dripped with ivy, and the dark, leaded windows peered through the climbing foliage like shadowy keepers of ancient secrets. At the centre of the forecourt was an empty, sunken fountain, and spreading each side of the steps leading to an enormous studded front door was a parterre where an assortment of black marble beasts surveyed their surroundings with stony disdain.

There was an endless amount of creepiness to be laced around this old estate when it came to describing it, but what was striking Cristy the most as they pulled up next to a black Lexus (presumably Olivia's) was the air of melancholy that made it seem more lonely than scary.

'It could be beautiful,' she said quietly to Connor as they began packing up, ready to get out of the car. 'The flower beds over there are stunning, and the topiary looks as though it's been shipped in for a film it's all so exquisitely done.' There were box hedges sculpted into the shapes of tortoises and squirrels, small horses and big dogs, and what looked like a flying saucer – someone was clearly having fun with the shears.

'The front door,' Connor stated darkly, recording himself, 'is brutal. I mean, really? It looks like it's been repurposed from the Munsters' gaff on Mockingbird Heights. Actually, maybe there's no repurposing about it.'

Cristy had to laugh. He was right: the old oak door with its impressive stone portico and gnarled dark wood did come over as forbidding, even prison like. She started slightly as one half of it began to swing open and then there was Olivia, easily recognizable from her photos. She was older now, of course, with touches of grey in her glossy sweep of thick, dark hair, held back by a red velvet band, but her sharp cheekbones, heart-shaped face and delicate mouth were very like her younger sister's. She was probably taller than Lexie had been, and seemed fuller figured, although she wasn't overweight or overstated in any way; in fact she was slim, dressed in plain black jeans and an oatmeal-coloured shirt with matching sweater draped over her shoulders.

Gathering up her bag, Cristy got out of the car, quickly recalling everything she knew about the Olivia Caldwell of today – fifty-three, mother of two, director of the Caldwell family business, keen equestrian, charity fundraiser, head of a local rehabilitation programme, and no doubt much more besides. No flower shops as far as they'd been able to find.

'Thanks so much for this,' she said, mounting the steps. 'It's good to meet you.'

Olivia's handshake wasn't firm, or warm; she seemed quite stiff as she glanced back at the car.

'Connor will be right with us,' Cristy said brightly. 'Just sorting out his gear.'

Olivia's pale green eyes became wary as she watched Connor clamber out into the drizzling rain and start towards them. 'I'm still not sure about recording,' she said, and turned to lead the way inside.

The entrance hall was as gloomy as Cristy had expected, with a vast inglenook fireplace at one end, exposed stone walls filled with antiquated tapestries and faded paintings, and nothing but dust on the flagstone floor.

'Through there,' Olivia said, closing the door behind Connor and pointing to another, already open, beside the fireplace.

Cristy led the way along a dimly lit corridor with rooms, closed off, either side of it, until she reached an enormous kitchen that might have been straight out of Downton Abbey. At first glance it seemed just about everything belonged to another era, even the musty smell; however, closer inspection revealed a fairly modern Aga (clearly not working given the room's temperature), a nifty little microwave on one of the much-scrubbed wooden countertops, and a Rise and Shine kettle plugged into the mains.

'I can offer you tea or instant coffee,' Oliva said, unhooking mugs from an old oak dresser. 'I know I ought to keep the place better stocked, just in case someone comes to view, but no one ever does.'

'Coffee's fine for us both, thanks,' Cristy said. 'Black.' She went to look out of the tall, rain-spattered window into a large cobbled yard surrounded by barns and stables, all boarded up and padlocked, it seemed, and a chained iron gate blocking access to the fields beyond. There was the rusting carcass of an old horsebox and a number of hitching posts with fraying ropes fluttering in the wind. She tried picturing the girls and the Gaudion boys, bringing this now deserted, derelict part of the estate back to life.

'We'll go into the parlour,' Olivia said. Placing three steaming mugs onto a tray, she backed into a door beside a large chest freezer and held it with her foot for them to follow along another dark corridor to a room at the end. It was comparatively small for the size of the house and warmed by an electric blow heater plugged in next to an empty cast-iron fireplace. There was a brass and leather fender, a couple of threadbare rugs over a neutral carpet, and a number of polished glass and wood cabinets pushed up against the pink silk walls. Surrounding an oval mahogany coffee table where Olivia placed the tray, were several elegant, if threadbare, parlour chairs.

'This was my mother's room,' Olivia said, gesturing for them to sit down. 'If she wasn't on a horse or haranguing someone in the kitchen, this was usually where she could be found. Sugar?' She was holding up a tiny silver spoonful.

'No thanks,' Connor answered as Cristy shook her head.

Putting the spoon back in the bowl, Olivia chose a chair close to the heater and sat down facing them. 'I heard your interview with Hannah Gains,' she told them, and reached for her coffee. 'This is where she'd come to sit with Mother, bringing her knitting and chatter along with her, carrying on as though she was a welcome guest.' The shadow of a smile crossed her lips. 'Mother always treated her as if she were a nuisance, but I think she was actually quite glad that someone bothered to care.' Her eyes drifted towards the French doors. 'We used to torment the life out of poor Hannah when we were kids,' she reflected, 'but she took it all, even seemed to play along. Secretly, Lexie and I used to wish she was one of our teachers, but she never taught around here, and Daddy . . . Well, I don't think there ever was an affair between them, but we used to like to make out there was.'

Surprised, Cristy asked, 'Would she have visited your mother if it was true?'

Olivia shrugged. 'He was dead by the time she started coming for her "pastoral" visits, so who knows what went on before. We saw him coming out of her cottage a couple of times, and you know how kids can't resist making up stories. I think there might have been some gossip, not put about by us, but what difference does it make now? It's not why you're here, obviously, but for what it's worth, looking back, I think Hannah has always been just a naturally kind person who sensed a loneliness in Mother that no one else could see.'

'Would you say she was Margaret's only friend?'

Olivia's eyes wandered back to the French doors. 'Certainly after Daddy went, but there were a lot of . . . *acquaintances* before that. There was a time when they'd throw parties or dinners and people would come from all over, but even then Mother never really knew how to make anyone feel welcome. She liked the cocktails and horse-talk, of course, and sometimes she'd want to show us off, me and Lexie. But mostly she forgot we were there, didn't even notice us watching from the gallery or main staircase, which we often did – if she happened to spot us she didn't much care, just carried on as if we were part of the furniture. Daddy was a far better host than she was, quite generous actually. I guess that's why people came.'

'How old were you when he passed?' Cristy asked.

'Eleven. Lexie was ten.'

'It must have been hard.'

Olivia's eyes flicked to her and away again. 'I don't really remember how we felt,' she admitted. 'It was a shock, of course, a tragedy, I guess, but I can't claim we were ever close to him. He was an aloof, self-involved sort of man who didn't want to be bothered with "girl matters" as he called them. He only took an interest in us if it was about our education or riding technique. Mother used to tell us she couldn't stand him, and we believed her. There wasn't any reason not to, although I do remember them having some fun together, and as far as I know they slept in the same bed until he died.' Her expression showed sadness now, and as Cristy watched her take another sip of coffee she began worrying about asking her to continue.

To her surprise, Olivia suddenly said, 'I think you can record. I don't have anything to say that . . .' Her breath caught and she took a moment before starting again. 'My husband and father-in-law didn't want me to do this,' she admitted. 'They know I'm here, of course, but right up until the time I left home they were trying to persuade me not to come.' She gave a wry sort of smile. 'And right up until the time you arrived, I thought I might leave and send a message to say sorry, I can't help you.'

Aware of Connor discreetly setting to record, Cristy was about to speak when Olivia continued, staring at the small mic on the table as she spoke almost to herself.

OLIVIA: 'I expect you've heard about my "collapse" after the murders. Some people would call it a breakdown or an emotional crisis. In our family we referred to it as the "collapse". Still do, I guess, although we hardly ever mention it now. I've had a lot of therapy since it all happened, but that still doesn't mean I find it easy to talk about.'

She broke off and took a sip of coffee, her eyes distant, her attention clearly elsewhere.

'My sister meant the world to me. Our experiences as children, the lack of proper parenting, the bond we shared . . .

'It wasn't a surprise to anyone when I took her death so hard. It was like losing a part of myself, and frankly I still miss her every day. I talk to her in my mind . . . I even asked her, before you arrived, if I was doing the right thing

214

talking to you. I can't say she gave me an answer, but I didn't get a bad feeling about it when I saw you coming up the drive, so I told myself she was OK with it. That sort of thing happens for a lot of people, doesn't it, when they lose someone they love? They continue as if they're still close by, listening, advising, approving or disapproving ... I know I'm not unusual in that, but what was unusual, in my case ... What none of us expected, me least of all ...'

She stared into the fireplace, fingers pressed to her lips, almost as if to stop the next words spilling out, but they came with the slight tremor of a sob.

'I had no idea that losing my mother would affect me so badly.'

She stopped again and fixed Cristy with wide, almost startled eyes, as if she still couldn't quite believe it now.

'Lexie was the one who always craved Mother's approval, feeling the need to get close, to make her smile and say something kind. She did have kindness in her, perhaps more than we gave her credit for, or maybe that's just something I want to believe now. Unlike Lexie, I ...I always told myself I didn't care what she thought about anything, I even used to wish her dead at times, but then, when it happened ...

'Of course it was the shock of how it happened that made it so much worse . . . I just couldn't seem to make myself believe she'd really gone. And I was so caught up in the horror of losing Lexie and my niece . . . It took a while for me to realize that my mother's loss was also hitting me hard. I needed to grieve for her too, a counsellor told me, but it was still almost impossible to make her the focus of my thoughts when Lexie was all that mattered . . . And Amelia, of course. And Cynthia.

'The Gaudions had been a part of our lives for so long, in many ways the most important part ... David, Richard, their parents . . . They were our real family. Lexie and I adored them, especially Cynthia. She was our mother really, the one we went to when things weren't good at home, or if we had something to show off, or a big decision to make. She was so easy to talk to, so loving and kind . . .

'After it all happened she was who I needed. I longed to go to her, to beg her to make sense of it all in a way I simply couldn't. Sometimes I felt I might go mad with the despair of not seeing her, but of course Rosaria, her granddaughter, was her main concern then. There was nothing she could do for me, especially after David was arrested . . .

'Richard came to see me a couple of times, which was decent of him, but he was in a terrible state himself. He couldn't, wouldn't believe his brother had committed such a horrible crime . . . I couldn't believe it either . . . But then . . .'

As her words trailed away and her thoughts deepened the crease between her brows, Cristy didn't prompt her to continue, sensing she would when she was ready.

OLIVIA: 'He was very angry with Lexie about the money. Do you know about that?'

CRISTY: 'The sums she was giving to Papilio?'

OLIVIA: 'Yes. They had some terrible arguments about it and we all . . . Once we knew how much was involved . . . It was hard to understand what was happening to her, and almost impossible to know what to do. On the one hand the amounts seemed preposterous – how could therapy or coaching, whatever it was, cost so much? And yet we could see what a positive effect it was having on her. She was finally coming out of this awful shell she'd put around herself ever since . . .'

Her eyes shot to Cristy's and then to the laptop that was recording her words. She looked at Connor in his headphones, and back to Cristy. For long moments Cristy expected her to ask them to stop, but in the end she continued in a voice that was quieter and somehow thinner.

'Something happened when she was young, at Oxford. You already know about it, you told me in your message . . . It affected her so deeply . . . Damaged her in ways . . .'

Once again she pressed her fingers to her lips as they shook, until, finally, after taking a breath she was able to continue.

'Over the years she lived through so much torment, mostly in her mind, but that doesn't make it any the less real. In many ways I think it makes it worse. She underwent endless amounts of counselling and therapy. Nothing ever seemed to work. We'd all but given up hope of her ever being able to lead a life free of anxiety and depression, with moods of such black despair we feared for what she might do to herself. Then she started to see Serena Sutton and the change in her . . . It took time, of course, it didn't happen overnight, but eventually we all began to notice how much calmer and more capable she seemed after her sessions. It's hard to describe the relief and hope we dared to feel as we saw her changing, blossoming before our eyes into the lovely woman she really was.
'Cynthia was the first to point out that it might be becoming a bit of an obsession, that even when Lexie wasn't actually seeing Serena she was always on the phone to her. At least, we thought it was Serena, but then we found out Lexie had progressed onto some kind of life-coaching programme with someone Serena had recommended.'

CRISTY: 'To be clear, we're talking about Papilio now?'

OLIVIA: 'Yes, but we didn't know what it was called at first, all I knew was that she was behaving like my sister again. She was brighter, more confident, loving with her girls in a way she'd struggled with before. Having our own mother as a role model was mostly what made things so difficult

217

for her, and not even Cynthia's guidance could get her over the fear of harming her own children in the way she'd been harmed herself. Not physically, you understand, we were never beaten, but the verbal abuse and neglect . . . How could it not leave a mark? But then Lexie joined this group and it seemed to, I don't know, set her free from the demons. I mean, she was still shy, sensitive, slightly reticent in a way, but the negatives of her character no longer seemed to dominate. She really did seem happy, and I hadn't seen her that way for so long that I didn't want to listen when Cynthia warned us that things might be getting out of hand.

'Then David found out how much she was paying for her treatment and that's when it all started to . . . fall apart, I suppose. Obviously I was as shocked, appalled even, as everyone else when I heard about the sums involved. There was no denying the results were good, but no amount of therapy, no matter its quality or uniqueness of approach, could warrant the thousands upon thousands of pounds she was handing over to Papilio. She was being taken advantage of, exploited, used . . .

'I tried talking to her, of course I did, and David and I even went to see Serena together, but we could tell we were wasting our time. She – and Lexie – were so caught up in the "ecstasy of healing" – that's what Serena called it – that both of them, Serena and my sister, were all but unreachable. Getting to Paolo Morelli was another story altogether. He just wasn't contactable, and yet obviously he was, because Lexie was seeing him regularly. She attended group-meets and one-on-one sessions all over the country, handing over small fortunes at the same time. We followed her once, David and I, thinking we might get to Morelli that way, but we ended up being locked outside the gates of some private estate in Worcestershire. It belonged to an American couple from Missouri, we found out later, and they told us they were perfectly aware of the meetings taking place inside their home and if Mr Morelli didn't wish to speak to us about his events then they had nothing to say either. It was bizarre, surreal, and I could see that David was getting more and more frustrated.

'Then the next thing we knew, Lexie was talking to our mother about the group, the last person on earth we expected her to confide in. I guess it proves how naïve we were at the time. It wasn't until later that we realized Morelli wasn't only after using the Hall as a venue for his events; he was also keen to recruit Mother into his programme. And because she was so contrary and unpredictable, and derived so much pleasure from playing Lexie and me off against one another, she apparently decided to join. Whether or not she'd ever have actually parted with any money, or let them use the Hall, I guess we'll never know, but she wasn't called Mean Margaret for nothing. What was it she said to Hannah Gains? "Olivia's going to be very cross with me, but who cares about her?" What kind of mother says something like that, mm? Not the kind it's easy to feel any affection for, but it seemed I had something going on where she was concerned, given how I reacted to losing her.'

She got to her feet and it seemed for a moment as if she was going to leave the room, but she simply went to the French doors and stood gazing out at the rain-soaked patio beyond. There was a rose garden out there, and a small, rusting table with two chairs.

Cristy could hardly begin to imagine what was in her mind now; the torment of her past must be incredibly hard to bear, never mind to share. Should they really allow this to run any further?

In the end, without any prompting, Olivia said:

'I don't want to speak ill of David. I promised myself I wouldn't. It won't change anything now. What's done is done and they're never coming back.'

Cristy and Connor looked at one another, Connor confirming with a nod that he was still recording.

Olivia's back was still to them as she said:

'Don't you have any questions?'

Momentarily thrown, Cristy scrambled to assimilate.

CRISTY: 'How long was it before she died that you last saw her?'

OLIVIA: 'I saw her that day. I went over there in the morning. We were supposed to be playing tennis, here at the Hall, but she was ... She kept laughing and behaving as though ... It's hard to describe, really, but she was in an impish sort of mood; I could see she was excited about something.'

CRISTY: 'Was David there?'

OLIVIA: 'Yes, he was. I'm sure they'd been arguing before I got there, but only he seemed upset by it. The girls were around too. They loved it when Lexie was playful with them and it had been happening more and more over the previous months. I thought to myself, you can't put a price on this, so maybe we should let the Papilio thing run its course. Provided it didn't bankrupt her and David in the process, of course. No one wanted to see that happen, I'm sure she didn't either, although it was hard to know when she refused to discuss the cost of it all.

'We didn't play tennis in the end. She wanted me to leave and drop the girls at Cynthia's on my way home. I could tell by David's expression that he was keen for me to do the same, so I piled them into the car and I was about to get in myself when he came outside to talk to me. He told me he'd found out – I'm not sure how – that Mother and Serena were visiting that afternoon and apparently there was some plan for Mother to join the group.

'Of course I was shocked, it seemed so unlike Mother, and yet it was exactly like her really, being as perverse as she was. I asked what he was going to do, and he said he wasn't sure yet, but it was good that I was getting the girls out of the way.'

She put a hand to her head and kept it there; her back was still turned as she struggled to continue.

'I'm sorry . . . I . . . I keep seeing their dear little faces and how thrilled they were when David leaned into the car window to kiss them goodbye. He told them to be good for Grandma and that he'd come to pick them up later. It was all so . . . normal. He even made a joke about how I'd picked up his phone instead of my own, so we swapped and then I drove away. When I checked the mirror before going through the gate, he was still standing there, watching us leave, and Lexie came to join him.

'I'm not sure if I had a bad feeling then. It's easy, with hindsight, to say that I did, but something wasn't right about the day. I didn't like the idea of Mother being drawn into Papilio, but I had no idea what to do about it – and anyway, I was fairly certain she was messing with Lexie. I just hoped it wasn't going to upset Lexie too much when she realized Mother was playing one of her horrible games.

'Cynthia was as concerned as I was when I told her. If it weren't for the girls, I think we'd have both gone back there . . . I'm not sure why; to talk some sense into Lexie, maybe, to prevent David from becoming angry again? Cynthia said we should leave it to him, he'd know what to do for the best. So I ended up getting back into the car and driving home.

'I got the call around five-thirty . . . I couldn't understand what I was being told. Will, my husband, took the phone and . . . They said we should wait, that someone would come to talk to us, but we drove straight over there . . . It was chaos, of course . . . They wouldn't let us through, even when I told them who I was. They just said that we should go home and someone would contact us again when they knew more.'

CRISTY: 'Did you see David while you were there?'

OLIVIA: 'No. We couldn't get close to the house, but we tried calling him. It just kept going to voicemail, so in the end we did as we were told and went home. I don't know why I didn't think to go straight to Cynthia's. It seems the most obvious thing now, but I guess the shock, the disbelief . . . I kept telling myself I'd wake up any minute and none of it would be real . . . It was terrible. I was so afraid . . . I'm not sure what of, the worst had already happened, but I remember I couldn't stop shaking.'

She turned around and her face was so haunted, so pale, that Cristy said, 'I can see how hard this is for you. We can stop now . . .'

Allowing herself to be led back to her chair, Olivia sat for a few moments staring blankly at the mic, seeming bewildered, as if she no longer knew what it was, or even where she was.

'Can I get you something?' Cristy offered.

Olivia shook her head and pressed her hands to her face as a small brass clock on the hearth with no hands and a tiny bird in its belfry whirred and chimed four times, before lapsing back into a monotonous tick. Another booming clock somewhere else in the house struck the hour before returning to silence.

Olivia finally looked up again and still seemed shaky as she said:

'Was it Fiona Mooney who told you about what happened to Lexie at Oxford?'

Though surprised by the sudden change of subject, Cristy was ready to go with it, but Olivia spoke again.

'It's OK. You don't have to answer. It doesn't really matter who told you, but Fiona's probably the only other one who knows, besides me, of course, and the . . .'

She swallowed her next words, the tightness around her mouth showing a sudden bitterness and even anger.

OLIVIA: 'It's a bit of a cliché these days, isn't it, rich boys behaving badly at our top institutions? I guess it was back then too, but cliché or not, it doesn't make it any the less true. There were five of them who forced themselves on her. They used her in some sort of sordid game, the object of some sick ceremony . . . They humiliated and even tortured her . . . It was obscene what they did to her, inhuman . . . I can't, won't go into detail, but she could never go back to Oxford after. She was so traumatized, so utterly broken by it . . .

'She came straight home once they let her go. She didn't even call me, not at first. Our mother was . . . She was at her worst, I'm afraid, drunk and angry that her night had been disturbed, but Cynthia, thank God, was at her best. She took care of Lexie in a way only she could . . . She tried to make her go to the police, or at least report it to the Proctor's office, but Lexie wouldn't. She didn't want anyone to know, said it would make no difference, no one could touch them anyway because of who they were, the families they came from.

'Imagine that, being so well-connected, so apart from normal, decent society, that you're actually above the law.'

As appalled by the reality as any woman would be to hear of another suffering the way Lexie had, Cristy gave it a moment before saying, very gently:

CRISTY: 'Does this mean that Rosaria . . .?'

OLIVIA: 'Yes, it does. Dear, sweet little angel that she was.'

She gave a long, tremulous sigh and stared at the mic again, though still not seeming to register it.

OLIVIA: 'I wonder where she is now, what she's doing? It was her thirty-first birthday last week, you know? I got her a card, same as I do every year, but I have nowhere to send it.'

223

Though Cristy was interested to hear more about Rosaria, for now she wanted to try to keep them on track.

CRISTY: 'I take it David knows about the attack and that he's not Rosaria's biological father?'

Olivia seemed baffled, as if she hadn't quite understood the words.

OLIVIA: 'Why would you say that? Of course Rosaria's his. David was one of them. He was there that night. It's why his parents made him marry my sister.'

CHAPTER TWENTY

'So what did you make of all that?' Connor asked as Cristy drove them out of the Kellon Estate to join the road that would eventually take them to the A38. The rain had vanished altogether now, but the sky was still a morose shade of grey and the countryside looked saturated and dull.

Cristy glanced in the rear-view mirror. Olivia had driven out after them then stopped, presumably to lock up. 'I need to hear it again,' she said. 'If you can play it back from where she told us David was a part of the gang-rape. That completely threw me, didn't it you?'

'Definitely didn't see it coming,' he agreed, 'but you followed it up pretty well.'

As he reset to the last part of the recording, Cristy began running through it in her mind until her mobile rang and Matthew's name popped up on the screen. 'Oh, God, I'd forgotten he wanted to meet me later,' she groaned and let the call go to messages. 'It's not going to happen anyway. We've got too much to do with this.'

'I'll just text Jodi to let her know we're going straight back to the office,' Connor said, reaching for his phone.

'Actually, before we get into what else Olivia told us,' Cristy said, when he'd finished his message, 'we need to find out if anyone during the initial investigation was aware of the rape at Oxford. We've found no mention of it, but given the other anomalies in this case I'm not sure that means anything.'

'It'll take some digging that can't be done here, in the car,' he pointed out, 'and we can't be certain it's connected to the murders.'

'But according to Olivia, it had some bearing on the trial being

225

abandoned. So let's listen again to what she said, and then we can take it from there.'

Connor hit play and a beat later Cristy's voice came over the car's sound system.

CRISTY: 'I need to get this straight – you're telling us that David Gaudion was there the night Lexie was raped?'

OLIVIA: 'Not just there, he was part of it. I believe he was the one who invited Lexie to join the party. It's unlikely she'd have gone otherwise.'

CRISTY: 'But I don't understand why she'd marry him if he allowed that to happen to her *and* was part of it himself.'

There was a long, shaky sigh from Olivia before she spoke again in a voice that sounded crushed by sadness.

OLIVIA: 'You'd have to know Lexie to understand why she married him, but I can begin by telling you that she was always in love with him. Right from when we were children. It wasn't a secret from me, of course, I was the only one she ever talked to about it. She was besotted with him. He could never do any wrong in her eyes, and he did plenty, believe me, but it never seemed to matter to her, or that he didn't feel the same about her. Oh, he cared for her, like a sister, same as me, I suppose, but he and Lexie were never going to have the future together that she always dreamed of.

'As we got older it broke her heart to see him with other girls, to never be his proper date, just a friend, when we went to parties or concerts or anywhere he didn't have a partner, or a better offer as my children would probably put it now. It was rare for him to be without one, but it happened from time to time and it meant everything to Lexie to get the call saying he needed her. She'd drop everything and go anywhere just to be with him, and after she'd spin all kinds of dreams and fantasies around those few precious hours. Precious to her, but not to him. Nevertheless, she was convinced that one day he'd realize they were meant to be together, she just had to be patient.'

CRISTY: 'But if the rape was as bad as you say it was . . . If it ruined her future at Oxford . . . How could she ever even look at him again?'

Another long, turbulent sigh from Olivia before she said:

'She could do it because she was Lexie and desperate to be loved. By anyone actually, but especially by him. And by our mother, of course. Lexie was so hurt, so damaged by our childhood, that it manifested itself in ways it's hard to describe now, but it devastated her sense of self-worth to a point where she made choices that were, frankly, more of a punishment than a right-thinking response to things. She didn't see it that way, of course, but it was as though she was on some endless cycle of self-destruct, forever destined to prove to herself that our mother was right not to love her.

'The funny thing is, she used to say she felt safe with Mother . . . I can still hardly believe that. It was the same with David, even after what happened with him. Maybe that gives you a measure of how horribly damaged she was. I guess Serena got there in the end with her therapy, and Papilio to a degree, because she definitely improved at that time.'

CRISTY: 'Was David ever violent towards her? Before or after the rape?'

OLIVIA: 'Not in the physical sense – or not that she ever told me, and he wasn't cruel to her the way Mother was, but after they were married he could be . . . impatient, dismissive, not always kind. She always forgave his criticisms and neglect, the way she forgave our mother for hers. These are my words, not Lexie's, you understand, but I think she believed in her heart that one day all the rejection she suffered, the confusion and humiliation would somehow turn into something wonderful and wholesome in a way that would make all that had gone before stop mattering. In other words, she told herself that Mother and David would suddenly start realizing how much she meant to them.'

CRISTY: 'I have to wonder why she went through with her first pregnancy considering how it had come about?'

OLIVIA: 'That's easily answered. First, she was too far along by the time she realized – or would admit it to herself or anyone else – to legally do anything about it. Second, I'm sure she'd have kept it anyway, either because there was a chance it was David's, or simply because she wanted something of her own to love. Probably both, actually. And when Cynthia and Don began putting pressure on David to marry her . . .'

CRISTY: 'Did he admit he was one of the rapists?'

OLIVIA: 'He had to once his mother got on the case. It was impossible to lie to her and Lexie had seen him, had begged him to make it stop, but he hadn't. He'd just put on some hideous robe and mask to take a turn himself.

'So rather than cause the kind of scandal that Lexie probably wouldn't survive in her fragile state, Cynthia took the decision that David had to marry her. It didn't matter to Cynthia then that the baby might not be David's. He needed to make this right – as if anyone ever could. So, if Lexie was willing to have him, he needed to commit to taking care of her, and the child, for the rest of their lives. Otherwise Cynthia would go to the police herself.'

CRISTY: 'Do you think she would have?'

OLIVIA: 'I don't know. It's possible.'

CRISTY: 'So when did David find out that Rosaria was actually his?'

OLIVIA: 'A few weeks after the birth.'

CRISTY: 'And how did he and Lexie take it when they realized the baby had Down's?'

OLIVIA: 'It didn't matter at all to Lexie. She would have loved Rosaria no matter what. The extra chromosome just made her even more special. As for David . . . Well, let's say I never saw him being unkind to her, and just like her mother she adored him. As for our mother, she was an absolute witch at first. Some of the things she said don't bear repeating, they wouldn't even be legal now. But then, to everyone's amazement, I think even her own, she started to connect with the child. As I said, Rosaria was the sweetest, sunniest little girl and impossible not to love.

'Amelia when she came along five years later . . . She was different. Wild, determined, defiant, always in some sort of scrape, a proper tomboy almost as soon as she could walk, but like everyone else she adored Rosaria.

'It was after Amelia's birth that Lexie started to struggle again. She had terrible postnatal depression and it never seemed to end. Some days she couldn't even make herself get out of bed. Cynthia took charge, obviously, because Cynthia would, but she didn't have the girls to live with her. She felt they needed their mother and Lexie needed them, no matter how hard it was for her to deal with things. I think Lexie was glad to know they were close by, in the same house, but sometimes she couldn't bear to have them in her sight. It was awful for them really, never knowing what mood she would be in, if they'd done something to make her feel bad, or sad, or angry. They blamed themselves all the time. Well, Amelia did, and it seemed to make her more rebellious than ever.

'As I've already told you, it wasn't until Lexie started to see Serena that she really began to cope. She'd had other therapists, and spells of being on top, but with Serena it was different. And then with Papilio. Everyone noticed the change in her, especially the children. It had a wonderful effect on Amelia. She settled better at school, made friends more easily and kept them . . . She still had a hot little temper, make no mistake about that, and seemed to delight in doing the opposite to what she'd been asked. But there was a new joy about her, an infectious ring in her laugh, and whenever she stayed with us, my children were happy to have her there. Before they'd been nervous of her, and in awe, I suppose, of how naughty and outspoken she could be. She was older, of course, but as she started to calm down they began looking forward to her visits and all the mischief she managed to cook up while she was there.

'The day she disappeared, she should have been at Cynthia's, where I'd dropped her. Typically, though, because she could never do as she was told, she'd made her way back to Kellon Hall to ride her pony. At least that's what we've always assumed.'

A long gap in the recording followed the breaking of Olivia's voice with only the faint sound of her struggling to control her emotions as Cristy went into the kitchen to find some paper towels. When she finally spoke again she sounded shaky and hoarse.

'It's very hard to think of my niece witnessing what happened to her mother and grandmother . . . That her father . . . I'm sorry, I shouldn't be doing this . . .'

Another minute or so passed before she continued.

'I never dreamt he was capable of hurting the children, I really didn't. I knew how angry he was with Lexie over the money she was giving to Papilio, but it never crossed my mind that he'd stop her like that. And for . . . for Amelia . . . to . . . to see it . . .'

CRISTY: 'Do you know that she did?'

OLIVIA: 'Not really, we've always presumed . . .'

As Cristy listened through the pause she was picturing Olivia at the time, hands pressed to her mouth in a futile effort to stifle the sobs. In the end, Cristy said softly:

CRISTY: 'Does this mean you believe he killed his daughter too?'

230

Cristy could see Olivia nodding, trying to find her voice, until finally she was able to say:

OLIVIA: 'If she'd got out of there she'd have run to Cynthia, but we know she didn't do that, so what else are we to think when we've never seen her again?'

There was another long pause and Cristy was about to tell Connor to stop the playback when Olivia suddenly said:

OLIVIA: 'What else would you like to know? Is there anything else?'

CRISTY: 'If you're sure . . .'

OLIVIA: 'Let's get it over with. What else do you need to ask?'

CRISTY: 'Well, if we could go back to the others who were involved in the rape . . .'

OLIVIA: 'You mean the monsters who should still be behind bars after what they did? Who should never be inflicted on decent society again. Nothing ever changed for them, did it? They were happy for David to be the scapegoat, to deflect all blame away from them so they could carry on at Oxford, a privilege they'd ripped from Lexie. They were free, untarnished by their own actions . . . They've gone on to all the greatness they dreamed of in a way Lexie never could. To look at them now sickens me to my soul. The success they've had, the positions they hold, their families, their wealth . . . But none of it matters because it'll never change who they are. They know what they did, and they know it'll never go away. David knows it too. How else do you think he managed to get his trial stopped? They were afraid he'd go public with what he knows and bring them down with him. That's how much influence they have.'

CRISTY: 'So who are they?'

231

OLIVIA: 'Believe me, you really don't want to know.'

CRISTY: 'How do *you* know?'

OLIVIA: 'Lexie told me, of course, but she swore me to secrecy. Partly to protect David in case they turned on him, but also because she didn't want to cause any trouble. She knew they'd get away with it even if she did report it, and so did Cynthia in her heart. That's why she made her son pay, because someone had to.'

CRISTY: 'Do you know if David continued to have any contact with them after the rape?'

OLIVIA: 'No, I don't, but he might have, considering who they are and what he used to do at Quantrell's. I'm sure he'd have run into them at some point. Maybe he even mixed with them while he was in London. Who knows?'

CRISTY: 'Do you think they could be involved in Papilio?'

OLIVIA: 'I – I don't know anything about their private lives, but it's my understanding that Papilio*'s* followers are mostly rich women, so maybe one of their mothers or wives . . .'

CRISTY: 'We've heard that satanism might have played a role somewhere. Did Lexie ever mention that?'

OLIVIA: 'No, never, but I'm aware there was a lot of gossip after the murders. It's what happens in small communities when something out of the ordinary happens. People make things up and try to find answers they think fit.'

CRISTY: 'But you knew about her branding?'

OLIVIA: 'Actually no, I didn't, until the police told me after. Are you saying it could have been part of something . . . evil? I don't understand how that's possible when the therapy was doing her so much good.'

Signalling for Connor to stop the playback, Cristy drove on quietly for a moment, thinking it all through, until finally she said, 'How convinced were you by her?'

Connor let out an incredulous laugh. Clearly not the question he'd been expecting. 'Well, she's given us quite a bit today that's making a lot of sense, so I'd say fairly convinced. Weren't you?'

Cristy frowned. 'Yes, I was. I just wish she'd revealed some names of the other rapists. Why keep them a secret? Especially after all this time. Doesn't she want them exposed for the monsters they are?'

'At a guess, I'd say she wants to shield her family from the fall-out, if these guys are as powerful as she's suggesting. We could try Fiona Mooney again, see if she'll change her mind about ID-ing them.'

Cristy's frown deepened. 'Maybe, but if you're right about wanting to protect a family from fall-out, she's not likely to talk either. Remember, she said she didn't want to end up with the same sort of thing happening to her. God, who are these people?'

'At risk of pointing out the obvious,' Connor said, 'we really need to talk to David Gaudion, although his brother could be the next best thing.'

'I don't suppose by any miracle we've heard back from him?'

Connor ran a quick check of their messages and shook his head. 'Nothing,' he confirmed.

'OK. See if you can find the bit at the very end when I asked Olivia if she had any idea where David or Cynthia might be now.'

A few moments later it was playing.

OLIVIA: 'I have no idea where he is. I almost wish I did, maybe then the nightmares about him suddenly showing up would stop. I see him sometimes while I'm out and about. It's not him, of course, just someone who looks similar, but it can set me back for days when it happens.'

CRISTY: 'And what about Cynthia?'

OLIVIA: 'Merely thinking about Cynthia makes me sad. She didn't even tell me she was leaving. She just left one night with Rosaria and never got in touch again. I found that very difficult. To think she didn't realize how much it would hurt me to be dropped like that. Or maybe she did realize, she just decided she had to cut all ties in everyone's best interests.'

OLIVIA: 'Do you think she's with David?'

CRISTY: 'I don't know about *with* him, but I'm sure, if she's still alive, she'll know where he is. Richard will too, of course.'

CRISTY: 'Have you ever asked Richard to put you in touch with his mother?'

OLIVIA: 'Back at the start, I did, but he wouldn't, and we don't have any contact now. My husband thought it was best to let it go after my "collapse" and I've never had a reason to disagree with him on that. Plenty of other things, maybe, but never on that.'

CHAPTER TWENTY-ONE

It was just after five by the time Cristy and Connor walked back into the office to find that Clover and Jackson were still busy at their desks.

'So, how did it go?' Clover asked, quickly removing her headphones and sitting back in her chair.

'There's a lot for you to listen to,' Cristy replied, letting her heavy bag sink to the floor. She glanced at David Gaudion's headshot, not expecting it to have changed, obviously, yet for some bizarre reason it surprised her to see it was the same. 'What's concerning me the most,' she said to Connor, turning on her computer, 'is how much of what we've just heard we can actually use.'

'That's on my mind too,' he agreed. 'We can't just weigh in with random accusations of rape, we'll get blown out of the water.'

'You're kidding!' Clover gasped. 'Olivia Caldwell accused Gaudion of raping her?'

'Not her,' Cristy corrected. 'As I said, you need to listen to it, and so do the lawyers.'

Jackson tore off his headset and got to his feet. 'This calls for a raid on Harry's fridge,' he announced. 'Don't start playback without me.'

'Mine's a beer,' Connor called after him.

'Bring wine if there is any,' Cristy added. 'Preferably white.'

'OK,' Clover said, busily tapping her keyboard, 'while we wait, let me fill you in on what's been happening here today.' She looked up to make sure everyone was ready. 'Right, first up, we've spent the past couple of hours putting the next episode together, following the structure you gave us focusing mostly on

Victor Green and Maria del Smet.' She looked up again. 'Does anything from today change it?'

'I don't think so, yet,' Cristy replied.

'Great. My guess is you guys will be fine-tuning what we've done most of the day tomorrow and we're happy to be here as back-up.'

Cristy smiled her gratitude as Connor raised a thumb.

Clover moved on. 'We've had an email back from Will Casson, the documentary producer. Apparently he didn't go ahead with the programme because he was diagnosed with prostate cancer. He's kind of OK now, but he didn't want to return to his old job. Too stressful, he said. I think that means we can rule out any sort of intimidation from quarters unknown. Although he did mention that David Gaudion's lawyer told him it wouldn't be a good idea to pursue the story.'

Cristy wrinkled her nose as she considered that. 'Kind of what you'd expect a lawyer to say, so let's not read anything into it. For now.'

'OK. Next, DSI Rush popped over a message with the name of Paul O'Malley's brief. Ferdinand Yarrow. That's the company, not the man. The guy himself is Lester Blower. I've looked him up and he retired about six years ago, so I dropped a line to the current managing partner, Charlie Blower, who I'm guessing is a whisper off the old windbag.'

Connor and Cristy laughed, and Clover took a bow.

'What did you say to him?' Connor asked, lifting his feet onto an open desk drawer.

'I explained who we are and that we'd like to talk to him, or someone at his firm, about Paolo Morelli. I thought it might get me a bit further if I used O'Malley's stage name. No answer yet, obvs, with it being Saturday.'

Cristy turned to Connor, her eyes narrowed thoughtfully. 'Did you get the impression Olivia Caldwell knew more than she told us about Papilio? As in, maybe she also belonged?'

He blinked in astonishment. 'Got to admit, it never crossed my mind.'

'No, nor mine, at the time, but now I'm thinking about it, she kind of talked it up, didn't she? Or she didn't have anything bad to say about it in spite of her sister's branding and all the money Lexie handed over.' She shrugged. 'Not sure where I'm going with that, but thought I'd put it out there. Ah, Jacks, you found wine!'

'And beer and snacks,' Jackson confirmed, dropping his burden of bottles and packets next to the coffee machine. 'Harry's there, by the way, said to go back for more if we need it.'

'Harry working at the weekend!' Connor exclaimed, sitting up straight again. 'Whatever next? Thanks, mate,' as Jackson flipped the top from a beer and handed it to him.

Clover went to uncork the wine while Cristy answered her mobile without checking who it was first.

'Hello, Cristy? It's Jess, Matthew's mother.'

Annoyed with herself for picking up, and with her mother-in-law for such a stupid opener, Cristy said, 'I know who you are, Jess. What can I do for you?'

'I'm fine, thanks. I hope you are too.'

'I'm good. I hear you're moving to a retirement village.'

'That's right. It's a lovely place, not far from here, actually, so no excuse for my family not to visit, although I expect to be quite busy with all the activities they have on offer. But that's not why I'm ringing. I want to know why you won't speak to my son.'

Cristy pulled back from the phone in disbelief. '*What?*'

'He called you and left a message earlier today, but you still haven't got back to him. Don't you have an arrangement to meet him later?'

Wondering if this woman would ever stop irritating her, Cristy said, 'It was mentioned, provided I wasn't working, but I am, so I'm afraid . . . Why isn't he making this call himself?'

'Because I'm making it. He needs to speak to you and I think you should make yourself available.'

'Well, thank you for your thoughts, Jess. I'll bear them in mind. Now, if it's all the same to you I'm in the middle of something. Good luck with the move when it happens,' and before the interfering old bag could say any more, she rang off.

'Sounds like you might need this,' Clover remarked dryly, passing over a large glass of wine.

'I did before,' Cristy muttered. 'I definitely do now.' She took a sip, closed her eyes as the pleasure of the taste swirled into her senses, and then was able to say, quite brightly, 'So what else have you guys achieved today?'

'Tons regarding music and sound effects for the next episode,' Clover replied, returning to her desk. 'That was my job alongside Jacks getting his head stuck into the first draft edit. Believe it or not, we're a great team. Oh, I managed to contact Berkeley Town Council – we're clearly not the only Saturday workers around here – and I was put through to someone who told me there had been a pine marten sighting in Seedown Woods and that's why it's fenced off. So that's the official line. Jacks and I are planning to head up there on Monday to see if any of the locals might have a different story to tell.'

'Like about voodoo ceremonies or zombie conversions,' Jackson said spookily.

Cristy smiled and drank more wine. 'OK, if Connor's ready, we ought to make a start on Olivia's interview . . . But before we go there, no more "Iris emails" or calls from the woman who's insisting Amelia is dead?'

'Not as of four-thirty,' Clover replied. 'I haven't run a check since then.'

'OK, well don't do it now. We need your take on this interview. Jacks, have you managed to track down either of Cynthia Gaudion's brothers yet?'

'Still working on it,' he replied. 'Hoping to have something by Monday or Tuesday. I'm guessing you'll want to make contact yourself if I come up with any possibles?'

Cristy nodded. 'OK, while you lot are listening to the playback I'm going outside to make a quick call.'

By the time she reached the door with her phone and wine glass, Olivia's voice was already filling the room. It was tempting to stay to take it all in again, but she had quite a bit fixed in her head and if need be, she could always play it back to herself later.

Matthew answered on the third ring. 'Hey!' he said brightly. 'I was starting to think—'

'Is your mother really still making phone calls for you?' she snapped. 'What are you, six?'

Laughing, he said, 'I'm not sure what you're talking about, but I think I can guess and I'm sorry if she rattled you—'

'She always rattles me. So why did she feel it was the right thing to do to call me up on your behalf to—'

'It wasn't on my behalf. I had no idea she was going to do it.'

'But you must have said something to trigger her.'

'Only that I was hoping to see you later, but you hadn't got back to me yet. So can you? See me?'

'No, and if this is about you being at a loose end because Marley's away for the weekend, you know what you can do with that loose end.'

'Actually, it's not about that, but if you're busy—'

'I am. If you're not I'm sure Aiden's around – where is he, by the way?'

'In the den with a couple of mates on the PlayStation.'

'Good. Is he showing any nerves about his end of year results yet?'

'What, our super-chilled superhero? He doesn't know what it is to be nervous.'

'That's what he wants you to think . . .'

'He's relaxed, because he's done brilliantly, the way he always does.'

It was true, Aiden unfailingly achieved high grades without ever seeming to try. 'So call Hayley, see if she and Hugo are free . . . Where are all your friends?'

'It's you I want to see. So when can you make it?'

'I don't know. There's a lot going on at the moment. I'll call you.'

'Except we know you won't.'

Not bothering to answer that, she said, 'I'm ringing off now and if your mother's upset that I won't see you, go have a chat with her instead.'

It was gone eight o'clock by the time they decided to call it a day. Connor had already forwarded the recording to Meena and Harry so they could weigh in with their thoughts before it was sent to the lawyers on Monday.

'Obviously there's a lot we *can* use,' Cristy said, switching off her computer and going to put her empty wine glass on the coffee bar. 'I'll mark it up over the next couple of days, but it definitely won't make Tuesday's episode. We'll tease it at the end, naturally, but it needs an airing of its own. The point is, we definitely won't be able to use anything about the rape.'

'Shame,' Jackson commented, 'because it's dynamite stuff. And you never know, the legals might come back with a green light for some of it.'

'Meantime, we have a cracking episode for Tuesday,' Clover reminded them, 'which we need to get back to tomorrow. See you all about ten?'

'Sounds good to me,' Jackson responded.

'Works for me too,' Connor said, patting his pockets in search of his keys.

'I picked you up earlier,' Cristy reminded him. 'I can drop you back . . .'

'I'm going your way,' Jackson said, stretching out his wiry frame.

'Can you take me too?' Clover asked. 'I've got a mate's birthday do somewhere in Southville. I'll find the address.'

After they'd gone Cristy lingered for a while, scanning the whiteboards again as she mulled everything she'd heard about David Gaudion to date. There were so many contradictions and ambiguities, personal biases and possible faulty recollections, that even Olivia's first-hand knowledge of it all seemed opaque in its way. Dutiful son, childhood friend, teenage tyrant of Lexie, ambitious student, powerful lobbyist, loving father, impatient husband, rapist, killer . . .

He was watching her again; she could feel those penetrating blue eyes absorbing her every move, the pleasant half-smile seeming a mocking reaction to what he'd heard here this evening.

It made her shiver and want to look away, but she didn't. She'd interviewed enough detectives in her time to know that it wasn't unusual to feel haunted, even stalked by a killer who was proving elusive. It was a trick of her own psyche making her think he was close by, in tune with her thoughts, maybe even laughing at her attempts to reach him. *It'll never happen unless I want it to,* he seemed to be saying, but that too was all in her mind.

Her eyes moved to Lexie's lovely elfin face and she felt a swell of sadness for all the poor woman had suffered in her short life.

So vulnerable and insecure, so needy, lonely and desperate to be loved. How utterly, unbearably tragic that her life had ended when, and how it did.

The others, Margaret and Serena, had always been considered collateral damage in Gaudion's plan to stop his wife giving away their money, and so far Cristy had heard nothing to contradict it. Except he'd known they were going to be there that day because he'd told Olivia, so collateral damage or not, the killings surely had to have been premeditated. Maybe he'd decided to stop any more of the Sallis estate finding its way to the cult. It might not have been his inheritance, but it was his daughters'. He wouldn't want it going to a charlatan who claimed miraculous healing skills and charged fortunes for them, no matter how improved Lexie had seemed by them. Had he even cared that Lexie was making progress?

Although none of this was feeling quite right, it didn't feel exactly wrong either.

She turned her attention to the pretty, lively features of Amelia Gaudion and felt a surge of pity for the terror she must have experienced that day – if she had witnessed the killings, and the general consensus was that she had. Why else would she have disappeared? Ten years old and the life she'd always known had come to such a shocking and violent end that she would surely never be the same again. It was heartbreaking to know that no one had ever found out where she'd been taken. What had her last minutes, hours, days been like? Had she known what was going to happen to her?

What *had* happened to her?

She went back to Gaudion and asked him, in her mind, if he really had killed his own daughter. 'Could you actually have done that?' she whispered aloud. 'Are you really that callous? That evil? Had you already worked it all out in your mind, right down to how you were going to escape trial if it should ever get that far? Or did that come later? Did you make contact with your fellow rapists and threaten to take them down if they refused to help you?

'Who are they? How well do you know them now? Are they men we see every day in roles that influence our lives? Men whose real personas are hidden from plain sight by some kind of exclusive chumocracy? Wealthy and powerful individuals bound by rites and rituals, ceremonies and sworn allegiances. Is it them you're hiding from? Or are they still protecting you?

'Maybe *they'd* had Lexie killed, after you'd warned them she was about to – or already had – confided in her master at Papilio.'

Enforcers, she thought to herself. That was what they were called, the minions who acted on behalf of people in power. It was they who carried out the dirty work in a way to make certain nothing ever got back to those who'd ordered it.

Enforcers: also known as hit men, eliminators, executioners.

On her way home she felt glad she was driving along Cumberland Road rather than walking beside the water, in spite of the Saturday night explosion of activity crowding the Harbourside. She didn't have a sense of being followed, but she had before and she didn't want the feeling again.

When she got home she put in a call to DSI Rush and talked the detective through what she'd learned from Olivia that day, and how her mind was working now.

When she'd finished Rush said, 'If you're right about any of it, then you need to be careful. The kind of people she was alluding to aren't to be messed with, and you know the force is riddled with them.'

'As is the judicial system,' Cristy replied.

'Exactly.'

'So is that what we're dealing with? Some sort of masonic allegiance?'

'It's always possible.'

Taking the conversation back to Olivia's worst allegations, Cristy said, 'So you didn't know about the rape?'

'I didn't, and I'm fairly certain that no one at my lowly level back then did either. Obviously, I can't speak for them upstairs. Do you know why Olivia hasn't come forward about it before? Why she failed to say anything at the time?'

'Because she knows who they are and what they're capable of.'

'Then why is she breaking her silence now?'

'Perhaps something's happened to change her mind about

speaking out. A lot can happen in sixteen years. Maybe this is her first step towards gaining some sort of justice for her mother and sister.'

'But she won't tell you who the rapists were.'

'She's exposed Gaudion – at least to me. I strongly doubt we can use it, but in her mind she's finally broken her silence, and I have a strong feeling that this is just the beginning of a journey she's needed to take for a very long time.'

CHAPTER TWENTY-TWO

On Tuesday evening the team, including Meena and Harry, were gathered as usual for drinks to mark the drop of another episode. Jodi was also with them, and was currently topping up everyone's wine glass as they listened to the interview Jackson and Clover had recorded with Iris Newman's fiancé, Joe Mead. They'd decided to open with this as Mead spoke eloquently about the failure to find the hit-and-run driver who'd killed Iris. It got Iris back into listeners' minds, especially when he talked about her attempts to start a podcast covering the Kellon Manse Murders. His interview ended as if he were speaking directly to Paolo Morelli and Miranda Ritchie.

JOE MEAD: 'If either of you, or Mr Morelli's lawyer, Lester Blower, know anything that could help us find out more about Iris's accident, please get in touch with me. Or with Cristy and Connor who are running this podcast.'

Next came Maria del Smet admitting to an affair with David Gaudion, and her second-hand insights into Lexie Gaudion's mental health. This interview was intercut with comments from Cristy and Connor wondering whether or not someone was feeding Maria del Smet her lines, and could that person have been David Gaudion himself?

CONNOR: 'What I also found curious – didn't you? – was how keen Gaudion's employer at Quantrell's was, when we spoke to him, to sound supportive of an ex-employee who'd been charged with the murder of three women, no less – and who, as far as anyone knows, was involved in the disappearance of his own daughter.'

CRISTY: 'Yes, I certainly found that interesting. Such loyalty from a boss after all these years made me wonder if David Gaudion might have something on one or more of his ex-colleagues they'd rather wasn't revealed. But maybe I just have a suspicious mind.'

CONNOR: 'It's true, you do, but it's definitely a question I'm asking myself. Maybe one of our listeners will have something to say about it that we'd like to hear.'

Moving on from that, Cristy delivered a precis of Fiona Mooney's call advising them to look more closely into the reason why Lexie had left Oxford. (They'd decided not to mention Olivia and her corroboration of events at this stage.)

CRISTY: 'The person who contacted us about the long-ago incident at Oxford has asked to remain anonymous, and of course we respect that. I'd like to be able to tell you about this person's shocking suspicions, but for the moment everything is in the hands of lawyers. We will, of course, bring you more as soon as we have clearance.'

After space for a short ad break, they introduced Sir Victor Green's interview and his belief that the police had had enough evidence to convict Gaudion. The ex-Chief Constable's claim that Gaudion had friends in high places who could have been involved in pulling the trial was included, as was his assertion that he was not one of them. They finished with Green's chilling words about whether or not Gaudion might have killed his own daughter:

VICTOR GREEN: 'It's hard to see what else happened to her. Worse things have been done to try and cover up a crime.'

Finally Cristy delivered the closing link.

CRISTY: 'I hope what we've presented you with in this episode, from the disturbing mystery of what happened to Iris Newman to the revelation of David Gaudion's long-time affair with Maria del Smet, something the police either missed or overlooked at the time of the original investigation, along with his old boss's high praise of a man most believe killed four people; right through to Sir Victor Green's extraordinary words, "Worse things have been done to try to cover up a crime", have proved how determined we are to bring you the inside story of the Kellon Manse Murders. There's clearly still a lot to uncover, but rest assured we are on the case, and if you'd like to hear more than we've included today, please go to our website where you'll find a lot of additional material regarding the butterfly cult, Papilio, and its elusive head of operations Paolo Morelli, aka Paul O'Malley. You can also catch up with what some of the Berkeley Vale residents had to say about Seedown Woods and satanic rituals. It's worth a listen, I promise.

'Now for next week's episode . . . It's shaping up to be truly sensational as we've finally interviewed Lexie Gaudion's older sister, Olivia Caldwell. What she has to say is fascinating on many levels, but there is something in particular that could blow everything wide open if we're given the all-clear to use it. It's currently with our lawyers, but we're hoping to share it by the next time we go to air. So get ready to learn things about this case, and about David Gaudion, that even the police didn't know until now.

'You have been listening to a *Hindsight* original podcast. I'd like to thank our sponsors . . .'

Connor stopped the recording and the room fell into a silence that no one hurried to break. It was as if they were already bracing for some sort of backlash, in spite of it being far too early for anyone even to have heard the pod yet, never mind to respond to it.

Harry was the first to speak. 'That was one powerful gauntlet you just threw down at the end,' he declared, looking between Cristy and Connor. 'Prepare to hear from Gaudion's lawyer. He'll want to know more about the Olivia Caldwell interview before it drops, you can bet your life on it.'

'Whether we agree to that or not,' Meena added, 'is a matter for our lawyers who, by the way, know we're keen for answers by the end of the week.'

Cristy picked up her wine. 'I just hope this doesn't send Olivia running for the hills. Or she doesn't get her own lawyer to try and rescind. We're going to have some serious egg on our faces if she does.'

'Just a quick aside,' Jodi said, rubbing a hand over the increasing mound of her belly, 'what did the locals say about the woods and diabolical practices?'

'Clover and I did the vox pops for that,' Jackson told her, 'and to be honest there wasn't anything particularly interesting or usable, which is why it's gone straight to the website.'

'Most of them spun us the pine marten line,' Clover continued, 'and for all we know it's true. The one we liked best, though, was from a couple of doggers who claimed they'd seen ghostly figures, like the Ku Klux Klan, floating in and out of the trees during full moons.'

'How do you know they were doggers?' Harry demanded.

'Because they told us. It's apparently why they were up that way when they had the sighting, which is obviously bollocks, unless they were in tractors or flying saucers.'

'Sounds like someone was having fun at your expense,' Cristy laughed, and immediately groaned as she saw who'd just texted her.

'Someone threatening us already?' Clover cried, rubbing her hands ready for action.

Rolling her eyes, Cristy said, 'It's Matthew's current wife.' She knew that wouldn't be lost on the people in this room, and it wasn't. 'Apparently, she's just about to run a bath and light some candles to make herself comfortable while she listens to the next episode of what she calls, KMM. This really is not an image I want in my head.'

'Why does she even want you to know?' Jodi protested. 'That is so weird.'

'Tell me about it,' Cristy sighed. 'This morning she sent me a list of her favourite podcasts that she thinks I might be interested in and if so maybe we could get together and discuss.'

'Beyond weird,' Clover confirmed.

'Maybe she's starting a podcast club,' Jackson suggested. 'You know, like a book club. What a coup for her if she managed to get you on board.'

'Never going to happen,' Cristy assured him, and putting her phone aside, she changed the subject. 'What I can't wait to find out,' she said, 'is how many cages we might have rattled tonight.'

Jodi was looking worried. 'If you're right about some sort of masonic involvement, then I'm concerned about the position you guys might be in now.'

'I think going public like this is a security of its own,' Connor reassured her, 'makes us kind of untouchable, or at least puts some kind of wall around us. But we're definitely expecting serious pushback in the next few days. It'll be interesting to see where, or who, it comes from first.'

It was the following afternoon while Cristy and Connor were at the lawyers' offices on Queen's Square, that they received a voicemail, forwarded by Clover with a covering message, telling them to listen to it NOW! *Not sure how on the level this is, but I reckon it's serious.*

Excusing themselves, they went outside and crossed onto the cobbles between the handsome Georgian buildings and tree-lined grassy quadrants to listen, in growing astonishment and alarm, to a hoarse male voice tinged with a cockney accent saying:

'I know who killed those women because I was there. I can tell you all about David Gaudion's involvement. I've got photos of the scene that even the police haven't seen. If you make it worth my while they can be yours. Here's a couple to be going on with. Call me on this number when you're ready to talk.'

Cristy quickly opened the attachment and almost immediately wished she hadn't.

'Holy fuck,' Connor muttered as they registered the ghastly close-up of Lexie Gaudion with half her face missing. The second shot showed three blood-soaked bodies in the exact positions the police photographer had also recorded them. The third showed the reflection of a masked man in the large, rococo mirror over the fireplace, using a phone to capture the scene.

Before either of them could say any more, another voicemail turned up from Clover, 'from the same source', she told them.

'Go to the police if you like, makes no odds to me, but remember it won't make anyone any less dead than they already are, and you will lose your exclusive.'

Cristy looked around the square where joggers, cyclists, scooter riders and dog walkers were going about their day. In a perverse switch of perspective, the normality around them seemed almost surreal in the light of these messages.

'I think all this needs to go to the police, don't you?' she said.

Connor shrugged. 'Eventually, but maybe let's find out if it's real first.'

'I don't think we can be in much doubt of that. You only have to look at them, and that figure in the mirror . . . Can something like that be faked?'

'I've no idea, but I'm sure Jacks is already on it.'

Cristy's instincts were striking all sorts of ominous notes. 'If it is real,' she said, 'then it's either the masked man who's just made contact, i.e. the killer, or it's someone who has come by these shots another way and wants paying for them. What do you think?'

Connor stared at her as he considered the question.

Cristy almost flinched as a new suspicion landed a blow. 'That voice, the person in the mirror . . . Could it have been David Gaudion?'

Connor balked. 'I can't see it,' he said. 'I mean, there's no knowing who it was in the mask, but why the hell would Gaudion send us this stuff? What would be in it for him?'

Having no answer for that, Cristy said, 'If it's not him, it has to be a hitman. Isn't that the kind of thing they do, take photos of their work to show it's been carried out?'

Connor nodded. 'So was he hired by Gaudion? That's what he seems to be implying.'

'Yes, it seems likely,' Cristy agreed. 'Obviously he's after money, he said as much, but he surely has to know it won't be as simple as us handing over a wad of cash and him going on his way.'

'Although he doesn't seem bothered about us going to the police, if what he said in his second message is to be believed.'

Shaking her head, Cristy said, 'We need to involve Harry and/or Meena in this. They, and the lawyers, need to assess it, because we sure as hell don't want to end up being charged for withholding evidence. If it even is evidence. You need to call Jacks to make sure he's trying to authenticate the shots.'

An hour later, after Harry and the lawyers had heard the messages and looked at the photo attachments in detail, a decision was made that they'd sit on everything while Jacks did his thing with authenticity. If it turned out the shots were real, they'd pass them to the police. If there was any doubt, they'd wait to see if the 'killer' called again.

By the following evening, Thursday, they'd received thousands of responses to episode three, including the predicted email from Gaudion's lawyer requesting details of Olivia's 'claims' and threatening action if they aired anything defamatory regarding their client. Cristy immediately contacted Connor who was working at home, Jodi having had a scare last night. They agreed right away to request an interview with Gaudion or his brother. They didn't, and wouldn't, reveal that they had been advised to omit any mention of rape at this stage. Let Edmond Crouch and his client stew.

The most surprising contact that day came from Paul O'Malley in the form of a short video fronted by the man himself. He looked relaxed and tanned and decidedly undevilish with large, brown, slowly blinking eyes framed by rimless specs, close-cut silver hair, goatee beard and sticky-out ears. Nothing to indicate where he was, and no sign of a butterfly either. It was just him in an open-neck blue shirt in front of a plain white background delivering his message in a quiet and melodic voice.

> O'MALLEY: 'Ms Ward and Mr Church, I am asking you kindly, and in person, to refrain from referring to Papilio as a cult. It is, in fact, a fully accredited order of holistic healing. Our counsellors' goal is to guide those who require assistance to a higher level of self-recognition and spiritual awareness. I must stress that we are not a secret organization, merely a private practice adhering to very strict codes of integrity, health and confidentiality.
>
> 'If you are desirous of a meeting with one of our practitioners, or a client, I'm sure it can be arranged. Or, Ms Ward, as most of our services are geared towards women who've been troubled by life's wayward and sometimes difficult challenges, particularly those around the break-up of a marriage, please let me extend the hand of friendship and welcome should you wish to join us and avail yourself of our services.'

'The nerve of him,' Cristy cried, 'mentioning my private life – and as if I could afford his butterfly package of betterment and branding even if I wanted it, which I don't. Anyway, this little movie of his might mean something if he'd told us how to contact him.'

'It was sent from a Hotmail address,' Clover announced. 'Could be as simple as hitting return.' She did it, and got ready to type in a message.

'Tell him we'd prefer to interview him, in person,' Cristy said, 'but if it has to be a practitioner or a client we'll await their details.'

'Iris was contacted by a client,' Jacks reminded them darkly.

Scowling at him, Cristy said, 'Send it to Connor, get his thoughts on it. The use of the word "order" intrigues me with its undertones of religion and discipline.'

'Anyone heard how Jodi's doing?' Clover asked as she whisked the video over to Connor's private email account.

'She's home again,' Cristy replied. 'Nothing to worry about, thankfully, but she has to take it easy for a few days. Jacks, how are you getting on with the crime scene photos?'

He pulled a face. 'They seem genuine enough to me, but can I tell you one hundred percent that they are?' He shook his head. 'If I could send them to a mate of mine, he'd be all over it, but I get that they can't be shared.'

Sighing, Cristy checked the podcast voicemailbox again, in case another message had turned up from the 'man-in-the-mirror', as they were now calling him, in the last few minutes.

Still nothing, but at least a dozen more destined for the trash.

She checked the social media outlets and found it astonishing, actually sickening, to read what some people felt they should share with the wider public: accusations of paedophilia against Victor Green; offers to do things to Maria del Smet no normal person would even think of never mind say out loud; and the trolling of Olivia Gaudion that was already starting to gain some momentum, though heaven only knew why, when no one even knew what she had to say yet. Added to that was all the nastiness levelled at her, Cristy, or Connor – just thank God for honest-to-goodness fan mail.

It was, in fact, Olivia who was causing Cristy the most concern right now, for two whole days had passed since the podcast had dropped and Cristy still hadn't been able to make contact with her. Was she regretting the interview, trying to figure out the best way to backtrack? Maybe someone had got to her, warned her to keep her mouth shut from here on?

Her silence felt odd, ominous even, if Cristy thought about it too deeply.

Realizing Clover was talking to her, she looked up from her laptop.

'. . . so Connor's saying we should put O'Malley's video on the website and use the soundtrack where appropriate in a future episode.'

Cristy nodded agreement. 'Is Jodi OK?'

Clover put the call on speaker and repeated the question.

'I'm good,' Jodi shouted out. 'Just a bit scary in the night when I started having pains. Apparently it's cool, a bit of indigestion and maybe I'm overdoing things. I just need to take it easy for a while and stop worrying, but try telling that to Connor.'

'Try making her relax,' Connor retorted.

Smiling, Cristy said, 'You both need to chill. I'll send my son over for some instruction if you like, he has it down to an art.'

Jodi laughed. 'He's always welcome here. So what's new with you guys?'

'Still can't get hold of Olivia,' Cristy replied, hoping Connor might have a suggestion on how to rectify that, while knowing he wouldn't. 'And obviously no take-up from Gaudion's lawyer regarding an interview,' she added.

'How about the "man-in-the-mirror"?' Connor asked.

'Nothing so far today,' Clover replied, 'and we're checking regularly.'

'And the phone tracker's still turned off, so no idea where he is,' Jackson weighed in.

'OK, I reckon if we don't hear anything by end of play tomorrow,' Connor said, 'we should at least consider calling him.'

'I'll email the lawyers,' Cristy responded, 'see what they advise, but in principle I agree.' Noticing the time at the top corner of her desktop, her heart sank. 'Sorry, guys. I'm meeting someone at six so I need to cut this short.'

'Sounds intriguing,' Jodi teased. 'Hot date?'

Cristy's laugh was mirthless. 'Hardly. I've run out of excuses not to see Matthew who apparently has something he needs to discuss with me. So, I've agreed to let him come to my place this evening, provided nothing urgent comes up beforehand. Which means,' she added, looking pointedly at Clover and Jacks, 'you need to come up with something.'

They regarded her helplessly.

'OK,' she sighed, 'but if a call does come in from the "man-in-the-mirror", you're to let me know right away. Same goes for Olivia Caldwell, although she has my personal number so I'd be more likely to hear from her on that. Will we see you tomorrow, Connor?'

'Yes,' Jodi answered.

'Provided we have a good night,' he said over her.

'We need to start finalizing Olivia's interview,' Cristy reminded him, 'but do it from home if you need to. We can always connect remotely. Let's just hope we don't get slapped with something horrible from her lawyer in the meantime trying to pull everything back.'

CHAPTER TWENTY-THREE

An hour later Cristy was grudgingly passing Matthew a gin and tonic, not wanting him to get too comfortable, sitting there on her sofa, looking for all the world as if he thought he belonged there. He didn't, although he used to, back in the day, when they'd used the flat from time to time. It had been a 'romantic escape' from all the hecticness of their home, somewhere they could be together, just the two of them.

Annoyed with her memory for coughing that up now, she went to open the French doors, letting in the headiness of damp, fragrant air; the music she'd been listening to when he'd arrived had been killed before she'd opened the door.

'You seem a bit . . . edgy?' he commented as she checked her phone while settling into the opposite sofa with her own drink. With a teasing laugh he added, 'Don't tell me I make you nervous. That would be taking us back to old times, first dates and all that.'

Trying not to grit her teeth, she said, 'You say the stupidest things sometimes, I hope you realize that.'

He grinned and she felt more irritated than ever. 'Come on, what is it?' he coaxed. 'Something's eating you. Maybe I can help.'

'You can't.'

'How do you know if you don't try?'

Resisting the urge to flatten him with a crushing put-down, she said, 'Jodi had a bit of a scare last night.'

His eyes widened in concern.

'She's OK now,' she added, 'but they told her she's probably overdoing things, which brings me neatly on to your decision to televise some of her podcasts. Have you met with her about it yet?'

'Last week. I'm surprised she didn't tell you.'

Surprised, too, although she'd been consumed with her own podcast and it wouldn't be like Jodi to make anything about her – unless Jodi had mentioned it and it had somehow passed her by. She seriously hoped *that* wasn't the case. 'So, is it going to happen?' she asked.

'Sure it is. The contract's being drawn up as we speak. No start date yet, I told her we're happy to work around her. We remember only too well how having kids can change the best laid plans, don't we, so I want to give her an out if she needs one.'

Disliking the reminder of their own early parenthood, Cristy said, 'I'm glad you at least made the offer. If she does take it up she'll bring some much-needed light-heartedness to the bulletins.'

'Indeed she will, and don't think I've forgotten it was your idea. Funny how they always come so easily to you.'

Slanting him a look, she was about to change the subject when he said, 'I'm enjoying the podcasts. I imagine you're getting a lot of positive feedback, and I'm keen to hear what the sister has to say. Don't worry, I'm not asking for the inside story, but I guess you've contacted the studios for footage from the time of the murders. I know we covered it . . .'

'Thanks, and yes, I've been in touch with Sandra, in the library. She was extremely helpful, which you'd know if you'd visited the website.'

Acting stung, he said, 'Well, if you need any more, just let me know.'

Moving past yet another urge to bring him down a few pegs, in spite of his friendliness, she said, 'Is that why you're here? To interfere in my podcasts?'

He gave a laugh of surprise as he held up a hand in peace. 'Not at all,' he promised.

'Then shall we get to the point of what this is all about?'

His eyes went down as he took a sip of his drink, and to her confusion, when he looked up again he seemed oddly less sure of himself, as though he might be working up to breaking something she wouldn't want to hear. He had form on that with their marriage, and his new baby. Well, at least he couldn't do

256

that again, so that only left the children. 'Is Aiden OK?' she asked snappishly.

Seeming baffled by her tone, he said, 'Yes. Of course. Why wouldn't he be?'

'I don't know. Have you heard from Hayley since she got to Oslo?'

'A couple of times. I know she's been in touch with you, because she's told me, and I guess you must be missing her. She said you guys had a great time hanging out together, even though you were working most of the time.'

If that was a criticism it didn't actually sound like one, so she let it go.

'Hugo seems like a good guy, don't you think?' he remarked.

'Yes, I do, but what's most important is that she does. Matthew, I have a lot to do, so will you please tell me why you're here.'

'OK, OK, I just . . . I guess you know that Aiden's going to Spain with Josh and his family at the end of next week?'

'Of course I do.'

'Then he's coming to join us in France for the rest of the month. I haven't sorted his flights yet, but I will. Uh, Hayley and Hugo are talking about coming for a week, which will be great—'

'For God's sake, Matthew, you're not here to invite me too, are you? Because if you are—'

'No! I mean, you'd be very welcome, of course, and I know how much you love Provence—'

'Stop,' she seethed as angered by the reminder of her favourite holidays as she was by the fact that he and Marley had, by the sound of it, chosen to go to the same place. Of all the beautiful villages in the world, were they really going to spend an entire month in Lourmarin? Was it Lourmarin? She didn't know and couldn't bear to ask; why would she want any more of her precious memories crushed by this new reality? 'Whose idea was it to go to Provence?' she asked, more tightly than she'd intended.

'Uh, I'm not sure. Marley's, I think. She saw some photographs of us from a few years—'

'There's something wrong with that girl,' Cristy blurted angrily. 'It's not normal the way she carries on, or tries to carry on with me, as if she's trying to live my life, which of course she is. And you're just as bad, making up to my friends, calling me all the time . . . What is going on with you, Matthew? Please don't tell me she sent you here this evening to try and persuade me—'

'She doesn't know I'm here, so calm down.'

She stared at him, wishing she could take back what she'd said about Marley, not because she hadn't meant it – she really did think something was odd about her – but because she'd allowed him to see that he was getting to her.

She watched as he got up to go and refresh his drink. 'You?' he offered, holding up the bottle.

'No thanks. And you shouldn't be doing that. This isn't your home. You're not the host, you're a guest and an uninvited one at that.'

For some reason this seemed to amuse him, so to stop herself sniping at him again, she turned to look out at the garden. She only turned back when she realized he'd had the gall to come and sit on her sofa. 'What are you doing?' she protested, putting more distance between them.

'I want to tell you why I'm here,' he said, 'and to be honest, I'm not finding it easy. Nothing to do with you . . . I mean, obviously it has everything to do with you or I wouldn't . . . What I'm saying is . . . Oh God,' he groaned, pressing his fingers to his eyes. 'The truth is, I've screwed up badly, Cris, and I don't know how the hell to put it right again.'

Confused, she said, 'Has something happened at work?'

He shook his head and glanced at her, before saying, 'It's . . . Marley. I . . .' He took a breath and blew it out slowly. 'I've made a terrible mistake,' he said hoarsely. 'I wish to God I could turn back the clock, could have seen then what is staring me in the face now. Was always staring me in the face, if only I'd opened my goddamned eyes. I love you, Cristy, I've only ever loved you and I can't bear the thought of us not spending the rest of our lives together, the way we were always meant to.'

She stared at him in disbelief, so stunned, so outraged even, that she could find no words.

'Marley is a sweet person,' he continued, 'she has so many qualities and I don't want to hurt her . . .'

Cristy shot to her feet. 'It's time for you to go,' she growled,

258

pointing at the door, 'before one of us says something we deeply regret, and I have a feeling it will be me.'

His eyes, as he gazed up at her, were so like Aiden's at his most guileless that she had to look away. 'Because you're going to turn me down and in your heart you don't want to?' he asked, seeming to mean it.

'No!' she cried. 'Because this is insane! You married her, Matthew, she's *pregnant*, for God's sake. She's carrying *your* child. You surely don't think you can just walk away from that. And what the hell happened to you being soul mates, meant for one another? *I'm sorry, Cristy, I didn't realize there could be more than one, and I can't give her up.'*

Flinching miserably, he said, 'I got it wrong, horribly wrong. I was . . . infatuated, in a mid-life crisis—'

'Oh, you're not falling back on that old chestnut, are you?' she broke in scathingly. 'Well, I don't care what kind of crisis you were in then, or now. You ruined our lives, Matthew. You threw yourself into an affair that would never even have happened if you had some moral decency about you. But you don't, and you sitting here like this, now, completely proves it. Jesus Christ!' she seethed, turning away in fury.

'Cristy, listen, please—'

'There's no going back,' she shouted over him. 'Surely to God you realize that. You didn't just betray and humiliate me, you destroyed our family, and I'll *never* be able to forgive you for that. We can't pretend none of it happened, go back to the way we were as if Marley and her baby don't exist . . .'

'That's not what I'm saying.'

'Then what are you saying? How the hell do you think I'm going to repair this for you, Matthew, when you don't even know how to do it yourself? And even if I wanted to help you, and I *don't*, the last thing I want is to put her through what you did to me. You can leave now.'

'Cristy—'

'Go,' she raged. 'Get out of here and don't even think about coming back. You're a weak, spineless, despicable man. And there you have it, me saying something I might regret, and yet I don't actually think I will.'

He put his glass down and rose to his feet. 'I deserve it,' he told her quietly. 'And a lot worse, because I know you're right, there isn't any going back; I've hurt too many people already, and I truly don't want to hurt her. But none of it changes the fact that I love you, I want to be with you and I always will.'

She turned away, hands covering her face as she fought down tears of fury and frustration. And regret and longing and such a soul-crushing need for her old life, her real life, that she didn't trust herself to speak or look at him again.

He tried to take her by the shoulders, but she snatched herself free. 'Do as I said,' she choked, not looking at him. 'Go now, and don't come back.'

'Cristy—'

'*Now!*' she seethed, somehow managing not to slap him.

Moments later, she heard the door close behind him, and sank back down onto the sofa, reaching for her drink. Her phone was ringing but she ignored it. She hardly knew what to do, or think, or even how to feel. This had thrown her so completely that she was in no fit state to answer whoever was trying to get hold of her, except if it was Olivia . . . Or something had happened to Jodi . . .

Reaching for her phone, she checked the screen, and a bolt of shock went through her. It was a call she absolutely had to take, regardless of her chaotic emotions.

Clicking on, she cleared her throat as she said, 'Cristy Ward.'

The voice at the other end said, 'Ms Ward. It's Richard Gaudion. My mother, Cynthia, would like to meet to you.'

CHAPTER TWENTY-FOUR

'Well, that's my thunder stolen,' Jackson exclaimed the following morning when Cristy broke the news of Cynthia Gaudion wanting to meet her. 'I've just found out where one of her brothers lives on Exmoor. *And* he's still alive.'

'Seems she is too,' Clover interjected dryly.

'So, have you rung her yet?' Connor asked.

'Apparently, she's expecting my call later today,' Cristy replied, peeling off her jacket. 'My instruction is to ring the number I've been given after five p.m. and his mother will answer.'

'Wow, bit James Bond,' Clover murmured. 'Did he say where she is?'

'No, but I guess she'll tell me herself when we speak. Or she'll want to meet somewhere.'

'Is Richard Gaudion going to be there?' Jackson wanted to know.

'No idea. He didn't say he would be.'

'Totally, mind-fuckingly amazing if David Gaudion turns up,' Clover declared, clearly relishing the prospect.

'My thoughts exactly,' Cristy responded, not quite sharing the relish.

'Any idea if we can record?' Connor asked, starting to unpack his heavy bag.

'Nothing like that was discussed, but obviously I'll ask when I call. So, until then, I guess we get on with our day and well done, Jacks, for finding the brother's address. He might still be worth an interview.'

Thanking Clover as she passed a coffee, Connor said,

'Whatever happens, this has the potential of being an amazing development, and fascinating that it's come *before* we air Olivia's interview. They've got to know she might have told us about the rape – that'll be what prompted the call, without a doubt. So chances are this contact is as much about getting information out of us as it is about us getting it from Cynthia. More so, even.'

Having reached the same conclusion, Cristy said, 'I won't be giving her anything if I feel she's trying to play us, but let's work through a few scenarios later so I can be prepared. Now, have we still not heard anything from the CPS since Victor Green told us – and the rest of the world – that the police always believed there was enough evidence to convict Gaudion?'

'I sent the extract to the Chief Crown Prosecutor's office the next morning,' Clover confirmed, 'just to make sure it reached them, but no word yet. My guess is we'll get the same spiel-bollocks we did at the start, about extensive investigations, professional opinions, lack of corroboration, or was it co-operation? Whatever, I'll chase it up.'

Checking it off her list, Cristy said, 'I won't ask about the bloke in the mirror; if anything had come in from him we'd be all over it by now. So are we agreed that we continue to wait till the end of the day before trying to contact him?'

As everyone was, they moved on to the subject of Olivia.

'I'm becoming increasingly worried that we haven't heard from her,' Cristy said. 'It doesn't feel right that she'd tell us so much and then start ghosting us. Apart from anything else, doesn't she want to find out why I'm trying to get hold of her, and which parts of her interview we're going to use?'

'She's got to know the lawyers will block any mention of the rape,' Jackson pointed out. 'She'd have known that ahead of time, surely?'

'If she did,' Cristy responded, 'and I agree with you, Jacks, she must have, then we have to wonder why she brought it up. What was she hoping to gain from it?'

'If we do hear from her,' Connor put in, 'what shall we do about the new crime-scene photos? Should we let her see them?'

Having already considered this, Cristy said, 'I think it would

262

be cruel to put her through the trauma of it. She doesn't need to see her sister and mother like that, or some ghoul in a mirror recording it all. Actually, the more I go over this, the more convinced I am that we should let police experts take a look at what we have. They have the resources to check if the images are real, and frankly, I'm not comfortable with us hanging onto something that's close to confirming a hitman was used. It kind of changes things a bit, wouldn't you say?'

Connor nodded. 'What we need is a clearer timeline of what happened on that day. Who saw what when, and who came and went from the house at what time.'

'All of which we have,' Clover put in.

'Yes, but it's worth going over it again,' Cristy said, 'so if you can put it into one document for us all to take a look at over the weekend, that'll be great. How's Jodi today?' she asked Connor.

He rolled his eyes and in a tone filled with fake exasperation, said, 'Irrepressible, insisting she's in great shape and, dare I say it, keen to know how things went with Matthew last night?'

Cristy's insides tightened as all her barriers went up against the reminder. She was trying to block out every part of what had been said, to stop herself connecting with the irreparable and senseless damage he'd inflicted on their lives, and for what? For nothing, apparently. Except it wasn't nothing now, because two other people were involved, one of them *his* unborn baby. Surely to God he wasn't intending to abandon them, throw them out, even? He'd lost his mind, woken up far too late from his mid-life crisis to get anything back on track now, because if he seriously thought, for a single minute, that she was going to entertain going back to him, he was certifiable.

'Let's just say,' she responded, 'he didn't cover himself in glory, but when does he ever? Anyway, why don't we stay focused where it matters? Did anything else interesting come in overnight?'

She was aware of Connor regarding her curiously, clearly sensing something more serious had gone down last night.

Jackson said, 'Nothing that can top your call from Richard Gaudion, but I've put O'Malley's video on the website and sorted out some of his tastier comments for a future episode. That's presuming the next one is all Olivia, although at this rate it could be all Cynthia. Or both.'

'Whatever, it has the promise of being a good one,' Cristy declared, opening up her emails. 'If you guys make a start on the edit, I'll catch you up . . . Oh my God! It's Olivia!' she cried excitedly, and quickly opening the message she read out loud.

'Sorry not returning your calls, a lot going on here, nothing to do with Lexie. Been digging around in her old boxes and found an unlabelled USB which I uploaded to my laptop. You might already have heard the attached if the police gave you a copy, if not you can judge for yourself whether it's worth using. It's dated May 14th, a little over three weeks before the murders. Painful for me to listen to, just hearing her brings home how much I still miss her and how conflicted I remain over Papilio's influence on her.'

'It's an audio link,' Cristy said, and hesitated for a moment as she took in the fact that they were about to hear Lexie's voice for the first time. It felt strange, disconcerting and even oddly intrusive, as if they were pushing too far into Lexie's private world. She glanced at the others and seeing they were waiting expectantly she put her qualms aside and clicked the link open, aware of Lexie's soulful eyes watching from the whiteboard behind her.

After a few moments of hissing, a gently spoken, young-sounding woman with no trace of an accent other than purely English, began to speak.

LEXIE: 'Thank you for seeing me today.'

O'MALLEY: 'You know my door is always open. Please come and sit down. How have you been?'

LEXIE: 'Tired, but better than I expected after ... everything.'

O'MALLEY: 'The tiredness is normal and I'm glad to hear you're feeling an improvement. Shall we talk about it? Is that why you're here?'

LEXIE: 'Yes. I— it was—'

O'MALLEY: 'Take your time. There's no rush.'

LEXIE: 'I just wanted to thank you, really. You know I've never been able to talk about it before, not to anyone – or not in the kind of detail and depth you took me to. I'm so glad you were there with me, holding my hand. I couldn't have done it otherwise. (A GIRLISH LAUGH.) It was like having a painful tooth extracted, only magnified a few thousand times.'

O'MALLEY: 'You were extremely brave, Lexie. You have my greatest admiration.'

LEXIE: 'David always says I should be careful who I tell, but I know I can trust you.'

O'MALLEY: 'Of course you can. We've already been through a lot together and please don't ever doubt that I'll always be here for you. Does David know you've told me?'

LEXIE: 'Yes. He said he hopes we don't live to regret it.'

O'MALLEY: 'Do you think you will?'

LEXIE: 'No, not at all, but it's not the same for David. As you know, it's something we've always tried to put behind us, to do our best to forget about. He feels it's better that way.'

LEXIE: 'But you know differently now?'

LEXIE: 'Of course. I think he's expecting me to do the same as before, when I used to let it overwhelm me, sometimes for weeks at a time, making me feel afraid and helpless, unworthy as a mother and a wife, and ashamed all over again.'

265

O'MALLEY: 'But you understand now that you have nothing to feel ashamed of?'

LEXIE: 'Yes, but it doesn't always stop me from feeling it. The things they did were very shameful. They hurt me a lot, physically and mentally.'

O'MALLEY: 'They certainly did. And it's made it hard for you to be intimate with David?'

LEXIE: 'Yes, because when I am, it's there, in my head, and I have to make him stop.'

O'MALLEY: 'And does he? Stop?'

LEXIE: 'Yes, if I tell him to, but sometimes I wait until he's finished.'

O'MALLEY: 'Does he get angry when you're unwilling to wait?'

LEXIE: 'No, not really. I mean, yes, sometimes.'

O'MALLEY: 'Have these difficulties continued since our cleansing?'

LEXIE: 'Um . . . They're not as bad as they were, but they haven't gone completely. I hope that doesn't mean I've failed.'

O'MALLEY: 'It doesn't. Nothing ever happens all at once, it can take time to reach the ultimate goal, but maybe we have a little more work to do. Tell me, has David ever tried to make you meet any of the men again? They are men, of course, no longer boys.'

LEXIE: 'Yes, they are, but we don't ever talk about them.'

O'MALLEY: 'But he sees them?'

LEXIE: 'He has to sometimes, for his work. Because of who they are, you understand.'

O'MALLEY: 'And how do you feel about that?'

LEXIE: 'Awful, sick, but mostly I try not to think about it.'

O'MALLEY: 'It's been a long time, but would it help to report what happened to the police? This could be the final step, what could put it all to rest for you.'

LEXIE: 'I don't know. Everyone tried to make me report them at the time, but I couldn't face it. I was afraid they'd deny it all, or blame me, or do something to make everything even worse, as if that were possible. It's only been since I started seeing Serena, and now you, that I've felt stronger, more able to cope, so maybe now could be the right time.'

O'MALLEY: 'Let's talk about it some more before you come to a decision. We want it to be the right one, for you and your children.'

LEXIE: 'Yes, it needs to be right for them.'

O'MALLEY: 'Meanwhile, perhaps speaking the names of your attackers out loud could start releasing the last of the demons, the ones that continue to interfere with your equilibrium and intimacy.'

LEXIE: 'Maybe, but I don't want them to hurt anyone I love.'

O'MALLEY: 'We shall do everything in our power to make sure that doesn't happen. Your sister-butterflies will support you. If you think it'll help, we can perform a capture.'

LEXIE: 'Yes, I think it will.'

O'MALLEY: 'OK. I'll make the arrangements. In the meantime, would you like to speak the names out loud here, between us? It might make it easier when you come to share with the group.'

Such a long, crackling silence followed that Cristy thought the recording might have ended, but then Lexie said:

LEXIE: 'Perhaps I can write them down first?'

O'MALLEY: 'Of course.'

A few minutes later, presumably after reading the names, O'Malley's voice was heard again.

O'MALLEY: 'Is this all of them?'

LEXIE: (Unintelligible)

O'MALLEY: 'OK. You've done very well with this. Your courage is proof of your healing. Soon you will become your true self with only love in your heart and no more fear or shame to weigh you down. In the next few days we will prepare you for this most important part of the transcendence.'

LEXIE: 'Will I be rewarded with a purple butterfly?'

O'MALLEY: 'Yes, my dear Lexie, you will.'

As the recording stopped Cristy sat back in her chair, feeling slightly winded by what she'd just heard as she tried to imagine where Lexie and O'Malley had been when the recording had taken place, how they'd looked, whether anyone else had been there, what might have been left unsaid, what had followed, even. Lexie's voice had sounded almost childlike in its vulnerability and trust, while the manipulation in O'Malley's words had, to her mind, rung clear.

'Powerful stuff,' Jackson commented, breaking the silence. Like the others, he was staring at Lexie's headshot on the whiteboard and Cristy turned to do the same. Now, having heard her, maybe they were seeing her with slightly different eyes. She felt, in some ways, more alive, or at least more real than she had before.

'What she says in that recording begs so many questions,'

she said, 'and I guess the first has to be, was David's name on that list? Or did she hold it back?'

'There was no sense, throughout the recording, of her planning to seek any sort of revenge on him,' Connor observed, 'so she'd either come to terms with his involvement, or O'Malley already knew about him so there was no need to reveal his name.'

Cristy nodded thoughtfully. 'So was she preparing herself – or being prepared – to see her husband disgraced and in prison? It might be a good motive for murder, but it didn't sound that way, did it?'

'What we don't know,' Connor said, 'is how she sounded during the "cleansing", as O'Malley put it. She could have been screaming in the depths of horror and swearing all sorts of vengeance for all we know.'

Cristy frowned. 'Did anyone else think that the tone of her voice was slightly too . . . calm? Is that the word I'm looking for? It was like she'd been . . . drugged? Hypnotized?'

'It's the kind of thing that happens in cults,' Jackson commented.

'What do you think performing a capture means?' Clover asked.

Cristy shrugged. 'I'm guessing it's some sort of ritual or ceremony to seize the "demons" as they're expelled. The demons, in this case, being the names.'

'And what then?'

'Without being a member, I have no idea.'

Looking up from his Google search, Connor said, 'The purple butterfly is about miracles and guidance. I'm not sure what that tells us. Didn't Serena have one?'

'Yes, she did,' Cristy confirmed, 'and we know she was a recruiter. So perhaps that was what Lexie was looking to become. It could explain why she took her mother into her confidence.'

'Funny that she didn't reach out to her sister,' Jackson commented.

'Maybe she did, or Olivia was next. Anyway, we're still no wiser as far as the rapists are concerned – unless Olivia changes her mind and decides to tell us.'

'She might turn up another recording,' Connor suggested.

'A recording of the transcendence would be good,' Clover put in. 'I'd love to know what it involves.'

'Wouldn't we all,' Cristy agreed, 'but whatever it is, it's not what killed her, at least not directly.'

'Well, for what it's worth,' Connor said, 'this puts O'Malley back in the frame big time for me. I don't know if he was grooming Lexie all along to get those names, but we know he got them, so did he contact someone to try to warn them they were about to be exposed? I'm ruling out blackmail or he'd surely have been the more obvious target for murder, and as we know, he's still making the most of his mortal coil.'

'While in some kind of self-imposed hiding,' Cristy pointed out.

'Same as Gaudion,' Jackson reminded them.

Cristy said, 'I think we're in danger of disappearing down a rabbit hole here, so let's work with what we have for now, which is Olivia's interview and this recording. We'll have to listen to it again, and I'm sure the lawyers will want to as well, but I don't see a problem with using Lexie's words.'

'I agree,' Connor said. 'She's not accusing anyone of anything, or naming names. She's just confirming that something happened to make her . . . what? Vulnerable? Afraid?'

'Ashamed,' Cristy said. 'A lot of women feel like that after a rape.'

'I reckon this confirms she was part of a cult,' Clover stated, 'no matter what O'Malley wants to call it.'

Cristy nodded. 'Let's get his video message up again and listen to it in light of what we've just heard from Lexie.'

After running through both recordings several times and finding nothing useful to link them, Cristy said, 'I'm going to reply to Olivia, thanking her for the tape and asking why she thinks Lexie had a copy of this one when she presumably had dozens of sessions with O'Malley.'

'Good question,' Connor stated, 'or maybe Olivia has more and has decided not to send them for some reason.'

'She seems to think the police have heard this one,' Cristy pointed out, 'but Frances Rush was all over the Papilio aspect of the case and she's never mentioned any tapes. So, if the detectives, or someone in the force, did get their hands on this, why didn't Rush bring it up when we met her?'

'Because,' Rush replied, when Cristy put the question to her, 'this is the first I've heard of it. As far as I knew, all Papilio's records were destroyed by the fire at Serena's place. Is there anything in this audio we should know about?'

'I'll send it over and you can judge for yourself,' Cristy replied. 'And while we're at it, there's something else you ought to see.' She was looking at Connor and, receiving a nod, she continued, 'We've been sent some shots of the crime scene, right down to a close-up of Lexie Gaudion's shattered face.'

There was a beat, before Rush, sounding both sceptical and intrigued, said, 'Better send them over too, and I'll make sure they get into the right hands. How long have you had them?'

'Since Wednesday. We don't know if they're genuine – our guy thinks it's possible, but he can't be a hundred percent.'

'I'm not sure anyone can be these days, the way technology is. So who sent them, and why?'

'No name, only a phone number that he's told us to call when we're ready to talk. You'll hear him claiming to have been there when the women were killed, and you'll see a shot of him, if it's him, in the mirror above the mantel. He's wearing a mask, so it's not possible to ID him, but he seems to be recording the scene on his phone.'

'OK, definitely worth looking into, but as you know, there's no end to what sickos can get from the dark web these days, and no end to what they can do with the material when they have it. So I'm not convinced yet. Have you called this guy?'

'No, we're waiting for him to contact us again.'

'Well, if he wants money, and I'm guessing that's what's behind this, maybe you should leave it to someone who's trained to deal with psychos, because whether this weirdo has anything to do with the case or not, that's exactly what he is.'

By five o'clock that day Connor had gone to meet with Frances Rush and other officers to make contact with the 'man-in-the-mirror', given that he, whoever he was, was expecting to hear from someone affiliated to the podcast. Jacks had gone along to organize the recording so that Connor could focus on what the man actually wanted and, whatever the sum, make it conditional on a face-to-face interview.

'He won't fall for it,' Rush had stated when she'd rung to set things up, 'not if he's got more than a single brain cell, but it's a start while the techies go to work on the photos.'

Minutes after they'd left, Clover had taken herself to the Crown Prosecution Service's South West HQ at Temple Meads, to meet with a 'spokesperson' who'd suddenly been put up for interview in response to Sir Victor Green's claims. Cristy would have gone herself, or at least accompanied Clover, were it not time to call Cynthia Gaudion.

Inexplicably, and somewhat ludicrously, she felt a fluttering of nerves as she checked to make sure her laptop was recording before entering the number she'd been given. She hadn't yet made the connection when a text arrived.

Have you given any thought to our chat last night? Matthew x

She deleted the message and listened as a ringtone came down the line.

'Hello?'

The voice was female, not young and lilted with a very gentle Gloucestershire burr, so it was presumably Cynthia.

'It's Cristy Ward speaking,' Cristy said, 'your son, Richard, told me you'd like to meet.'

'Yes, dear, that's correct. Thank you very much for calling. I had hoped to suggest tomorrow, but I'm afraid that won't be possible now. So would Sunday afternoon be convenient?'

'Yes, of course,' Cristy replied. If she had anything else on, it had already slipped to second place. 'Where is convenient for you?'

'I'll give you the address if you're ready, and Richard will send directions. It isn't easy to find, even with a satnav. Are you gluten-free?'

Cristy blinked. 'No, I'm not,' she replied.

'Good. I'll bake a cake and hopefully you'll help me to eat at least some of it. Now, are you ready to write down the address?'

After doing so, and making a quick calculation of how long

it could take to get there, Cristy said, 'Can I ask if you're open to us recording our chat?'

There was concern in Cynthia's voice as she said, 'I'm not sure, maybe we can discuss that when you get here. And when you say us?'

'My co-producer Connor usually works with me.'

'I see. Would it bother you terribly to come alone? There's only me here, you see, and I think I might find it easier to talk if I'm not outnumbered.'

After ringing off, Cristy went to pour herself a glass of wine left over from Tuesday's 'drop party' and took her laptop to the sofa to relax while she read through all the notes they had on Cynthia Gaudion. For the moment she wasn't sure how she felt about meeting her alone – on the face of it, she was just a sweet old lady loved by all, apparently, but the address was quite remote and there was no getting away from the fact that she was the mother of a suspected killer. This didn't make her a killer, of course, and she, Cristy was one of the first to damn those who judged someone by another's actions, no matter how close their relationship might be. Connor would almost certainly take the same view, but how was he going to feel about being excluded? Actually, he'd probably welcome the chance to take a day off, given Jodi's recent scare, and he could always continue working on Olivia's interview at home.

She'd go alone, as Cynthia had requested, and if David Gaudion did show up . . .?

She looked over at his headshot on the whiteboard, still watching her, still seeming to read her in a faintly mocking sort of way. If he did turn up, he was hardly going to murder her, was he, not when everyone would know where she was that day, and presumably not in front of his mother who he surely wouldn't use to set a trap. And why on earth would he harm her when he had absolutely no reason to? True, there was still the unresolved issue of Iris, enough on its own to make her uneasy, and then there was the fact that he'd been hiding for so long. Why? Where? What or who was he afraid of? She had so many questions whirling around in her head, so much she wanted to clarify with him, and could only bring it to a stop when she reminded herself that it was his mother she was meeting, not him. It was a chat with Cynthia that she needed to prepare for.

She became so engrossed in her notes over the next half an hour or so that when she finally looked up she'd almost lost the sense of where she was. Her heart gave an unsteady thud as she realized someone was standing in the doorway, shoulder resting on the frame, arms crossed over a wide chest as he stared down at her, apparently amused and totally comfortable with being there.

She sat up so quickly it made her head spin as her laptop slid to the floor. 'Who are you?' she asked, not recognizing a thing about this man in a navy pinstriped suit and garish tie. 'Can I help you? Are you lost?'

He merely raised an eyebrow. His balding head gleamed in the evening sunlight, while his thin, taut face was partly lost in shadow, but she could see the smile and feel his intrusion as if it were sucking air from the room.

'Mrs Ward,' he said.

'Ms,' she corrected, not sure if she wanted to find out how he knew her name.

'Ms Ward. I'm sorry to barge in on you—'

'Who are you?' she repeated uneasily. 'And what do you want?'

'I'm here to let you know that it wouldn't be wise to use any of the names Olivia Caldwell might have given you.'

Tensing, but refusing to be intimidated even though she was, she said, 'Is that a threat?' She felt certain it was, although there wasn't anything overtly menacing about his manner.

'It's simply a piece of advice from a friendly source.' He looked slowly around the room, taking it all in until his eyes came to rest on the whiteboard. He went to it and leaned in towards the shot of ten-year-old Amelia. 'You have children, don't you, Mrs Ward?' he said, turning back. 'And I believe your colleague's wife is expecting.'

Suddenly terrified, Cristy said, 'What's that got to do with anything?'

He shrugged and smiled as he said, 'Just forget what Olivia

Caldwell might have told you, that's all,' and returning to the door he left as quietly as he'd come in.

Quick as a flash she was on her feet. 'Who sent you?' she shouted after him, running out to the car park.

He was already in the lane getting into the passenger side of a dark green Jaguar.

'Who sent you?' she shouted again, but the driver was pulling away and with the vehicle side-on to the car park's entrance she couldn't see a registration plate.

CHAPTER TWENTY-FIVE

'Really, I wouldn't put too much store by it,' Frances Rush advised when Cristy finally got hold of her late on Sunday morning. 'I get that it was scary with him talking about your children, and Connor's wife, but it's the kind of thing lowlifes like him do to exert pressure. Rarely does anything come of it.'

'I realize you're more used to those types than we are,' Cristy retorted, indicating to leave the M5 at junction 25, 'but I can tell you it seriously spooked us. I wasn't even sure I should tell Connor . . .'

'But you did, and take it from me, his wife will not be harmed. Is he worried?'

'What do you think?'

'But he's not talking about abandoning the podcast?'

'Not yet, no, but if anything like it happens again . . .'

'If it does, I'll have someone look into it, but I'm sure it won't. As I said, it was a bit of muscle-flexing, a clumsy attempt to bully you, but you're too high profile for anyone to make a move on you or your family, especially when you don't have any names to reveal. I guess you didn't tell him that?'

'Actually, he didn't ask if I knew, just advised me not to use them.'

'Which is kind of proving my point – nothing to be worried about. If he really meant business, he'd have tried getting them out of you to be sure you had the right ones.'

'But who the hell was he? That's what I'd like to know.'

'Tell me, who do *you* think he was?'

'Someone sent by one of the rapists is the most obvious answer. Or O'Malley, but I can't quite get my head around that.'

'So you don't think it was a message from Gaudion?'

Although it had crossed her mind, she'd dismissed it after talking it through with Connor and the others. 'Why? Do you?' she countered.

'I'd say it seems unlikely now you're about to talk to his mother, but as we've no idea what's actually going on in that family I wouldn't rule it out.'

As unsettled by that as she was by Rush's casual dismissal of the ominous visit, Cristy circled yet another roundabout on this slow road to the middle-of-nowhere, and said, 'I guess there's no way of connecting my visitor to the "man in the mirror"?'

'You're right, there isn't, but as we know, connecting anything to that guy at this stage is eluding us.'

Knowing that he hadn't picked up when Connor had rung on Friday, nor again yesterday when he'd made another attempt, Cristy said, 'Do you know where the call was made from?'

'It's been narrowed down to a small town in Somerset, but that's as far as they've got with it.'

'Will someone be following up on it?'

'They will, I'm sure, but remember I'm running an entirely different division. Whatever I can get on this case will only come second hand.'

'OK, but does anyone know yet if the images he sent are genuine?'

'Way too early. Sorry, I know that's disappointing, but I don't think you were really expecting another answer. This isn't a live enquiry, so it isn't being treated as a priority. At least not yet. Keep going the way you are and that could change.'

Glad to hear this, Cristy said, 'You know, what intrigues me – actually, it scares the hell out of me really – is that there doesn't seem to have been any hesitation when it came to dealing with Iris Newman.'

'You don't know if she had a visit first and refused to back off, which is what I think is worrying you. Did she have the names?'

'Not that I'm aware of.'

'So it could be it was no more than unfortunate timing that she was knocked off her bike soon after beginning her investigations.

Maybe some toerag, probably drunk, just drove off and left her and we're reading too much into it.'

Knowing that was entirely possible, in spite of how unconvinced she felt right now, Cristy said, 'Have you had a chance to listen to Lexie's interview with O'Malley yet?'

'Some of it, yes. Have you made contact with him?'

'We reached out yesterday, but no response so far. Even if we get one, is he really going to give us the names?'

'I doubt it, but look at it this way, just mentioning you've spoken to Olivia has already started flushing them out – I'm talking Gaudion's brother and mother, the bloke in the mirror, the mouthpiece who dropped in on you Friday . . . Seems to me you're doing something right. And don't forget the authorities – police or CPS – can't shut you down the way they managed with an official investigation, and a trial, although I wouldn't be surprised if they try.'

After the call was over and Cristy finally turned from the main road onto Exmoor's Galloping Bottom Lane, she was thinking about the secretive, shadowy fraternity that was very probably operating around this case. Exposing any one of them, or anything about them, was going to be next to impossible, so were she and her team being naïve, delusional, arrogant even, to think they could ever get to the truth of what had really happened that day in June of 2008? More to the point, how much danger were they putting themselves in simply by trying?

It was just after two by the time Richard Gaudion's detailed directions steered her off a narrow, potholed road sunk between hedgerows to begin a steep and winding drive up another rough track. According to a sign she'd just passed, awkwardly propped against an old tree stump, she was now on private land.

She'd been going for a while, higher and further into the moor, heading in the vague direction of Lynton and Lynmouth but with no glimpses of the sea through the dense foliage she was passing, nor any other signs of life, apart from a few sheep and a handful of wild ponies. She hadn't passed another vehicle for at least ten minutes, and she'd lost a phone signal somewhere around Simonsbath. So much for being able to keep in touch with

Connor, or for anyone finding her if she didn't make contact by six, as promised.

Not entirely sure how worried she was, she took a right fork at a giant oak, as directed, and a hundred yards further on she crossed a small field to pull up alongside an old Land Cruiser with rusted hubcaps and a cavernous dent in the rear fender. There was a tractor nearby, and a quad bike, and something she really hadn't expected: a child's trampoline, a slide, tyre-swing, and a giant paddling pool. However, it was the house itself that was the biggest surprise. With its lichen-green tiled roof, triple dormer windows, and glorious wraparound porch, it looked straight out of the American mid-west. It gleamed with newness; a dream hideaway that she already knew belonged to Cynthia Gaudion's brother, Ronald Phelps, for this was the address Jackson had found on Exmoor.

Hauling her bag from the car, she started towards the ranch – that was all she could think to call it – taking in the magnificent panorama of gorse and heather tumbling over the expanse of hillside in front of her, and a sparkling blue-grey sea in the distance. She and Matthew had brought the children to Exmoor any number of times when they were young, but they'd never come across anywhere this remote or spectacular. If they had, she could imagine Matthew would have wanted to buy it on the spot simply for how magical the whole place seemed.

'Hello, hello,' a cheery voice rang out. 'You must be Cristy.'

Cristy turned to see a slight, grey-haired woman in her seventies, maybe early eighties, coming stiffly down from the porch to greet her. She was wearing a short-sleeved summery dress, sandals and the biggest of smiles, as though she was truly thrilled to be meeting the stranger who was raking up her family's pain. But it wasn't only the gentleness of this woman's eyes that had caught at Cristy's heart; it was the stunning smoke tree she'd just noticed at the side of the house, tamed into a bush and protected by a tall wire fence. She hadn't seen one in so long and to come across one now, in this remote hilltop place with all its conflicting associations, seemed to be saying something, though heaven only knew what.

'I'm Cynthia,' Mrs Gaudion declared, taking Cristy's hand and shaking it warmly. 'And that's what you must call me. We don't stand on ceremony here. I'm so glad you got here safely. Not easy to find, is it? But Richard's always very good with directions.'

'They were excellent,' Cristy confirmed, glancing back to the smoke tree's feathery pink flowers, not quite ready to stop looking at them yet.

'Beautiful, isn't it?' Cynthia commented, following her eyes.

'It was one of my mother's favourite's,' Cristy told her. 'You so rarely see them.'

Cynthia smiled. 'It's one of my favourites too, so I think your mother is a person of very good taste. They're poisonous, you know? That's why there's a fence around it, to protect the children. Funny that it does so well up here in all the winds and weather, but as you can see . . . Teresa, my sister-in-law, was very proud of it. She had a way with trees. Now, come along in, let me get you some tea, or lemonade, or you can have a little tipple if it's your thing. We have plenty of it.'

Understanding already why everyone seemed to warm to this woman, Cristy said, 'Lemonade sounds perfect, thank you.' Adding, as she followed Cynthia up the steps and into the house, 'This place is . . . *amazing*.'

Cynthia twinkled over her shoulder. 'You mean this little house on the prairie? Ronnie, my brother, only moved in a couple of months ago, so it's all still spanking new, but heavens, you should have seen what was here before. The old farmhouse was so decrepit we kept expecting it to fall down around us, but in the end a crew had to come and clear it to make space for this. It's one of those flat-pack affairs. I expect you've come across them before. Very handy. The project was finished in next to no time.

'Now, make yourself comfortable at the table there while I pour some drinks. I made a banana cake, a bit of a favourite with my family, so don't worry if you can't finish it all.'

The kitchen was homely and spacious with a large, square oak table at its centre, antique dressers and rustic units around the walls and green gingham curtains at the windows. A stable door was fully open to the back deck, allowing a soft breeze to blow through. It was picture-book, Cristy was thinking, as she dumped her bag next to a spindle-back chair and inhaled deeply, drawing in the pleasing fragrance of the place. Timber, cake and freshly cut grass. 'Do you live here with your brother?' she asked, gazing up at the vaulted ceiling to where a helium star-balloon had become trapped in the rafters.

'Oh no, he wouldn't be having any of that,' Cynthia chuckled. 'Likes his solitude, does our Ronnie, though he gets precious little of it with his grandchildren descending on him all the time. Of course, he loves them being here really, and they'll be coming a lot more now this place is ready, having their own bedrooms and all. Here we are, my own recipe with cream cheese frosting and no sprinkles – I'll add them later for the little ones.'

As she set down the biggest and most delicious-looking banana cake Cristy had ever seen, she seemed momentarily puzzled as a phone started to ring. Laughing, she said, 'I've no idea where I put it, but if it rings long enough I expect I'll get a clue. Did you want to connect to the WiFi, by the way? It's a bit hit-and-miss up here, but luckily we're not entirely cut off. I'll get you the code.'

'It's really not necessary,' Cristy assured her as the old lady began to rummage in a drawer. 'It's actually quite freeing to be incommunicado for a while.'

'Yes, I find that too,' Cynthia agreed, 'but I'm under strict instructions, if I'm here alone, as I am today, that I have to be connected so I can be reached, or in case of emergencies, I suppose, but no one ever actually says that.' Her smile suddenly widened at she turned back to Cristy. 'I hope you don't mind me saying, but you have a lovely look about you. Did anyone ever tell you that? It makes me feel like I know you already. Of course, I've heard your podcasts, so your voice is familiar, I just hadn't expected you to be quite so *familiar*-seeming in person. And so *young*.'

Laughing, Cristy said, 'I'm almost fifty.'

'Well, you don't look it, and believe me, when you reach my age that's young. Now, I'll just fetch the lemonade and a couple of plates and we can settle down for a chat.'

As she headed to the fridge, Cristy said, 'Aren't you going to answer your phone?'

Cynthia cocked her head. 'Is it ringing again? Ah, so it is. Now where did I put it?'

Following the ringtone to a fruit basket full of Play-Doh fruit,

Cristy plucked it from under a potato that might actually have been a pineapple and handed it over. Cynthia smiled her thanks and clicked on. 'Hello, yes, I'm all right if that's why you're ringing . . . Yes, I thought so. Yes, she's here. Ronnie's with Rachel and the children today, I thought you knew . . . At their place, it's Lottie's birthday. I told you all this . . . OK, I'll be sure to ring if there's a problem. I won't ask why you think there will be . . . Oh, stop fussing now. I'll speak to you later,' and she abruptly rang off. 'My son,' she declared. 'I wish he wouldn't treat me like a child, but he seems compelled to.'

Going for it, Cristy said, 'Richard or David?'

Cynthia tugged open the fridge. 'Richard,' she replied. 'He was checking you'd found the place without any trouble, and to make sure you're not about to do something drastic. You're not, are you?' she asked, turning around with a mischievous gleam in her eyes.

'No plans for the moment,' Cristy responded dryly. 'Unless you call recording our chat drastic?' she ventured.

Bringing a jug of chilled lemonade to the table, Cynthia took two plates and cake forks from the nearby dresser and sat on one of the old wooden chairs. 'I've been thinking about that,' she replied, hovering a knife over the cake for Cristy to choose the size of her slice, 'and maybe it's best for us to get to know one another a little first, what do you say? I might be a bit less nervous then.'

Unable to imagine her being nervous of anything, Cristy pinched her thumb and forefinger together to indicate smaller, and said, 'That's fine.'

'Are you sure no bigger?' Cynthia encouraged.

'I might come back for seconds.'

Clearly happy with that, Cynthia plunged in the knife and as she set a huge wedge of cake onto a plate Cristy's mouth watered. 'Mm,' she swooned after tasting her first mouthful of moist, buttery bananas with a fragrant hint of vanilla, 'this is to die for.'

Cynthia beamed. 'I don't share the recipe very often, but my daughter-in-law, Astrid, Richard's wife, bullied it out of me and now she's even better at it than I am, but don't ever tell her I said that.'

Enjoying the little glimpses into her family life, Cristy said, 'So, if you don't live here, on Exmoor, where do you live?'

Cynthia's eyes narrowed playfully; clearly she'd been expecting the question but apparently she wasn't yet ready to answer it. 'Not far away,' she said, glancing up as a wayward gust filled the curtains. 'Well, maybe it is quite far; I suppose it depends on your perspective. I should move that vase,' and getting up she went to rescue an arrangement of giant horsetails from the windowsill.

'Another of my mother's favourites,' Cristy told her as she returned to the table.

'Sounds like she and I would get along very well,' Cynthia responded. 'Is she a keen horticulturist?'

'She was, but she passed away about ten years ago.'

'Oh, I'm sorry to hear that.' She regarded Cristy closely. 'And you still miss her,' she stated. 'Of course you do. Was it sudden?'

'She was diagnosed in early April and we lost her just before Christmas of the same year.'

Cynthia shook her head in dismay. 'And your father?'

'He died when I was still in my teens. I guess that's why Mum and I became so close.'

'Do you have brothers and sisters?'

'A brother, in Canada. We were close with him too. I still am, I guess, but we don't get to see one another often.' Realizing what was happening, Cristy broke into a chiding smile. 'I didn't come here to talk about me,' she said gently, 'but it's kind of you to ask.'

'I'm always interested in other people and their families. Perhaps one of these days you'll tell me more about yours.'

'Perhaps,' Cristy responded, thinking she'd probably like to, if the circumstances ever arose, although they were hard to imagine. 'So,' she said, after another delicious mouthful of cake, 'we were talking about where you live now.'

Cynthia laughed. 'And I avoided the question.'

'Does it have to be a secret?'

'Oh, napkins! Silly me,' and yanking open a drawer in front of her, she pulled out a pile of strawberry-covered serviettes. 'I was with Teresa when she bought these,' she sighed, handing one over. 'That's Ronnie's wife. They spent years talking about this place, you know, what it was going to be like when they gave

283

up farming. It was one of those property programmes that gave them the idea for what you see now. They visited the factory in Germany and got all the planning permissions – not easy, I can tell you, with the land being right at the heart of a national park – then they arranged for a local builder to come and knock the old place down. They even bought a caravan to live in while it was all happening. Then one day, just after it was all delivered ready for the build, Teresa's heart gave out and she wasn't with us any more.'

'Gosh, I'm so sorry,' Cristy responded, meaning it.

'Yes, we all were. She was a lovely lady, devoted to Ronnie and their children, but it was carrying on with this house, trying to get it the way she wanted, that kept him going. He's done a marvellous job, hasn't he? We all weighed in, of course, but now all the big stuff is done, I'm a bit worried he might start going downhill again. Still, we're keeping an eye on him and thankfully his daughter lives in Taunton, so not too far away, and his son's in Exeter. Do you have children, dear?'

Dabbing crumbs from her mouth, Cristy said, 'A girl and a boy, nineteen and soon-to-be-sixteen.'

'Ah, lovely, but they can be tricky in their teens, can't they? I remember what my boys were like, the girls too, Olivia and Lexie, although the girls weren't mine, of course. Sometimes it felt like they were. I loved them dearly, and I'm sure poor Margaret did too in her way, but being a mother never came naturally to her. I expect you've heard a lot about that already, haven't you?'

'Some, but it matters more to hear it from you.'

Cynthia smiled and circled a hand around her lemonade glass as her eyes drifted to a place somewhere in the past.

'Olivia was really sad when you left,' Cristy told her softly.

Cynthia's gaze remained unfocused as she nodded. 'I was sad to do that to her,' she replied, 'but she had her lovely husband to take care of her and . . . Well, it was a long time ago. I hope she's forgiven me by now.' She looked at Cristy. 'Has she?' she asked. 'I know you've spoken to her, so has she?'

'I think so,' Cristy replied, 'but I'm sure she'd like to hear from you why you left the way you did.'

Cynthia sighed. 'It was a very difficult time,' she said, 'and we all made decisions we maybe came to regret. Abandoning Olivia was certainly one of mine, but she was a grown woman, and not alone.' After a moment she added, 'Of course, she'd just lost her mother and sister, and believe me, losing Lexie had broken my heart too, but I had to put Rosaria first. I think, deep down, Olivia understands that.'

Certain she did, Cristy said, 'Can I ask where you went when you left?'

Cynthia tapped the table. 'We came here, to Ronnie and Teresa. It felt safe and far enough away from what had happened for us to live without the police and press constantly bothering us. And our friends and neighbours back in the Vale . . . They were good people for the most part, but the gossip, and the way we were stared at, or avoided . . . All that stopped when we got here.'

'Did Rosaria understand why you'd left?'

'Oh yes. She's a bright girl – young woman now – but back then, losing her mother and sister . . . She idolized Amelia, you know, Lexie too . . . Her grief was no less than any of ours.'

'Where is she now?'

Cynthia's smile returned. 'She wanted to come with me to see you, but something cropped up at the last minute . . . It's why I couldn't get here until today. She'll want to hear all about you when I get home. She's very inquisitive, and talk about Miss Sociable.' She laughed softly and drank some lemonade.

'Have you ever found out what happened to Amelia?' Cristy prompted gently.

Cynthia inhaled deeply and continued gazing into the past as she said, 'Amelia's gone.'

Moved by the finality of the words, Cristy said, 'You know that for certain?'

Cynthia glanced at her and away again. 'There is a lot about my family,' she said, 'that most people don't know and probably never will. Of course, I realize you're here to try to find out more, but if you don't mind, I'd rather not talk about Amelia.'

Realizing she had to accept this, at least for now, Cristy said, 'Do you ever see David?' Strange how saying his name made her feel as though he was watching her, the way she often did in the office.

'He's my son,' Cynthia replied.

As it seemed more of a yes than a no, Cristy pushed a little harder. 'Do you know where he is?'

Clearly, Cynthia's thoughts had returned to Rosaria, as she said, 'I'm not saying the tragedies haven't left their mark on our dear girl, but we've done our best with her, got her all the help she needed, and I think, if you met her, you'd consider her a happy, well-rounded person with a very definite naughty streak.'

Touched by her evident love for her granddaughter, Cristy said, 'Does she ever see her father?'

Cynthia didn't answer, and as her eyes went down, the hand on her glass trembled slightly. In the end she said, 'To be honest, we almost never refer to those times any more. We've found it easier not to – that's why I'm concerned about your podcasts and what they're bringing up again.'

Experiencing the inevitable guilt, Cristy said, 'But don't you want to find out who was behind it all? You must have so many questions yourself, especially about your granddaughter?'

Cynthia continued to sit quietly staring at nothing.

Cristy waited, feeling dreadful and intrigued and unsettled by the sense of them not being entirely alone. She looked around, but there was no sign of anyone else, nor had she heard anything to suggest someone was close by. There were no watchful cameras as far as she could make out, and no listening devices either, and yet . . .

'I do have questions,' Cynthia said, 'of course I do, but maybe the answers will deliver things we don't need to know.'

Did that mean she suspected her son too? 'How so?' Cristy queried.

Cynthia's eyes came to hers with a gentleness that was almost searing when Cristy considered the pain behind them. 'What did Olivia tell you about David?' she asked.

Cristy hesitated, not sure how much to reveal. 'She talked about how close they all were as children, and about Lexie's crush on him during their teenage years.'

Cynthia nodded slowly. 'Is that how she remembers it? Funny how differently we see things, but no one was closer to Lexie than her. What else?' she prompted.

'She told me he was never really interested in Lexie and how it used to break her heart to see him with other girls.'

After absorbing this, Cynthia said, 'Did she tell you what happened to Lexie at Oxford?'

'Yes, she did.'

Seeming neither surprised nor upset, Cynthia cut another sliver of cake and put it on Cristy's plate.

'Are you willing to talk about it?' Cristy asked.

Cynthia lifted her head and looked past her, as she said, 'Do you want to take it from here?'

Cristy spun round and her heart flipped over so violently it hurt. David Gaudion was standing in the doorway and had clearly been listening to every word.

PART TWO

CHAPTER TWENTY-SIX

'Are you angry?'

Cristy glanced at Gaudion and away again, out towards the glowering clouds starting to close in on the estuary.

They were seated on the ranch-style porch, in Adirondack chairs either side of a small round table where glasses of lemonade that Cynthia had poured remained untouched.

Was she angry? Certainly it was a part of what she was feeling; perhaps tricked would describe it more accurately, and uneasy, although she wouldn't admit to that.

'I didn't want you to announce on your podcast that you were coming to see me,' he explained.

'We don't go live with it until Tuesday,' she replied shortly.

He nodded and batted away a persistent fly.

Though she'd known all along that he was a good-looking man, this older, living, breathing version of him was, she decided, somehow almost too powerful in spite of him being greyer, more weather-worn and even . . . Even what? There was something about him that was eluding her, but for some reason it seemed to matter. Certainly his eyes were the same, blue, penetrating and . . . chilling? Maybe, but it was too soon to be sure of that, and she didn't want prejudices or clichés to start mixing up her thoughts in ways that wouldn't be helpful.

'I'm sorry if I'm making you nervous,' he said, lifting a foot to rest it on one knee. He was wearing jean shorts and old moccasins, a faded blue polo shirt and an expensive-looking wristwatch.

'You're not,' she lied. She needed to say something, to get herself out of this shocked stupor she seemed to be trapped in, but gathering her thoughts was still proving difficult. 'If you'd asked me to keep my visit confidential,' she said, 'I would have.'

He nodded, though it was impossible to tell whether or not he believed her. 'I had to do what I thought was right,' he responded.

He was disconcerting, too *present* somehow, as if he was taking up more space, more air even than he should.

'So how long were you listening to my conversation with your mother?' she asked, picking up her drink and hoping he didn't notice the slight tremor of her hand.

'From the start. I wanted to get a feel for how open-minded you might be; how willing to listen to another side of the story.'

Though intrigued by that, and of course interested, she said, 'Are you saying my podcasts are weighted in one direction?'

'Not exactly, but I know you think I murdered my wife . . .'

'How can you know what I think? I haven't said I believe in your guilt.'

'Not outright, no, but you do, deep down, and I understand that. I don't even blame you for it. And I guess your ultimate goal is to bring me to justice, because a mere retelling of events will, for someone like you, be less than satisfactory. It will ultimately achieve nothing, other than to get people talking about the case again, throwing up all sorts of speculation and half-cocked theories, misinformation and skewed truths, distressing my family, censuring me—'

'So you got me here to tell me to back off?' she broke in tightly, still stung by the *someone like you*. 'You have to know that it's not going to work.'

'Yes, I think I do know that, although I wish you would. However, I understand it would seem extremely odd to your thousands of listeners – maybe you're in the millions by now – if you suddenly abandoned your commitment to exposing the truth as you see it.'

'And how do I see it?' she challenged, wishing she could find a way to wrongfoot him, but not sure how to – yet.

Seeming to smile he said, 'You've got me there, so perhaps we're both guilty of making assumptions. Tell me,' he continued, turning to fix her with his disturbing eyes, 'do you want me to be guilty?'

Thrown by the oddness of the question, she said, 'Why on earth would you say that? It makes no difference to me whether you—' She broke off as his hand went up. It was strong and tanned, as were his legs and arms, and not for the first time since they'd sat down, she wondered if he spent a lot of time outdoors. Maybe he'd taken up farming, fulfilling his father's wish that one of his sons would.

'I guess it was a fatuous question,' he said, 'but I hope you'll allow me one or two.'

'I'll allow you the truth,' she countered.

'Ah, but how will you know if it's real?'

'It's not my place to judge you, but I am offering you a platform to tell your side of the story.'

He nodded slowly and let some time pass before picking up his glass and drinking. 'Why do you think you and your colleagues can reach a resolution now?' he asked. 'Nothing's changed over the last sixteen years; no new evidence has come to light, or not that I've heard about, and if it had you can be sure I'd know.'

'How would you hear about it?'

He shrugged. 'Because it would make the news? Or were you thinking I have someone on the inside?'

Since it was what she'd thought she said, 'Do you? Have someone "on the inside"?'

He shook his head. 'But you do – I'm talking about the police officers you've interviewed – and it doesn't seem they've changed their original opinions of me.'

'Why would they if you haven't given them a reason to?'

Seeming to concede the point, he rose to his feet and went to lean against the balustrade, turning his back to the view to look at her. She felt suddenly uncomfortable, exposed under his unabashed scrutiny. Was she looking at someone who'd fired the shots to end the lives of three innocent women, who'd done away with his own daughter? Could he be the 'man-in-the-mirror', masked and recording his handiwork? Or was he the person who'd hired the killer?

'I'm considering giving you the interview you require,' he told her, 'but I'd like to get to know you better first.'

She frowned, slightly annoyed. 'What exactly does that mean?' she demanded.

'Just what I said. You know a great deal about me . . .'

'Actually, I don't feel I know you at all.'

'And yet you're spending all this time digging into my life, my thoughts, my motives, my family . . . You must surely have learned something by now.'

'If I have,' she replied, 'then clearly it's not enough, because I honestly wouldn't want to give an opinion on you as things stand.'

He laughed and she was taken aback by the way it made her smile too. She had sounded a little ridiculous, pompous even, although she decided she was allowed that if he was to get away with being fatuous.

She looked past him as thunder rumbled across the distant horizon.

'I'm sorry about what happened between you and your husband,' he said.

She looked at him sharply.

He shrugged. 'If you can read about me, surely I'm allowed to read about you,' he said simply.

'That's not why I'm here,' she reminded him. 'I came to talk to your mother, but I'm happy to talk to you instead.'

'And that's what we're doing, talking, and getting along quite well, I think, unless you want to tell me differently.'

'Well, I suppose no punches have been thrown yet.'

He laughed again and to her dismay so did she. Her absurdities were going to outnumber his if she didn't stop biting back so quickly.

'Let me answer a few things Olivia told you about me and Lexie,' he said, glancing across the field to where his mother was taking washing from a rotary line.

'Can I record?' she asked.

His eyes came to hers and to her surprise he gestured for her to go ahead.

Quickly she went inside for her device and when she came back he'd returned to his chair. After identifying the interview, she placed the recorder between them and invited him to begin.

GAUDION: 'It isn't true that Lexie always had a crush on me, or was in love with me. In fact, it was the other way around. I was the one who was in love with her, right from when we were small children. I used to find her captivating, exciting, clever, funny . . . She was brave and yet shy, afraid of her parents and yet devoted to them in spite of the way they treated her. Olivia was older, although only by a year, more outspoken and somehow better able to cope with the neglect and verbal abuse than Lexie was. She was Lexie's protector, but I liked to see myself in that role too.

'By the time we were in our teens I was head over heels in love with her and I had eyes for no one else. Which isn't to say I didn't date other girls, because I did, but only because Lexie wasn't interested in me. Oh, she liked me well enough, and we were close, the way brothers and sisters are, but as for anything else . . . Her great love was for the science of human beings, not the mundane reality of them. She was fascinated by the evolution of culture and ethnohistory. Even when she was at school she belonged to all sorts of societies and movements dedicated to the behaviour of our species . . . I expect you know all this already?'

CRISTY: 'Actually, this is the first time anyone's talked about her as a scholar or intellectual.'

GAUDION: 'I guess that's what happens when you become the victim of a terrible crime. It's all about that after, but before she was . . . She had everything going for her, or everything she wanted, and that's what counts, isn't it? She had no interest in following conventional paths, she told me, like getting married and having children; she was only interested in devoting herself to her research. Of course I told her it was a waste – not for her, obviously, but it was the way I saw it as someone who hoped to share his life with her.

'Typically, arrogantly, I thought I'd be able to change her mind eventually, and we were still so young when we went to uni . . . I had a lot of wild oats to sow, we both had a great deal of growing up to do, so I wasn't expecting anything to happen between us then. We stayed in touch, and I saw her from time to time, at parties when I visited other friends at Oxford, maybe at concerts in London. Richard and I met up with her and Olivia from time to time for birthdays, or some other special occasion. We were still close, the four of us, like family, and at Christmas, during the holidays, that's just what we were, family. Unless one of us was travelling, obviously, and she did a few times, for research, of course. I remember being terrified she'd find some profound scientist-type with a big beard and head full of knowledge who'd sweep her off her feet and she'd never come back. She always did come back though, and she'd tease me for being worried. She'd say, "I swear, David, if I ever do decide to throw myself into a romance, or a marriage, it will be with you, but please don't wait for me, because there's someone out there for you, I promise, it just isn't me.'"

He stopped speaking and stared into the distance for a moment, as if hearing echoes or seeing ghosts maybe.

Cristy waited, saying nothing, while thinking that, at least on the face of it, he seemed genuinely moved by the memories of his dead wife. Then she recalled Frances Rush's words during their first interview, *I will say this, he was clever, personable, actually quite easy to like. He had us all taken in at one time or another, but we soon learned that he was a consummate actor. Or, put another way, he conformed very well to the profile of a psychopath.*

GAUDION: 'I wish Olivia hadn't told you about the rape, but I'm not surprised that she did, because it changed everything for Lexie. It ruined her life, shut down her dreams; you could say it destroyed everything. I know that's how she saw it, although she never used those words. In fact, in the early days she didn't speak much at all. What was done to her, the trauma and degradation she suffered . . .'

He turned his head away from the recorder, but he wasn't speaking any more, was merely gazing out at the darkening

296

afternoon as rain drew closer. Watching him, Cristy wondered how truthful he was being, how real his appearance of grief actually was. If it was an act, it was certainly convincing.

Still not looking at her, he continued with a question.

GAUDION: 'How much did Olivia tell you about the attack? I know you haven't gone public with it yet, but she has told you, hasn't she?'

CRISTY: 'She said there were five involved, that they used her in some sort of ritual, but she didn't go into detail about what was done.'

GAUDION: 'That's good.'

Long pause.

CRISTY: 'She told me you were there.'

His head came round, his eyes suddenly dark and his frown unnervingly deep. He pointed at the recorder, an indication to turn it off.

Cristy did so and for a long time neither of them spoke. In the end, he said, 'So that's why you told your listeners they were going to learn things about me that even the police didn't know, until now?'

Cristy nodded.

He looked away again, and she could see a pulse throbbing in his temple, his hands tight on the arms of the chair.

'Why would she say it if wasn't true?' she prompted quietly.

He got to his feet. 'Why don't you ask Olivia?' he responded, and moving past her he went back into the house.

CHAPTER TWENTY-SEVEN

'Didn't he even try to deny it?' Connor demanded when Cristy reported back the next morning.

She shook her head, and ended the playback.

Now they'd all heard the recording, and she'd listened to it for at least the sixth time since leaving Exmoor, she was still no closer to deciding what she'd really made of that very short time with Gaudion. Certainly it had given her a disturbed night's sleep as she'd gone over and over it, from the shock of turning around to find him standing in the doorway, to the tone of his voice as he'd talked about Lexie and bringing her to life in a way no one else had so far, to the moment he'd got up and walked away.

'What happened after?' Clover wanted to know. 'I mean, he must have said something else before you left. Even if it was only goodbye.'

'Actually, he's invited me back there so we can talk again,' Cristy admitted, hearing the tightness in his voice as he'd said it, and the strain in his face had been unmissable. 'Apparently he's going to be at his uncle's place for the rest of the week, so I can call to set a time.'

'I'm completely blown away by this,' Jackson informed her. 'You've actually got David Gaudion on speed dial?'

'So do you think he was there when the Oxford attack happened?' Connor pressed.

Reaching for her phone, Cristy said, 'I called Fiona Mooney, Lexie's friend, on the way back. The recording isn't great, but here's the most salient part of what she had to say.'

Finding the audio link she'd put together, she pressed play and frowned as she listened.

FIONA: 'Olivia told you David was there? David *Gaudion*?'

CRISTY: 'It's what she said. It doesn't sound as though you've heard that before?'

FIONA: 'No, I haven't, but remember, Lexie didn't tell me anything. All I know is what I heard through rumour and gossip. He was friends with those guys, though. Or he knew them, anyway. I guess everyone did, one way or another. But she married David, so this can't be right. I mean, why would she if he'd done something like that to her?'

CRISTY: 'Olivia says she was always crazy about him, and his parents more or less forced him into it. So maybe she got her man in the end?'

FIONA: 'Wow! I have to be honest I'm quite stunned by this, but if Olivia says he was there, she's the one who'd know.'

Cristy handed her phone to Jackson for him to upload the call onto the main computer. 'I've left a message for Olivia, asking her to get back to me today.'

'Meantime, do we run any of this in tomorrow's pod?' Connor asked.

'Obviously not Fiona's comments – we're still not cleared for using anything about the rape yet – but I made some notes last night about how we could intercut David and Olivia both talking about Lexie – almost as if they're addressing one another's points. Or contradicting, more like.'

'Are you sure Olivia's going to be up for that?' Clover queried worriedly. 'It's like they're talking about two different people at times.'

'Exactly. Curious, isn't it?' Cristy responded. 'They're both incredibly convincing, but there's still a way to go, and he's probably been preparing for this for years. Anyway, Olivia will get to hear it before we upload. So, we're going to need two versions in case she doesn't go for it.'

'Is that all?' Connor responded dryly as he went to his keyboard. 'Just send me your notes. Jacks, work with me, will you? We don't have a lot of time if we want to be ready for tomorrow's drop.'

'Wait up!' Clover cried, waving her hands. 'I've got some pretty sensational news myself. It's not going to top yours, Cristy, but I think you'll want to hear it.'

'Bring it on,' Connor encouraged, reaching for his coffee.

Clearly thrilled to be the bearer of something important, Clover picked up her notebook and flipped to the relevant page. 'Right, well, you all know I went to see the CPS on Friday, and I was spun the usual guff about evidentiary value being insufficient, blah, blah, blah . . .'

'And the guy they put up to talk to you turned out to be an old mate from uni,' Jackson put in.

'Exactly. His name's Carl Evans, by the way. Well, he got in touch with me over the weekend so he could talk "off the record".'

Everyone's eyes widened with interest. 'Go on,' Cristy prompted.

'Well, apparently someone very senior at the CPS – he didn't give me a name, but I got the impression it's right at the top locally – has been talking to police about "other information that's come to light" in the Kellon Manse Murders. He doesn't know what this info is – he's going to try to find out – but I'm guessing it's the crime scene photos from our man-in-the-mirror. So, it could be our podcast is getting some serious attention at last.'

Impressed and energized by this, Cristy said, 'I wonder if this has something to do with the new Chief Crown Prosecutor. She's only been in position since . . . when? Early last year, I think, so she won't have been part of the original investigation, or had anything to do with blocking any others. Things could be getting very interesting.'

'Do you know her?' Connor asked.

'Not personally, no, but Frances Rush might know what's going on. Jacks, if you've finished with my phone . . .'

Passing it back he said, 'Have we told Rush about the rape? I'm trying to keep up here.'

'Yes, we have.'

'I'm thinking,' Connor said, 'that whether Gaudion was there at the time of the attack or not, he'll know who the others are/were. Which begs the question, why has he never reported them?'

'Because he *was* there.' Clover concluded.

Connecting to Rush's voicemail, Cristy left a message for her to get back to her when she could and rang off as another call came in. Seeing it was Marley, she let it go to voicemail. Matthew's second wife was not someone she wanted to speak to right now, or even think about, come to that. 'OK,' she said, going to refresh her coffee, 'I want us to work on a list of questions for David Gaudion so I can make sure I cover everything on my next visit.'

'Are you going alone again?' Connor asked.

'I can ask when I call, if he has any objection to you coming with me,' she replied. As he seemed OK with that, she continued. 'Next up, I'm going to send you notes on my chat with Cynthia Gaudion. When I asked what had happened to Amelia the answer I got was "she's gone". So does that mean she's accepted her granddaughter is dead? Perhaps it's something I should put to Gaudion when we talk. I also need to ask him about Rosaria, who Olivia seemed certain was his, even though she was conceived during a gang rape.'

Grimacing, Clover said, 'That's going to be tricky to bring up.'

'Tell me about it,' Cristy said, 'but a lot depends on what Gaudion has to say about the rape, presuming he'll talk about it at all. For now, what Cynthia's words about Amelia have brought back to my mind is the anonymous woman who's twice insisted Amelia is dead. I don't think Cynthia's behind it, the voices aren't the same, but we need to try harder to track this person down.'

Connor said, 'I think we should deliver a recap of events in the next pod, stating where we are with the case, what we're still looking to uncover, who we need to talk to.'

'Good idea,' Cristy agreed. 'If we don't use it tomorrow, we can always expand for a later episode.'

'OK, but staying with tomorrow, if we don't end up using any of Gaudion's interview, are you going to make public the fact you've met and spoken to him?'

'Oh yes, we should definitely do that. If nothing else, it'll be a brilliant tease for the following episode.'

'And what about your visit from some "mouthpiece", as Rush called him?' Clover pointed out. 'Are we going to include that?'

'I'm still thinking that through. Someone put him on their list of things for me to ask Gaudion about, will you? And add

O'Malley to it.' Returning to her desk, she checked to see who was calling her mobile. 'Great! It's Olivia,' she exclaimed. 'I'll try to set up another meet for some time this afternoon. Failing that, she might be willing to do a video chat, so stand by to record.'

'Right there,' Jacks assured her as she said:

'Hi Olivia, thanks for getting back to me. How are you?'

'I'm OK, thanks,' Olivia replied. 'Actually, to be honest, I was a bit thrown by your message. You said you've seen David?'

'That's right. Yesterday.'

'Well, that's . . . Um . . . Surprising, obviously, and probably a good thing from your point of view, but I have to admit my husband and I are quite worried about it. Can I ask how you found him? We've never been able to.'

Wondering how hard they'd been looking, or why they'd even want to find him, Cristy said, 'Actually, his brother contacted me to set up a meeting with their mother and when I got there David was waiting.'

'Gosh! That must have been a shock, if you weren't expecting him. Where was it?'

She hadn't been asked to hold the information back, so she said, 'At a relative's place on Exmoor.'

'You mean Cynthia's brother, Ronald?'

'That's right.'

'Has she been there all this time?'

'No, but she didn't say where she's currently living.'

'I see. I haven't ever been to Ronald's myself, but Lexie went a few times. She said it was a lovely spot.' After a pause she said, 'So you saw Cynthia? How is she?'

Hearing the sadness in her voice, Cristy said, 'She seemed fine, and she said how sorry she was that she left you the way she did. She wanted to know if you've forgiven her.'

Olivia's voice was tender as she said, 'I'd forgive Cynthia almost anything. Do you think she'll let me be in touch with her again?'

'I can always ask if you'd like me to.'

'Thank you. I would. I still miss her, which probably sounds odd after so long, but she meant so much to me. To Lexie too, of course. Did you see Rosaria?'

302

'No, she wasn't there, but I think she's doing well.'

'That's good. I think about her such a lot. It's like he took everyone away from me that day, every last drop of blood that I shared with Lexie and her children. Cynthia was gone too . . . Thank goodness I still have my family here. I couldn't have got through it without them, and I've always told myself that Cynthia would have done what she thought was best, because she always does.'

Wondering when she was going to ask more about David, Cristy said, 'We're working on the edit of your interview now. We'll send it over for you to approve before we finalize the episode. Obviously, we haven't changed anything, just trimmed a few lines here and there, but the reason I wanted to talk to you is to be sure that you understand we can't include anything about the rape at this stage?'

'No, of course not. I didn't think it would be possible, but I wanted you to know about it anyway. It's absolutely central to everything as far as Lexie was concerned. Do you think you will ever be able to use it?'

'That could depend on whether or not you're prepared to give me the names of those who did it.'

'Yes, I've been thinking about that, and I want to, really I do, but my lawyers are advising against it for the moment.'

Unsurprised, though disappointed, Cristy said, 'The second reason I wanted us to talk today is because of something David said yesterday.'

Olivia's voice sounded hollow as she said, 'Oh?'

'I told him what you told me about him being there during the rape, being a part of it, even.'

'Yes, he was, but of course he denied it.'

'Not exactly, but when I asked why you'd lie about something like that he told me to ask you.'

There was a moment's silence before a dry, miserable laugh came down the line. 'He knows the truth as well as I do, but of course he's managed to make you question what I said. Well, I'm sure you were doing that anyway, it would be odd if you didn't, but he's very good at making people think things that are totally contrary to what they believe. I'm not sure how he does it, it's a strange sort of . . . *insight* that he has, to know what's going on in your head, and then he somehow uses it for his own purposes, or to mess with you. It almost drove my sister out of her mind, and would have if she hadn't started to see Serena.'

'Did David find Serena for Lexie?'

'I'm not sure. I know his old mistress told you he did, and it could be true, because he did bring people in from time to time, but I don't recall Lexie ever telling me where the recommendation to use Serena came from. Unfortunately that went too far in the end, as we know.

'I don't suppose, while you were with him, that he told you anything about his toxic mind games, did he? Did he mention how manipulative and controlling he can be, or frightening when things aren't going his way? Of course he didn't – he's hardly going to admit to the evil side of his character, is he? For you he'd have turned on all the charm, but believe me, he's rotten to the core and nothing you say could ever convince me he's changed.'

Unwilling to think she could have been so easily duped, while knowing it was highly possible, Cristy stored this away for future use, and said, 'He told me he was always in love with Lexie, not the other way round.'

Olivia barked out a laugh. 'You're proving my point,' she said. 'He says things that are patently untrue; we all know they're lies, but in this instance you didn't, so you're easier to deceive. Take it from me, he treated her appallingly at times, and it's only because she was afraid of losing her girls that she stayed. If you'd like to ask my husband about it, he's willing to confirm what I'm telling you, because he knows very well what David is like. So does Cynthia, of course, but I'm not sure she'll ever speak ill of her son. My mother would have, and she did, quite often, but being the way she was no one ever took much notice of her.'

Wishing they were already recording this, Cristy said, 'Would you be willing to see me later today so we can go through this again? I could explain, at the same time, how we're proposing to use it alongside your main interview.'

There was a moment's hesitation before Olivia said, 'I'm not sure . . . I mean, I guess it would be OK, but I'd like my husband to be there, so can I check with him first? He's just outside, I'll call you straight back. What time are you suggesting?'

'I'm happy with whatever suits you.'

As she rang off, Cristy let go a tremulous sigh. 'The way she sounded,' she said, staring at Olivia's picture on the wall, 'made me think of the breakdown she suffered, so I wouldn't be surprised if her husband steps forward now and vetoes the whole thing.'

'Christ, let's hope not,' Connor responded, 'or we won't have much of an episode for tomorrow.'

'There's nothing wrong with most of what she told you,' Clover pointed out, 'it's only when she talks about the rape that it gets tricky, but we can't use that anyway.'

Cristy nodded. This was true. Just as long as they stayed off the main subject, there wouldn't really be any reason for Will Caldwell to object.

Ten minutes later Cristy received a call from Frances Rush. After explaining that they'd been told the police might be looking into the murders again, Cristy said, 'Have you heard anything about that?'

'No, I haven't,' Rush replied, 'but I've been tied up with other things all weekend, which you'll probably hear about in the news later. A dawn raid, five arrests for trafficking and three Somali girls taken in by social services. Anyway, let me look into what you've said and get back to you. Incidentally, how did it go with Cynthia Gaudion?'

'I'll tell you about it next time, but it was interesting.'

Finally, after a further ten minutes, Olivia rang back. 'Will is suggesting we do it over Zoom,' she said, 'to save you coming all this way. He'll take part as well, but can it be after two, he's about to go into a meeting.'

By the end of the day they'd managed to record everything Olivia had told them in response to David's question: why would she lie, about the way he twisted things, played mind games with people and had come close to driving Lexie out of her mind. Although Olivia's answers second-time around lacked some of the shock and concern that had been in her voice when Cristy had first put them to her, they were still impactful. Surprisingly, both she and her husband, a silver-haired, round-faced, almost boyish-looking man in his fifties, agreed to Olivia's interview being used alongside Gaudion's without needing to hear what Gaudion had to say.

'Whatever it is, he's lying,' Will Caldwell stated forcefully, 'and it'll come out that way.' He was sitting shoulder-to-shoulder with his wife, a family portrait behind them and one of his hands clasping hers on the desk in front of them. 'I have no doubt,' he continued, 'that he'll lace his inherent mendacity with the odd truth here and there, a clever but despicably deceitful way of trying to discredit Olivia. As you know, I've never been happy about her getting involved in your podcast, but it has to be her decision. I just hope she isn't going to live to regret it.'

'We very much hope the same,' Cristy assured him. 'And we really appreciate you talking to us today.'

'I did it for her, but before we go, let me tell you this: David Gaudion is charm personified when it suits him, he'll probably even try to make out he's some sort of victim in all this, but don't forget, he's already proved, in the most heinous of ways, that he doesn't like to be crossed.'

As the screen went dark Connor waited a beat before saying, 'And there we have the final words of the next episode.'

'I wonder how understanding Gaudion will be about that?'

'Does it matter?' Connor countered.

Realizing it probably didn't, she said, 'I just don't want it to stop him from talking to me again. Maybe I should call now to set it up?' Unlocking her phone, she scrolled to his number and was surprised when he answered on the second ring.

'I wasn't expecting to hear from you so soon,' he told her, his tone not warm, but not entirely unfriendly either. 'Have you decided when you'd like to meet?'

Putting the call on speaker, she said, 'I'm sure I can make myself available at a time that would suit you. I just wondered how you'd feel about my co-producer, Connor Church, coming with me.'

'If it makes you feel more comfortable, safer even, to bring back-up, I have no objection, but I've been giving this some thought and I'd like to make a suggestion.'

Her eyebrows rose as she looked at the others. 'I'm listening,' she told him.

'I'd appreciate it if we could talk first and record after. That way I'll have a good idea of what you're going to ask and it'll give me a second shot at my answers. Not that they'll change – obviously you'll know if they do – but if we go about it that way, I could probably be clearer and more detailed where it counts. Are you agreeable to that?'

As the others scowled discouragement, she said, 'Yes, I'm sure that'll be fine.'

'Good. So shall we say three o'clock tomorrow?'

She hesitated. They were already running down the clock trying to prepare everything for a six o'clock upload. Losing both her and Connor would make it virtually impossible.

Connor was mouthing, *go for it.*

'OK,' she said, frowning at him, 'we'll see you then.'

'You go,' Connor told her as soon as she'd rung off. 'I'll just be extra to requirements anyway, and someone has to get the next pod to air.'

'And we definitely don't want to miss out on his version of events,' Jackson put in.

'That's right, you go back down there all on your own,' Clover said sarcastically, 'have a nice cosy little chat with a killer and let him decide if things are going his way before he lets you record. Yeah, I can see how that will work for him.'

Cristy shot her a narrow-eyed look. 'If you think I'm that easily manipulated,' she retorted, 'then I'm afraid you don't know me at all.'

Later, as Cristy stepped off the cross-harbour ferry to find Aiden waiting for her on the jetty, early for once, she was impressed to see that he'd taken her advice that morning to get himself a haircut. In fact, he was extremely pleased with himself, he told her, as they circled the harbour wall to start heading towards Millennium Square.

'I got up just after you left this morning,' he boasted, 'and apart from my quick fix at ChopBox, I've been at home all day washing and ironing ready for tomorrow.'

'You were ironing!' she cried incredulously.

He shrugged. 'Well, I got it out of the cupboard, but then I figured it would all get creased in the bag anyway, so why bother? How about you? Cool day at the podcast hive?'

'Busy. A lot going on, but I'm looking forward to this evening. Where are we going?'

'Steak of the Art. Josh and his parents are going to be a few minutes late. Apparently someone parked across their drive so they couldn't get out.'

'The joys of living in Clifton. So what time are you all setting off tomorrow?'

'About seven, I think. I am so up for this. We're doing kayaking, mountain biking, hang-gliding – we've signed up for everything. You know what Josh's dad is like, Mr Action Man. He's the dude, *and* he knows where to get some stash while we're there.'

Cristy turned to him. 'Seriously? He's supplying drugs for you? I think I've just changed my mind about you going.'

'Joke! Just wanted to see your reaction. No way is he into the magic stuff . . .'

'And you shouldn't be either. The only reason Dad and I turn a blind eye now and again is so you won't do it behind our backs and get into the hard stuff.'

'And it's working. I'm a good boy, just a dabble here and there, same as you guys when you were my age.'

'Same as Dad, I was never really into it.'

'Says you. Anyway, I got to tell you this, Mum, I wish you were going to be in France when we get there. The thought of spending two whole weeks with Dad and the Marley is already doing my head in. That woman is such a ball-ache.'

'Charming.'

'Well, she is. Hey, man!' he cried, stopping to fist-bump a lad Cristy recognized from his school. 'How's shit?'

'Shit's good. What's going down with you?'

'Off to Spain tomorrow, France after. Catch up when I'm back?'

'Cool. See you then.'

Smiling at the exchange, Cristy waved to someone she knew and resisted taking Aiden's arm as they walked on. Chilled though he was, he probably wouldn't like it. 'You'll have Josh to keep you company,' she reminded him, picking up where they'd left off, 'and Hayley and Hugo will be there for some of the time, so you'll be fine.'

'Oh yeah, I know that, it's *her*, the Marley, who won't. She's desperate to be your friend. It's all she bloody talks about these days. "What do I have to do, Aiden?" "Please speak to her for me. I know Dad's tried, but I think you'll have more influence." She even cries about it, sobbing and trying to put her arms around me. It's like, woah, no hugs here, baby. I'm telling you, she's like a kid who forgot to grow up. Hormones, Dad calls it. And get a load of this, she actually asked me what I thought she'd done to turn you against her.'

Cristy stopped walking. 'You don't mean that.'

'I swear, it's what she said. I told her, like duh. "But we're all over that now," she says, "it's in the past. We have to move on, especially with the baby coming. We need to be one big happy family."'

Cristy stared at him in disbelief, and yet she did believe it, because Marley really wasn't like normal people. In fact, she was so unlike anyone else Cristy knew that she had no idea how to begin figuring out what was in her head.

'Does she say all this in front of Dad?'

Aiden shrugged. 'Sometimes. He never engages, though; makes out like he hasn't heard or his phone's just rung so he has to take a call. Hayley and I reckon he's regretting this big time and wishes he hadn't been such a horny-ass-stupid-cunt when he first met her. Bit late now he's got her up the duff though, innit?'

While wincing at the language, Cristy was thinking how right the children were about their father, and what a hopeless predicament he'd got himself into. Of course, it wasn't anything she could help with, and nor would she, were it in her power, but she couldn't deny that a small part of her was actually starting to feel sorry for him. There was no way he could escape the marriage without proving to the world at large what a total bastard he was, and that was something a man like him, who lived so much of his life in the public eye, would find impossible to deal with. In fact, it was a miracle he'd come through the negative publicity he'd received at the time of his affair and their break-up with his ego intact, although maybe that just showed how big it was.

'Earth to Mother,' Aiden called, waving a hand in front of her face.

She glanced at him, and moved on. She was wondering now if Matthew had decided that reuniting with her might in some way mitigate his abandonment of a young, pregnant woman. Was that what lay behind his ludicrous declaration of undying love? If so, he was completely out of his mind.

Realizing her phone was vibrating, she checked the screen. Her heart did a giant flip when she saw who it was. 'Please don't be cancelling on me,' she muttered as she debated whether or not to take the call now.

'Who is it?' Aiden asked.

'It's to do with work,' she replied. 'Go on ahead in case they get there on time. I'll catch up as soon as I've dealt with this.'

He ambled off in the direction of the restaurant, mobile in hand, while Cristy took the call, 'Mr Gaudion. What can I do for you?'

'David,' he replied, 'unless you prefer to remain formal.'

Realizing how pompous she'd sound if she said she did, she repeated his name and said, 'I hope there's not a problem about tomorrow.'

'I'm afraid there is. Something's come up that I have to deal with in person, so my mother and I will be leaving Exmoor in the morning.'

Trying not to feel frustrated or angry, she said, 'I'm sorry to hear that. Nothing too serious, I hope.'

'It'll be sorted. Meantime, if you're prepared to travel, I should have some time free on Thursday or Friday. Would that suit?'

Was he kidding? 'Travel? To where?' she asked, already knowing she'd go even if it was Sydney.

'Not far, just to Guernsey.'

The Channel Islands. 'Is that where you live?' she asked.

'It is.'

'With your mother?'

'And two of my three children.'

Thrown by him telling her this so freely, she skipped the 'three

310

children' for now and said, 'Is it where you've been since . . .?' How was she going to end that question?

'Since losing Lexie?' he provided. 'Yes.'

'I see. Well, I'd be very happy to come there. If you can give me your address . . .'

'I'll arrange your flights and see that you're picked up at the airport. Perhaps I should book a hotel in case you decide to remain overnight.'

'No, really, I can sort myself out.'

'As you please.'

'I'll text you the details as soon as I have them.'

'OK,' and without as much as a goodbye he'd gone.

She put her phone away and walked on, still trying to take in the last few minutes. Guernsey. A place she'd never even considered he might be, although why would she when it had never been mentioned? It was, apparently, the place he now lived with two of his three children. So had he married again? He hadn't mentioned a wife, but it was ludicrous to think a man like him had spent the past sixteen years alone. Curious that no one on the island had come forward to reveal his presence there – or maybe they had, and sums of money were required for the information. She'd get Clover to check, although it hardly mattered now that he'd told her himself where he was, and sometime in the next couple of days she was going to be heading there.

CHAPTER TWENTY-EIGHT

Forty-eight hours later, after a lengthy delay at Bristol airport, Cristy was on her way south to the Channel Islands. As the small plane took off, heading for the Devonshire coast, she was listening to the latest episode of *Hindsight*. The pod had finally been uploaded last night after a crazy day of laying down Olivia's full interview and interlocking later parts with David's comments. It was lucky that she, Cristy, had still been around or they probably wouldn't have made the six o'clock drop. As it was, she'd have preferred another couple of hours of fine-tuning, but at least the programme contained all the information they'd foreshadowed at the end of episode three. This one closed with a promise to bring more from David Gaudion in the next instalment, something in itself that would guarantee listeners stayed with them and very probably increase in number. She'd also mentioned the tip-off they'd received that senior police and CPS lawyers were looking into the Kellon Manse Murders again, after receiving information passed on by *Hindsight*.

Somehow Clover had managed to revisit the ever-swelling cache of listener messages and had managed to unearth several 'sightings' of David Gaudion that could be genuine. If they hadn't all required some sort of reward for their information, they wouldn't have been ignored, but to enter into negotiations of that sort was almost always a waste of time and money, since they were usually from chancers who knew nothing at all. However, if they'd thought to look up Gaudion's surname, as Jackson had yesterday, they'd have discovered that it had originated in France, and was not exactly uncommon on Guernsey. So, did this mean that David Gaudion had relatives on the island, and that was why he'd chosen to go there?

Once they'd known what to look for – his digital footprint was extremely light to the point of mostly obscure – they'd discovered that he was now a wealth manager advising high net-worth individuals on how to invest their portfolios and plan finances to meet their fiscal goals. Given where he lived, he presumably didn't have to work hard to find clients.

There was nothing about his immediate family – Jackson was still looking – so as yet Cristy didn't know anything about the mother of his two younger children, presuming Rosaria was the eldest. Nor was she sure who'd be picking her up when she got to the island; he'd simply texted back to say someone would be waiting. *Good choice of hotel,* he'd added. *Should be comfortable there if you decide to stay over.*

Having no idea yet whether or not she would, she began searching the latest pod for the part Olivia had contacted her about an hour after it had dropped.

'I didn't realize you were going to do that,' she'd complained. 'I wish you hadn't.'

'I offered to let you listen first,' Cristy reminded her, 'but I'm sorry if it's upset you.'

'I'm not sure upset is the right word, or maybe it is. It seems to devalue what I told you, and I know Lexie wouldn't have wanted that.'

'I don't think it detracts from what you said at all,' Cristy argued, 'and if the early feedback is anything to go by, nor does anyone else. We've already received dozens of comments praising your courage for speaking up and offering sympathy for what you've been through. I can ask Clover to send the messages on if you like.'

'No, that won't be necessary. I guess it was hearing my voice with David's, almost as if we were . . . *challenging* one another, that I found unsettling. What are they saying about him?'

'Not much that I'd want to repeat,' Cristy replied. 'In other words, he doesn't seem to have won any friends so far.' This wasn't strictly true. The response to him had been mixed: some inevitable fan mail (funny what a handsome face and hint of ruthlessness could do), others claiming it was high time he was brought to justice, while still others criticized her, Cristy, for giving airtime to a murderer. A few shouty ones labelled him a liar and child killer who should have been locked up years ago. However, Olivia probably didn't need to know those details yet. 'For what it's worth,' she continued, 'I think you're right not to engage with any of the feedback. The trolls haven't really got started yet, but when they do, none of us will be spared. Makes you wonder about their mental health.'

The call had ended just after that, and though she'd known Olivia was still troubled, at least she'd agreed to meet up again after Cristy returned from Guernsey. Of course, she wanted to hear what David had to say so she could correct the record, as she'd put it, and Cristy would be more than happy to give her the chance.

Having found the section Olivia had objected to, she pressed play and sat back to listen, pen poised, ready to take notes.

CRISTY: 'Here's Olivia talking about Lexie's early relationship with David, followed by David's comments on the same subject.'

OLIVIA: '. . . she was always in love with him. Right from when we were children . . . She was besotted with him. He could never do any wrong in her eyes, and he did plenty, believe me, but it never seemed to matter to her, or that he didn't feel the same about her.'

DAVID: 'It isn't true that Lexie always had a crush on me, or was in love with me. In fact, it was the other way around. I was the one who was in love with her, right from when we were small children.'

OLIVIA: 'As we got older it broke her heart to see him with other girls, to never be his proper date, just a friend, when we went to parties or concerts . . .'

DAVID: 'By the time we were in our teens I was head over heels in love with her and I had eyes for no one else. Which isn't to say I didn't date other girls, because I did, but only because Lexie wasn't interested in me.'

OLIVIA: 'She'd drop everything and go anywhere just to be with him.'

DAVID: 'Her great love was for the science of human beings, not the mundane reality of them.'

CRISTY: 'Was David ever violent towards her?'

OLIVIA: 'Not in the physical sense . . . but he could be impatient, dismissive, not always kind.'

DAVID: 'How much did Olivia tell you about the attack?'

CRISTY: 'He's referring to an incident at Oxford here that, for legal reasons, we can't yet go into. I told him that Olivia had claimed he was there when it happened and he asked me, quite abruptly, to stop the recording. He was visibly upset, so I gave him a few moments before asking why Olivia would say it if it wasn't true. His answer was, "Why don't you ask Olivia?" So I did. We weren't recording when she gave her first answer, but what you're about to hear is virtually a repeat of what she told me.'

OLIVIA: 'He knows the truth as well as I do, but of course he's managed to make you question what I said. He's very good at making people think things that are totally contrary to what they believe. I'm not sure how he does it, it's a strange sort of . . . insight that he has, to know what's going on in your head, and then he somehow uses it for his own purposes, or to mess with you. It almost drove my sister out of her mind.'

CRISTY: 'We've already heard Olivia talking about Lexie's emotional struggles and how she became a member of Papilio. We haven't yet had a chance to put any of it to David Gaudion, but we will.

'Before we end this, I brought up the contradiction over Lexie and David's childhood relationship again. Here's Olivia's reply.'

OLIVIA: 'You're proving my point. He says things that are

patently untrue; we all know they're lies, but in this instance you didn't, so you're easier to deceive.'

Cristy clicked off the recording and sighed out a long breath as she turned to gaze at the passing clouds. If Gaudion really was the master manipulator Olivia and others were claiming him to be (Cristy didn't actually doubt it, given how he'd already set ground rules for his interview and was trying to take control of the time she spent in Guernsey) then this was going to be an interesting trip.

It wasn't easy to say what happened, or even how it happened, but almost from the moment Cristy set foot off the plane in Guernsey she had a sense of entering a slightly different world. Although it was essentially British – same language, same currency, same side of the road for driving – the feel of the place wasn't quite what she'd expected. Nor could she say exactly what made it different. She just felt as though she'd stepped from the confines of her normal life into . . . Well, into something else.

Cynthia and Rosaria Gaudion were waiting in arrivals as she came through, Rosaria, a blonde-haired, bouncy woman-child, lighting up with joy as if they already knew one another.

'*Bianvnu, bianvnu,*' she'd called out, waving and smiling all over her dear, sweet face.

Realizing this must be a version of the French *bien venue,* Cristy laughed as Rosaria hugged her and Cynthia, smiling on fondly, said, 'Welcome to Guernsey, my dear. We're your taxi service. The car is just outside.'

It turned out to be a four-seater electric smart, and as Cynthia drove them steadily along narrow, winding roads lined with quaint stone cottages, towering wrought-iron gates, forested hillsides and sweeping fields with occasional glimpses of a shimmering blue sea, it was like being in a sublime mix of the familiarly rural and the temptingly exotic. Rosaria sat in the back explaining where they were going and what they were passing, throwing out such useful information as: 'My friend Lydia lives in that house,' or 'That's the church we go to at Christmas,' or 'You can get really good fish and chips there.

'Granny's booked us into Pier 17 for lunch,' she chattered on cheerfully, 'it's in St Peter Port. That's our capital, like London or Paris, only smaller and on the sea. Daddy's office is there, and I work with him sometimes.'

'Really?' Cristy queried, turning to get a better look at the guilelessly sunny face that struck her as so precious she was already having doubts about why she was here. The last thing in the world she'd ever want to do was hurt this young woman who'd already been through so much in her life. 'What do you do?' she asked.

'Oh, depends which office he's in. He's got two and another at home. I'm a big help sometimes, aren't I, Granny?'

'You are indeed,' Cynthia confirmed. Then to Cristy, 'With your flight being delayed, I thought you'd be hungry so I'm taking us straight to the restaurant. Is that OK?'

'Absolutely,' Cristy replied, touched that they'd thought of it, while still inwardly trying to hold back from being too drawn in by these apparently guileless women. 'Will David be joining us?'

'If he can,' Cynthia replied. 'Otherwise we'll meet up with him after. Rosaria, darling, you're blocking the rear-view mirror.'

'Sorry! Do you like pantomimes, Cristy?' she asked, bouncing to move behind her. 'I'm going to be in ours this year. It's *Beauty and the Beast* and I'm playing Beauty.'

'You're the understudy,' Cynthia gently corrected.

'Oh yes. We start rehearsing in a couple of weeks. Judy Moore is directing, and we all love Judy, don't we, Granny? I was in last year's as well. She always lets me be in the panto. I do other plays too, but I like Judy's pantos the best. Would you like to see the theatre while you're here? And the rehearsal room? It's full of costumes and props and things. Very interesting. Oh! We've just gone past the Ladies College where my sister went to school, but this is Elizabeth College where my brother, Laurent, goes. He's in France this week with his *maman*, Juliette.'

'And how old are your brother and sister?' Cristy asked, knowing full well that Cynthia would be on high alert now.

'Laurent's eleven,' Rosaria replied. 'He's very good at sports, especially cricket and rugby – oh, and sailing which he does a lot with Daddy. Do you sail, Cristy?'

317

'Not really,' she replied, feeling, absurdly, as if she was letting Rosaria down.

'Nor me, but I crew for Daddy sometimes. And for Maggie and John if they'll let me. They're our neighbours at the cider farm. We see them a lot. You can do a tour of their farm if you like. It's very interesting. I work there sometimes, giving out chutney to the visitors.'

Sighing out a laugh, Cynthia said, 'You're a proper little chatterbox, Rosie Gaudion. You're hardly giving Cristy time to think, and you know she's here to see Daddy . . .'

'Yes, but there are lots of other things to do. Did you know that Victor Hugo lived here?' she asked Cristy.

Cristy absorbed this with interest, because no, she hadn't known that, but she did know that the great master was reputed to have been a freemason. Did that mean there were still lodges on the island? Undoubtedly there were, given they were everywhere.

'Laurent's been studying him at school,' Rosaria was telling her. 'We can visit his house, if you like. He's very interesting. He wrote *Les Misérables* when he was here. Have you seen it?'

'I have,' Cristy smiled. 'And you?'

'Yes, three times, twice in New York and once in Sydney. Oh, we've got a surprise for you, haven't we, Granny?' Before Cynthia could respond, Rosaria clapped a hand to her mouth. 'Sorry, I wasn't supposed to say anything. Anyway, it doesn't matter because I've forgotten what it is.'

Laughing, Cynthia said, 'Well, that's a good thing or it wouldn't be a surprise any more. Now, let's hope we can find a parking space somewhere around here.'

As they drove onto a pier where parked cars were lined up either side, Cristy looked out at all the yachts and motor boats, grey stone harbour buildings and strolling tourists. It was certainly picturesque, and though she was in no doubt that Gaudion – apparently pronounced the French way here – had sent his mother and daughter to open up some sort of charm offensive, she had to admit she was quite glad he had. Rosaria really was a delight, and this time with her and Cynthia was allowing Cristy to get something of a feel for the family and how they lived today, although there was still clearly much to learn about Laurent's other sister and presumably French mother.

The restaurant turned out to be at the end of the pier overlooking the quay, where boats of all shapes and sizes were bobbing at anchor in the full tide, or coming and going from the ferry terminal across the port. Large parasols were protecting a dozen or so terrace tables from the midday sun, and as they settled at one close to the water's edge, Cristy watched Rosaria and Cynthia greeting many of the staff and other diners. It was clear they were well known in the town, which presumably meant Gaudion was too.

No sooner had they placed their orders than three large glasses of lemonade arrived and Rosaria suddenly shot up from her chair. 'There's Daddy!' she cried, waving frantically. 'Daddy! Daddy!'

'He can't hear you from here, sweetheart,' Cynthia said as Cristy looked across the basin towards a boatyard where a dozen or more vessels were raised up on blocks.

'I'll text him,' Rosaria decided, sitting down again.

Having spotted Gaudion now, talking to another man, Cristy watched for a moment as he gesticulated and laughed, shook his head and turned to call out to someone else.

Apparently Rosaria's text didn't arrive before he and the other man disappeared inside an enormous steel grey warehouse with *Maritime Maintenance* blazoned across it.

'That's Daddy's boatyard,' Rosaria told her proudly.

'He's a part-owner,' Cynthia corrected.

Rosaria nodded agreement. 'He's got an office over there and another close to the high street for when he's doing finance things.'

'Do you live in town?' Cristy asked, picking up her drink. The port was overlooked by some pretty enormous properties and she couldn't imagine Gaudion's being small.

'Actually, we're inland,' Cynthia replied. 'Only about fifteen minutes from your hotel, in fact, which is on the west coast, if you didn't already know that.'

'We're on the east coast here,' Rosaria chipped in. 'The Cobo Bay Hotel where you're staying is very nice, right across from the beach. We go there sometimes for dinner or cocktails. And to swim when the tide is in.'

Thinking how lovely it was of Ruth, Harry and Meena's PA, to have booked her somewhere that sounded so appealing, Cristy said, 'I'm not sure yet that I'll be staying,' but even as she uttered the words she realized that her delayed arrival made it almost certain that she'd have to.

'Dad's on his way over,' Rosaria informed them, looking up from her phone. 'He says he doesn't want to eat, he'll have some of my *frites*. He's cheeky.' She laughed, perhaps a little too loudly, but the joy of it was infectious anyway.

For the next twenty minutes as their food arrived and more drinks were ordered Rosaria continued to chat about the island, showing off a little of her *Guernésiais*, the local patois. She even recited a few lines from the national anthem before going on to talk about the new horse in their stables.

Since trying to badger Rosaria with reminders of events she'd no doubt put a long way behind her would be unforgivably insensitive, even cruel, Cristy was happy simply to listen. It was a beautiful day; the surroundings were idyllic and the burble of chat mixing with gulls' cries and clanking yacht masts was wonderfully relaxing. She could almost be on holiday; however, she wasn't so lost to the moment that she could stop herself wondering how much Rosaria remembered of her mother, and what she actually knew about why she and her grandmother had left Berkeley Vale when she was fifteen.

After a while, as Rosaria fell into a chat with someone on the next table, Cristy said to Cynthia, 'What made you come to Guernsey? I know, of course, why you wanted to get away, but why here?'

Cynthia smiled as she replaced her knife and fork on her plate. 'My husband has family here that go way back,' she replied. 'He used to say to 1066, but I'm not too sure about that. They were farmers mostly; a couple were scoundrels and a couple more financiers – we always say they're one and the same thing.' She chuckled at the tease. 'The first time I came here was with my parents on holiday, back when I was still in my teens. That's how Don and I met, and after a couple of years of writing letters and phoning once a week, a few more holidays as well, he moved to England to work our farm with my dad and my brothers. As you probably already know, he took over in the end, got properly settled in, while Ronald and George went off to do their own thing.'

'Do you miss England?' Cristy ventured.

Cynthia frowned as if trying to remember. 'I did, at first,' she confessed, 'but you can see for yourself how lovely it is here, and it's always been much better for the children. Rosaria's blossomed in ways I'm not sure would have been possible if we'd stayed in Gloucestershire, not after all that happened, although she was always a little ray of sunshine, weren't you, my pet?'

Rosaria was about to reply when two large hands claimed her shoulders, and spinning round she broke into a delighted laugh.

'Dad!' she cried. 'You made me jump.'

Stooping to kiss the top of her head, Gaudion reached out a hand to shake Cristy's and she was surprised to discover how self-conscious she suddenly felt, as if she was some sort of interloper they were too polite to try to exclude. 'Welcome to Guernsey,' he said. 'Sorry I couldn't get away to meet you myself, but I hope these two have been keeping you entertained.'

Before Cristy could reply, Rosaria said, 'We're going to take Cristy to see the theatre while she's here, and the rehearsal rooms. I should probably text Judy Moore to make sure it's OK.'

Folding a hand over hers as she started her message, Gaudion said, 'I'm not sure Cristy's going to have time for all that, but it's lovely of you to be so friendly.'

Rosaria beamed at Cristy, then shrieked a protest as David helped himself to her chips.

'I told Cristy you were cheeky,' she informed him.

He threw out his hands in mock despair. 'Now she'll have an even lower opinion of me than she already has,' he grumbled.

Rosaria looked bemused and Cynthia said, 'He's only joking. Now, are you going to have a dessert?'

Rosaria's eyes went to her father.

'I promise I won't steal it,' he said, crossing his heart. 'Unless it's ice-cream. Then I might have to.'

'I always have ice-cream,' Rosaria cried, clearly enjoying the tease. 'It's my favourite.'

As David ordered, Cristy found herself wondering what was

really going on his mind now, how he actually felt about her being here, what he was expecting to gain or lose from it. He was hard to read with eyes masked by dark glasses, but his manner was easy and nothing in his tone was unfriendly or resentful, or even cautious. On the surface he came over as just another yachtie-type in a navy polo shirt and knee-length shorts, tanned skin and leather flip flops. No one here today would look at him and see a man who'd once been charged with a triple murder and perhaps a fourth; a man who still, in fact, had that very same charge hanging over him.

CHAPTER TWENTY-NINE

Half an hour later, after Cynthia and Rosaria had driven off in the smart, Gaudion showed Cristy through the chandlery at Maritime Maintenance and up a back staircase into a conference-room-cum-office. It was one of the most impressive meeting rooms she'd seen with its wall-to-wall windows onto the port and open sea beyond; in fact, it was almost like being on board a small ship. If it was meant to distract her, it could succeed, given how tempting it was to sit and watch the ebb and flow of the world outside.

'So, here you are in Guernsey,' he stated, taking two small bottles of water from a fridge and passing one across the table to her. 'Your first time?'

Nodding, she unscrewed the cap and took a sip as he sat down facing her, back to the view. She could see his eyes now he'd taken off his sunglasses, and she realized it was slightly unsettling to find herself under their scrutiny. 'Seems I chose a good day, weather-wise,' she added with a smile.

'With it being mid-summer the chances were good,' he said dryly, regarding her in a way that stirred her defences. This wasn't going to be easy, she could tell that already, but she wasn't as daunted by him as he might like to think. What mattered was not letting him get the upper hand. 'So you asked Olivia why she lied,' he stated, 'and she, of course, denied that she had.'

With the confirmation that he'd heard the latest episode, she said, 'Is that what you expected?'

He shrugged, as if it didn't make much difference. 'I'm not sure what's going on with her,' he said, 'or who might have got to her, but tell me this, if I was involved in the attack on Lexie,

323

why the hell would she have married me? You've got to have asked yourself that question, so please, I'm interested to know the answer.'

Trying not to feel on the back foot, she said, 'According to Olivia, your parents had a hand in it.'

He looked confused.

'She said they more or less forced you into it, and as it was what Lexie always wanted, she agreed.'

His expression was pure incredulity. 'And you swallowed that?' he challenged with something akin to a laugh.

'Are you telling me it isn't true?'

'I don't have to tell you anything, but you've met my mother and you've met me, so do you really think either of us would have tried to force Lexie into a marriage she didn't want after what had happened to her?'

Having no choice but to concede the point when, for the moment at least, she really did consider it unlikely, she said, 'Then it brings me back to the question, why would Olivia lie about it?'

For a long time he said nothing, simply stared past her to the mirrored back wall, not at his own reflection, but, she suspected, into a world it was impossible for her to see. She noticed the gentle rise and fall of his chest as he breathed, the glint of sunlight threading through the hairs on his arms. His physical presence was as compelling as she'd been told it was, although she had yet to detect much of the famed charisma.

In the end, he said, 'Has she told you *who* was involved in the rape?'

Her eyes widened slightly. She hadn't expected that. 'Apart from yours, she hasn't divulged any names.'

He didn't seem surprised. 'I guess she wouldn't have. She'd be too afraid to go there after what happened to her mother and sister.'

'So you're telling me that the rapists were behind what happened to Lexie and Margaret?'

'And Serena,' he added.

She nodded. 'And your daughter?'

His face darkened, but he only stared at her, as if trying to gauge what she was really thinking, or perhaps where they should go next with this.

'Olivia believes you killed them all,' she told him.

He shook his head slowly. 'It's beyond me,' he said, 'the way some people can convince themselves of a story that they know isn't true. It's like she has to believe I was the killer, because if she doesn't, she'll have to try and find out who did it, and she knows that really wouldn't be wise.'

Grabbing onto that, she said, 'So these people, the rapists, presuming you're not one of them, remain a threat?'

He frowned slightly. 'I'd appreciate you counting me out of their number.' After a beat he continued, 'I sent you a message when you started your podcast, warning you to look at what happened to the girl, Iris.'

Cristy blinked. 'So the email was from you?' Of course she'd considered it, but it was a surprise to hear him admit it. 'Does that mean you know it wasn't an accident?'

'Actually, I don't know anything, but the coincidence was . . . How should I put this? Let's say it concerned me.'

'And now you think they'll come after me and my team?'

His eyes narrowed slightly. 'Have they?' he asked.

Deciding to be truthful, she said, 'It's possible. Someone came to my office and advised me not to use the names Olivia had given me. He didn't say who'd sent him.'

'Mm, no, he wouldn't.'

Not quite sure why she was trusting him with this, she said, 'He mentioned my children and the pregnant wife of my partner.'

His eyes hardened.

'Should I take him seriously?'

'Have you told the police?'

She nodded.

'Then you've already taken it seriously. Personally, I don't think anything will happen to them; it was more likely a well-used tactic intended to make you back off. You see, no one wants this case opened up again. There is too much to lose, for everyone.'

'Including you?'

'Yes, including me. If I tell you what you want to hear, I'll be putting my own family at risk. I haven't done that for a very long time, and I wouldn't be talking to you now if you hadn't managed to get as far as you have.'

Feeling slightly discomfited, she said, 'So you believe that having met your family – your mother and eldest daughter, anyway – I will want to protect them too and so shut everything down?'

'Don't you want to protect them?'

The obvious answer was, of course, but she could tell he was manipulating her now, pushing her into a place she couldn't escape without doing as he wanted. 'Tell me,' she countered, 'how much of what you've just told me would you be prepared to say on tape?'

He gave a laugh and quite suddenly the tension was gone. 'Good move,' he said approvingly, 'and the answer is, some, but not all, and not right now.'

Sensing that to try to push it wouldn't achieve the right result, she decided to return them to the rape, hoping the sudden change of direction would wrongfoot him into saying something unguarded. 'It's hard to think of Rosaria coming from such a violent act when she's so sweet,' she commented, not liking herself much for it, but it had to be done.

His eyes were like flint as he regarded her closely. 'Your point being?' he asked.

'Olivia says you're Rosaria's real father, so doesn't it follow that you were there that night?'

'All you need to know,' he replied coldly, 'is that she's mine in every way that matters.'

'So not biologically?'

He sat back in his chair. 'I understand why you've drawn the conclusions you have about Rosie,' he said, 'I'm just sorry that Olivia has chosen to paint me in the kind of light she has.'

'Why would she do it?'

'Maybe she believes I was involved in the attack.'

Cristy frowned. 'You intimated just now that she's convinced herself you were, even though it isn't true.'

'Precisely.'

Feeling they were starting to go in circles, she said, 'Have you ever determined the identity of Rosaria's natural father?'

'I am her father. That is all she, or you, need to know.'

In spite of the ambiguity, she accepted the answer, for now, and said, 'And your other children?'

'Are mine in all the ways that will satisfy you.'

Taking that as an oblique suggestion that Rosaria wasn't actually his, she found herself wondering how much more subtext she might be missing. If she'd cheated and recorded she'd be able to play it back later to assess it, but she hadn't, so she simply noted his answer down and said, 'Will you tell me about them?'

'What do you want to know?'

'Maybe we can begin with their mother, Juliette? I believe that's her name.'

He crooked an eyebrow. 'Juliette is French,' he said. 'A talented artist and not-so-good poet. We were together for several years before she decided to move back to Paris. Laurent, our son, has remained here with me.'

'And is being educated at Elizabeth College. Rosaria told me. What about your other daughter?'

'Anna? She is not Juliette's, but she too lives here on the island, mostly with me, but she has a place of her own in town.'

'How old is she?'

Their eyes locked and for a bizarre moment it was as though time itself came to a stop. She could tell he knew exactly what she was thinking, and she wanted him to know, wanted to find out if she was right. If she was it would be explosive.

In the end, he said, 'Why haven't you asked me anything about Serena Sutton or Paul O'Malley, aka Paolo Morelli?'

Disappointed by the back-down, but deciding to go with the flow, she waved a hand for him to continue.

'Have you met O'Malley?' he asked.

'Not in person. Have you?'

'Just the once. Serena several times. She was . . .' He considered his words before saying, 'Lexie was very attached to her, and actually with good reason. They shared a rapport, a trust, that Lexie hadn't really found with anyone else. Not even me, or Olivia. Sometimes it takes an outsider, someone who isn't going to be hurt by your memories or your fears, to get to the heart of you. That was how Lexie described her to me, as a friend who couldn't be scarred or damaged by her past the way I had been.'

Surprised by this admission, she said, 'Did you feel damaged by what had happened to her?'

His smile wasn't real. 'It's impossible not to be affected by the pain of someone you love.'

Knowing the truth of that, she said, 'The last time we spoke you said she wasn't in love with you. Do you think that changed after you were married?'

Once again he took some time to consider his answer, until finally he said, 'I told you then that she loved me like a brother. That didn't change, but of course we were closer than that, a lot closer, but it wasn't always . . .' He stopped and started again. 'The intimate side of our relationship was never easy. I hoped, once she started to see Serena, that things might improve, that she could start tolerating . . . Maybe that's not the right word, enjoying might be better. The therapy was having a positive effect on her in every other way, and it continued to after she was drawn into O'Malley's sphere.

'I know Olivia's told you how appalled I was by the money that was changing hands, and it's true, I was. Anyone would be, and all the secrecy around it made things worse, but it was hard to argue with Lexie when I could see her breaking out of the shell she'd shut herself in. She used to say she was a butterfly hatching from a chrysalis, but that won't surprise you given the name of the cult.'

'So you do think of it as a cult?'

He shrugged. 'It's hard to see it any other way, but I wouldn't consider it particularly harmful given what they did for Lexie's state of mind.'

'So you don't think O'Malley was involved in the killings?'

'Not directly.'

Cristy frowned. 'What does that mean?'

'She told him the names of the rapists, and if he's connected in some way to one or more of them, and I believe he is, he'd have considered it his duty to alert them to the fact that she was finally speaking out. It's the only scenario that makes sense, when he was making good money out of her and she was about to introduce her mother. So what would be in it for him to end their association by killing them?'

It seemed a reasonable deduction, if anything he was telling her was true. 'Did you know that when Iris lost her life, it was just after making contact with O'Malley?' she asked.

He looked surprised. 'No, I didn't.'

Deciding to leave that there for now, she said, 'Did you know Serena was coming to the house the day of the murders?'

Appearing unperturbed by the change of direction, he said, 'Yes, I did. I also knew that Margaret was very probably playing one of her monstrous tricks on Lexie, letting her think she was happy to join the "butterfly bimbos" – her words, but whether she would have – I doubt it very much. Her reputation for being mean was well-deserved, so I can't see her parting with the kind of sums O'Malley was after.'

'Did you and Lexie discuss her mother joining Papilio?'

'Not at any length. She knew I wasn't convinced by Margaret's interest, and because she so desperately wanted to help Margaret defeat "her demons", she allowed herself to believe that the cult was going to do it, and might even end up bringing them closer together.' His voice was quieter as he added, 'She was like the puppy that always returns to a cruel master where her mother was concerned.'

While feeling the poignancy of that, she decided to move them on. 'I'm guessing you timed your run that day for when you knew Serena would be visiting?'

He nodded. 'Like everything else that happened that day, it's in my police statement.'

'Which has mysteriously disappeared.'

His eyebrows rose in surprise, but he didn't comment.

'You were out for about three hours, I believe, and when you returned you came up the drive?'

'To utter chaos and all hell breaking loose,' he confirmed.

Watching him closely, she said, 'I've followed your route that day, and it took me to the hill behind Kellon Hall where you can see all over the Vale, but most particularly down to the front drive of the Manse. Didn't you notice the emergency vehicles then? And if you did, why didn't you run down through the fields, which would have been a much quicker route home?'

For a moment he seemed almost confused as he looked at her. 'I think you're presuming I carried on to the hilltop after leaving the woods,' he said, 'but there's another route from there that circles around the brow to the far side of the fields and eventually brings you down onto the road. That's the route I took. It's in my statement.'

Since she hadn't seen the statement, had only had Kevin Break's old files as guidance, she could only say, 'So when you got to the house—'

'Flora Gibson and a whole lot of police officers saw me come back. If you want to know what happened, then you need to ask them. Actually, Flora's already told you, of course. Personally, I'd rather not relive it.'

Remembering Flora describing how he'd forced his way into the house and had thrown up the instant he was outside again, she said, 'Did you see Amelia that day? Not then, but earlier?'

'Yes. We all had breakfast together, and after she and Rosie left to go to my mother's.'

'With Olivia?'

'That's right.'

'Did Olivia know Lexie was going to introduce their mother to Serena?'

'I believe Olivia's already told you that she did. She was no more approving of the cult than I was, but equally as torn given the results.'

'So Olivia took the girls to your mother and you have no idea what happened to Amelia after that?'

'As a matter of fact, I do know, but before I tell you I'd like you to tell me why you think the police and CPS are opening up the investigation again. You said in your podcast that it's based on information you passed to them.'

He was looking pale now, and as though he'd like to bring things to an end, but not before he'd received an answer to his question. It was, she guessed, the only reason he was speaking so frankly – at least in places – to try to draw her out on this potential new development.

Aware of the crime-scene photographs on her phone, the terrible shot of Lexie, the blood, the brain spatter, the masked man in the mirror, she decided she couldn't show him, at least not yet. However, she said, 'Someone sent us photographs of the scene. He says he was there when it happened, not that he did it, but that he was there.'

Gaudion looked so shaken that she wasn't surprised when he didn't respond right away. Did it mean he'd hired the hitman and was now terrified it was about to explode in his face, or were his thoughts somewhere else entirely? In the end he said, 'I told them at the start that someone had been paid to do it. I could have – probably should have – given them names, but I had the rest of my family to consider.' He got to his feet and walked to the window, staring down at the rippling water and anchored boats while she sat quietly watching him, wishing she knew what he was thinking, what kind of images his mind's eye – and his conscience – might be conjuring.

Eventually, with his back still turned, he said, 'I'll give you the names.'

Feeling a thud of surprise and unease, she said, 'OK.' Then, 'Can I ask why?'

He turned around and with the light behind him she couldn't make out his expression. 'Because then you'll know why I haven't spoken out before – and why you shouldn't now.'

Going to open the door, he called to someone in the outer office then returned. 'My assistant will drive you to your hotel now, and I, or Mum, will pick you up from the Cobo Bay at six.'

There was only one person Cristy wanted to speak to as soon as she'd left the boatyard and that was Connor. However, with Gaudion's PA beside her, she had no choice but to wait until she'd checked into her hotel. Maybe Connor could help bring some clarity to the conversation she'd just had with Gaudion, some sense of reality even, or of what they should believe, because right now she had no idea whether she considered the man a master manipulator, a great actor and mind reader, or someone who'd been horribly maligned and misunderstood for years.

'Wow!' Connor murmured after she'd related all she could remember – thank God she'd taken notes. 'I'm not sure I've ever known you to get quite so worked up over an interviewee, although I can see why you did. He laid a lot of stuff on you.'

Closing her eyes in an effort to stop her mind racing, she said, 'The problem is, I keep hearing Olivia in my head. She knew something like this would happen, that he'd somehow manage to convince me that everything I believed until now was wrong, and whatever *he* tells me is the truth.'

'Where are your instincts on it all?'

She took a breath and reached for the wine she'd brought upstairs with her. 'Still waiting for them to kick in,' she replied, after taking a sip. 'Hearing about a hitman upset him, a lot. He said he'd tried to convince the police of it at the time, and might have been successful if he'd been willing to name who was behind it.'

'Did he tell you who was?'

'No, but he says he's going to. I'm being picked up from here at six and taken to his house. I'm assuming his mother will be there, and Rosaria, and now here comes the bombshell – I'm pretty sure Amelia is still alive and living right here on the island so I could be meeting her too.'

There was a beat of astonished silence before he said, 'Are you serious? Did he say that?'

'No, not at all, but when I asked about her . . . The look he gave me . . . You needed to be there, but he obviously knows what happened to her.'

'You realize, if she is still alive and with him, then it's a total game changer? I'm not sure in what way right now, but this could be huge.'

'Tell me about it. I wonder if Olivia knows.'

'If she does, why would she keep it to herself?'

'Why anything with that family?' she cried in frustration. 'She had me convinced she didn't know Gaudion and his mother were on Guernsey, but what if she did know and she's the one who's been lying to us, not him?'

'Why would she? And we were both there, she seemed completely on the level to me, and I can't say you've told me anything yet to change my mind about that.'

'I'm not trying to, but he's definitely the more convincing when it comes to Lexie's attack. He asked me today why the hell would she have married him if he'd been involved in doing that to her, and obviously I didn't have a good answer, other than to parrot what Olivia told us.'

'That his parents forced him into it? I'm with you, I find that a hard one to swallow. On the other hand, we know from experience that sometimes the simplest, or even unlikeliest version of events is the one that turns out to be true. And let's not forget, she was unequivocal when it came to telling us how besotted Lexie always was with David.'

'And he tells it the other way round, but they're just words, easy to say and even easier to coat with sincerity, especially when you've had a very long time to practise.'

'Precisely. Are you going to contact Olivia before you see him again?'

'I'm not sure. I think, at this stage, I need to get him to record what he told me earlier, then I'll be able to play her what he said rather than just repeat it in my own words.'

'Good call. Now, do you want to know what's been happening here today? It's not going to upstage what's going on at your end, that's for sure, but it's pretty significant.'

'Go for it.'

'OK, so we got a call about an hour ago from a pompous-sounding old git calling himself Detective Inspector Trevor Thompson. Apparently he's taken over the Kellon Manse Murders case and wants to talk to us about the pod, and any other information we might have that could assist him in his enquiries. Of course I said we'd be happy to help, so he's coming here on Friday, when you're back.'

'So it's official, they really have reopened the case,' Cristy muttered thoughtfully. 'Do we know anything about this detective?'

'According to our old friend Kevin, who I called as soon as I put the phone down, he's a bit old school, but he's got a stellar track record when it comes to solving cold cases.'

Cristy's eyebrows arched. 'Interesting. I wonder if he'll be willing to let us interview him?'

'I didn't ask, thought I'd give you the pleasure, given how much more persuasive you can be when it comes to blokes with attitudes.'

She laughed. 'Maybe, by the time we see him, I'll be able to share the names of the rapists, and if they turn out to be as elevated as we're led to believe . . . Well, God only knows where that will take us, unless this Trevor Thompson has his own special connections and has been assigned to the case simply to shut it all down again.'

By five-thirty she'd showered and changed into a simple mint-coloured linen dress that didn't exactly disguise her figure, but didn't accentuate it either. It was, she decided, studying her reflection, a statement of casual elegance that didn't make it appear as though she was trying, but that she'd at least made an effort.

Not that it mattered a jot what she was wearing, so she couldn't think why she'd even brought the thing, but it was here now, and she was in it, and there was just enough time to sit out on the lovely spacious balcony to watch the sun turning to a burnt orange glow as it sank towards the sea. Or maybe she could WhatsApp with Hayley and Aiden, if they were online, and read the many messages that had come her way since she'd got off the plane.

In the end she settled for sending the children some shots of the glorious view, accompanied by a cheesy *wish you were here* video, and in response to Matthew's texts asking where she was and why she'd stopped speaking to him, she said:

I'm on Guernsey. Very busy. We don't have anything to discuss because you're a married man and I've moved on.

To Marley's plaintive request to know when they could get together – *I urgently need to talk to you* – she said nothing at all. If Matthew's wife had to be dealt with, she'd do it when she got back, not now.

Her phone rang and stupidly, before checking who it was, she clicked on.

'What are you doing in Guernsey?' Matthew demanded hotly.

Irritated, she said, 'What are you doing calling me? I sent you a text—'

'Yes, I have it, and what do you mean, you've moved on?'

'Oh Matthew, grow up, please. I don't want to talk to you now and I won't be bullied into explaining myself either.'

'Do you have any idea what this is doing to me?' he cried desperately. 'I need you, Cristy. I'm going out of my mind—'

'Matthew, for God's sake! I'm about to go out for the evening—'

'Where? Who are you with?'

'What business is that of yours?'

'Are you with someone?'

'Not right now, but I will be later, and that's where this call is going to end.'

Almost as soon as she'd rung off, she felt bad for leading him to believe something that wasn't true. However, she had no intention of calling him back to change or even ameliorate her story when he was a distraction she really could do without this evening.

Realizing she was about to become emotional and detesting herself for allowing him to have this effect on her still, she picked up her key card and purse and left the room. She'd wait outside on the bar terrace where the cocktail hour was already underway and the atmosphere would surely lift her mood – or at the very least allow her to refocus on the reason she was here. Not that she'd lost sight of it, for the impression David Gaudion had made on her earlier was proving as deep as it was conflicting. She kept picturing him in her mind's eye, darkly intense, aloof, engaging, someone who commanded the space he was in, who clearly harboured secrets, and who was extremely wary about allowing anyone to get too close. And yet he'd invited her to his home this evening, and was talking to her in a way he'd spoken to no one else since the murders, at least as far as she knew. For her it meant she could have a scoop on her hands like no other, but what was it meaning for him? Why had he chosen her to open up to, and why now when he could have remained here on this island in relative anonymity and continued refusing to give interviews to anyone at all?

Unless the police came for him, of course – he wouldn't be able to refuse them.

CHAPTER THIRTY

'Are you OK?' Gaudion asked as they pulled away from the hotel to start heading south on the coast road.

Cristy glanced at him in surprise. 'I'm fine, thanks,' she replied. 'Are you?'

For some reason he laughed, and just as inexplicably it made her smile. 'You were looking worried as you got into the car,' he explained.

She turned to gaze towards the sunset and the sea wall where many were gathered to watch the slow, exquisitely colourful end to another day. 'I had words with my ex before leaving,' she admitted, not sure why she was telling him, although if she shared confidences, maybe it would make it easier for him to do the same. An old tactic, but usually a trusty one.

'I'm sorry to hear that,' he said. 'I hope it didn't upset you.'

With a dry laugh, she said, 'Almost everything Matthew does upsets me, and that in itself upsets me more.'

She was aware of him glancing at her but kept her eyes averted, suddenly finding herself more aware of his proximity than she'd like to be. The car wasn't small, some kind of Toshiba estate, but the front seats seemed closer together than they needed to be, and his hand, as he changed gear, came close to her own. Moving hers to the equipment bag in her lap, she changed the subject: 'Will your mother be there this evening?'

He indicated to turn inland. 'She will,' he confirmed, 'and Rosie's excited to see you again. As you've probably realized by now, my eldest loves everyone and, I'm glad to say, most people seem to love her.'

Cristy had to smile. 'It's hard not to,' she said, and almost sucked in air as the road suddenly narrowed and steepened, as if she could somehow make them smaller. She guessed they were heading into the high parishes now, a forested area she'd found on the map, or maybe it was called Forest? Whatever, it seemed to encompass most of the south-west of the island with dramatically steep cliffs along the coastline and some exotically white sandy beaches. It was also, she'd read, home to many of the island's wealthier residents. 'She's a sweetheart,' she added as they rounded a hairpin bend to go even higher.

'And an innocent who could be easily taken advantage of,' he stated.

She turned to look at him. 'Is that what you think?' she said sharply. 'That I'd use your daughter to try and get information you're not willing to share?'

Appearing unruffled, he said, 'You wouldn't be the first, but for what it's worth, I'm ready to believe you have a little more integrity than that.'

'Then why bring it up?'

Slowing to take another curve in the road, he said, 'Don't let's start the evening on bad terms. Please just accept that, as a father, I'm very protective of my children. However, I also understand that you have a purpose to being here. I'm going to help you with that, as far as I can, but I can't promise everything will go as smoothly as you might like.'

More intrigued by that than nettled, she said, 'All I ask of you is the truth.'

He smiled and it threw her, although she wasn't quite sure why. 'But even if I give it, will you believe me?' he countered.

'I guess that depends on what you tell me. Will we begin with the names of Lexie's attackers?'

He braked again as they approached a white five-bar gate between two high laurel hedges. As it started to swing open she noticed the name of the property and her heart thudded a beat.

Papillon.

The French version of Papilio.

Why on earth would he call his home after the cult that could have played a part in his wife's murder? It didn't make any sense. He couldn't be a part of it, could he? What the heck had she missed? Unless this wasn't his home they were entering. Had he tricked her into coming with him to get her to a place she very probably didn't want to go?

'I don't understand,' she said as he drove them along a winding, tarmacked lane between an apple orchard and a field full of brown and white cows. 'Is this where you live?'

Seeming surprised, he said, 'Yes, why? Is there a problem?'

'No. I just . . . It's called *Papillon*.'

He frowned as if not quite following, then laughed. 'Of course, how could I have forgotten? That's not its official name, just the one Rosaria gave it when we completed the rebuild. I guess when you see something every day you stop noticing it.'

'Why did she choose that?' Cristy asked, still disconcerted.

'Because she loves butterflies and has Lexie's collection in her jewellery box. So I guess you could say she chose it to honour her mother. That's how we like to think of it, anyway. Juliette wasn't so impressed when she first saw it, but she's her own person and she'd already moved to Paris by then, so she didn't really get a say.'

With twilight now succumbing to night, and bats starting to swoop overhead, they rounded a handful of stone cottages and the drive suddenly lit up ahead of them to show such an unexpectedly beautiful house that Cristy couldn't stop herself whispering, 'Wow!'

It was a quintessentially Italianate villa, white, with four tall sash windows each side of the arch-topped front door, six more on the level above, and a black filigree balustrade forming a wraparound veranda. There was wisteria climbing the walls, no longer in flower but still managing to look as decorative as the twin windmill palms standing sentry at the entrance. The impressive size of the place, and its easy symmetry was only surpassed by its sublime elegance.

'You built this?' she asked as he brought the car to a stop beside his mother's smart.

'Not personally,' he admitted. 'I didn't design it either, but I did pay for it and now I get to enjoy it.'

'It's stunning,' she murmured, feeling almost as drawn to it as she was to the story behind this man.

'Anna will be pleased to hear that,' he told her, opening his door to get out. 'It's mostly her creation, with a lot of back-up from a firm of local architects. She's started her own interiors company, with her partner Patrick. I could say he's her fiancé, but I'm not sure if that's an outdated word these days. I thought they'd be here by now, but no sign of their car.'

Aware of a faint nervousness starting to stir inside her, all wrapped up in a heady sort of anticipation, Cristy followed him across the gravel forecourt and up a wide set of steps onto the veranda. It took a moment to make herself believe she was actually here, at the home of David Gaudion, the man at the centre of the Kellon Manse Murders – the suspected killer whose whereabouts had been a mystery until a few days ago – and she was about to interview him for the second time that day. In a professional sense that alone could put her on a high.

Noticing that he didn't use a key to get in – the doors were apparently unlocked – she accepted his gesture for her to go ahead and came to a laughing stop as a large, ecstatic Golden Retriever bounded up to greet her.

'Henry, try to behave,' Gaudion scolded as the dog's tail whipped up a wind and he pressed his face into Cristy's crotch. 'Sorry,' he grimaced, dragging the beast away by its collar. 'He's like Rosaria in many ways, always thrilled to meet someone new, although I'm glad to say her manners are better.'

Still laughing, Cristy said, 'He's adorable.'

'And far too talkative,' Gaudion responded as the dog started to howl. 'Yes, it's lovely to see you too, but no, I'm not letting you jump all over our guest.' Still holding onto the collar, he walked the dog over to a large crate and popped him inside. 'Just for now,' he promised. 'You can come out when Anna gets here.'

Obediently, Henry flopped down on his bed and seemed to grin happily as he watched Cristy taking in the enormous, oval entrance hall with two movie-set staircases each side curving up to a mezzanine level and overlooked by a huge Victorian-style roof lantern. The walls were covered in watercolours, from racing yachts to country landscapes and beach scenes, to portraits, easily recognizable cities and impenetrable abstracts.

Gaudion, apparently unaware of how much she was admiring

340

his home, was already opening a door beneath the mezzanine for her to go through. It turned out to be a kitchen-cum-dining-cum-sitting room that surely encompassed the entire back of the house. The ceilings and limed beams were high, the furnishings deep and luxurious, and the table where Rosaria appeared to be working was round and spotlit by a trio of old ship's lamps.

'Ah! You're here,' Cynthia declared, abandoning a triple-fronted Rangemaster to come and embrace Cristy as if they were old friends. 'Welcome, welcome.'

'*Bianvnu,*' Rosaria sang out, bouncing up from her chair. Her hug was awkward with her bottom sticking out and her face not quite touching Cristy's, and yet it was undeniably sincere if the loving way she gazed at Cristy was anything go by. Cristy smiled at the blue paint smears on her cheeks and smoothed her pretty blonde hair.

'It's lovely to see you again,' she said.

Rosaria beamed. 'Granny's making a special oyster casserole for us, and a gâche, which we usually only have at Christmas, but it's one of my favourites so we're having it tonight.'

'Do you like seafood?' Cynthia asked, returning to her task as if Cristy were there every day of the week.

'I love it,' Cristy replied, 'but I haven't heard of gâche.'

'Ah, yes, it's a kind of sweetbread made with all sorts, raisins, cherries, orange peel, peas—'

'What will you have to drink?' Gaudion interrupted. 'We have wine, or gin and tonic . . .'

'I'm having some cider from Maggie and John's,' Rosaria told her. 'It's a special one they make just for me.'

Guessing it might be apple juice, Cristy smiled and said, 'White wine, if there's some open.'

'If there isn't we can always remedy that. Mum, will you have one?'

'Silly question,' Cynthia chided, with a wink in Cristy's direction.

Rosaria was back at the table. 'I'm making crowns for the panto,' she explained. 'Judy asked me to. Oh, I told her you were here and that you'd like to see the theatre and she said that's fine, we just have to let her know when.'

341

In a low voice as he passed her a drink, Gaudion said, 'She won't take offence if it doesn't happen, so don't feel obliged.'

'I heard that,' Rosaria told him without looking up.

Cynthia said, 'Richard rang while you were out, dear. He wants to speak to you before he comes over on Friday.'

'OK, I'll call him later.' Gaudion looked up as the dog suddenly came skidding into the kitchen followed by a tall, slender young woman with a mass of dark, wildly curly hair, stunning blue eyes and an exquisite heart-shaped face.

Cristy's heart turned over as she froze. Although she'd suspected this, had even hoped for it, she hadn't been able to convince herself until now that it might be true. The shock was almost palpable, for there was no doubt at all that she was looking at Lexie Gaudion's younger daughter – and Amelia Gaudion was glaring right back at her.

'Anna, Patrick,' Gaudion cried cheerily as a young man came in behind Anna, 'let me introduce you to Cristy—'

'I know who she is,' Anna snapped, eyes flashing, nostrils flaring. 'And frankly I'm amazed you have the nerve to come here—'

Though still reeling, Cristy started as Gaudion barked, 'Anna!'

'I know what you want,' she snarled at Cristy, 'but you can just leave us alone. No one asked you to come—'

'Actually, I did,' Gaudion interrupted.

'We don't need you poking your nose into our lives,' Anna raged on, 'trying to turn us into some kind of podcast sensation—'

'That's enough!' Gaudion growled as Patrick took Anna by the shoulders.

Shaking herself free, she cried, 'I don't know how you persuaded him to see you, but I swear, if anything happens to my father after this, I'll find you and make you pay.'

'Oh, Anna,' Cynthia groaned as Gaudion dropped his head to his hands.

'What's going to happen to Dad?' Rosaria wailed.

Going to her, Gaudion said, 'You can go to your room, Anna, or you can leave. Either way, I won't have you—'

'You're a fool!' she shouted over him as Patrick tried leading her away. To Cristy, she seethed, 'It might be fun for you dredging up old ghosts and trying to prove to the world that you're the big investigator who can solve cases no one else can, but what you're really doing is trying to destroy our lives. There's so much you don't know and you never will, so why don't you do us all a favour and go back to wherever the hell you came from and pick on some other poor family?'

As the door closed behind her, the dog whined, and Cristy put her glass on a countertop. 'She shouldn't have to leave,' she said, slightly shakily. 'This is her home, so if you don't mind taking me back to the hotel, perhaps—'

'No! Don't go,' Rosaria cried, coming to clutch Cristy's hands. 'Anna always gets angry, but she doesn't mean it. Please don't go.'

Gaudion picked up Cristy's wine and handed it back to her. 'I'm sorry for what just happened,' he said. 'She had no right to speak to you that way—'

'Actually, she did,' Cristy interrupted. 'Protectiveness works both ways, remember? We don't have an exclusivity on it as parents, children feel it too, and that's what's happening here.'

'She's always been a feisty one,' Cynthia said, shaking her head in dismay, 'but please don't let her drive you away.'

'You still need to record what I told you earlier,' Gaudion reminded her. 'Or as much of it as I'm prepared to repeat.'

There was a smile in his eyes that went some way towards easing the embarrassment she still felt.

'You must also,' he continued, 'be keen to know how Amelia ended up here. That was her you just met, obviously, although we call her Anna now.'

'She prefers it,' Rosaria said.

Unable to deny the depth of her curiosity any more than she could allow herself simply to give up without answers, Cristy said, 'If you're sure . . .'

'We are,' Gaudion assured her as Rosaria said, 'What ghosts are you looking for, Cristy? Because I don't think we have any here.'

By the time they'd finished a scrumptious meal of creamy seafood casserole dipped with Cynthia's homemade gâche, it was pitch dark outside, but still warm as Gaudion led the way into a large, glass room filled with exotic plants and sylphlike sculptures. Cristy could see lights leading from the back terrace down over a sloping lawn to surround an ornamental lake in the shallow valley below. There was a fountain at its centre and clusters of lilies floating around the inky black surface, and a quaint little duck house tucked in amongst a cluster of broadleaf cattails. All feminine touches that were undoubtedly Anna's. Amelia's. Lexie and David's youngest daughter, and now, it would seem, Cristy's sworn enemy. In spite of the enjoyable hour since the outburst which had thrown her so badly, she was still feeling uncomfortable, and wished there was a way she could speak to Anna, to persuade her that she wasn't here to try to destroy their lives at all.

Except maybe she was.

'Your mother's a great cook,' she commented as Gaudion directed her to a cushioned wicker chair and took a matching one next to it.

'Yes, she is,' he agreed, 'and fortunately for us all she loves it.' He gave a small laugh and lifted a foot to rest it on the opposite knee. 'My brother keeps threatening to steal her when he comes to visit, so I might have to lock her up on Friday.'

Cristy smiled. 'How long will he be here?' she asked.

'Just for the weekend, with his wife, Astrid. His children are due to arrive the week after, a source of great excitement for Rosaria. She loves to have visitors, especially her cousins.'

Thinking of her other cousins, Olivia's children who she must surely have had a relationship with once, Cristy put it aside for the moment and said, 'Are you happy for me to record what we discussed earlier? I can remember most of it, so no trying to skip the important parts.'

His eyebrows rose with humour. 'OK. Why don't you start us off and we'll see how we progress?'

Happy with that, in spite of him calling the shots already, she prepped the handheld device and after testing to make sure it was working, she glanced up to see if he was ready.

'Are you sure you're not going to find it tedious, going over it all again?' he asked, deadpan.

With a roll of her eyes she said, 'Nice try, but I'm not falling for it.'

He laughed. 'OK, but before you press the red button, you understand I won't be giving you the names of Lexie's attackers for the recording.'

Her eyes sharpened.

'I'm happy for you to write them down,' he continued, 'or I can do it for you; I just don't want them coming from my lips to the wider world.'

She frowned, and because they were on the subject now, she said, 'Can I ask again why you've decided to speak out about them after all these years?'

He took a while to mull the question, his eyes travelling to the darkened windows, his thoughts in places she couldn't follow, until finally he said, 'You're going to find them out sooner or later – it's inevitable now, given how far into it all you are – so I've taken the decision that your high profile, plus the sheer number of listeners you've acquired for this podcast, is providing its own sort of protection. For you, I mean. And for my family.'

Both surprised by his frankness and moved by his admission, she said, 'Meaning that with so much attention on the case no one will dare to harm anyone?'

His eyes came to hers. 'Are you recording this?' he asked.

She shook her head. 'Not yet, but I'd like to.'

'I think you should,' he told her, 'and when it comes to the names we'll stop while I give them to you.'

'Will you be OK with me speaking them into the tape at a later time?'

He considered it. 'Why don't you decide that when you know who they are?' he suggested. 'Meantime, let's follow your directive to go over what we talked about earlier, keeping in mind that we won't discuss anything about the rape. That remains off limits, at least for now.'

Since she still didn't have clearance from the lawyers, she didn't argue, simply opened her notebook and said, 'OK, so we began with me asking you if you'd expected Olivia to lie about the attack, you said yes, and then you asked me why I thought Lexie would marry you if you'd been involved. Shall we pick it up from there?'

Gesturing for her to go ahead, he appeared perfectly relaxed as she hit record and for the next half an hour or so they carried out a repeat of what they'd discussed at his office. As she listened, she couldn't help regretting that they'd lost the sense of immediacy by going over it again, the changing nuances in his tone that often said more than words, but she could find no fault with his recall. His answers remained more or less the same, some shorter, some slightly longer, but at no point did he try to alter the essence of what he'd told her. So, no obvious attempts yet at subtle manipulation, unless she wasn't seeing it, or – and this was still a possibility – the truth was so interwoven with lies that even he might be unable to extricate it intact.

Eventually, inevitably, they came to his version of what had happened that day at the Manse. She'd already prepared herself for it, knew how she wanted to approach it, so, still recording, she said:

CRISTY: 'We know that the police, at the time of the murders, looked into the possibility of a contract killer being involved, possibly hired by you, but it was never pursued. What do you say to that now that it's arisen again?'

He took a breath, and let it go slowly before replying, carefully and, she had to admit, fairly convincingly.

GAUDION: 'I have never been in any doubt that someone was hired to kill my wife. What I can't tell you is why Margaret and Serena were also victims that day, although I believe it's been decided they were in the wrong place at the wrong time.'

CRISTY: 'So you had nothing to do with it?'

GAUDION: 'Nothing at all.'

CRISTY: 'Can you tell me who you think would want to harm your wife, or the others?'

GAUDION: 'As far as Lexie was concerned, the answer is yes, I can, but as you know, I'm not prepared to name names for this recording.'

CRISTY: 'OK. Let's move on to the fact that no one saw you out running that day when you were, by your own admission, gone for three hours and stayed in an area where you were well known. Can you explain that?'

GAUDION: 'I'm afraid I can't. It just happened that way.'

CRISTY: 'Did you usually see people you knew when you were out for a run?'

GAUDION: 'Yes, but that day, for some reason, I didn't.'

Already hearing the cries of 'liar' and 'killer' zinging their way through social media, Cristy checked her notes, taking a moment to consider whether or not to ask him to repeat why he hadn't seen the emergency vehicles from the top of the hill. As they'd already recorded his reason – that he hadn't actually taken the exact route she'd followed – she decided to move on.

CRISTY: 'I'd like to ask you about Maria del Smet, who was a colleague of yours when you worked for the lobbying firm Quantrell's.'

His eyes darkened and she half-expected him to stop the recording, given that this hadn't been discussed beforehand, nor had she even hinted that she might bring it up. However, for whatever reason, he clearly decided to roll with it.

GAUDION: 'Yes, I remember Maria. I also heard her on one of your earlier podcasts.'

CRISTY: 'So did you two have an affair as she claims?'

GAUDION: 'Our relationship was much as she described.'

CRISTY: 'Did Lexie know about it?'

He pointed at the recorder, and she turned it off.

'I had an arrangement with Lexie,' he told her. 'She knew that I sometimes slept with other women, she understood that I had those needs; in fact, she encouraged me to satisfy them elsewhere.

I never gave her names or dates, or anything else about them, because she didn't want to know. It didn't change how I felt about her. She was still my wife and I had no intention of ending my marriage over her difficulties with intimacy. Which, I must add, were not constant, because sometimes we were as close as I wanted us to be. Does that answer your question?'

Inwardly flinching at his tone, she said, 'I understand why you're not keen to go on the record with that, but it might help you to win people over if they have some sort of understanding of why you had other relationships.'

His smile wasn't pleasant. 'I'm not trying to win anyone over,' he retorted harshly. 'I don't care what people think of me. All that matters to me are my children. I've already made it clear I don't want to discuss the rape, which is, of course, at the root of Lexie's problems with intimacy. It's already out there in general terms, thanks to Olivia; if I add anything to it, it would be like a betrayal of Lexie's memory, and neither Rosaria nor Anna deserve that.'

Knowing she could do nothing more than concede his point, Cristy apologized and said, 'As someone who's had her own personal life picked over by the media and public, I should have been more sensitive.'

His eyes softened slightly as he looked more deeply into hers. 'You have a job to do, and I'm sorry you had to go through what you did with your husband. It can't have been pleasant.'

She smiled at the understatement, but didn't want this to become about her, so she went on, 'I'd like to talk about Amelia – Anna – now, if that's OK. Would you prefer to discuss it first, without the tape running, or are you willing to go straight to record?'

He didn't take long to consider it. 'You can record,' he told her, 'but I want Anna to hear it before anyone else. She knows the story, obviously, but she might not want to share it with the wider world.'

Suspecting she wouldn't, Cristy said, 'I understand your concern and her desire for privacy, but you must know that it's going to come out anyway. Wouldn't it be better told by you?'

'Possibly, but she's nothing if not unpredictable, so she might want to tell it herself.'

Suspecting that would happen this side of never, Cristy restarted the recorder and began again.

CRISTY: 'It's going to come as quite a shock to everyone when they discover your daughter, Amelia, is still alive and has been living with you here in Guernsey all this time. Are you ready to explain how it came about?'

GAUDION: 'I am, but I'd prefer to call her Anna, if you don't mind. It's the name she goes by now and how I think of her.'

Cristy nodded agreement, glad to have that settled early on. However, she reinforced the point, making it clear that Amelia Gaudion was now Anna Gaudion, before continuing.

CRISTY: 'So, talk us through, if you will, what actually happened at the time she was believed murdered, or kidnapped, by the killer.'

He shifted position in his chair, and stretched out his legs in a way that made him seem even more relaxed than he had during the previous recording.

GAUDION: 'She was supposed to be at my mother's that day – actually, she was there, until she decided to take off without telling anyone. It wasn't unusual for her to do that, she was – and is – an independent spirit, and the previous week her grandmother, Margaret, had bought her a pony. She was mad about horses, and having one of her own meant the world to her. She was at Kellon Hall stables morning, noon and night, grooming, mucking out, exercising . . . She'd have slept with the pony if we'd allowed her to, so when she didn't show up for lunch that day my mother guessed where she was and decided she'd either come back when she was hungry or go home.

'It wasn't a wrong assessment, because Anna did get hungry and probably because it was closer she went over to the Manse. She was in the kitchen, making herself a

349

sandwich, when she heard loud noises coming from the sitting room and went to see what was happening. She got as far as the door when she came up against a man with his back to her, blocking the way, but she could see past him to where her mother was slumped across the sofa and covered in blood. The man was holding up his phone, or a camera, she wasn't sure which, then he took off his mask and that's when he saw her in the mirror.

'Before he could grab her she raced down to the basement. You might ask why the basement, but you wouldn't if you knew Anna. I had no idea then that she knew where to find the key to the gun cabinet, but she did. She grabbed a rifle, pointed it back at the stairs and started to climb.'

Stunned by the child's actions, the courage and foolhardiness, it was a moment before Cristy was able to ask if the gun was loaded.

GAUDION: 'No, but her reasoning was that he didn't know that.'

CRISTY: 'Ten years old and she had reasoning in a situation like that?'

GAUDION: 'It always was, and still is, typical of Anna to do the unexpected, the foolish, I should probably say. It's in her nature to act first and think later, and all she had in her head in that moment was that a man who'd hurt her mother was in the house and she had to get rid of him before he hurt her too.

'He was in the hall, calling out to her, when she came up behind him. He tried to seize her, but she slammed the rifle into his groin and ran. I've no idea if he attempted to go after her; all I can tell you is that she kept on running, across the garden, over the gate, up over the hill and across the top field into the woods. And that's where I found her the following day, fast asleep in the hollow of a tree, still clutching the gun, brambles in her hair, scratches all over her, filthy, and missing a shoe.'

CRISTY: 'How did you know where to look?'

GAUDION: 'I didn't, at first. Like everyone else, I was terrified that she'd seen the killer and he'd taken her. It was more an act of desperation on my part when I started searching our secret places, and the nook of that tree was one of them.'

CRISTY: 'I can hardly begin to imagine how relieved you must have felt when you found her.'

GAUDION: 'Looking back, I was probably more relieved she didn't shoot me. She was delirious, terrified, suffering with exhaustion and exposure, and yet she still tried to defend herself, fighting me like a wild cat, until she finally realized it was me.'

CRISTY: 'What happened then?'

GAUDION: 'Before we left the woods, I got her to tell me what had happened, and as soon as I realized she'd seen the killer I knew she wasn't safe. Of course I didn't know for certain who was behind it all then, but I had a fairly good idea and I was never in any doubt that they'd take whatever measures necessary to make sure she didn't identify their man.

'That's when I decided no one could know she hadn't been taken. It was better for the police and public to think that she had – even though it turned out they thought I'd killed her. Anything rather than put her in danger again.

'So I bundled her into the back of my car, made her lie down and took her to Mum's. She remained hidden there for the next few weeks – even she realized how important it was for her to stay out of sight. And Rosaria has always been good at secrets – actually less so these days, but back then she played her part in keeping Anna safe by staying hidden too.

'After I was arrested, Richard, my brother, and Mum's brothers helped her to pack everything she and the girls needed and took them, in the dead of night, to Exmoor. Obviously, Mum had to tell the police where she was, but she'd already given her statement and there was no reason to interview her again.'

CRISTY: 'So while the search for Anna was at its height and everyone was getting involved, she was at her uncle and aunt's place on Exmoor?'

GAUDION: 'And it's where they remained until a year after my release. I went back to the Manse at first, not wanting to draw anyone's attention to my mother's whereabouts, then when the time felt right we all came to settle in Guernsey.'

CRISTY: 'Did the police know where you were?'

GAUDION: 'I don't think so. The charges against me had been dropped, I was a free man, so I didn't have to tell them my plans, and no one ever tried to make contact either before or after I left England.'

CRISTY: 'But surely people in Guernsey must have known who you were – or, more to the point, who Anna was?'

GAUDION: 'Some did, of course, and now you're going to ask why they never contacted the police. Well, they'd be able to answer that far better than I, but this much I can tell you: for the most part we're a community that takes care of one another. And I should add that the authorities here have always been fully aware of who she is. Luckily no one has come looking – until now – or if they have they were headed off at the pass, so to speak.'

CRISTY: 'This is clearly a tightknit community.'

GAUDION: 'My grandfather, Cyril Gaudion, and his wife, Grandma Jean, were prominent and popular islanders who did a lot for the Bailiwick back in the day. My grandfather was Chief Minister for a number of years, and Grandma Jean was active in many social matters.'

CRISTY: 'Were they still here when you came?'

GAUDION: 'No, they'd both died by then, but their reputation for kindness and generosity lived on, as did two of their sons and a daughter, all of whom are still alive and who we see quite often with their families. So I guess you could say it became an unspoken understanding between our family and the rest of the islanders that Anna needed to live her life as free of her past as we could make it. And of course, over time, no one even thought about it any more. That only changed when you decided to resurrect it all as effectively as you have.'

Experiencing yet more guilt, along with the shame of knowing she hadn't given nearly enough consideration to what her podcast might do to the Gaudion family, she stopped the recording without telling him that there were islanders who'd been prepared to betray him for the right amount of silver. They never had, because *Hindsight* didn't pay for information, so there was no need at this time for him to know.

'I'm sure,' she said, 'I'll have a lot more questions after I've listened to this back, but for now, if it's not too late, I'd like to start asking about your release from custody, and as it's sure to include names, I know you'd rather not commit it to tape.'

Checking his watch, he said, 'I'm guessing you're booked onto a flight back to Bristol tomorrow?'

She nodded.

'So no time for us to get together in the morning. However, it's not yet nine. So, what do you say we take a break and get ourselves a drink before we continue?'

CHAPTER THIRTY-ONE

Twenty minutes later they were back in the garden room with a bottle of red wine on the table between them alongside a selection of handmade chocolates, provided, apparently, by one of his artisanal cousins. They were delicious, far too moreish in fact, although Cristy was now completely distracted by the names Gaudion had written in her notebook.

She was aware of him watching her as she processed them. She recognized only two: Russell MacAnany, the controversial and radical head of a powerful right-wing think tank known to be strongly influencing the current government. The second was Kenneth Cribbs-Right, a high court judge famed and greatly revered for his vocal and effective support of women's rights. Since both men were too old to have been at Oxford at the same time as Lexie, Cristy guessed that they were in some way related to two of the rapists.

'Correct,' Gaudion confirmed when she asked. 'I've given you the father's names because I suspected you'd be more likely to have heard of them. The sons are Liam MacAnany and Joshua Cribbs-Right. Incidentally, if you haven't already figured out that there is an exclusive fraternity operating around this case, then I can tell you it's known as Frumentarii and both fathers belong to it. *Frumentarii* is the name of an ancient Roman intelligence agency.'

Cristy's eyes widened.

'You can read about the originals online,' he continued, 'but today's version, in a nutshell, is a secretive and highly influential organization focused mainly on politics, finance and the judiciary. Much like the freemasons, it can be a force for good, and again like the masons, allegiance to their society and to one another is paramount. It enables them to disappear matters that might embarrass, inconvenience or even criminalize one of their number, or someone close to them. As I'm sure you know, Cribbs-Right has a long-standing and well-earned reputation for championing women's causes; he would not have wanted his only son caught up in a rape scandal, then or now, especially one as violent as the one inflicted on Lexie. The same goes for MacAnany, who you probably know wields immense power in the UK; no one gets into Tory high office without the backing of his policy institute. Some say he should be a politician himself, but why would the puppet-master want to hand someone his strings? His son, Liam, works for him at the institute as some kind of emissary with particular focus on similar neo-con organizations in the US and Canada.'

Already starting to see what powerful enemies these men could make, Cristy said, 'What about the other three? I've never heard of them.'

Glancing at the names, he said, 'Carlton Greenberg is South African, an Oxford graduate – all five of them are, as are their fathers. Greenberg is from billionaire mining stock, mostly gold, some platinum. The last I knew of him he was more of a playboy than a businessman, although I doubt he'd describe himself that way. He's onto his third wife and fourth superyacht and I believe he remains a prolific drug user. On the surface it could be said he's the least influential of the five, but he's equally well connected and practically untouchable.

'Yiannis Christakos is the nephew of a pretty ruthless shipping magnate who it's said murdered his business partner to gain control of the company, but nothing was ever proved. Yiannis himself is a lawyer these days, based in Zurich, and has a client list that could make your eyes water if you moved in the world of top-flight industrialists or small African nations.'

Swallowing dryly, she said, 'And Friedrich Fischer?'

'Fischer is also a lawyer, based in London. He and Christakos work closely together, and both have sons currently studying at Oxford. Recently, maybe a year ago, the younger Fischer's name came up during a grooming scandal that ended with a less well-connected young man going to prison. I don't know if the convicted man is innocent, but I strongly suspect that he is, and if I'm right it shows you the kind of things Frumentarii can make happen if they need something cleaned up.'

Feeling faintly stunned, Cristy sat back in her chair and stared at their ghostly reflections in the windows. With the lake still lit up in the distance, it appeared as if they were floating in the rippling water, and in a way it was how she felt, cast adrift in a world where rules were made and broken for the purposes of serving some sort of elite while others drowned.

'So which of them do you suspect of hiring the killer?' she asked.

He poured more wine into their glasses. 'In a way it doesn't matter who it was, because you can be certain that the others all knew about it and a ring of protection has been thrown around the one who organized the saving of all five necks.'

Cristy looked down at her drink, deeply worried about what this could mean going forward. After a while she said, 'By telling me these names you've put me and my team, possibly my children as well, at their mercy.'

He didn't deny it, but said, 'You never have to reveal that you know them.'

'But then they win.'

'They always do.'

Getting up from her chair, she walked to the windows where moths and night-flies were throwing themselves against the panes. It was like a reminder of what she was up against, a solid, impenetrable wall of privilege, a select group of insiders who could crush them all if necessity compelled.

'What do you want me to do with this information?' she asked, turning to look at him again.

'Nothing,' he replied. 'I told you so you'd know what kind of people you're dealing with. They won't harm you, or anyone else, unless you strike at them. Lexie and I learned that the hard way sixteen years ago.'

'Because she told O'Malley the names.'

He inclined his head.

'Is he one of them?'

'I don't know, but I'm certain he sent out the warning.'

She was trying to get a grip on the level of coercion, duplicity and betrayal involved in Lexie's therapy, but it wasn't easy.

'You probably want to know how my trial came to be cancelled,' he said.

She nodded.

'My lawyer, Edmond Crouch, was contacted by someone at the CPS and told in veiled terms, although they were clear enough to us and I'll make them clear to you, that the case wouldn't need to go ahead if I gave my word never to reveal what had happened at Oxford.'

Her throat was dry. 'You could have brought them all down,' she said quietly. 'Made them pay for what they'd done.'

'Of course I could, but Lexie was gone and I had my daughters to think of, Anna most of all considering the position she was in. They needed me, and I knew they'd be safer if I accepted the deal.'

'But it means you've allowed people to think, all this time, that you were the one who got away with murder.'

'People will always think what they want to, or in some cases what they need to. Olivia probably won't have told you this, but her husband and his father belong to Frumentarii.'

Cristy's eyes widened.

'Oh, don't worry, I'm not saying they were involved in what happened to Lexie, or to me – they probably don't even know the details of it – but their loyalty to fellow members will have meant they'd encourage Olivia to think the worst of me.'

Cristy was incredulous. 'To the point she'd claim you were one of the rapists?' she exclaimed.

His eyebrows rose. 'In her defence, I think she really does believe I killed her sister and mother.'

'But why? I don't understand this.'

'All I can tell you is what she's already told you herself, that she went through a very rough time after Lexie and Margaret died. Her breakdown, the treatment she received, the therapy – and I believe O'Malley was involved in that – any of it could have made her vulnerable to suggestion, and ultimately confused about what had actually happened.'

Cristy stared at him, dumbfounded. 'Are you saying she was brainwashed into believing you were involved in the murders, *and* the rape? But Lexie would have known if you were one of her attackers, and wasn't *she* the one who told Olivia you were?'

'So says Olivia, but doesn't that bring us back to the question of why Lexie would have married me if I was?'

Putting a hand to her head as if to stop it spinning, she said, 'This is all so . . . *twisted* and crazy and frankly, right now, I don't even know if we've still got a podcast.'

He got to his feet and went to switch off the exterior lights. 'I've given you a lot to think about tonight. You need some time to process it, but you'll still have doubts and questions, more fear, even. So you know where I am and you have my number.'

Not sure how comforted she felt by that, though she was glad to hear it anyway, she went to pack up her things and turned back to find him watching her. A strange sort of current seemed to pass between them, making her pause for a moment as if she was seeing him, maybe even understanding him, for the first time and at a level she couldn't yet fathom. A moment later the feeling was gone, swept away by the reminder that she had no idea how much of what he'd just told her was true. How capable was he of fabricating such an elaborate and convoluted tale to keep her at arm's length and himself out of prison? 'Will you drive me back to the hotel?' she asked.

'Of course,' he replied. 'I'll also take you to the airport in the morning so we can talk again before you leave.'

CHAPTER THIRTY-TWO

The following afternoon the entire team, including Jodi, was gathered in the production office to discuss Cristy's time with David Gaudion and the shock news about his daughter, Amelia, now Anna. She'd briefed everyone by email late last night, and had followed up with more thoughts before getting on the plane this morning. She hadn't named names regarding Frumentarii, deciding it would be reckless at this stage, although she'd been careful to include a sense of urgency and concern in her messages.

'So are you going to tell us who these guys are now?' Meena asked, after Cristy finished a fuller briefing of what she'd managed to learn in the past twenty-four hours.

'I don't think that's wise,' Cristy replied. 'Not yet, anyway.'

'Not even me?' Connor protested hotly.

'It's for your own sake,' she told him. 'The less you know, the less chance there is that someone will attempt to stop you speaking out.'

'Do we need to be that scared?' Jodi said, confused.

'Think Iris,' Cristy reminded her.

As Jodi blanched, and the others fell silent, Cristy continued. 'Frankly, I'm not sure how scared we need to be, but we do know that I've already had a visit from someone's Mr Muscle advising me not to name names, so for the time being at least we won't do that.'

'Especially in light of what happened to Lexie after she did,' Clover added gravely.

Cristy threw her a look of gratitude, although it was a far harsher reminder than her own mention of Iris.

'So are we assuming Gaudion's on our side now?' Harry ventured.

Not sure how to answer that, Cristy said, 'I've been going over and over it in my mind . . . Part of me wants to trust him – actually, I found it very easy to when I was with him – but something that keeps jarring for me is why a man as attractive and personable as he is, someone who had a great future ahead of him and any number of women to choose from, would have tied himself to someone as . . . fragile as Lexie?'

'Because he was always in love with her,' Jodi stated. 'Isn't that what he claims?'

'Yes, but do we believe it? Olivia tells it quite differently and there doesn't seem any good reason why she'd lie about it.'

'What about her being "brainwashed" by O'Malley while she was in therapy?' Clover asked. 'What did you make of that?'

'Good question,' Cristy responded approvingly. 'She never even told us she'd met the man, much less that he'd treated her "collapse", as she calls it.'

'You need to speak to her,' Meena advised.

'I've left a message.'

'So what did you and Gaudion discuss en route to the airport this morning?' Connor wanted to know.

'Nothing about the case. Rosaria insisted on coming with him so it wasn't possible to talk.'

'Convenient,' Clover remarked into her coffee.

Though Cristy had thought so too when they'd arrived to pick her up, in fact she'd been glad of Rosaria's presence. After a near sleepless night, and her mind still trying to absorb everything she'd learned in the past eighteen hours, she hadn't really been ready to talk to Gaudion again at that point.

'So how have you left it with him?' Connor asked.

'I've promised to send over the interview he gave about Amelia – who we're now to call Anna. As I said in my email, he feels it's her story to tell, so he wants her to hear it first.'

'And if she doesn't want it to go public?'

'We cross that when we come to it, but I'm guessing she won't, so we have to decide what we're going to tell this Detective Thompson when he comes tomorrow.'

'The truth, obviously,' Harry declared. 'We can't be withholding information like that from the police.'

'It's not my intention,' she assured him, 'but hopefully we'll know by then how she feels about being exposed so we can at least forewarn him.'

'And meanwhile,' Connor stated, clearly not happy, 'a fucking great big scoop like the one you have and we're just going to sit on it?'

Cristy regarded him helplessly. 'Let's just wait to see how things play out over the next twenty-four hours,' she said. 'Jacks, if you can package up the interview to send, I'll let Gaudion know it's on its way.' Noticing the way Meena was staring at her, she said, 'What?'

Meena shook her head. 'Nothing,' but clearly there was something even if she didn't want to spit it out now.

Deciding to take it up later, Cristy continued, 'We need to work out what we're comfortable with running in next week's pod. Obviously, the exclusive about Amelia – Anna – is top of the list if we can use it—'

'I still don't see what's stopping us, even if she doesn't want to play along,' Connor interrupted tetchily.

'I agree,' Harry said. 'We can't let Gaudion start calling the shots. It's bad enough that he's persuaded you to keep the rapists' names to yourself. In fact, do we even know that there *was* a rape?'

Thrown by that, Cristy said, 'We've heard it from other sources – Olivia, of course, and Fiona Mooney. There's also the fact that Lexie dropped out of university when she did and Rosaria was born nine months later.'

Harry regarded her sceptically. 'I'm just not sure I trust this bloke,' he said grudgingly.

Picturing Gaudion during the time they'd spoken last night, seeming both solemn and sincere, and the concern in his eyes this morning when he'd waved her off, Cristy said, 'I guess the jury's still out on whether or not we should.'

'A great phrase about someone who's never faced one,' Jackson commented wryly.

Meena said, 'Well, it has to be your decision about what you put into next week's pod, as long as it doesn't land us in court, or worse, but for what it's worth I don't think it's a good idea to start alienating Gaudion at this stage by going against his wishes. Especially where his daughter's concerned.'

Connor and Harry glared at Meena, but Cristy said, 'Harry, I'll share the names with you so you'll understand why I don't want to reveal them to anyone else at this stage. Is that OK?'

'No! It's absolutely fucking not OK,' Connor exploded. 'I'm the one co-producing this pod, so I'm the one who should get the intel.'

'You also have a pregnant wife,' Cristy reminded him tartly, 'and you know very well that fact was mentioned by the arse who came to see me.'

'But if I know who they are I'll know who to look out for.'

'We know already that they don't come themselves, but OK, look up Frumentarii on the web then you'll have some sort of idea of who we're up against.'

'Fruit what?' Jackson demanded, tapping into his computer.

Cristy spelled it out and said, 'Do it after. We still have things to discuss, such as the point made just now about Gaudion's claim to have always been in love with Lexie. I want you guys, Clove and Jacks, to go back to the Vale and see what more you can find out about that. There've got to be plenty of people who remember them when they were young, not least your lovely old lady, Hannah Gains. Talk to her again, try to get her to be more specific.'

Noting it down, Clover said, 'I asked my mate at the CPS if he was prepared to talk on record about the case being reopened and I think he might be, so I'll chase him up.'

'Great,' Cristy responded. 'Do we know yet if Detective Inspector Thompson is prepared to be interviewed?' she asked Connor.

'I told you, I thought you'd do better getting a positive out of him than I would,' he answered, still tight-lipped, 'but I got the impression he wants to find out how much we know first.'

'He admitted the pod had influenced the decision to look into the case again,' Jackson put in helpfully.

Cristy nodded, interested to hear that, then promptly moved

362

on. 'I guess no more contact from the "man-in-the-mirror"?' she asked.

Connor shook his head. 'You can be sure I'd have told you if there was.'

Taking it as the dig it was meant to be, Cristy turned to Harry as he said, 'OK, so here's your next big question. Are you going to reveal the names to Thompson when he comes?'

Cristy had been thinking about that, and while she didn't feel comfortable holding them back from the police, what if Thompson had been put in place by Cribbs-Right, or someone else in the judiciary? 'Let's discuss it when you know who they are,' she countered, glancing at her phone as it rang. Her heart tripped when she saw the name on the screen. 'Gaudion,' she told them, and getting up from her desk she took the phone outside.

'Hi, I just wanted to be sure you'd got back safely,' he said when she answered. 'And to apologize again for not being able to discuss anything this morning.'

'It's fine. I wasn't ready to actually, and it was good to see Rosaria.'

'She's asked if she can email you, but I said I needed to check with you first. I'm afraid she wants to give you updates on the panto rehearsals.'

Though she sensed the charm offensive coming on again, Cristy couldn't help but smile. 'I'd love to hear from her,' she said, meaning it. After all, what harm was there in a few messages from a very sweet girl who just wanted to be everyone's friend?

'Thanks,' he said. Then, 'So do you want to talk? Maybe now isn't a good time, but if you—'

'Possibly later,' she interrupted. 'One of the team is about to send you the recording of what you told me about Amel— Anna. Do you think she'll listen to it?'

'I'm sure she will, but I can't say how she'll respond. I'm guessing you want to use it sooner rather than later?'

'Of course, but more than that, we're seeing the detective in charge of the cold case tomorrow. I feel we have to tell him what we know.'

There was a pause. 'You mean about Anna? Or about . . .?'

'Yes, about Anna. Actually, I think I should tell him the names too, but I don't know how to find out if he's operating for someone who has a vested interest in seeing this all go away. Has anyone from the cold case team contacted you yet?'

'No, but I'm sure they will. As for whether there's any other-party involvement in the new investigation, send me what you already know about the lead detective and I'll look into it.'

After thanking him, she rang off and checked to see if there was any word yet from Olivia.

There wasn't, so she went back inside. 'Jacks,' she said, 'when you send Gaudion's interview to Olivia, make sure you include what he told us about Amelia.'

Connor's eyes rounded with shock. 'You're going to break it to her like that?' he cried incredulously.

Confused, Cristy said, 'How else should we do it?'

'Like face-to-face,' he said, making it a no-brainer. 'I mean, it's going to be a pretty big deal for her finding out that her sister's daughter is still alive sixteen years on and hasn't been in touch for all that time. Don't we at least want to see how she reacts when she's told?'

Conceding the point, and actually troubled by not having seen it herself, Cristy said, 'OK, let's hold back until we see her. Meantime, send the first part of Gaudion's interview over to her, Jacks. With any luck it'll prompt her to get in touch before we see Thompson.'

Meena and Harry got up to leave. 'Send me the names,' Harry said as they reached the door.

'I don't want to commit them electronically,' she told him. 'I'll come and find you shortly and we can go through it.'

Once he'd left, Meena said casually, 'Fancy a drink later?'

Realizing this wasn't an invitation to be refused, Cristy said, 'Your place or mine?'

'Let's say six at the Pump House, shall we? Unless Olivia gets in touch first. She has priority.'

After she'd gone, Cristy turned to Connor. 'Listen, I'm really sorry. I didn't mean to upset you—'

'It's OK,' Jodi interrupted, 'he's a big boy, he'll get over it.'

Glowering at his wife, Connor said, 'I just thought we didn't keep secrets from one another.'

'We don't,' Cristy told him forcefully, 'and it wouldn't be happening now if I was a hundred percent certain Gaudion's story was false, but I'm not, so I'm afraid this is how it has to be until things are clearer. I swear, I'm thinking of Jodi, otherwise you'd have been the first person I told.'

'So,' Meena said later as she and Cristy settled at a table outside the Pump House with their drinks, 'I hear Harry agrees that you're right not to share the names for now.'

Cristy eyed her over the rim of her glass as she sipped her wine. 'Do you think he'll tell you who they are anyway?' she asked, waving to an old colleague who was jogging along the towpath.

'Not if he thinks it's better for me not to know,' Meena replied, 'but I have to confess I'm madly intrigued.'

Cristy smiled. 'So you looked up Frumentarii?'

'I did, and it's clearly an interesting organization with some even more interesting affiliations. Would I have come across any of the infamous names while I was browsing?'

Cristy shrugged. 'I guess it's possible, but it's a global affair so a pretty big membership.'

'Mm, I noticed a lot of Indians. It made me wonder if I might even be related to one or two.'

Cristy's eyes sparked with humour. 'They're not all bad,' she assured her.

'No, but a lot of my family are. Anyway, there's no doubting the kind of influence a society like that can bring to bear on a situation, or a government, or an industry, or even a person, if the need arose. So, perhaps I'm happier staying in the dark.'

Almost wishing she was there, too, Cristy raised her glass. 'Olivia called just before I left,' she said. 'We're seeing her tomorrow at her home in the Cotswolds. Incidentally, her husband and father-in-law belong to Frumentarii.'

Meena's eyebrows shot up, and a moment later her eyes crossed, making Cristy laugh. 'Don't tell me any more,' she begged, 'I'll wait to find it all out along with everyone else.'

'Wise,' Cristy told her. 'Now, how about we get to the real reason we're here?'

Meena regarded her curiously.

'Don't look at me like that. I know you've got something on your mind, so come on, out with it.' A sudden suspicion seized her, 'Oh God, please don't tell me Matthew's been in touch again? Or Marley . . .'

'No, no, I haven't heard from either of them for over a week, but there is something of a more personal nature I'd like to ask you.'

Intrigued, Cristy encouraged her to continue.

'I'm just wondering,' Meena began, seeming unusually awkward for her, 'if you're in danger of doing a Jay Wells on us.'

Cristy started in surprise. Jay Wells was one of Bristol's most successful defence lawyers who'd managed to fall in love with a client who'd turned out to be a murderer. It had almost destroyed Jay's career, and her marriage, and had done absolutely nothing for her reputation. 'Why on earth would you say that?' she demanded, already guessing the answer, while wondering how the heck Meena had managed to work out that she could hardly stop thinking about Gaudion and his family, his home, the beautiful island, the terrible injustice he might have suffered, the horror of him going to prison for something he hadn't done . . . And right there was the similarity with Jay Wells' situation. She'd believed in Edward Blake until, in the end, he'd confessed to killing his wife.

'I noticed you took his call outside today,' Meena told her, 'and the way you talk about him—'

'How can I not talk about him?' Cristy cried defensively. 'Everything we're doing is about him.'

'Of course, and I swear I'm not criticizing you; I'm simply trying to be your friend and maybe save you from the awful experience dear Jay went through. She's back at work, by the way. Did you know that?'

'No, I didn't. I should give her a call.'

'I'm sure she'd love to hear from you. You were a great support to her when Edward Blake first gave himself up. There weren't many prepared to speak out on her behalf the way you did. It showed a lot of courage and loyalty at a time when she needed it most.'

'She couldn't help who she fell in love with,' Cristy pointed out, 'and her husband . . . Well, we know Tom had a child with another woman, so he could hardly start shouting about betrayal, could he?'

'Of course not, but that's them, and right now I'm more concerned about you.'

Realizing that to continue protesting would only makes things worse, Cristy put on a smile and covered Meena's hand with her own. 'You don't need to be,' she assured her gently. 'Yes, Gaudion's attractive and charming and, as far as I can tell, available, but there are so many sides to him, some of them pretty dark, I'm sure, that I doubt anyone will ever get the full measure of him. Besides, the last thing I need in my life now, or ever, is another man screwing it up. Especially when Matthew's still doing such a great job of it.'

Meena looked worried. 'In what way?'

Cristy shook her head and though glad to change the subject, gave a sigh of despair. 'Apparently the new wife isn't what he'd been hoping for, and for some extraordinarily deluded reason he seems to think I might go back to him.'

Meena blinked, clearly shocked. 'But Marley's pregnant, for God's sake!'

'Indeed she is, but that doesn't seem to be making a difference.'

Meena glared back in anger. 'This is terrible,' she declared. 'Does she know how he feels?'

'I shouldn't think so. Although she's extremely keen to see me, so maybe it's what she wants to talk about. I'm afraid I keep putting her off, because – you're probably going to hate me for this – I don't want to get involved.'

'I don't hate you at all,' Meena assured her, 'and I don't blame you either.' She tutted angrily, impatiently. 'God, what a mess.' Then, 'But you will see her, if she insists?'

Cristy sighed. 'I expect I'll have to at some point, but I'd rather not do it now, while I've got so much else to think about. And yes, one of those things is David Gaudion, but as I said—'

'It's OK, I heard you and I promise I won't go there again. I just felt I should bring it up in case you really were doing a Jay on us.'

Cristy eyed her carefully, loving her as a friend, but wondering if she was really connecting with what she was saying. 'You do realize that you're implying you think Gaudion is guilty, don't you?' she said.

Meena frowned. 'Mm, I guess it does sound that way,' she conceded, 'but actually, all this conspiracy stuff, secret societies and the like . . . I'm not doubting its existence, obviously, and it seems that rape really was covered up, which is why Harry is fully on your team. But speaking for myself, I just wonder if it's really as complicated as that.'

'And if it's not, it has to be Gaudion?'

With a grimace, Meena nodded.

'That's exactly what I think,' Cristy told her, truthfully, but as they knocked their drinks together she couldn't deny, at least to herself, how very much she didn't want it to be him.

CHAPTER THIRTY-THREE

As Cristy watched the colour drain from Olivia's face, she couldn't feel anything but profoundly sorry for her. Clearly the shock of learning that her niece wasn't only alive, but living with her father and his mother in Guernsey, was so unexpected and so deeply shattering that it had robbed her of the power to speak, perhaps even to properly process the news.

They were in the large, classically styled drawing room of the Jacobean manor house that Olivia called home, with ancient family portraits staring down at them from elaborately carved walls, and tall leaded windows offering views of the gardens outside.

Understanding that Olivia still needed time to collect herself, they sat quietly watching as she began to pace up and down, seeming every now and again as though she might stop, but then changing her mind. They were ready to answer her questions when they began, insofar as they could, and the recording of Gaudion telling the story of what had happened to Amelia on that terrible day, and after, was in an audio file ready to be shared as soon as Olivia was ready to hear it.

So far there had been no sign of anyone else in the house, although every now and again the sound of voices drifted in from outside, and at one stage a young woman in full riding gear, possibly Olivia's daughter, trotted a horse past the window towards the stable block Cristy had noticed coming in.

Finally Olivia paused in front of the hearth, shoulders hunched, hands clutched to her face, although a small amount of colour had returned to her cheeks by the time she turned to look at them. 'I'm sorry,' she said hoarsely, 'but you have to understand, this is . . . Actually, it's breaking my heart. All this time . . . Lexie's little girl . . . How can so many years have passed without her being in touch, without *him* letting us know she was safe? Why would he do that to us?'

The first question, and Cristy was unable to answer, at least not in the way Olivia might be hoping for. 'I think you should listen to what he told me,' she said. 'It might give you a better understanding.'

Olivia's eyes sharpened, making her seem doubtful, even cynical. 'I'd rather not hear his voice if I don't have to,' she said, 'so perhaps you can tell me what kind of story he's invented to excuse kidnapping his own daughter and taking her from her family.'

Refraining from pointing out that Amelia had, in fact, been with family this whole time, Cristy took out her notebook and shot a quick glance at Connor. He was holding a remote device that could start a discreet recording at the touch of a button, but she wasn't sure if he'd used it yet.

For the next few minutes Cristy summarized Gaudion's account of Amelia's movements the day of the killings, and how Cynthia had hidden her away after, until they'd moved to the Channel Islands.

Olivia's face was ashen again. 'Cynthia kept her from me right after it happened?' she asked, sitting down as though her legs were too weak to hold her up any longer. 'But she'd have known – she *knew* – how terrified I was that Amelia had been harmed, that someone was holding her and we might never see her again. Oh God,' she sobbed, pressing a hand to her mouth. 'I don't understand why Cynthia let me go through that when she, of all people, knew how much Lexie's children meant to me. I couldn't have loved those girls more if they were my own, and Lexie was the same with my children. You have to know that.'

Not doubting it for a moment, Cristy said, 'It was done for your sake as well as Amelia's.'

'What?' Olivia asked, clearly confounded.

'Your brother-in-law, David, is adamant that someone was hired to kill your sister and mother. Serena too, obviously . . .'

'You know he had an affair with Serena, don't you?' Olivia asked.

Cristy's heart contracted with shock. She looked at Connor as he said, quietly, 'No, we didn't know that.'

Olivia looked pinched and increasingly upset. 'I can't give you any details,' she said, 'but I can tell you it's what Lexie suspected.'

'Did you ever tell the police that?' Cristy wanted to know.

'Yes. I'm sure I did. I must have. It's so long ago now, I can hardly remember what I told them, but it's the kind of man he was. Every time Lexie made a friend he would make her his "friend" too.'

Repelled by this image of Gaudion, Cristy said, 'Did Lexie mind about Serena?'

'Of course. It hurt her a lot to know that Serena was betraying her, but it kept him away from her, that was the most important thing.'

Hoping they were recording, Cristy decided to continue unpacking this. 'I'm still not quite seeing his motive for killing Serena,' she said.

'Only he knows the answer to that,' Olivia said harshly, 'but of course, if you ask him he'll deny, deny, deny, because that's what he does.'

'And what about Lexie and your mother? Why would he have killed them?'

Olivia regarded her incredulously. 'I thought we'd already established that. Lexie was giving all their money to Papilio, and as far as we knew Mother was about to do the same. It was his daughter's inheritance he was concerned about, nothing more, nothing less.'

Since she'd brought them onto the subject of Papilio, Cristy said, 'Is it true Paul O'Malley was the therapist who helped you during your collapse?'

Olivia seemed to flinch. 'Yes, he did for a while. He'd done such wonders with Lexie that Will thought it would be a good idea to call on him to help treat me too.'

'And was he helpful?'

'I – I would say so, yes, but I didn't join Papilio, if that's what you're thinking. Will would never have allowed it for one thing, but it wasn't something I needed, anyway. With Lexie it was different. She was so horribly damaged by what had happened to her at Oxford, and for years nothing else had seemed to work. That's another part of why David wanted her dead. Thanks to Papilio, she was regaining a sense of herself and he was losing control of her – and of what she might decide to reveal about her past.'

Connor shifted the heavy bag beside him and Cristy realized he was recording. Obviously, they'd have to clear everything with Olivia before they could use it, but this way it meant they wouldn't have to ask her to go over it again.

'So it's still your belief that David carried out the killings himself?' Cristy prompted.

'And then apparently took Amelia to his mother,' Olivia retorted. 'I don't believe a word about her grabbing a gun and him finding her in the woods a day later, and I can't imagine you do either.'

Not ready to admit that she was having some difficulty with it, in spite of feeling close to convinced when she'd listened to Gaudion telling it, Cristy said, 'Will it surprise you to know that David has shared the names of Lexie's attackers with me?'

Olivia's eyes widened with shock and something that looked like fear. 'Yes, it does,' she replied, 'but maybe it shouldn't. He'll have had his reasons for doing it, and they probably involve using you in a way that will only work out well for him. It's never been easy to read his mind, and you need to be careful of him. You really do.'

Taking over for the moment, Connor said, 'I don't know the names myself, but you do, don't you?'

Olivia nodded. 'Of course, Lexie told me. She could never forget them. How could she after what they did to her?'

'And she told you David was one of them?' he prompted.

'That's what she said and I've never had any reason to doubt her. I know he's denied it, but as I've just told you, that's what he does, he denies everything, unless something changes and he finds it more beneficial to amend his story.'

Taking a moment with this, Connor said, 'He's still asking the question – we are too – why would Lexie have married him if he'd done something so terrible to her?'

Olivia's eyes showed impatience, exasperation. 'At risk of repeating myself *again*,' she said, 'his parents put enormous pressure on him to make things right once they found out Lexie was pregnant. And she, God rest her soul, was always so desperate to be loved, for *him* to love her, that not even his vile actions that night managed to change it. At least not then, though it did, over time. It's why she couldn't bear him anywhere near her. And nor could I, knowing what he'd done.'

'But he was a good father,' Cristy interjected. 'That's what you told us when we met at the Hall.'

'I'm not sure I said "good", but he was certainly a lot better with the children than he ever was with Lexie.'

Cristy said quietly, 'The first time we spoke you didn't seem quite so . . . scathing about him as you do now.'

Olivia seemed perplexed by the comment. 'I didn't know then that he'd taken my niece and kept her from me all these years,' she pointed out crossly, as if Cristy must be some kind of fool if she didn't understand what had changed. 'But I'm sure I told you that I thought he'd killed Amelia, his own daughter – doesn't that show what kind of man I think he is? That he could be capable of something like that?'

Unable to argue with that, Cristy said, 'OK. So to be clear, you still don't think someone was *hired* to kill your mother and sister, even though . . .'

'And Serena. Why does everyone keep forgetting her? She mattered too, you know.'

Cristy apologized and continued, 'Even though the police are looking into it again.'

'OK, it could have been a stranger,' Olivia conceded, 'I can see that, but if it was, he'd have been hired by David.'

'Not by one of the rapists?' Connor queried, wading right in.

Olivia started and shook her head. 'I'm sure that's what David wants you to think, and I know it probably seems possible to you, but I don't believe it and nor does my husband or his father.'

'Who,' Connor continued seamlessly, 'apparently belong to the same network of high-worth and extremely well-connected individuals as said rapists.'

Olivia's eyes widened. 'What makes you say that?' she asked nervously.

'Their names are on the Frumentarii website,' Cristy told her.

Olivia regarded her stupidly. It was several moments before she managed to say, 'Are you trying to tell me Will and Horace had something to do with . . . They were *not* involved . . . They loved Lexie . . .'

'No, that's not what we're saying,' Cristy assured her, 'but we do know how certain societies such as Frumentarii operate, and covering up for fellow members can be a part of it.'

Olivia was shaking her head and Cristy wondered if she'd actually ever heard of Frumentarii before. 'You see,' she said in the end, 'this is what David does. He throws things out there to create all the smoke and mirrors he needs to change the narrative to how he wants it to be. And now he's trying to blame my husband and father-in-law for something they'd *never* do.'

'Actually, he isn't,' Cristy told her. 'He simply said they belonged, but he doesn't believe they were involved.'

Olivia inhaled deeply, as if Cristy's last words were providing a rare source of oxygen. 'Well, that's one good thing,' she responded shakily. She started to get up, but sat down again as if she had no idea where she might go. 'This is all so awful,' she said, using a hand to dab away her tears. 'I keep thinking about Amelia, what she might have seen, what she's been told . . .' Her eyes went to Cristy. 'What's she like now? Is she as lovely as her mother? She was always the image of Lexie as a child.'

'She still is,' Cristy assured her, deciding not to mention the fiery temper and angry threats.

'What does she do? You say she's living with David, but she'll be in her mid-twenties by now.'

'I think she might have her own place outside the family home,' Cristy replied. 'She works as an interior designer, and she's engaged to be married.'

Olivia clasped a hand to her mouth. 'Is she really? My goodness. A serious boyfriend. So she's happy?'

'In the way you mean it, yes, I think so, but I'm afraid she isn't thrilled about the podcast.'

Olivia started to nod. 'No, I don't suppose she is. It'll be so disruptive for her, all the drama and publicity of people finding out she's still alive, and why would she want to relive so many terrible memories?' She looked at Cristy beseechingly. 'Do you think there's any way I could be in touch with her? Would she welcome that? Or has he poisoned her against me?'

'That's hard to answer,' Cristy admitted, 'but I can put it to David the next time we speak.'

'Or Cynthia? Please will you ask her to call me, or email? I'd give almost anything to hear from her.'

Realizing she must be feeling as though her loved ones had suddenly come back to life, Cristy said, 'I'll ask her too.'

'You promise?'

'Of course.' She gave it a moment, then said, 'I'd like to clear up something else now, if that's OK?'

Olivia nodded, almost like a child, willing to help in any way she could, provided the sweetie of reconnecting with Cynthia and her nieces could be the reward.

'After David was released from prison,' Cristy began, 'he returned to the Manse for several months and you visited him there?'

Olivia frowned. 'Is that what he's saying?' she asked. 'Because I don't—'

'Actually, it was someone else who saw you,' Cristy told her.

Olivia blinked several times until finally she started to nod. 'Yes, I did go, once,' she admitted. 'I'd forgotten until . . . It was about six weeks after he was released, as I recall. I went to beg him to tell me what he'd done with Amelia, but he just kept saying it was best that I didn't know. We had a terrible fight. I remember asking him why he wasn't out there looking for her, and he accused me of not knowing anything so I should just go home and leave him alone. In the end he practically threw me out, and I didn't go back again. Will didn't think it was good for me to engage with him when I was in such a terrible state anyway, and of course he was right. Being anywhere near David made me crazier than ever, and that was horrible for my own children, as you can probably imagine.'

Cristy nodded and after checking her notes to see if there was anything she'd missed, she turned to Connor who gave a small shake of his head. Closing up her book, Cristy said, 'Before we go, I need to tell you that we've recorded this chat . . .'

Olivia's eyes widened with alarm.

'Don't worry,' Cristy jumped in, 'we won't be using it without your permission. If you'd like to listen to it back now, while we're here, we're happy to wait. Or we can email it to you and you can let us know your decision some time over the weekend. Should you decide you don't want us to run any of it, of course we won't.'

Olivia stared at Connor's bag, clearly running back over the last twenty minutes and all she'd told them. Although she looked pinched and worried, in the end she said, 'I don't think I said anything I wouldn't want you to use, but yes, I'd like to listen first, so if you have the time . . .'

'No problem,' Connor assured her, and reached for his laptop. 'I'll line it up and anything you don't feel happy with, just let us know.'

Finally, after sitting through the wretched experience of hearing herself discussing events that could only be painful for her, she began to nod and press her hands together. 'I don't want to change anything,' she declared when it finished. 'I hope you'll use the part where I ask to be in touch with my nieces. And Cynthia.'

'I'm sure we will,' Cristy told her. 'We could even send it to David and Cynthia as an extract before we upload the episode on Tuesday, if you'd like us to.'

Olivia nodded right away. 'Yes, I would. Thank you. And will you let me know when you've done it? It's going to be a long wait anyway, but no point putting myself through the agony of it if they haven't already heard it.'

Cristy smiled her understanding and rose to her feet. 'Thanks very much for seeing us this morning,' she said. 'I'm sorry it's all so difficult for you, but maybe something good will come of it.'

'If I can see my nieces and Cynthia, it will,' Olivia assured her, standing up too. 'And him paying for what he did would be the right outcome, but I realize that won't be easy for them. Not now.'

She walked them out to the car and watched them get in, clearly distracted, and yet not looking away from them. In the end she said, 'So the police really are looking at the case again?'

'Yes, they are,' Cristy replied. 'A detective was supposed to be coming to see us yesterday, but he cancelled at the last minute. Has anyone been in touch with you?'

Olivia shook her head and shivered. 'I don't want to go through it again, ever, but if I have to . . . Have they questioned *him* yet?'

Cristy said, 'Not unless it happened while we've been here.'

'It makes me wonder,' Connor commented, 'who they *are* talking to?'

The answer to that came the following Tuesday, but by then quite a lot else had happened.

Clover and Jackson had reported back from the Vale with even more conflicting memories of the young Gaudion boys and Sallis girls than they'd had before. Some claimed it was Richard that Lexie had been keen on, others that David had always seemed sweet on Olivia, while still others recalled Olivia dating Richard when they were in their teens, or was it David? Even Hannah Gains wasn't as clear as she'd seemed before, saying that she could only really remember the time after Lexie left uni and she and David were together.

As there wasn't much from those interviews they could use for the next episode, they spent a good part of the weekend trying to get some information out of the police on what was happening with the new investigation. It appeared no one working on the cold case was available to take their calls, and Clover's contact at the CPS was laid up with flu (such timing!). Frances Rush was 'out on manoeuvres', as she put it when she rang Cristy back, but she'd find out what she could asap.

Meanwhile they worked on pulling the next episode together, focusing mainly on Gaudion's and Olivia's interviews, with some reflective and speculative chat between Cristy and Connor. Still being unable to use anything about the rape meant they had to tread extremely carefully, although, to Cristy's amazement and relief, Anna had not objected to them running her father's account of what had happened to her at the time of the murders. She wasn't willing to give an interview herself, nor was she open to a chat on the phone, but she seemed resigned, Cynthia said in her email, to having her *alive and kicking status revealed. She knows it's going to cause a lot of inconvenience for a while, but she's bracing herself for it.*

Inconvenience was one way of putting it; Cristy imagined it was going to be a lot worse than that when the time came, largely thanks to her aunt, Olivia, not believing a word of David's story. The contradictions in their accounts, the passion and heartache in Olivia's, was making for a sensational episode, there was no doubt about that, not least because Anna was steadfastly supporting her father.

'Of course he didn't do it,' she'd shouted during the one brief call Cristy had had with her. 'For one thing, don't you think I'd have recognized him if I'd seen him? And for another, it's crazy even to think it.'

'You know, someone we haven't heard from in a while,' Clover remarked late on Sunday afternoon, 'is the anonymous caller who claimed that Amelia was dead. She's going to have a bit of shock when she hears the next pod.'

'Actually, she's another good example of how convincing someone can be when they're not telling the truth,' Cristy commented, keeping her head down, though acutely aware of Gaudion's eyes on her the way she so often was. In truth, she'd avoided looking at him since returning from Guernsey, and for the most part she was communicating with him by email rather than phone. She was all too conscious of how easily she'd been swayed by him when they were together, and she didn't want it happening again. She needed to remain objective, neutral and of course professional. For the most part she was exactly that, though it fell apart slightly during her email exchanges with Rosaria. Having any sort of contact with his daughter couldn't be considered wise, and yet how could she refuse it when Rosaria seemed so thrilled to be in touch with her, and excited to share her news?

And how could a man who'd killed three people be such a wonderful father?

Ridiculous question, and she knew it, which was why she didn't even attempt to voice it, or try to answer it for herself.

Instead, she made sure Connor was there on Monday morning when she and Gaudion arranged to connect via Zoom. She'd have made it happen sooner were it not for wanting to be sure they covered everything that the edit kicked up during the interview.

At eleven o'clock prompt he appeared on the screen looking, she thought curiously, not very much like the man she'd met. His shock of light brown hair was neater, he was cleanly shaved and wearing a white shirt and slightly skewed tie. Presumably he was being a wealth manager today, as opposed to the boss of Maritime Maintenance. His eyes, of course, were exactly the same, pale blue, arresting, penetrating and, at least to her mind, all-seeing.

'Hi,' she said, only turning her camera on once she knew Connor was also on screen. 'You guys haven't met before, so Connor, this is David, and David, meet Connor, my co-producer. He's more technically gifted than I am, so he'll make sure we get everything recorded. Provided that's OK with you, of course.'

Gaudion appeared his usual relaxed self, as he said, 'I'm guessing we're just going to cover what we've already discussed by email? That Olivia doesn't believe her niece was capable of going for a gun, or hiding out in the woods overnight?'

'Correct,' Cristy replied.

'What do you say to that?' Connor asked. 'We're recording now, by the way.'

GAUDION: 'Well, what can I say, apart from I'm sorry she doesn't believe it, but maybe she's forgotten just how headstrong and gutsy her niece was – still is. I could also ask how she thought the gun came to be in the woods if Anna didn't take it there.'

CRISTY: 'You could have taken it yourself.'

GAUDION: 'But why would I if, as Olivia seems to think, I'd already taken Anna to my mother's? I guess she'd probably say I was trying to create a false narrative, and I suppose some will think she has a point, but I can assure you I didn't take the gun to the woods, and nor did I take my daughter to my mother's – until the next day, after I'd found her.'

CRISTY: 'As we have your account of how you discovered your daughter in the hollow of a tree, I'd like to ask you about something else Olivia told us. She says you were having an affair with Serena Sutton.'

Gaudion's eyes widened with so much surprise that Cristy could only feel thankful that Connor was there, so he was seeing it too, and presumably being equally taken in by it. Gaudion ran a hand over his chin and sighed out a long breath.

GAUDION: 'Well, I admit I didn't see that one coming. I'm presuming it's the first you've heard of it too, as you haven't mentioned it before.'

CONNOR: 'So are you denying it?'

GAUDION: 'I am.'

CONNOR: 'Any idea why Olivia would say it?'

GAUDION: 'I think you must be aware by now that Olivia's saying a lot of things that aren't true.'

CONNOR: 'We know that you're contradicting one another's accounts of events.'

Gaudion nodded slowly at that, seeming to accept it, and realizing how tense she'd become, and how under scrutiny she was from Clover and Jacks in the background, Cristy quickly gathered herself, ready to continue. However, Gaudion spoke first.

GAUDION: 'There's something I'd like to ask you, but not on the record, so can we cut for a while?'

After Connor had complied, Cristy said, 'We're still here, as you can see, but no longer recording.'
Speaking directly to her, Gaudion said, 'Have you shared the names I gave you with any of your colleagues?'
She shook her head. 'Not yet.' No need to mention Harry at this stage.

'So, Connor, you're not aware of them?' Gaudion said. 'That's OK, I just wanted to get an idea of how things currently stand. I'm presuming Cristy's told you that it's better if you don't know, and if she has, believe me she's right. Did you tell Olivia you know who they are?' he asked Cristy.

'I did, and she said she wasn't surprised you'd shared them. In her opinion, you're using them as a smoke screen to cover up for yourself.'

He seemed impressed, intrigued even. 'So she still thinks I carried out the killings myself? Or does she accept it might have been someone else?'

'Hired by you,' Connor told him.

'Of course, she would assume he'd been hired by me.' He sounded philosophical, unperturbed, and for the first time, as his eyes went down, Cristy had a horrible feeling he was lying.

'She's still insisting,' Connor continued, 'that you were involved in the attack on Lexie at Oxford.'

Gaudion shook his head sadly and as he sat forward in his chair, coming closer to the camera, Cristy almost found herself pulling back. 'You know that doesn't make any sense,' he said, looking straight at her. 'It never has and never will.'

'She's adamant Lexie told her you were there,' Connor told him.

'Lexie didn't say that,' he responded quietly but firmly, and still looking at Cristy. 'But as she can no longer speak for herself, it seems Olivia feels free to make things up for her.'

'But why would she?' Cristy challenged.

His eyes remained on hers. 'I think we dealt with that while you were here,' he replied. 'She very probably believes what she's telling you, because the power of suggestion when someone is in the drugged and highly emotional state she was in after the murders can be extremely effective.'

'So you're still maintaining,' Cristy said flatly, 'that O'Malley brainwashed her on behalf of a few members of Frumentarii?' She simply couldn't make up her mind whether she was believing this or not, and at the moment she didn't think she was.

'I don't *know* if that's what happened,' he told her, 'but I suspect it did. Unless you believe in coincidence to the point that would stretch most people's credulity.'

'The coincidence being,' Connor interjected, 'that O'Malley became Olivia's therapist when she was at her most vulnerable?'

Gaudion nodded. 'Let me tell you something,' he said, shifting position slightly. 'Olivia has a lot of secrets she wouldn't want to share, that she *isn't* sharing, at least it doesn't seem to me at this time that she is. I'm not about to reveal them, it's not my place to, but please tell her, the next time you speak to her, that I'd really appreciate it if she'd stop claiming I was one of the rapists. Even if she believes it's true, surely some sort of prevailing logic must tell you it isn't.' He checked the time. 'You said in your email that this would be brief, so if there isn't anything else, I'm afraid I need to get to a meeting.'

'Can we speak again later?' Connor asked.

'If you find it's necessary, of course.' He looked at Cristy again and a moment later he'd gone.

As she turned off her own camera, Cristy looked around at the others and began to shake her head. 'So, you see for yourselves how persuasive, *believable,* he can be one minute, and then not at all.'

'If Aiden was here,' Jackson said, 'he'd take one look at those eyes and declare him a psychopath.'

'Then lucky for us that Aiden's in Spain,' she retorted. 'Anyway, was that a threat he just asked us to relay to Olivia? Did it sound like one to you?'

'I guess it could have been,' Clover replied, 'but think of it this way – if he really wasn't there at the time of the rape, he must be pretty fed up with hearing it by now.'

Deciding to accept that as an answer for now, Cristy said, 'OK, he's given us quite a bit to work with, so let's get his response to Olivia's disbelief into the final cut, and we'll definitely include his denial of an affair with Serena.'

'Actually, I've been thinking about that,' Clover declared, 'and if it's true, surely Serena would have told *someone*, and no one's ever come forward that we know of.'

'What are you, some kind of defence lawyer for Gaudion now?' Jackson put in.

Clover shrugged. 'I'm just saying it's odd that it's only come up now.'

Connor looked at Cristy. 'Olivia wasn't clear about whether or not she'd told the police, so maybe there's a chance she did make it up?'

Having no answer to offer, Cristy looked up as Harry came in. 'I think we should record what we've just said,' she told the team, 'and include it.'

'I'm not here to interrupt,' Harry insisted. 'I'd just like a quick word if you can spare a moment, Cristy.'

Slipping on a jacket, she followed him out to the car park and regarded him curiously. 'I'm concerned about the names,' he said. 'Just one of those guys could bring everything Meena and I have built up here down around our ears should he choose to.'

Cristy's mouth turned dry. 'Are you asking me to shut the podcast down?' she asked incredulously.

He shook his head. 'It would be too difficult to explain at this stage,' he replied, 'but I am asking you not to use them.'

Confused, she said, 'You know I don't intend to, so what's brought this on?'

He glanced out to the street just as two mounted policemen trotted past towards the waterfront. 'It's been preying on my mind,' he confessed, 'all we stand to lose if there's ever any suggestion of that rape. Or at least who was involved in it.'

Understanding and sharing his fear, she said, 'Maybe we should pass the names to our lawyers, just in case?'

'I've been thinking about that too, and the answer's yes, maybe we should. I'll talk to Sherman. He's back from his holidays, so he's taken our case over. With the way things stand, we need someone at the top to start advising us.'

'OK. Then I'll leave it with you, but you'll let me know how it goes?'

'Of course.'

'Ah, there you are,' Meena declared, coming outside to join them. Registering their sombre expressions, she scowled. 'I can guess what you're talking about,' she said, 'so do you want me to go away again?'

'No, it's fine. We're done,' Harry assured her. 'Are you looking for me?'

She grimaced. 'Cristy, but you can stay if you'd like to.'

'Unless it's about the pod, I probably don't want to.'

'OK, off you go then.'

Cristy had to laugh as he obediently disappeared inside and Meena, looking her usual radiant and mischievous self, watched him go. 'Got to love him,' she murmured. Turning to Cristy, she regarded her closely for a moment as if searching for some hidden secret deep in her eyes.

'This isn't about Jay Wells again, is it?' Cristy protested, knowing she'd hate it if it was.

Meena shook her head. 'No, although I still think you need to be careful where David Gaudion is concerned. No, this is something you won't want to be bothered with while you're pulling together tomorrow's pod, but I thought I should alert you anyway to the fact that Marley's been in touch with me.'

Cristy's heart sank.

'She really is desperate to see you,' Meena continued. 'I felt quite sorry for her when we spoke, but don't worry, I've explained how busy you are at the moment—'

'She shouldn't have dragged you into this,' Cristy interrupted. 'I'll speak to her.'

'It's OK, I've told her that we'll be breaking something big tomorrow evening – Amelia/Anna's story?'

Cristy nodded.

'So you won't be able to see her before that. She asked if after six would be good, but I managed to put her off again by explaining that we'll all be working late dealing with the fallout from our big reveal.'

It was true, they would be. They'd even put in food and drink orders to keep them going. 'The biggest reaction will come from the police, obviously,' Cristy predicted. 'They're going to hate finding out this way, but if the high and mighty DI Thompson or one of his apparently brilliant cold-case team won't get back to us, I don't feel particularly inclined to tip them off. Anyway, you're right, I definitely won't be able to see Marley before Wednesday, and even then . . .' Her eyes closed as she groaned at the prospect of having to give in. 'Why can't Matthew deal with her, for God's sake? She's his bloody wife, not mine.'

'Have you spoken to him recently?' Meena asked.

Cristy shook her head. 'Not since I was in Guernsey. Just thank God both children are away at the moment, because I wouldn't want to be trying to deal with them as well, although frankly they're a lot easier than their father and his child-bride.'

With a smile, Meena linked arms with her and they started back inside. 'Just let me know if you need to lean on me at any time,' she said, 'it's what I'm here for.'

Reminded of just how good a friend she'd been over the past few years, Cristy turned to give her a hug. 'When this is over,' she said, 'why don't we treat ourselves to a lovely spa weekend somewhere? I think we deserve it, don't you?'

'We do, and I know just the place, so give me a heads up when you're ready.'

As they parted Cristy returned to the office and found herself staring straight at Gaudion, as if somehow, against her will, he'd drawn her to him. She wondered what he was doing now, if he really had had a meeting to be at, or if he'd cut them off before talking himself into a trap he couldn't get out of.

'OK,' she said, sitting down at her desk, 'let's try Thompson and his A team again. Some input from them for tomorrow could send us stratospheric if they have something meaningful to tell, and surely to God they do by now.'

CHAPTER THIRTY-FOUR

It was early on Wednesday morning when Connor rang Cristy from home to tell her to put on the TV news. She was only still in bed because they'd stayed so late at the office last night, inundated by calls and messages from a stunned, cynical and agitated public reacting to the revelation about Amelia Gaudion and conflicting stories between David and Olivia.

Strangely, nothing from the police yet.

'Why?' she asked, pushing back the duvet and checking the time. Eight fifty-four.

'You're about to find out,' Connor told her soberly. 'I'll hang on.'

Locating the remote in Aiden's room, she pointed it at the TV. 'Where am I going? ITV, BBC? Sky?'

'Either will do. I'm on the Beeb.'

Going there, Cristy watched the screen come to life, and as she realized what she was seeing she sank into the sofa behind her in mute disbelief.

The reporter was saying, '. . . *he has always been the chief suspect in this triple-murder case, and now we're told that the police have new evidence leading them to bring charges again. You can see Gaudion here at the airport in Guernsey with plain clothes officers who apparently flew over just after daybreak to make the arrest.*'

Cristy felt lightheaded, disoriented, as she watched Gaudion in jeans and leather jacket, climbing the steps of a small plane, hands in cuffs, head turned from the cameras.

'Are you there?' Connor asked.

'Yes, I'm here,' she murmured.

386

'. . . As yet we don't know what the new evidence is, but according to some early reports it was first acquired by the Hindsight podcast team who are currently covering this case for their latest true-crime series.'

Cristy swallowed dryly. 'It has to be the crime-scene shots,' she said. 'They've obviously made progress, and it sounds as though there's something we missed.'

'Or that allowed the experts to go deeper than we were able to see.'

She continued staring at the screen, hardly hearing the reporter now as she pictured what must have happened on the island during the last few hours. Had he received any warning they were coming for him, a call from his lawyer, the local police even? Or had the UK officers just turned up at his home? Did Rosaria know what was going on? What about Cynthia? And Anna . . . Her eyes closed as a terrible sense of dread came over her. 'She warned me,' she said to Connor. 'Anna. She told me there were things I didn't know and never would . . .'

'And?' he prompted.

'I think she knew how possible it was it would come to this . . .'

'But how could she?'

'Maybe because she lied for her father?'

Connor fell silent and the report continued.

'. . . you can find a full background of this case on our website, but if you've been following the highly popular podcast from Cristy Ward and Connor Church, you'll already be aware of how Gaudion's wife, Alexandra – Lexie – Gaudion, his mother-in-law, Margaret Sallis, and family friend, Serena Sutton, were shot to death in Gaudion's Gloucestershire home back in 2008. It's long been held that his ten-year-old daughter was witness to the event and was taken from the scene by the killer. However, it was revealed last night on the Hindsight pod that she has been living with her father in Guernsey since the murders.'

Cristy's chest felt tight; her eyes seemed to hurt as she searched the screen, wishing, hoping that her mind was playing tricks, that she was still asleep and would catch up with reality any minute.

Gaudion had been swallowed into the plane now, the propellors a blur in front of the engines, while several men remained standing at the foot of the steps, talking amongst themselves. Was his lawyer with them? Were Cynthia and Anna watching this? Surely no one would allow Rosaria to.

What did they, she and Connor, need to do now?

Shock was making it hard to think. It was as though they'd hit a brick wall in a road they'd thought was completely clear.

'This will be why Thompson and his crew haven't spoken to us yet,' Connor stated. 'They didn't want to risk us tipping him off.'

Suspecting he was right, Cristy said, 'We need to find out what made them so confident that they actually flew over there to bring him back when the case has barely been reopened a week.'

'Just what I was thinking. It has to be something pretty major or the CPS would never have signed off on it. They wouldn't want to be pulling a trial again.'

Cristy looked at her phone. Twenty missed calls, but she was only interested in the crime-scene photos. What was there that they hadn't seen in spite of all their scrutiny? Or maybe they had seen it but had misunderstood it. 'Have you checked the shots?' she asked Connor.

'Sure, and I'm doing it again now, but we don't have the kind of equipment the police have, nor does Jacks. What we need is to try to get ahead of the news, the way we've been up to now, because this has left us fair and square on our asses.'

It certainly had. 'I'm already getting calls from the press,' she said, recognizing some of the names and numbers, 'I expect you are too, but I, for one, don't fancy giving any statements until we're better prepared. We need to get everyone to the office . . . Actually, we should meet here, we're too easily found at the studios. If you call Jacks and Clover, I'll get hold of Harry and Meena . . . Oh shit, Matthew's trying to get through to me now. He'll be after an exclusive, I just know it.'

'Hit decline and don't take calls from anyone until the rest of us get there.'

After they'd rung off, Cristy quickly messaged Harry and Meena before switching her phone to silent while she jumped in the shower. Her mind was racing so fast now she could hardly keep up with her own thoughts as they veered from Gaudion and the shock – or was it inevitability – he'd surely felt when they'd come for him; to his family and how afraid they must be feeling now; to the glimpse of him getting onto the plane; to the crime-scene photos; then to the masked man and Anna's promise that if anything happened to her father she'd find Cristy and make her pay.

Though Cristy's heart tightened at the thought of Anna's outrage and fear, she knew she couldn't allow herself to be distracted by personal feelings in spite of how hard this was going to be for the family. Right now she needed to focus on Thompson and how he'd managed to get a warrant for Gaudion's arrest so quickly after his enquiries had begun.

As soon as she was dressed and had put some coffee on, she sat down with her laptop. Thankfully her personal email account wasn't under attack from reporters or listeners yet, although it was filling up fast with messages from people she knew. Ignoring them, she scrolled on down, hoping to find something from Gaudion, a few words that might tell her what was happening, or simply saying WTF?, but there was nothing. However, Rosaria had been in touch, and as Cristy read the jolly-sounding email she realized it had been sent last night while Rosaria's world had still been full of small things that made her happy: the panto, her job at the tourist office, painting hulls at her dad's boatyard, helping Cynthia pickle walnuts in the kitchen.

Hello Cristy,

I thought you'd like to know that we've chosen some music for the panto and I have a special song that I am going to sing all on my own. It's called Kiss from a Rose *and is when the Beast and Belle meet in the ballroom of his castle. Dad says I'm already hurting his ears (he's very cheeky) but Granny says practice makes perfect. I don't know all the words off by heart yet, but when I do I will sing it for you and Dad will help me attach it to an email.*

Lots of love
Rosaria

PS: Laurent is going to be in the panto too, as a monster, and my boyfriend, Pierre, is playing the beast.

PPS: (Cynthia here) She's actually singing a few lines solo, but we're certain she'll be a star whatever she does.

Cristy ached with so much feeling that it brought tears to her eyes. This dear young woman with the heart and mind of a child, who deserved nothing but sweetness and joy in her life, had been completely unprepared for what was going on in her world now. And she, Cristy, had helped to bring it about.

'You can't blame yourself,' Jodi scolded when she and Connor turned up a few minutes later. 'It's not your fault this is happening . . .'

'The pod was my idea.'

'And it was a good one. And if Gaudion did do it . . . Well, it seems he did, or we wouldn't be where we are, would we? Did you speak to Matthew earlier?'

'No,' Cristy shuddered. 'I guess he's tried to contact you,' she said to Connor.

'I told him we'd get back to him as soon as we had something we could share,' he responded, pouring himself and Jodi a coffee.

'Well put. We need to use that line with everyone, at least for now. How's Clover's CPS contact? Please tell me he's not still laid up with man flu.'

'Either that, or he's ducking her.'

'Do you have a number for Trevor Thompson? We can but try.'

Finding it, Connor made the connection. 'Voicemail,' he told her, and after leaving a message for the detective to call him or Cristy if he could tell them more about the arrest, he said, 'Have you contacted Frances Rush?'

'About half an hour ago. And Kevin Break? Have you spoken to him?'

'He's trying to find out who's on Thompson's team in case there's anyone he knows from old times. Even if there is, he's doubtful we'll get any information out of them at this stage, but he's doing his best.'

For the next few minutes as they called their many contacts in the hope of learning more, Jodi noted down who they spoke to and who they left messages for.

'I'll do Matthew if you like,' Connor offered as the buzzer sounded, announcing someone at the front door.

'I'll go,' Jodi said, heaving herself up from the sofa.

'Matthew won't know even as much as us,' Cristy declared. 'On the other hand, he's got some pretty good contacts he might be willing to put us in touch with, so yes, go for it.'

Moments later Clover and Jacks traipsed in with Meena and Harry right behind them.

'So where is he now?' Harry demanded, positioning himself in front of the TV as the others went straight to the coffee. 'Has the plane landed yet?'

'I wouldn't think so,' Cristy replied, 'they've only just taken off.'

'Where will they land him?' Meena asked.

'Best guess, Bristol airport,' Cristy answered, 'but it could be any of the smaller airfields around. We've been trying to find out what the news outlets know, but so far no one seems to have any inside info – or none that they're prepared to share.'

Putting his phone on hold, Connor said, 'Matthew's willing to make a few calls for us, but he wants something in return.'

Cristy's jaw tightened. 'Isn't that just like him,' she muttered. 'Tell him to fuck off.'

'Hang on,' Harry stepped in. 'Let's at least find out what he wants.'

Connor looked at Cristy. 'He's keen for you to meet with Marley,' he told her awkwardly. 'Apparently she's been trying to get hold of you and he thinks you should see her before they go off to France next week.'

Hating being cornered like this, Cristy said, 'Tell him I'll call her by the end of the day, but he's got to understand this is a pretty busy time for us.'

After relaying the message, Connor put the call on hold again. 'He says we're producing a weekly podcast that drops on Tuesdays and today's Wednesday, so he doesn't understand the urgency.'

Gritting her teeth, Cristy held out a hand for the phone. 'My answer to your insufferable condescension,' she said, 'is this: as soon as you put us in touch with someone useful I'll see her.'

There was a smile in his voice as he said, 'I think that can be done within the hour. Shall I get back to you or Connor?'

'Connor,' she replied, and rang off. 'God he's a shit,' she seethed, meaning it, although deep down she couldn't help admiring and envying how many people he knew, and how he always managed to get what he wanted.

Her phone rang and seeing it was Frances Rush she immediately put the call on speaker. 'Hi, thanks for getting back to me. Can you tell us anything yet?'

'I'm still working on it, but they'll almost certainly take him to Keynsham or Patchway for processing when they get here, and I should think, once he's charged, he'll be in front of a magistrate by tomorrow. As for what evidence they've found, apparently it's connected to some old phone records.'

Cristy frowned, not expecting that. 'His, or Lexie's?'

'That's all I have right now. Apparently, trawling through old phone records is what got them a warrant to bring him in. Apologies, but I have to go. I'll be in touch again if I can find out more.'

As soon as Rush rang off, Connor said, 'It could be the masked man's phone records. They'll have his number from the photos we sent.'

'She said "old" phone records,' Clover pointed out. 'Would he still have the same number after all this time?'

'It's a long shot,' Jacks replied, 'but I could have a go at tracking it again.'

'Yes, do that,' Cristy said. 'Meantime I'm going to try Edmond Crouch.'

'Remind me who that is,' Meena prompted.

'Gaudion's lawyer. Of course we don't stand a snowball's chance of him speaking to us, especially as he's probably on that plane right now, but no harm in trying.'

'Mr Crouch,' she said into his voicemail. 'It's Cristy Ward here. I realize this is a difficult time, but if there's anything we can do on our podcast to help the situation you know we are at your disposal. You have my number.'

As she rang off, Meena said, 'Was that you being disingenuous, or were you telling him we think his client could have been wrongfully arrested?'

It took Cristy a moment to understand how Meena had come to that conclusion. 'I have to make him think we're on their side or he'll never speak to us,' she explained. 'And I'm sure everyone in this room is aware of the coincidence of him being arrested right after he told me the names.'

'But how would anyone know he'd told you?' Clover asked, confused.

Cristy looked at Connor. 'We told Olivia,' she reminded him.

Connor hit his head as a light went on. 'Her husband and father-in-law,' he stated. 'Of course, so we can assume all the bastard rapists have been briefed and clearly they've acted pretty swiftly.'

Seeming not to follow, Harry said, 'But I thought he presented more of a risk to them if he was in danger of going down.'

Cristy nodded. 'That's always been our assumption, and he basically confirmed that when we spoke, but frankly, we have no idea how they operate, so we definitely can't rule out the fact that they could be behind this arrest.'

'And if we rule it in?' Clover asked. 'Where do we go with it?'

'Too early to say without speaking to his lawyer,' Connor replied, 'but you do realize, don't you, that the way we're talking now makes it sound like we're assuming he's innocent when we have no idea if that's true.'

Discomfited by the way Meena was looking at her, Cristy said, 'It's not so much an assumption as a hope that he is.'

Meena scowled.

'He has a family,' Cristy cried, throwing out her hands. 'A mother, two daughters, a son, people who depend on him and love him. They're going to be completely traumatized if it turns out he is guilty, so please forgive me for hoping he isn't.' Turning to Connor, she said, 'In fact, I've been wondering . . . Would it be inappropriate to try calling his mother?'

'Just a bit,' Harry jumped in.

'I don't see why,' Jodi protested. 'It's a considerate thing to do when the woman is probably terrified of what's going to happen.'

'I'm sure she is,' Harry responded, 'but if you're going to ask how it went down over there, what time the police came, what they said and so on, it's going to make you no more than one of the pack.'

'That wasn't my intention,' Cristy told him tartly. 'I just thought it might help to let her know that *we* haven't given up on him.'

'Great! And what happens when we do?' Meena demanded. 'What are you going to tell her then? Sorry, we got it all wrong, your son's clearly a cold-blooded killer who deserves to be where he is, and we're glad we played a part in bringing him to justice.'

Cristy eyed her balefully.

Undeterred, Meena said, 'I think you should hold off speaking to her at least until you've heard from Gaudion's lawyer—'

'Which might be never.'

'Even so, it's too soon to start reaching out in the way you're suggesting.'

Aware she hadn't really suggested anything, Cristy turned to Jacks as he said, 'No go with the phone. Completely off air, but I'll stay on it.'

Unsurprised, Cristy said, 'Maybe we should try finding out if anyone else has been arrested in relation to the case.'

Quickly following her train of thought, Connor said, 'They've got the phone number and pics, so I guess there's a chance they could now have the hitman himself.'

'Or he's under surveillance,' Cristy added, 'which we wouldn't be able to penetrate. However, arrests are usually a matter of public record.'

'On it,' Jacks declared, and returned to his laptop as Clover said, 'This is weird.'

Everyone looked at her as she turned the podcast's mobile phone for them to see the screen. 'It's from the anonymous caller who kept claiming Amelia was dead,' she explained.

'How's she taken the good news?' Connor asked dryly.

'I'll read it,' she answered. '"I heard what you said last night about Amelia, but whoever that is in Guernsey, it can't be her. Amelia is dead and he killed her. I know because I saw him do it, and that's why they've arrested him this morning, because I told them everything."' Clover looked up. 'She's given us her name – Wendy Grails – and a phone number.'

Cristy gave an incredulous laugh. 'Amelia is not dead,' she assured them. 'I saw her while I was there, and I can tell you, apart from Gaudion's eyes, she's the image of her mother. In fact, see for yourselves, there she is now.'

As they turned to the screen Cristy increased the volume and a moment later almost wished she hadn't as a red-eyed, furious Anna Gaudion rounded on a pursuing reporter, saying, '. . . Of course he didn't do it. It's insane even to think it, but I know most of you in the media want to believe it, and no one more than the *podcaster* Cristy Ward. She came here playing nice with my family, getting everyone eating out of her hand, even my dad, but I could see straight through her. I knew what she was doing. It was all about adding ratings to her *libellous* podcast and now look where we are. I've no idea what lies she told the police, but I can assure you that my father *did not kill my mother or anyone else*, and I should know.'

It was mid-afternoon and they were all at the office by the time Matthew called to relay the unhelpful news that none of his police contacts would speak to them; however, he did have something to share.

Connor hit speaker so the others could listen and told him to go ahead.

'OK, so I was told that Gaudion's original police statements and other materials have recently come to light following an archive search.'

As Cristy's eyes widened, Connor cried, 'You're kidding me. That's a bit convenient, isn't it? How do they go from "Nowhere-to-be-found, straight to oh-look-here-they-are and hey, they contain everything we need to charge him again"?'

'I can only agree,' Matthew replied, 'that it's odd they've turned up again now.'

'*Odd*,' Cristy shot back. 'It's un-frigging-believable, is what it is. Corrupt is another word that comes to mind.' To the others she said, 'We're definitely including this in the next pod.

395

It's the only way we can call them out. Anything else?' she asked Matthew.

'Apparently the new evidence is connected to some old phone logs,' he replied. 'I don't know whose phone, or how many calls, or when they were made, just that.'

'Yeah, we've heard the same,' Connor told him, 'but thanks anyway.'

'You're welcome. Don't forget, Cristy, you owe me. We'll be waiting for your call.'

'Just tell me *why* she wants to speak to me,' she cried before he could ring off.

'With everyone listening?'

'Yes, why not? What the heck is it about?'

'Actually, I can only guess,' he admitted, 'but please see her. It seems to mean a lot and I'm sure she won't take up much of your time.'

As he ended the call, she gave a growl of annoyance and turned to her own phone as her family WhatsApp came to life again. It had been going on and off throughout the day with Hayley and Aiden demanding updates on the arrest, but so far she had no more to tell them than they were already hearing on the news. Gaudion was now at Patchway Police Centre 'helping with enquiries', and charges were expected to be brought within the next twenty-four to forty-eight hours. There had been no official statements from investigating officers or from his lawyers as yet, and none of them had got back to Cristy either.

'Kevin Break!' Connor announced, and bounced the call onto speaker. 'Hanging on your every word,' he told the ex-cop.

'OK, so here's what I know,' Break responded. 'I'm afraid it's not much, but he's likely to be charged sometime in the next couple of hours and will spend the night where he is before appearing in front of a magistrate in the morning. The expectation is that he'll be remanded in custody . . .'

Refraining from pointing out that they could have guessed as much themselves, Cristy said, 'Did you learn anything about the phone records?'

'Just that they're at the centre of it, but sounds like you already know that.'

'So no idea whose records they are?'

'I can't say for certain, but I'm getting the impression they're his. Unfortunately, everyone's being really tight-lipped about this and as I don't know anyone on the inside, I can only get what little my guy is managing to pick up.'

'OK,' Connor said, 'thanks for this anyway, and let us know if you hear anything else.'

'Sure will.'

As he rang off everyone sat quietly for a moment, formulating how to incorporate these small but important events into the next pod.

Cristy checked her emails. Still nothing from Cynthia, who she'd messaged earlier to say, *Here if you want to chat. Not looking for info, just concerned about you.* She knew, courtesy of the news crews in Guernsey, that Richard Gaudion had flown to the island earlier and was now at the house, while his wife, Astrid, was still at their London home refusing to give interviews to the media camped outside.

Olivia and her family had also been bombarded, but no one there was speaking out either, apart from one short statement from Will Caldwell, delivered at the gates, asking everyone to respect their privacy at this very difficult time for his wife.

Cristy had called Olivia without much hope of getting through, and she hadn't, but Olivia had sent a text about an hour ago saying:

Finally looks like justice is going to be served. Feeling very conflicted about it, relieved, obviously, but upset for Cynthia, Rosaria and Anna. If you're in touch with them please send my love. Police have been here most of the day, a horrible rerun of what we went through before, but hopefully I'm stronger now. We – Lexie, Mum and I – want to thank you for all you've done to help bring this about.

Cristy had started a message back insisting she hadn't done anything, but of course she had. Gaudion wouldn't be facing charges, and Olivia wouldn't finally know that her murdered loved ones were receiving justice, if it weren't for the podcast. So yes, she was responsible, even if she had no idea what had actually happened since her return from Guernsey.

'I hope this wasn't a crazy thing to do,' Clover announced to the room at large, 'but I've contacted this Wendy Grails to see if she'll talk to me.'

Cristy blinked; Connor looked confused.

'OK, I get we all think she's a whack job,' Clover pressed on, 'but she's so adamant, and if she really has spoken to the police in the past forty-eight hours, I think we'd like to know about it. Wouldn't we?'

'Of course we would,' Cristy confirmed.

Connor said, 'Even if it turns out to be a red herring, it could provide some interesting material for next week's pod, because the way we're going, we'll be struggling to fill it with anything other than regurgitated news.'

Cristy nodded. 'You're right. So OK, Clove, do it, but only if she's not too far away. There's no point wasting time going to Scotland or the outer reaches of Wales for something that might not be used anyway.'

'She's in Oxford,' Clover informed them, and gave it a moment to resonate.

'Serena Sutton's home town,' Connor stated, turning back to Cristy.

Frowning, Cristy said, 'Could be just a coincidence—'

'Unless,' Connor interrupted, 'it turns out we've been missing something major that's about to leap out and bite us on the collective backside.'

Cristy turned as someone came into the room. Realizing who it was, her mouth literally fell open with shock.

'Sorry to interrupt,' the sharp-suited man with a bald head and thin face said with a smile, 'I'm here on behalf Mr MacAnany who is, at this moment, very close by and hoping to meet you.'

Cristy stared at him, too thrown to answer right away. How could the man who'd dropped in unannounced before and threatened – or at least advised her how to deal with her own business – have just come waltzing in again as if he was welcome?

'Why doesn't Mr MacAnany come here?' Connor challenged.

'He would prefer to speak with Ms Ward privately,' he replied, 'and would appreciate an assurance that the conversation will be off the record. No hidden cameras or microphones.'

Realizing this was why it had been sprung on them, giving them no time to prepare anything covert, Cristy said, 'Where is he, exactly?'

'He's waiting down by the Harbourside, in full view of passersby, so there is nothing to be concerned about. He assures me it will only take a few minutes of your time . . .' He stepped back and gestured for Cristy to join him for the short walk to the water's edge, clearly assuming she wouldn't refuse.

'I'll be right behind you,' Connor told her, 'not letting you out of my sight.'

Seeming to have no objection to that, the messenger waited for Cristy to follow instructions, then fell in beside her as they crossed the small car park into the narrow street leading to the SS *Great Britain*.

'Tell me,' she said, glancing round to make sure Connor was behind them, 'am I about to meet MacAnany senior or junior?'

'Junior,' came the reply.

So, she thought with no small revulsion, *a face-to-face with one of the rapists*. That alone was enough to send chills down her spine, but the fact that he was here, in Bristol, wanting to talk to her so soon after Gaudion's arrest, surely meant that someone was in a panic.

She spotted the man right away, in spite of never having seen him before. The father, yes, on TV, plenty of times, but this was the first time she'd laid eyes on the son. She knew it was him, because his air of sophistication, the expensive suit and oily black hair would make him stand out anywhere; here on the Harbourside where most were casually dressed and getting on with their day, he didn't even begin to blend in.

'Ms Ward,' he said, stepping forward to shake her hand.

She glanced down at his and decided not to take it. 'What is this about?' she asked bluntly.

Accepting the snub with sublime equanimity, he indicated the nearby café terrace. 'Maybe I can get you a drink?'

'That won't be necessary,' she told him. 'I'd like to know what you want to see me about.'

'Of course.' He nodded to the messenger, apparently an instruction to step away out of earshot. She turned and saw Connor seating himself at one of the café's tables, making no secret of watching them.

'I'm aware,' MacAnany began, 'that David Gaudion gave you several names while you were in Guernsey, and one of them was mine.'

She neither admitted nor denied it, simply realized that his information could only have come from Olivia's husband or father-in-law via Olivia herself.

'I'd like to ask if you've shared your information with anyone,' he went on quietly.

Although several answers presented themselves, the one she went for was, 'If I say I haven't, how will you know if I'm telling the truth?'

His eyes narrowed as his mouth crooked into a grudging smile. He was a handsome man, no doubt about that, not unlike Pierce Brosnan on a good day; however, she'd never been taken in by looks and it certainly wasn't happening now.

'Of course, I won't know,' he conceded, 'but maybe I should tell you this: if you are intending to use the names in a future podcast, or in any other way that makes them public, it will end up being your own reputation that suffers the most.'

Her eyebrows rose. 'How?' she asked, realizing he'd just threatened her.

Seeming surprised by the question, he said, 'I'm aware of the allegations Lexie Gaudion made against us many years ago – none of which are true by the way – but at least she was sensible enough never to go to the authorities. As far as we know, she only ever told two people: her sister, Olivia, who understood right away how harmful it could be for her sister to take matters any further, and Paolo Morelli. Fortunately, Mr Morelli and his family share a long association with my own – I'm sure you know his name is really O'Malley and he's as Irish as we MacAnanys are, but that's beside the point other than to say loyalties run deep. He was concerned to hear Lexie accusing me and others of the savage act

400

that she'd been subjected to during her time at Oxford. Whether or not it really did happen, I can't say, but for obvious reasons none of us wanted – or indeed want – to be forced into a position where we have to defend ourselves over serious offences that none of us actually committed.'

'Would that include murder?' she asked, holding his gaze.

He appeared puzzled, until enlightenment dawned. 'Ah, you think we were behind Lexie's tragic end, her mother and the other woman too, but you're wrong about that, Ms Ward.'

God, he was smooth; nothing seemed to ruffle him, and he lied with such ease she could almost be persuaded to believe him. 'It's quite a coincidence, isn't it,' she retorted, 'that she was murdered right after she told O'Malley about the *rape*.' She pronounced the word deliberately and had the satisfaction of seeing him flinch.

'It was unfortunate timing,' he conceded, 'but no less of a coincidence for that.' He glanced away for a moment, and back again. 'I can assure you, Ms Ward, you will never find anything to tie any of us to those murders, for the simple reason that they were as much of a shock to us as they were to the rest of the world.'

'Is that so?' she asked derisively.

'It is the truth.'

'Just like your claim not to have raped her so brutally that she was never the same after?'

Shaking his head in dismay, he said, 'Believe me, I'm truly sorry for her experience. She was a popular, intelligent and ambitious young woman. We all had a lot of respect for her—'

'Spare me,' she cut in scathingly. 'You left out someone very important just now when you said Lexie only confided in two people, because her husband knows, as you're clearly aware, and that's the real reason you're here, isn't it? Not to see me, although I'm sure I qualify as some sort of important business to be dealt with, but to wield your influence, or use your contacts, or whatever you do to keep people in check, to make sure David Gaudion doesn't reveal your names to the police. Have you seen him yet?'

He regarded her levelly, almost admiringly. 'No, I haven't seen him,' he replied. 'I doubt it would be permitted while he's still being questioned.'

401

'But you'll be able to get word to him, I'm sure, make sure he knows you're listening and watching, just in case he's tempted to say things you'd prefer he didn't. But what if he doesn't reveal your names? What happens then? Are you going to get another trial cancelled to make sure they don't come out in court? You could already be too late for that. There's a new investigative team on the case, a new Chief Prosecutor, maybe they're beyond your reach.'

'Nobody is that,' he assured her, 'but once again you are confusing the issue by imagining David Gaudion will try to drag us down with him. He won't. You see, I didn't mention him just now as someone Lexie told, because he knew all along.'

Cristy felt her throat turn dry. Surely to God this wasn't going where she now thought it was.

'I know,' he continued, 'that Olivia told you he was involved in the attack, if we're to agree there was one, so this surely can't come as such a surprise.'

Cristy tried to speak and found she couldn't.

'He's the one who's been lying all this time, Ms Ward, about everything, including the rape. And I'm here trying to spare you – actually to spare us all – the expense and public humiliation of becoming embroiled in allegations that cannot be proven when they are entirely without foundation. So, please, for your own sake, keep what you've heard to yourself – and if you have told anyone else, they would be well advised to do the same.'

CHAPTER THIRTY-FIVE

'Did it sound like a threat?' Connor asked as she finished recounting the bizarre and wholly disorientating last few minutes.

They were on their way back to the office now; MacAnany and his lackey had merged into the Harbourside foot traffic, presumably heading for a car left somewhere around Wapping Wharf.

'Not exactly, but I'm sure it was,' she replied. 'I mean, why else would he come here if not to let us know that it wouldn't go well for us if we name him and his cronies as potential rapists? I'm guessing the intention would be to tie us up in law suits that we, at our lowly level, don't stand much chance of winning when pitched against the crack teams they could muster, so we'd end up broke and totally discredited.'

'I think we need to get Harry and Meena in on this,' Connor said as they entered the building. 'Hold fire on telling the others while I go get them.'

Ten minutes later the team was gathered for the second time that day, listening intently as Cristy took them through the conversation with MacAnany, this time with an equal focus on Gaudion as a liar as on MacAnany as an existential threat.

'So what do you believe?' Harry asked when she'd finished.

Cristy shook her head and felt suddenly weighted by it. 'I don't know,' she groaned, burying her face in her hands. 'It's such a terrible story for Gaudion to have made up, that Lexie was raped—'

'But MacAnany didn't say it was made up,' Meena interrupted. 'If I heard you correctly, he said he didn't know if she'd been raped, but if she had, then he and the others had nothing to do with it.'

403

'Then answer me this,' Cristy said, looking up again, 'if he wasn't involved, how did he know Gaudion was there?'

'Good point,' Connor commented to Meena.

'Why didn't I think to ask MacAnany while he was here?' Cristy growled. 'It all happened so fast, and he was so . . . *subtle* – is that the word I'm looking for? I guess it'll do for now. He was also, I've got to admit it, believable, but practised liars usually are.'

'And Gaudion wouldn't be an exception to that,' Meena pointed out.

Cristy flashed her a look. 'You've got such a down on him,' she said accusingly. 'Aren't you prepared to give him the benefit of the doubt at all?'

'Right now I'm not giving it to anyone,' Meena retorted, 'and frankly, I'm worried you're not seeing straight as far as that man's concerned. The police won't have taken him in without being certain of their ground, not after last time, and fabricating some sort of story about five high-powered men raping his wife and trying to cover it up would be an effective way for Gaudion to pull these men's strings. As MacAnany's just told you himself, even if they didn't do it, they don't want the publicity, so, in my opinion, it's highly possible Gaudion approached them the last time, blackmailed them if you like, forcing them to use their influence to get himself off—'

'Just a minute,' Cristy broke in hotly, 'let's not forget that it was Lexie who repeated the names to O'Malley and ended up getting herself killed. Doesn't that put the Frumentarii fraternity more squarely behind the murders than Gaudion?'

'Or maybe MacAnany was right about it being no more than a coincidence that it happened after she confided in O'Malley.'

'And you believe that?' Cristy cried incredulously, suddenly wanting to scream.

'OK, OK, let's calm this down,' Harry advised, holding up his hands for peace.

Cristy and Meena continued to glare at one another until Cristy turned away, realizing she really didn't want to fall out with someone who mattered so much to her when she was no more certain of the truth than Meena was.

'The way I'm reading this,' Harry said, 'is that you've just been warned, Cristy, not to mess with people who can only win, whatever the reality. But that's OK, because as we keep saying, we're not intending to use those names, so if they do come out it'll be down to Gaudion, or someone else, not to us. As for whether or not Gaudion was involved in the rape, or the murder of those three women . . . Frankly, I've no idea how we get to the truth of that, but remember, it isn't our job to. That's what the police are for, and your role is to make a podcast that relates events as they unfold, not to solve the crime.'

Reluctantly accepting that she was allowing herself to get far too close to this, Cristy took a breath and sighed it out loudly. 'I just wish I could find a way to talk to Gaudion,' she said, reaching for her phone in case something had happened in the last half an hour that they'd missed.

'Actually, I might be able to help with that,' Clover piped up, speaking for the first time since Cristy and Connor had returned from the Harbourside.

Cristy looked at her in astonishment.

'Well, not with actually speaking to him,' Clover quickly added, 'but his lawyer rang while you were gone – not Crouch, one of the minions. He wants you to call back when it's convenient.'

'Did he say why?' Cristy asked, quickly opening up her contacts. 'Do I use Crouch's number?'

'Here's the one he left,' Clover replied, pinging it over.

Seconds later Cristy was speaking to someone whose name she'd already forgotten as he said, 'Mr Crouch is asking if you can meet at his office tomorrow morning.'

'In London?' she asked, confused.

'No, we're using the premises of another law firm on Queen Square while we're here. I'll text you the details. Would ten a.m. be too early for you?'

'Ten will be fine. Thank you,' and ending the call she looked disbelievingly at the others. 'Well, that's got to mean something,' she declared, almost wanting to cheer without knowing if there was anything to cheer about. 'Gaudion's lawyer reaches out just when we think we've hit a brick wall.'

'It sounds like he might not be going in front of a magistrate

405

in the morning,' Jackson pointed out. 'His lawyer would obvs be there if he was.'

'He could have a barrister repping him already,' Connor said, 'so we'll keep an eye on that, and if you're with Crouch when it happens, Cristy, Clove and I will go to the court.'

Cristy sat back in her chair, stretching her arms overhead in an effort to release the tension in her limbs. 'Now all I have to get through,' she said, already feeling the dread of it creeping over her, 'is this bloody meeting with Marley.'

A couple of hours later she was feeling as though she'd stepped into a parallel universe, going straight from the peak of what was happening with Gaudion and the Kellon Manse Murders, right into the crisis that was Marley's world.

What she'd heard so far wasn't just stunningly unexpected, it was extremely worrying.

'Let me get this straight,' she said, bringing the olive-skinned, raven-haired beauty a glass of sparkling water with ice and a slice of fresh lime. She'd been advised by Aiden what his pregnant stepmother liked to drink when she'd WhatsApped to ask. His reply had continued with, *You know why she wants to see you, don't you? 'Please, please, Cristy, be my friend'*, and a row of teary emojis and praying hands had ended it. Minutes later Hayley had weighed in with, *Dying to hear what it's about. Let us know as soon as she leaves.*

Sitting down on the opposite sofa with a glass of white wine for herself – she needed it after the day she'd had – Cristy continued trying to lay out her alarmed and incredulous understanding of what Marley had just told her. 'You're saying you don't want to be married to Matthew any more, but you don't want to break his heart either, so you'd like *me* to come to France with you next week to help as some sort of . . . mediator?' Had she really just spoken those words out loud as if they were some sort of credible option? It was never going to happen – surely to God Marley realized that? – except maybe she didn't. Just looking at her sitting there in all her youthful eagerness, so exquisitely lovely and keen to be reasonable and, presumably, approved of, showed how terribly naïve she really was. Or stupid – it was hard to say for certain.

'I know you all used to go to France for your holidays,' Marley responded, her low, throaty voice lending a melodious note of maturity to her weirdly juvenile grasp of reality. 'It's a place where you have so many happy memories, and I was thinking, perhaps you could make more of them if I bowed out of your lives while we're there. You'd be around for Matthew, and I know that'll mean a great deal to him, because he's still very attached to you. And after I've gone and the children arrive, you can take the opportunity to become a family again.'

Cristy sat staring at her, still unable to believe she was really this delusional, or that she was actually serious, although it seemed she was. There was so much she could say now, so much build-up of pain, grief, loss and fury she could heap all over this beautiful cuckoo who'd taken over her precious family nest, pushing her out and claiming Cristy's husband as her own, but all she said was, 'Aren't you forgetting one extremely important little factor here?'

Marley's hand went to the small mound of her belly, suggesting that she was at least not in denial over her condition, and now Cristy was fascinated to hear what she was going to say next.

'My agent,' Marley began, her sad, sloe eyes lowering and raising again as if she was playing some sort of tragic heroine, which, in a way, Cristy supposed she was, 'is very keen for me to go to Los Angeles. He thinks there are more opportunities for me there than here, and apparently he's already spoken to a few producers who are keen to meet me. Nothing definite, you understand, it's a fickle and unpredictable business as I'm sure you know, but becoming a mother at this time of my life, having to put everything on hold for heaven knows how long . . .' She broke off, reaching into her sleeve for a tissue to dab the tears from her cheeks.

Hoping to God she wasn't about to be asked to arrange a termination, Cristy sat transfixed, having no idea of what she was going to say if she was proved right.

'So I thought,' Marley went on tearily, and yet hopefully it seemed, 'that if I was to go there and meet people, sort a few things out, maybe I could give birth over there and then you and Matthew can become its parents.'

Cristy gaped at her open-mouthed, certain she couldn't have heard that right, while knowing she had. Not in a million years could she have seen it coming, and yet there it was, the hope, the insane belief that *she* would want to take on the child her ex-husband and his new wife had created as if it were her own. She was so completely dumbfounded she wasn't sure she'd ever find a way to respond.

'You've been such a brilliant mother to Hayley and Aiden,' Marley reminded her, 'that I know this little one will be far better off with you than he or she would ever be with me.' She managed a smile, and seemed almost as if she was discussing a fait accompli now. 'Of course, I'd want to see it now and again,' she ran on, clearly thinking that was the right thing to say, 'and don't worry, I'd contribute financially, because I know babies – children – can be expensive, but as I said, you and Matthew know how to be parents, whereas I don't.'

Finally finding her voice, Cristy said, 'Have you discussed *any* of this with Matthew?'

Marley quickly shook her head. 'I knew I had to run it past you first, because obviously it all depends on you wanting to get back with Matthew, and I think you do, don't you?' Her tone was so pleading she might as well have got down on her knees to beg for the answer she wanted.

Once again Cristy could only stare at her, while wondering fleetingly what Aiden and Hayley were going to make of this when – *if* – she told them. Then for one crazy moment she almost wanted to laugh, even though there was nothing remotely funny about Matthew's mid-life crisis coming to an end like this. How hurt was he actually going to be when he was told about this outrageous, unbelievable plan that was absolutely never going to come to fruition?

In the end, she said, 'I'm afraid you have a very strange way of seeing the world, Marley, and the people in it. I can't speak for Matthew at this time, but I can tell you that I have no interest whatsoever in becoming a mother again, either to your baby or to you, and that, I think, is how you're seeing me. You seem to be under the impression that it's my role to fix your problems, or correct the mistakes you've made, but I'm afraid I can't do that, not only because I don't even want to try, but because you have to do it for yourself. In fact, as I see it, it's time for you to grow the hell up and face how much heartache you've caused to me and my family since you came into our lives, and that you're now intending to inflict on your own child.'

Marley blinked as if in shock.

Cristy hadn't finished. 'Strangely, I don't think you're deliberately malicious or cruel – that doesn't seem to be in your nature – but these past few minutes have shown me that you're not only painfully naïve and self-centred, you are shockingly lacking in any kind of insight when it comes to other people's feelings.' She didn't add that it made her wonder how Marley did her job. It was a step too far, and anyway, the girl had a director and acting coach and God only knew who else helping her to get into character, so empathy might not have to be a strong point for her.

Marley's tears were flowing again. 'I'm sorry,' she sobbed, 'I didn't mean to upset you, I was just trying to find a solution that will work for us all.'

'You mean that works for you, and apparently with no serious consideration for how it would impact the lives of those you're trying to draw into this *solution*, as you call it. No thought to what any of us would have to give up in order to comply with your . . . *dream*. Worst of all, I don't think you have any idea of what it will be like to give that baby up when it comes, how likely it is to break your heart, to haunt you for the rest of your life. And if it doesn't have that effect on you, well, maybe you really shouldn't . . .' She stopped abruptly, aware that what she'd been about to say could push Marley down a road she really didn't want any responsibility for.

'Listen,' she said, more gently now – was she actually starting to feel sorry for the girl? She didn't have a mother to advise her (Cristy was still feeling insulted that Marley had actually tried to cast her in that role), and her father, the so-called Olivier of his time, was probably too involved in his own world to be overly concerned with his daughter's, especially now she was married to such a stable and capable man as Matthew Jennings. She'd clearly grown up with a skewed or at least completely different way of seeing the world than most, and that wasn't her fault. She was simply the way she was, and now she was doing her best to find a way through the mess she'd created when she'd got her own way over a man more than twice her age. 'You need to go home and talk this through with Matthew,' Cristy told her. 'Only he can help you decide what to do about your future together, but whatever you decide it can't involve me. I won't be coming to France to help you sort through it; in fact, I don't want to be part of the discussion even if it's here in Bristol.' Without really meaning to she added, 'Maybe, a couple of years ago, when I was so devastated by Matthew's betrayal, I'd have found myself considering any possible way to win him back, but that's not how it is now. I've moved on, my feelings for him have changed and while I still care for him deeply, it's really only as Hayley and Aiden's father, not as someone I want to share my life with.'

It wasn't until after Marley had gone, hugging her first and thanking her for her kindness and being such a wonderful human being (more proof that she didn't think the same way as most), that Cristy gave herself some time to consider her own words. Oddly, the fact that what she'd said was true – she really didn't want to share her life with Matthew again – made her want to cry. They were never going to get back what they'd once shared; it was all too broken, too steeped in the pain of betrayal ever to be good again. However, it didn't mean their memories would be any less precious, or that they couldn't be friends in the future, in spite of how much he annoyed her now.

He didn't deserve the hurt that was coming his way.

There again, maybe he did.

CHAPTER THIRTY-SIX

'Hi, Cristy here. I'm recording this the morning after David Gaudion was charged with the triple murder of his wife, mother-in-law and Serena Sutton. He's due to appear at the magistrate's court around ten o'clock and Connor is heading over there now in the hope of getting an interview after with Gaudion's barrister, Andrew Fogarty KC.

'Meantime, yours truly is on Queen Square in Bristol, a beautiful Georgian enclave close to the city centre, on my way to talk to Gaudion's defence solicitor.

'Unfortunately, there is much background we're still unable to bring you, for legal reasons, but as soon as that changes you'll be the first to know. And I want to assure you that we'll be staying on this case no matter what happens, bringing you as much as we can of the story behind the scenes.'

Turning off her handheld device, she came to a stop in front of the elegant townhouse she'd been directed to by Crouch's assistant – only a few doors from Quinn's lawyers – and, ignoring the rain, gave herself a moment to prepare for what might be coming next.

It hadn't been easy refocusing her thoughts after the extraordinary hour with Marley last night, especially when Matthew called wanting to know what it had all been about and the children kept WhatsApping, asking for updates. In the end she'd told them all that she'd been sworn to secrecy, but they'd find out soon enough – in Matthew's case from Marley herself; in Hayley and Aiden's, probably from their father.

411

It was the best she could do given her completely justified, in her opinion, determination not to become embroiled in the nightmare of it. In fact, she'd spent half the night doing her damnedest to put it out of her mind, and now, with an extremely intriguing meeting in front of her, she was finally having some success.

After checking to make sure she hadn't missed a message from Connor while recording – she hadn't – she pushed open the small black iron gate in front of the house and went to press the law firm's entryphone. A buzzer sounded, releasing the door, and as soon as she stepped into the hall a slim, boyish-looking man in a navy suit and pink tie came out of a side office to greet her.

'Mrs Ward,' he said, holding out a hand to shake. 'I'm Simon Wren, Mr Crouch's assistant. We spoke on the phone yesterday. Please come in, he's waiting for you.'

Following him into a spacious, well-equipped office with the typical high ceilings and decorative cornices of the Georgian era, Cristy received polite smiles of welcome from two secretaries busy at their computers and a moment later she was in a smaller, though no less elegant room where Edmond Crouch was already rising from an impressive antique desk to greet her. He was shorter than she'd expected, and seemed older than the photographs she'd seen of him, but appeared every bit as stern, until the hard lines of his features were faintly softened by a smile.

'Ms Ward, thank you for coming,' he said, gesturing for her to take a seat as Simon Wren closed the door behind them. 'I'm afraid this meeting will have to be brief. As I'm sure you already know, my client is appearing in front of the magistrate today, and I'd like to see him before he's taken into custody.'

Finding herself picturing Gaudion in the court, watching proceedings with those pale, impenetrable eyes of his, unable to utter a word as the formalities of remand and referral were gone through, she said, 'So no expectation of bail?' Of course she already knew the answer, but it seemed the right thing to ask.

'I'm afraid not. Can I get you a coffee? Tea perhaps?'

'No thanks, I'm fine. Just interested to know why you've finally agreed to see me now when I could hardly get an emailed reply from you before.'

Acknowledging that with no apparent discomfort, he said,

'I'm sure you understand that it isn't possible for me to speak to you about a case without the client's permission. That was never forthcoming in this instance. However, David has asked me to see you today in the hope of finding out what you might know that could help mitigate matters from his point of view.'

Cristy balked slightly as her eyes widened in surprise. 'What makes you think I know anything?' she countered. 'I've been getting all my updates from the news, so I'm as in the dark as anyone else regarding the actual detail of what's happening and why.'

Crouch nodded, almost as if he'd expected this answer. 'When I spoke to him last night,' he said, 'he seemed certain you'd be contacted by certain persons he'd named for you during your recent trip to Guernsey.'

Cristy regarded him steadily, not entirely sure how to answer that yet, although her preferred course was to be as truthful and upfront as she wished everyone would be with her.

'Have you been contacted?' Crouch urged.

She nodded. 'As a matter of fact, I have, by Liam MacAnany. And now I expect you want to know what the man said to me?'

Crouch smiled. 'That would have been my request had I not received an instruction from David this morning releasing me from my third-party role in the exchanges between the two of you.'

Cristy frowned, not sure she was following this very well. 'Exactly why am I here?' she asked, needing to have it spelled out.

'Simply so I can ask if you'd be willing to talk to David yourself.'

She blinked as her heart contracted. 'You mean in prison?' She'd meant to say person, but prison served just as well so she didn't correct herself.

'That's where he will be for the foreseeable future,' Crouch replied, 'most probably here in Bristol where they held him before. I can arrange the visit for you, but rather than take up valuable family time – his closest relatives will want to see him, of course, and he's keen to see them . . .'

'Including Rosaria?'

'Yes, I believe so. While she doesn't have a full understanding of what's happening, she will naturally want to see her father. So, as I was saying, I am going to try to arrange for you to visit him with me.'

She simply looked at him, having no idea what to say to that.

'I'm not sure yet that I can make it happen,' he continued, 'but if I can, please know that it has to be on the understanding that no recording can take place, and no reporting afterwards either, unless approved by myself or David.'

Still assimilating, while knowing she wasn't going to pass up an opportunity to speak directly with Gaudion, she said, 'When can we go?'

'Probably not until sometime next week at the earliest. There will be a lot of channels for me to go through to get you clearance, strings to pull, et cetera, but if, in the end, we can't make it happen, we'll use one of the family visits.'

She looked back at him, still taking it all in and trying to second-guess what Gaudion was hoping to get out of meeting her face to face. For an unsettling moment she found herself distracted by the thought of Jay Wells and Meena's warnings about falling for a man who'd been charged with murder and how badly it could end. Except this was different. For one thing she wasn't Gaudion's lawyer; nor, more importantly, was she falling for him. She was simply keen to see him for all the reasons any right-minded journalist would be.

'If I have your agreement,' Crouch ran on, 'I'll call as soon as I can get the consent we need. In the meantime, should you wish to be in touch with me, for any reason, you have my number. I assure you I will answer, or get back to you if you have to leave a message.'

And that was that. He had to leave now before his client was transported to the prison, but thank you for coming.

Minutes later Cristy was back out on the square and connecting to Connor. 'What news?' she asked as soon as he answered.

'Remanded in custody, as expected,' Connor replied. 'What about your end?'

Looking round as Crouch hurried out of the building and into a waiting car, she said, 'Apparently Gaudion wants to see me.'

'You're kidding!' Connor exclaimed in disbelief. 'When? How? Please tell me you said yes.'

'Of course I did. Crouch is going to let me know when. It could be as soon as next week.'

'This is bloody stupendous,' Connor cried excitedly.

'It would be even more so if we could record or report it, but I'm afraid we can't, not without their say-so. Anyway, maybe don't mention anything to Meena about it just yet, OK? She has some strange ideas going on regarding it all at the moment and if she hears about this she'll only be encouraged in her beliefs.'

'Which are?'

'You don't want to know.'

'Actually, I think I can guess. If I say Jay Wells am I getting warm?'

Sighing, Cristy said, 'You are, but please don't you start down that road as well, because this is an entirely different situation.'

'Not seeing how,' Connor responded, 'but OK, this is the last you'll hear of it from me.'

Realizing that he too had, for some reason, misinterpreted her interest in Gaudion, she rang off and tried to swallow down her frustration. What was the matter with people? Just because Gaudion was a personable man of around her age, and she was someone with no personal life to speak of, it really didn't follow that she was developing some extremely inappropriate sort of attachment to him. For his eldest daughter, maybe, and his mother, but they weren't him and nor were they in any way involved in what had happened at Kellon Manse sixteen years ago.

Still, none of that was important right now. What was, was the fact that she had absolutely no intention of trying to stand in the way of justice taking its course. So, if Gaudion had killed those three women, and it was looking more certain than ever that he had, then he was going to find out very soon that he was completely wrong if he thought he could use her in some way to try to pull off another miracle release from the legal process he was now trapped in.

CHAPTER THIRTY-SEVEN

More than two weeks passed before Cristy finally got a call from Emond Crouch asking if she could make herself available the following Thursday morning to accompany him to the prison. By then a lot had happened in her professional world, while in Matthew and Marley's fool's paradise it seemed as though nothing had at all.

They'd driven off to France together two days ago, him still not any the wiser as to why his wife and ex-wife had got together, and Marley, according to the texts she kept sending, continuing to hope that Cristy might join them. Cristy had to wonder what the woman was on to make her so bewilderingly convinced it was even a remote possibility; however, she knew better than to ask, or to engage at all if she didn't want to open up an unstoppable floodgate of persuasion.

Fortunately the children had stopped pestering her for 'the goss', as they called it, although both had sworn to get it out of her the next time they saw her – or out of Marley while they were in France.

Cristy could only hope that Marley didn't confide in them before speaking to Matthew, although given how strangely the woman seemed to be wired, she knew there was a chance she would.

Still, that was their problem to deal with almost a thousand miles away. Her focus, here in Bristol, since meeting Crouch at the Queen Square office, had been on getting the next two podcasts together. Although they hadn't been able to add anything new for the time being, they'd used the time to recap, comment and speculate on what could happen next, and what it might say about the original case if this time around Gaudion did go to trial and was found guilty.

One interesting, although terribly sad development, had materialized when Clover had gone to talk to Wendy Grails, the caller who'd kept insisting Amelia was dead. It turned out the poor woman had had a daughter with the same name, who'd been taken by her father, David Grails, and stabbed to death in a wood near the ten-year-old girl's home. Clearly it was the similarities in names, location and age that had triggered a reaction in Wendy, whose ex-husband, now serving a life sentence, had later been diagnosed with severe mental health issues. Wendy, apparently, was similarly afflicted, and was receiving little in the way of support, although she lived with a sister these days who'd apologized profusely for Wendy's calls when Clover showed up, and hoped they hadn't put the *Hindsight* team to too much trouble.

There had been no more contact from MacAnany since the day of Gaudion's arrest; however, Olivia had been in touch by email a week after her brother-in-law was remanded in custody. She'd wanted Cristy to pass a message to Cynthia letting her know that she, Rosaria and Anna, would be welcome to stay at her home if they were intending to visit Gaudion. *Please be sure to tell her how very much I'd love to see them all again*, she'd added, and Cristy had almost felt the longing coming off the screen.

Of course she'd forwarded the invitation to Cynthia, and had added a message of her own asking the old lady simply to let her know if they were all OK. So far neither she nor Olivia had received a reply.

It wasn't until Crouch's call came to confirm her visit could go ahead that Cristy really allowed herself to believe it would happen. Neither she nor Connor had mentioned it to the others yet, had simply been waiting to find out whether or not Crouch could pull it off the way he'd hoped. It could so easily be overtaken by other developments, or worse, Gaudion might change his mind and decide he didn't want to see her after all. She could only wish that the wait for news hadn't made her feel so ridiculously like a teenager willing the damned phone to ring.

417

However, the call had come, and it was now Thursday morning and Connor was driving her along the Gloucester Road to Horfield where Crouch would apparently be waiting at the barrier outside the prison. Fortunately, the heavy rain overnight had stopped about an hour ago, so no umbrellas necessary, and the sun was doing its best to peek through the dense mass of morose grey cloud. So much for mid-summer – August was turning into a wash out and the forecast wasn't all that great either. Still, she could hardly have cared less about the weather as Connor turned into Cambridge Road and came to a stop outside the huge concrete and red-brick monstrosity that had no place in the middle of a built-up residential area.

'I'll find somewhere to park,' he told her. 'Text me when you're leaving and I'll come pick you up.'

'Thanks,' she said, glad he couldn't see the nervous flutterings she was experiencing inside.

Spotting Crouch at the barrier, she got out of the car. Luckily Connor had no way of knowing that she was thinking about Jay Wells now, her friend the lawyer who'd come regularly to this very prison to see the killer she'd fallen in love with. As far as Cristy knew, Edward Blake was serving his sentence at Guy's Marsh in Dorset – maybe Jay was a visitor there these days.

What hell it must be to fall in love with a man who'd killed his wife and was now serving a life sentence.

'Ms Ward,' Crouch said, pocketing his phone as he came to greet her. 'Thanks for being prompt. I can't promise we won't be made to wait – it's what usually happens, I'm afraid. I take it you don't have any hidden recording devices on you? Security will pick them up if you have . . .'

'I haven't,' Cristy assured him, slightly irritated that he thought she'd be so foolish.

'Good. Is there anything you'd like to ask before we go in?'

In spite of feeling there ought to be, she couldn't seem to think of anything, so she countered with, 'Is there anything you'd like to tell me?'

His smile was small. 'I'll let David do the talking. He's grateful you're here, as am I.' Touching a hand to her elbow, he steered her towards the main door. 'Andrew Fogarty, his barrister, had

418

hoped to be here,' he said as they were allowed entry, 'but he's in court today, so I'll brief him later.'

The clearance process involved several phone calls and even more assurances from Crouch that all was in order, followed by a thorough security screening and body search. She could see Crouch was becoming impatient, until finally they were allowed upstairs to wait in a small glass walled cube that allowed them to see, though not hear, other lawyers and their clients in neighbouring boxes.

'We have an hour,' Crouch said, checking his watch, 'and already they've used up half of it with all their nonsense.'

Cristy looked up as the door opened and she felt one small, swift blow hit her heart. Gaudion was every bit the same as he'd been before: tall, powerfully built, seeming to exude the kind of presence that dominated a room – or maybe today his self-assurance was a front, an effort not to be diminished by his surroundings. His movements as he shook Crouch's hand first, then Cristy's, were easy, assertive even. His grip was firm but not overly so; nevertheless, she found herself wondering if it was the hand of a killer.

'Thanks for coming,' he said, and took a chair the other side of the table. She noticed that his pale eyes seemed somehow darker and were shadowed by fatigue, and his fading tan made his pallor seem perhaps more drawn than it really was. 'We don't have long,' he said, 'so I'll get straight to it. I'm sure you've heard about the phone records they used to get me here?'

Cristy nodded.

'They're mine from two weeks before the killings, and the day of. Apparently, they show three calls to the same number that, so they're telling us, showed up in another crime committed a few weeks after Lexie and the others were murdered. In that case it was aggravated assault and was carried out by someone called Wayne Ryall.'

As the name meant nothing to her, Cristy waited for him to continue.

'The police have managed to identify the person who sent you photographs of the scene at Kellon Manse as Wayne Ryall,' he told her.

She tensed with shock.

Gaudion continued, 'Apparently, Ryall has been in and out of prison for most of his adult life, mainly for petty crimes, until he was sentenced to eight years in late 2008 for the assault I just mentioned. This was increased to fourteen years for offences committed while in prison. He was released eighteen months ago and seems to have stayed below the radar since, only to resurface when your podcast began.'

Cristy swallowed – sobered by the thought of how far-reaching their broadcasts could be, of what they could actually stir from the shadows that they had no idea was lurking.

'It's our assumption,' he continued, 'and the police agree, that he took the photographs at Kellon Manse to send as proof he'd carried out his instructions, but apparently he kept them, presumably as some kind of insurance for later, which he's now calling in by sending them to you. I'm guessing he asked for something in return.'

She nodded and looked from one man's intense gaze to the other's, needing a moment to process this. 'We haven't given him anything,' she assured them. 'It's our policy not to, but we weren't able to contact him after anyway.'

'And he hasn't been in touch again?' Crouch prompted.

She shook her head. 'If the police know it was him who sent them, why don't they just arrest him?' she asked, guessing it was a stupid question, but she needed it out there anyway.

'They can't find him,' Gaudion replied, 'but obviously there's a pretty intense search going on right now, not least because they want him to confirm that it was me who hired him and who he sent the photos to back in 2008. If he admits it, he could find himself with a more lenient sentence.'

Her voice was slightly hoarse as she decided to spell out her understanding of what had been said so far. 'So they think you paid him and now they've tied the number on your phone records to one that was used by him . . .' She swallowed dryly.

'I don't know how that number came to be on the log,' he told her quietly, 'but I do know that I never rang the man, not even once. Until they started questioning me I'd never even heard of him.'

'But the records can't lie – can they?'

'No, they can't. Only people do that, such as those who have more contacts than anyone would ever need to make things happen in their favour. So you could say this is another example of how far MacAnany and his friends will go to protect themselves.'

'Are you saying they've doctored your phone records?' she asked incredulously.

'That's exactly what I'm saying.'

Seeing the contradiction right away – that they'd been at pains to keep him out of prison before, but were now apparently trying to put him there – she started to point it out, but he was speaking again.

'I'm sure I heard on your podcast,' he said, 'that you'd been told my case file was missing, and yet suddenly it's come to light again right when the police reopen investigations.'

'And you're saying these three calls have been added?'

He nodded. 'If they'd been there before,' he said, 'don't you think someone would have asked me about them at the time?'

It was a good point – why hadn't they? *If* they'd been there. Except they'd had nothing to match the number to at the time of the killings; that had only come later and maybe the process simply hadn't been carried out.

'And, if I was behind the murders,' he continued, 'would I really have been stupid enough to use my own phone to contact the man I'd hired to commit them?'

Sitting back in her chair, she glanced at Crouch again, knowing that it was his apparent belief in these false phone records that was, at least in part, helping to keep her on board. 'So how,' she asked, 'are you going to prove that the log has been tampered with?'

'We're working on it,' Crouch assured her, 'and we also have our own people looking for Ryall. MacAnany and his crew aren't the only ones with friends in low places – most lawyers have them, especially those of us working in crime.' Checking the time, he said, 'Are you willing to share what Ryall said in his message to you?'

Since there seemed no reason not to, she said, 'He told us that he was there when the murders happened, and we wondered if that meant he hadn't acted alone.'

Gaudion and Crouch exchanged confused glances. 'Anna only saw one man,' Gaudion said. 'If anyone else had been there she'd have seen them too, I'm sure of it, but obviously I'll get her to confirm it.'

Thinking of how wretched this must be for his younger daughter, having to be put through it all again, and with her father where he was, she found herself wishing she knew how to help her, but of course she couldn't.

'What else did Ryall say in his message?' Crouch prompted.

'He wanted to be paid, obviously, you already know that, but then, in a later message, he told us to go ahead and contact the police if we wanted to, it didn't bother him, but we'd lose our exclusive if we did.'

Crouch said to Gaudion, 'Why wouldn't it bother him to involve the police?'

Gaudion shook his head, clearly having no answer for that. He turned back to Cristy. 'Have the police interviewed you, or any of your team yet?'

'I'm sure they'll get round to it,' she replied, 'but before we go any further, I'd like to ask you something. It's probably not significant, but it's bothering me slightly and I'd like to clear it up. I remember taking a conscious decision when I was in Guernsey not to show you the crime-scene photos I'd received, so have you seen them now?'

Gaudion looked strained as he nodded. 'I saw them at the time,' he told her, 'but yes, I've seen the ones sent to you with the masked man in the mirror – who, for the record, is not me.'

She held his gaze, not wanting to admit that she'd considered it, but clearly he'd guessed it anyway.

'I'm sure,' he said, seeming to take no offence, 'when the police first received the shots you forwarded, they assumed I was in the mask, but now, thanks to the number, they're assuming it was Ryall. As they see it, I called him that morning to give the go-ahead for him to act. Once again, I have to ask, would I really have used my own phone?'

'Surely you've asked them that?'

Gaudion almost smiled. 'Of course, but in these sorts of circumstances they're under no obligation to provide answers.'

'But they must see the logic of what you're saying?'

'You'd think so, but maybe there's something else going on that we still don't know about.'

Hoping for his sake there wasn't since this was surely enough, she said, 'What do you want us to do if this Ryall contacts us again? I can't think that he will, given everything that's out there now, but just in case.'

'We're hoping,' Gaudion said, 'that you might find a way of reaching him through the podcast, say something that might encourage him to get in touch. He's the only one who can tell us who paid him.'

Her eyes widened. It made sense, of course, but off the top of her head she had no idea how they'd do it; however, she could at least give it some thought. And it surely meant, didn't it, that Gaudion wasn't behind it if he was so eager to know the identity of who was? 'And in the unlikely event it works?' she said. 'Do you want us to pay him?'

Crouch jumped in. 'We cannot be seen to be bribing a witness,' he told her, 'so no money must change hands under any circumstances.'

Relieved about that, she turned back to Gaudion as he said, 'If you do hear from him, you must report it to the police, but we'd appreciate it if you told us too. Actually, the same goes for MacAnany, should he happen to raise his head again.'

'Do you think he will?'

'I've no idea, but it's possible if he feels there's a reason to exert some sort of pressure.'

Not relishing the prospect one bit, she said, 'He told me something the last time I saw him that I need to ask you about.'

Gaudion cocked his head, an encouragement to continue.

'He told me you were there when Lexie was raped.'

His eyes closed as he dropped his head in his hands and gave a low growl of frustration. 'Please tell me you didn't believe him,' he said, looking at her again.

'I didn't want to,' she admitted, 'and—'

'He'll know what Olivia's told you,' he reminded her, 'which is presumably what he or O'Malley fed her in the first place, and now he's reiterating it to keep sowing the doubt. If it helps, I'll say it again, I was not there when Lexie was attacked. I didn't even know about it until my mother called to tell me to come home as soon as I could.'

'But it was Lexie who told Olivia you were there.'

He shook his head. 'Lexie didn't tell her that. I know we can't call on Lexie to confirm that now, but I assure you she didn't. Olivia just . . . Well, we discussed this before, these accusations of hers only started after her therapy with O'Malley. It's one of the reasons, perhaps the main reason, we haven't had any contact with her.'

Taking that in, she said, 'So you returned to the Vale when your mother asked you to and then, after finding out what had happened to Lexie, you married her?'

'A few months later, yes, because I loved her and wanted to keep her safe.'

She stared back at him and found herself, perhaps for the first time, considering just how terrible it must all have been for him if he was telling the truth. And still was. Before she could go any further with the thought, or ask anything else, the door opened and they were informed that their time was up.

Gaudion rose to his feet. 'Thanks again for coming,' he said, reaching over to shake her hand. 'Can I call you?'

'Yes, of course,' she replied, without thinking. 'Do you still have my number?'

'I'll make sure he gets it,' Crouch said. 'I'll be in touch,' he told Gaudion, going to slap him on the back, 'and try not to worry, we'll get this sorted.'

Cristy waited until they were outside on the street, alongside the barrier, before saying to Crouch, 'You really believe he didn't do it, don't you?'

'I do,' the lawyer confirmed. 'I know what he's up against, and I also know how difficult it will be to prove those phone records are false, but I'm going to do my damnedest.'

'Here's what I don't get,' she said. 'Last time they used their influence to get your client out of a trial, presumably in exchange for not connecting their names to a rape accusation, even if it couldn't be proven. Now, according to you, they're trying to get him sent to prison for life. That's one hell of a one-eighty, so what's changed?'

'It's a good question,' he told her, 'and the first answer is that your podcast has clearly shaken things up in ways that are probably still playing out. The second is that all of us working on David's team believe that Ryall's contact with you is key to finding out what's really going on. And that would be a lot easier if we could find the man himself.'

'Shit,' Connor swore under his breath as Cristy finished telling him about the visit. 'It's blowing my mind to think they can get to phone records like that. Do you believe it?'

'His lawyer seems to,' she countered, still undecided about it herself.

'If it's true,' he said, 'you know what it tells us, don't you? That someone on the inside is being worked again.'

Not disagreeing, she flipped up the vanity mirror after checking to see if she was as pale as she felt. The past half an hour had been far more draining than she'd realized until she and Connor had driven away from the prison. 'So apparently,' she said, 'they "located" the missing case files and slipped in the new phone records, either before, or after, Trevor Thompson reopened the case. Personally, I'd like to think he's one of the good guys, and if I'm right the convenient discovery would have been before he took over, but at a time when they knew it was going to happen. If it was after, and he's in on it, well . . . God knows where that's going to lead us.'

'Unless Gaudion decides to open up about the rape. All sorts of shit would hit the fan then. So, I have to ask myself, why doesn't he?'

Wishing she'd asked Gaudion that very question while she was there, she said, 'Maybe because proving it now, after all this time and with Lexie gone, just isn't possible. Also, it would hurt Gaudion's daughters and he won't want that.'

'Not even to save his own skin?'

'He's obviously trying to do it another way first, but even his lawyer thinks the chances of them proving those phone records were doctored are vanishingly small.'

'Then I guess I have to say good luck to him, and meantime we have to try and come up with a way to reach out to this Wayne Ryall character through the pod?'

Nodding, she said, 'We'll have to couch it in the right terms so only he will know we're talking to him. What we won't know is if, or when, he hears it, unless he goes for it right away, of course. I don't think he will, personally. He'll think it's some sort of police trap, and who could blame him when it kind of is. Not set by them, obviously, but we're not being asked to hold back from them if he does get in touch.'

'Nothing wrong with flying blind,' Connor commented cryptically as they pulled into the car park outside the office. 'So, do we tell the others about your visit now?'

She nodded. 'I think we have to if we're going to formulate some sort of hook for Ryall. Anyway, I don't like holding back on them, and now we know what it was about there's no reason not to share.'

'Even with Meena?'

She shot him a look and started to get out of the car. 'By the way,' she said, turning back, 'I've told Gaudion he can call me, so read into that what you will.'

He laughed. 'I'm just a bloke,' he reminded her, 'I don't read anything into anything where women are concerned. I usually find it's safer.'

Later, after a lengthy and useful team discussion about her visit to Gaudion followed by the floating of ideas on how to reel in Ryall, Cristy decided to walk home in spite of the rain. Sometimes, in the small personal space of an umbrella, with the world going about its business around her and with little to distract her, she found it easier to think than when she was in front of a computer, or brainstorming with the others.

This evening was no exception. In fact, she was so caught up in her thoughts about Gaudion and the many conflicting instincts and beliefs she had where he was concerned that she didn't realize at first that her mobile was ringing.

Wondering if it was him, already, she dug the phone out of her cross-body purse and saw, to her surprise and relief, that it was Cynthia's name on the screen.

'Hi,' she said warmly, 'I've been hoping to hear from you. How are you, if it's not a silly question.'

'I'm fine,' Cynthia replied, sounding tired, but at least not overwrought, although Cristy suspected she was. 'I just wanted to thank you for going to see David today. It meant a lot to him, to us all, actually. I hope he's managed to make things clearer for you, and that maybe he's . . . Won you over? Sorry, you don't have to answer that, but the fact that you're going to try to contact that man . . .'

'Even if we do, there's no telling whether or not he'll respond to our message, or that he'll say what we want to hear if he does get in touch.'

Sounding dejected, Cynthia said, 'No, I suppose not, but at least it's a start, and David has great faith in you, you know.'

Cristy hesitated in her step, thrown, and then wondering if Gaudion had told his mother to say that.

'Sorry if that sounds like pressure,' Cynthia continued, 'it's not meant to be; it's just that after listening to your podcasts, which he did, avidly . . . Well, he has a lot of respect for you. As do I. Naturally we'd have preferred them not to have happened at all, but it was always going to one day, and so we consider ourselves fortunate that it was someone like you who took it on.'

Someone like her?

'Tell me, if you don't mind,' Cynthia said, 'how did he seem when you saw him today? Is he holding up, do you think? I worry about him all the time.'

'Of course you do,' Cristy said sympathetically, 'and honestly, he seemed fine. At little stressed perhaps, which is only to be expected, but it's possible you and his children are a bigger concern to him than anything else.'

'Yes, I'm sure we are, but I keep telling him we're OK. Ronald and his family are taking good care of us here on Exmoor. It's a long drive to go and see him, but not as long as if we'd stayed in Guernsey.'

'You know Olivia is happy for you to stay with her? It's much closer to Bristol.'

'Dear girl, it's very kind of her, but this isn't the right time, not with the things she's been saying about David. I know she doesn't mean any harm, that she wouldn't be doing it if she hadn't been spun a web of lies by her husband and father-in-law, that O'Malley man as well. He was so good with what he did for Lexie, but what they've done to Olivia . . . Still, there's no point going into it all again now. As I said, I just wanted to say thank you for seeing David.'

'How are the children?'

'Yes, yes, they're OK. Laurent's gone back to his mother in Paris, the girls are here with me. Rosaria's not herself though, poor lamb. Not that you'd expect her to be, going through something like this all over again. She's very sad and afraid and all she wants to do is talk to her father. Anna's on the phone to him at the moment. She's the strongest amongst us, but it's hitting her hard too. By the way, she's not as angry with you as she was. David had words with her, and now she knows you've been to see him . . . Well, it's made a difference, let's say that, but like the rest of us, Richard included, none of us finds it easy to tear ourselves away when we go to see him. It's terrible having to leave him in that place. It's all wrong, Cristy, really it is. We just have to find a way of making it right.'

'Of course,' Cristy agreed, 'and thankfully he has a great legal team, very supportive and loyal.'

'Yes, his brother, Richard, was at university with Edmond, so they go way back.'

'Is Richard with you now?'

'Yes, he is, and Astrid, his wife. They'll have to go home at the weekend, they've both got work on Monday, but it's lovely to have them here. Oh, Anna's shouting for me – shame that girl has to do everything so loudly, but I expect David wants to talk to me before he has to ring off. Thanks for listening to me ramble on, and please call if you have time. David wants us to be in touch with you now that he's seen you.'

It was only as she rang off that Cristy realized she'd come to a stop outside the River Station, a restaurant that had once been a favourite with her and Matthew. Passing it without remembering the happy times they'd shared there had always been impossible, and apparently it still was; however, it didn't seem to hurt quite as much any more. It was simply making her think about Gaudion and what his meal might have been this evening, and whether or not he'd call her after he'd finished speaking to his family.

CHAPTER THIRTY-EIGHT

It was early on Sunday evening when Gaudion rang, catching Cristy in a tetchy mood after she'd spent the entire afternoon dealing with a mountain of paperwork, always an onerous task and how did so much of it pile up in such a short space of time? Hearing his voice was a welcome distraction; now she could put it all aside and focus on him.

'Is this a good time?' he asked. 'Sorry if I'm interrupting . . .'

'You're really not,' she assured him, closing her laptop, 'it's a very good time. How are you?'

'I guess OK, considering. Mum told me she'd thanked you for coming to see me, time for me to do the same.'

'You did, when I was there,' she reminded him, 'and there was no need. It gave me some . . . clarity, I guess, although there's still some way to go.'

'Indeed, but Edmond Crouch is one of the best, and he has a great team around him. Can I assume that if you'd heard anything from Ryall you'd have let him know by now?'

'Of course, and we haven't, but we're seeing Edmond tomorrow to discuss how to try and reel Ryall in. We thought his input would be useful.'

'Is it going to be in your next podcast?'

'That's the intention.'

'I guess the important, and probably most difficult part, will be trying to avoid it coming over as a trap. Have you done your own research on him by now?'

'We're still on it, but so far we've only come up with what you already know – born 1980, making him forty-four; grew up in Harold Hill, Essex; no further education following school;

first arrest aged fifteen for a stabbing that got accepted as self-defence; several more arrests for petty crime, three prison terms for theft and drug offences before the aggravated assault that landed him inside for almost fifteen years. No address for him currently, but he has to be living somewhere and on something, unless he's being taken care of by other parties, thereby allowing him to stay under the radar. Obviously, we're seriously hoping that isn't the case or we're unlikely ever to hear from him.'

'What gives me hope is that he made contact with you in the first place. That suggests he's calling his own shots, or he was then – and I could have phrased that better.'

With a small smile, she said, 'You've seen his mug shots, presumably, so you don't recognize him?'

'I have and no, I don't recall ever seeing him before.'

Picking up on how sad he sounded, as though he might be losing heart, she said quietly, 'We'll find him, or the police will, so don't give up.'

'I'm not doing that,' he assured her, 'but as you said, there's still a way to go and I'd be a fool if I weren't bracing myself for whatever might come next. As if this isn't already enough.'

Feeling the awfulness of his situation, the dread that must fill his every hour, the fear that he wouldn't be able to fight it off this time, she said, 'I was wondering if you'd be OK with me mentioning my visit during our next episode? I realize we won't be able to reveal a lot of what was discussed, but maybe the fact that you're willing to talk to us at all might help things along in some way.'

Sighing, he said, 'If you don't think it'll put Ryall off taking the bait, I see no reason not to.'

'Of course we'd have to keep that in mind, but we'll talk to your lawyer about it tomorrow and make a decision then. Obviously, the most important thing is connecting with Ryall.'

'Who, let's not forget, might be of no use to us at all if he's now decided to turn to MacAnany for funding.'

Hearing the note of despondency in his voice again, she said gently, 'We don't know if that's the case, so let's try to keep positive. Now, tell me, when did you last see your family?'

Going with the change of subject, he said, 'They came yesterday.'

'And how was it?'

After a pause he said, 'It's hard seeing Rosie so upset when it comes time to leave. She arrives all sunshine and smiles, is lovely and chatty while she's here and then it all falls apart at the end. She weeps like a banshee and the other visitors aren't always kind. Anna's very good with her, always has been, but I can see how much she's struggling too. And as for Mum . . . Just thank God Richard is around for her to lean on, and her brother, of course.'

'Are they staying on Exmoor until the trial?' she asked, and instantly wished she could take it back. 'If things get that far,' she hastily added.

'They'll have to go home to Guernsey soon, and it'll be good for them to be surrounded by our friends and family there. They'll receive a lot of support.'

As she imagined it, she belatedly realized that she could hear no other voices coming from his end, no background noise at all in fact. 'I don't know much about making calls from where you are,' she said, 'but you sound as though you're alone, with no one around you?'

'There's some football match on that everyone wanted to watch,' he explained, 'so the phones are free, at least for now, so I thought it was a good time to try you.'

'I'm glad you did, and I'm only sorry I don't have any useful news to share, but that's going to change, I feel sure of it, and hopefully for the better. Have you spoken to your family today?'

'Richard's taking them out for a meal this evening; they deserve a treat, all of them, so I guess you could say I'm home alone.'

She couldn't quite smile.

'What about your family?' he asked. 'Are they with you?'

Looking at the photos on the mantel, she said, 'The children are in France with their father for the next couple of weeks.'

'Do you mind?'

'No, as long as I don't allow myself to remember the times we spent there as a family.' She was glad he couldn't see her now

432

as she poured herself a glass of wine; it might seem insensitive when he was unable to do the same.

'Can I ask how old your children are?'

Understanding his need to focus on something else for a while, she said, 'Hayley, my daughter, is nineteen, studying International Relations and French at Edinburgh, and Aiden was sixteen last month.'

'Do you miss them when they're not around?'

'More than I'd admit to them, but they rang this morning and we had a very long chat about not very much.'

He laughed. 'I know those chats,' he said, and she felt warmed by the reminder that he was a father who loved his children too. 'And what about your ex?' he prompted. 'Are you on good terms with him, when he isn't upsetting you?'

Remembering how she'd told him that everything about Matthew upset her, she chuckled and said, 'We have an extremely strange situation going on at the moment, one I certainly didn't see coming, and right now I don't have the first idea what to do about it.'

'Well, it seems I've still got time,' he said, 'so if you want to talk about it . . .'

Seeing no reason not to, she sank into a sofa with her drink and stretched out her legs as she began recounting her last two encounters with Matthew and Marley.

Maybe it was because the rain had stopped and the sun was breaking through the clouds and a cooling breeze was blowing into the stuffy room that she felt herself relaxing as she talked openly and freely, and in a way she hadn't for far too long. Or perhaps it was because he was a stranger, and a good listener, that she was sharing so much, allowing the words to pour out of her as if even they were relieved they'd finally found her voice. She became aware of feeling lighter, easier in herself, as if she was letting go of a burden she hadn't even known she was carrying.

Then they were laughing at the absurdity of her ex-husband's new wife seeing her as some sort of mother figure which was outrageous, insulting, and yet hilarious.

In the end he said, 'I'm sorry, I have to go, but I've enjoyed this. Thank you.'

'Thanks for listening,' she responded, 'and sorry if I went on too long . . .'

'You didn't, but I have to give the phone up now. Good luck with Edmond in the morning. I'll call again when I can.'

After he'd gone she continued to sit where she was, holding the phone in her lap and trying to sort out how she was feeling about the way she'd just opened up to him, without actually meaning to, at least not to the extent that she had. It had felt as though they were old friends with the easiest rapport, instead of . . . What were they exactly? Was there a way to describe their relationship (for want of a more appropriate word, maybe affiliation was better) that didn't cast her as some sort of media predator and him the prey? It wasn't how she saw him, and surely he didn't see her that way either. However, there was certainly a truth to it, and she couldn't help wondering, now she could no longer hear his voice or his laughter, wasn't waiting for his response or enjoying his humour, if he'd just used some sort of manipulative power to draw her to him, to make sure she continued onside to help him escape his nightmare.

Jay Wells knew to her cost just how charming and controlling a killer could be; but she wasn't Jay Wells, and Gaudion wasn't a killer, she was convinced of that now. He simply wasn't.

It was Tuesday evening and Edmond Crouch had joined them in the production office to listen to the closing minutes of the latest episode. It had been decided that Connor should try speaking to Ryall, man-to-man as it were; maybe the chumminess would have a better chance of eliciting a response, although no one was hugely optimistic about it working at all.

CONNOR: 'So that's about it for this week's pod. We're sorry we couldn't bring you Cristy's recent chat with David Gaudion – not very surprisingly the prison authorities wouldn't allow her to record it – but I hope her report gave you some insight into the man and how he's coping with his time in custody. He is, as you no doubt gathered, still adamant that he was in no way involved in the Kellon Manse Murders.

434

'Now, before we go I want to reach out to someone who sent us some extremely interesting photos a couple of weeks ago. You'll know who you are if you're listening. We've tried getting back to you, mate, but no luck so far, so if you'd like to get in touch again, I think you'll find it'll be to our mutual benefit. You have my number; I can meet you wherever you choose, and be sure that anything you tell me will stay between us if that's how you want it to be.'

'Do you really think he's going to fall for the confidentiality line?' Meena said, once he'd stopped the playback.

'Probably not,' Cristy replied, 'but there was no harm in putting it in. If nothing else, it might encourage someone else to come forward who we don't even know about yet.'

'Will Gaudion hear this, where he is?' Harry asked Crouch.

'I'll take it when I next visit,' Crouch replied. 'Have you contacted the police?' he asked Cristy. 'Do they know we're trying to connect with Ryall?'

'They do now, if any of them are listening,' she responded, watching Jodi smoothing her bump and thinking of Marley and of how things might be progressing in France. No news is good news, she kept trying to tell herself.

'OK, well, thanks for doing this,' Crouch said, getting to his feet. 'It's a long shot, that's for sure, but we're all for taking them with so much at stake.'

The first non-troll, non-smart-ass response they had to Connor's request came three days later, when Liam MacAnany's trusty messenger fell into step with Cristy as she walked past the M Shed towards the studios.

'Mr MacAnany would like to speak to you,' he told her, hopping over a puddle.

'Would he?' she responded, keeping up her pace and not bothering to look at him.

He held out a mobile phone and gestured for her to take it.

Realizing MacAnany must be on the other end, she stopped and put it to her ear. 'How can I help you, Mr MacAnany?' she said coldly.

'Your latest podcast,' he replied.

'What about it?'

'You were, or are, trying to make contact with someone. Can I ask if you've been successful yet?'

Realizing if Ryall was under this man's protection he'd surely already know the answer to that, she said, 'Why does it matter to you?'

'Everything about what you're doing matters to me. What are the photographs of?'

Experiencing more surprise, and now a deepening suspicion, she said, 'I'm afraid we're not sharing that information at this time.'

'I think it would be in your interest to do so.'

She blinked. 'Excuse me. Was that some sort of threat?'

He laughed. 'It was an offer, actually. If you're prepared to share the photographs with me, or even tell me what they're of, ways can be found to be equally helpful to you, perhaps not now, but in the future.'

It had taken a moment, but she finally realized he was afraid the photos were from the night of Lexie's rape, if such photos even existed. Hoping she wasn't going to live to regret what she was about to say, considering his reach, she said, 'I don't foresee a time when we'll need your help, thank you,' and promptly passed the phone back to the messenger.

'So could there be any photos of what happened at Oxford?' she asked Gaudion when he called later for the second time since Sunday.

'I've never seen or heard of any,' he replied, 'but the man's obviously worried, so maybe something does exist. Did he mention anything about Ryall's photos?'

'No, nothing.'

'And still no word from Ryall himself?'

'I'm afraid not.'

Sighing with frustration, he said, 'Have you told Edmond about MacAnany's call?'

'Yes. He thinks more or less the same as you, that MacAnany's nervous, and it could be because he doesn't know where Ryall is either. That's kind of good news for us, but only if Ryall does decide to get in touch.'

'And we have no way of knowing if he's even heard the podcast yet.'

Taking the point, she swivelled her chair to look at his photo on the wall behind her and was aware of how different it seemed now she'd actually met and spoken to him. There was no longer a pervading menace to it, no sense of him watching or listening; it was simply an old photograph of someone she was getting to know. 'How's today been?' she asked, wanting to get him onto a more cheerful subject, if that was even possible considering where he was. 'Did you have any visitors?'

'None today,' he replied, 'but Richard's coming tomorrow and bringing Laurent.'

'Your son.' She hardly wanted to think about how difficult that was going to be.

'I've no idea how long I'm going to be in here,' he said, 'so he has to start dealing with it before he goes back to school.'

'Are you two close?' she asked.

'Yes. He's upset about being shut out of this already, so after they've been here Richard is taking him to Exmoor to be with his sisters before they all travel back to Guernsey together.'

Thinking of how difficult it was going to be for him when they left with no more visits, only phone calls, she considered offering to go and see him herself, but now wasn't the right time to mention it. Instead she said, 'I'm sorry there's still no news to share with you, but obviously as soon as we have any I'll make sure it gets to you. And you can call any time. I'm always here, at the end of the phone.'

'Thanks,' he said. 'Good to know. Now, let's forget me for a while, shall we, and talk about what's happening in France? Has Marley broken her big news yet?'

'I'm guessing not or I'm sure Matthew would have been in touch.'

'Well, I have to admit, I can't see how they're going to work it out, unless of course you go along with it and have a reunion with—'

'Not going to happen,' she assured him quickly. 'Maybe once, when the break-up was still fresh, but after everything we've been through, that he put me through . . . You know, it makes me sad to say it, which is a bit crazy in itself, but we really are in the past now. Too much damage has been done, too little respect is left – for him, I mean, not for myself. I'd lose all mine if I were to go back to him, and I want that even less than I want the baby, which I don't want at all.'

With a laugh he said, 'I can still hardly believe she thought you might . . .'

'And at my age, after bringing up two of my own and only just getting to grips with what it's like to have my freedom again.' Her eyes closed as she heard herself a beat too late. 'Sorry,' she groaned. 'I didn't mean—'

'It's OK. I understand what you're saying, and I'm glad for you it's how you're feeling. Hang on . . . All right,' he said as someone yelled in his ear to *get off the fucking phone.*

Hating that he was being spoken to like that, and knowing he'd hate that she'd heard it, she said, 'I'll let you go, but call again whenever you want to, even if it's not about your case. I enjoy talking to you.'

Before handing over the phone he said, 'There's not a lot that makes me feel good at the moment, but that just did. Thank you.'

CHAPTER THIRTY-NINE

The next two weeks passed with virtually no new developments in spite of Cristy and Connor's appearances on both TV and radio asking again for 'their listener with the photographs' to be in touch. Of course, it caused much speculation in the public and media alike, while they, along with Crouch and his team, remained acutely aware of what a poisoned chalice finding the man could turn out to be when they had no knowledge of what he might say, but that was a problem they'd have to deal with when, if, they came to it.

The only positive aspect of it all at the moment was the fact that the police hadn't caught up with him either.

On the other hand, if he had returned to MacAnany's protection it was likely they'd never hear from him again.

By now Clover and Jackson had been re-assigned to another pod on the understanding they could return to *Hindsight* as soon as they were able to go live again. Although they'd expected the hiatus – such pauses often happened during the course of these sorts of podcast – it was hard letting them go. However, they continued to pop in all the time and would no doubt continue to do so for as long as Cristy and Connor were cleared to remain in the production office.

Their whole focus now was on assisting Edmond Crouch and his investigators to find Wayne Ryall.

Because she was speaking to Gaudion fairly regularly, Cristy knew from him, as well as from Cynthia who was emailing her own occasional updates, that the family had now returned to Guernsey. This left Gaudion with only his lawyer and brother as visitors, so Cristy had arranged to go herself the following week. She wanted to see him, very much in fact, and sensed that he was equally keen to see her, although neither of them had put that into words. They mostly talked about his situation, or Matthew and Marley, who were now in crisis following Marley's announcement of her bonkers plan for their future. According to Matthew, she, Cristy, should get herself down to the Riviera asap to help sort things out.

As she had no intention of doing any such thing, she'd told him so in no uncertain terms, but it didn't stop him demanding it on virtually a daily basis, or the children from saying they were being driven crazy by all the drama.

Best stay away Hayley had advised in one of their WhatsApp chats. *They're supposed to be grown-ups so let them sort it out.*

Aiden added, *I told the Matt-man that he's the prat-man now who got himself into this mess so good luck getting out of it. Fuckwit.*

Cristy had winced at that, and didn't ask how Matthew had responded – it wouldn't have been good, but the children were right, he had got himself into it, and it wasn't her problem to deal with. She had plenty else on her plate that required her to stay right where she was.

'So here's what I've found,' Connor said, glancing up as she came into the office following a lengthy budget review with Meena and Harry and headed straight for the coffee. Not that the meeting had gone badly; on the contrary, everyone was beyond thrilled with the success of *The Kellon Manse Murders*; it was simply that she couldn't shake the feelings of restlessness and frustration she'd had building for days.

'Go on,' she prompted, stepping back to watch him entering some dates onto the whiteboard. 'Any word from MacAnany or his useful idiot, by the way?'

'Nothing,' Connor replied, underlining a date. 'If they're holding their collective breath over the photos coming to light, with any luck they'll have expired by now.'

'We can only hope. So, what have you found?'

Recapping his marker pen, he said, 'We've had news from the cold case team via Kevin Break's insider. Apparently they've discovered that Ryall signed up for target practice at a range in

South Glos a month before the killings, meaning May 2008. I called said range about half an hour ago and they confirmed he'd completed a course, but they haven't seen or heard from him since.'

'So how does that help us to find him now?' she said, trying not to sound irritable.

'It doesn't; it's the police building a case against him should he, by some strange quirk of the brain, decide to plead not guilty when they finally get hold of him. To continue: I asked the bloke at the shooting range if anyone else ever came to the practice sessions with Ryall. He didn't know, he wasn't working there then; however, his records show that someone else paid for the course. He couldn't tell me who – apparently the police have instructed him not to talk to anyone – but he was willing to say that the name wasn't Gaudion's; it was some sort of company.'

Feeling the relief of Gaudion being ruled out, although of course she'd known he would be, she frowned as she sipped her coffee. 'A company,' she repeated, 'that will no doubt be impossible to trace. At least for us, maybe for the police too if MacAnany and his crew set it up, and we can be fairly certain they did. This still isn't getting us any closer to Ryall.'

'No, but it's giving us material for a future pod, and actually, I still haven't finished. Fast forward from 2008 to now – this next bit is from Frances Rush who rang while you were in the meeting – and apparently it's come to her attention that Ryall, or someone they're pretty certain was him, was picked up on CCTV a couple of weeks ago coming out of a fast-food place in Southmead.'

'Southmead, Bristol?'

He nodded. 'I've passed this on to Crouch's team, by the way.'

'OK.' She glanced at his phone as it rang, and reaching for it said, 'So he was in Bristol recently getting himself some food . . . Hello, Connor Church's phone.'

'Is he there?'

Her heart somersaulted as she swung round to Connor. 'Can I ask who's calling?' she said carefully, eyes wide as she stared at Connor.

'He'll want to talk to me.'

441

Clasping a hand over the mic, she mouthed, '*It's him. Shit,*' and quickly hitting speaker she said, 'I'll put him on.'

Assimilating fast as Cristy quietly shut and locked the door, Connor said, 'Hey, Connor here, how can I help you?'

'You mean how can I help you,' came the drawled response, an unmistakable cockney twang, a little rougher than before, but it was definitely him.

Just to be clear, Connor said, 'Am I speaking to the person who sent us certain photos . . .'

'Of the crime-scene. Yeah, that were me. Wayne Ryall's the name, if you don't know it already, but I'm guessing you do. I'd have got in touch sooner, but I didn't hear your pod-thing till yesterday. I've been a bit undisposed, if you get my meaning. Stuff going on, and all that. Anyways, I know the police are after me now, so you obviously went to them, but like I told you before, it don't bother me. I got nothing to lose, so tell 'em whatever you like. Meantime I'm telling you, Connor my friend, they've got the wrong man.'

Cristy's heart stopped as her eyes shot to Connor's.

'What do you mean?' Connor asked cautiously.

'What I said, they've got the wrong bloke locked up for this. They did it before, after it all kicked off. I could have told them then that it weren't him, but it would have been . . . *awkward* for me if I did, so I decided to keep out of it. And that was OK, because it all worked out anyway. Trouble is, they're doing it to him again, and this time around I ain't going to just stand back and let them. I'm the one what pulled the trigger that day, three shots, took 'em all out, bang, bang, bang. Course, it was only supposed to be the wife, but the others was there so I dealt with them too. Suffered a lot of stick for that, I did, but hey, it was already done, so no point crying over spilt milk is what I say.'

Reading from the note Cristy had hastily scribbled, Connor said, 'So if I'm understanding you correctly, sorry, we need to spell this out, are you saying it wasn't David Gaudion who hired you?'

'That's right, it weren't him. He's a good bloke, he is, helped me out once when I got in a bit of a jam. Nothing serious, probably didn't mean anything to him. Shouldn't think he even remembers me now, but I remember him.'

Looking at Cristy, Connor said, 'His phone records show that he called you the morning of the killings. Can you explain that?'

'Nah, nah. Makes no sense, that. I've never spoke to him on any phone, only in person one time when I drove a quad bike off the road. So nah, something not right there, if that's what they're saying.'

'But did you get a call that morning, giving you some sort of instruction?' Connor persisted.

'If you're meaning the one to tell me it was on, sure I did, but like I said, it definitely weren't from him.'

'So who was it from?'

Ryall coughed and started to wheeze. 'Excuse me,' he said, his voice strained by the effort to breathe. 'Just getting me puff back. That's it, yeah, yeah. So, I'll tell you who it was and I hope you're sitting down, because from what I've heard on your pod-things you're either a long way up a blind alley, or you're not very good at what you do. One an' the same thing, I suppose, but you get my meaning. Anyway, it weren't David Gaudion who rang me that morning, it was her, the sister. She's who ordered it.'

Cristy gaped at the phone, as stunned as Connor. For an instant she felt certain that Ryall was making this up, or had got himself confused somehow, or had been put up to it by someone, but even as she reeled she was starting to see how it could be true.

She sat down heavily, still trying to put it together. The pieces were moving in so fast that the full picture wasn't yet clear enough to see, but what she did know was that Olivia, by her own admission, had been at Kellon Manse that morning. 'Are you sure about this?' she said, forgetting she was supposed to be listening, not talking.

'Is that Cristy Ward?' Ryall asked chirpily. 'Yeah, thought you might be there too. Hope I haven't shocked you, but I've got a feeling I have. Anyways, she's who called me that morning and she's the one what got me into it all. To be honest, I never knew if she was acting as a front for someone, but I didn't bother to ask. The payout was good, that's all that mattered to me.'

'But how did she find you?' Cristy asked, plucking a random question from the hundreds that were forming.

'Oh, that's easy. I was on one of the rehab programmes her family runs for ex-offenders. Good gigs they are too. Didn't do me much good in the end, I suppose, but I know they've worked out well for some.'

Cristy and Connor looked at one another, needing more time to take in the fact that Olivia had been behind the killings of her own mother and sister. And she'd made it happen by exploiting a young man, albeit an ex-con, who'd presumably been chosen by her husband and father-in-law as someone they could help to turn his life around.

Unless one of them had been involved too.

'You still there?' Ryall coughed.

'Where are you now?' Connor asked. 'Can we meet? If you want to help Gaudion, and I think you do, will you speak to his lawyers?'

'Sure, I'll talk to anyone, me, even the cops, but I'm happy to see you guys first if you can get here in time.'

'In time for what?'

'Well, got a bit of a pressing appointment with Him Upstairs, so I have. The old big C has got me in the guts, well, everywhere now, bastard that it is. It's why I didn't hear your pod-thing right off, they've been trying me out with new pain meds. Palliative stuff, you know the sort.'

'So you're in hospital?' Cristy said. 'Southmead, by any chance?'

'No, I'm in a hospice in Somerset. Lovely place it is, nice people. They calls me George here, not sure why – think there was some sort of mix-up with records when I got moved from Musgrove Park Hospital, and it stuck.'

Knowing Musgrove Park was in Taunton, Cristy said, 'Did you receive any treatment at Southmead in Bristol?'

'Nah, never been there in me life. Why do you ask?'

Putting the sighting down to mistaken identity, she said, 'If you can give us the address we'll come right away.'

'Sure, I'll text it, just as soon as you've given me your word you'll do the right thing for my daughter and make sure she's

444

taken care of when I'm gone. I reckon a hundred grand will do it, more if you're feeling generous.'

Daughter? Connor mouthed, looking at Cristy.

'You have my word,' Cristy said rashly. If she didn't promise it he wouldn't see them, and no way could they let him slip through their fingers now.

Moments after the call was over a text arrived with the hospice address. Connor quickly got the place up online and rang the number, wanting to be sure that Ryall, aka George, was actually there. As soon as he gave Cristy the thumbs up, she rang Edmond Crouch who, it turned out, was on his way to Bristol, no more than thirty minutes away.

'Keep going on the M4,' she told him, 'then take the M5 south to Weston-Super-Mare. Connor will send you the exact address and meet you there.'

'Where are *you* going?' Connor demanded as she rang off.

'To talk to Olivia.'

Astounded, he cried, 'No! No, no, no. You can't go blundering in there with what we've just heard. You've got no idea what she might do. We need to let the police deal with it.'

'Then we'll never know why,' Cristy pointed out. 'Have you sent Crouch the address yet?'

'Done. Listen, I understand why you want to see Olivia, I want to know why she did it too, but if you go there first, without the police, what if she ends up doing a disappearing act before they can get to her? Or worse, topping herself? No one will ever know anything then.'

She stared at him hard as she thought.

'And it's not our job to interview her,' he added forcefully. 'Sure, we want the story, but we can't do it like that.'

Pressing her hands to her face, she continued to think.

'There's got to be a good chance Gaudion can tell us why,' Connor reminded her. 'Once he knows it was her, I mean. Much better that you speak to him.'

Realizing he was right, she looked up as she said, 'How did we miss it? The whole time we were talking to her . . .'

'She was believable,' he cried, 'and who the hell would suspect her of killing her own sister and mother? No one else did, not even those who'd known them for years. Not even Gaudion, come to that.'

Realizing what a shock this was going to be for him, for Cynthia too, Cristy gave it only a moment before refocusing on Olivia. 'She was there that morning, at the Manse,' she reminded him. 'She told us that herself. She must have used his phone; for the other calls, too.' As the shocking truth of it sank in, spreading its horror ever deeper, she said, 'Why would she do that to him? She must really hate him.'

'Or was she being used?' Connor ventured.

Cristy's thoughts flashed to MacAnany, but she started to shake her head. 'Her "collapse", as she calls it, the brainwashing Gaudion suspected, although that's obviously in doubt now, happened *after* the killings. So if she was in her right mind before – something else that's in doubt considering everything – why would she have allowed someone to use her to kill her own sister? She had to have wanted it herself.'

They stayed silently looking at one another as all the questions, the need for understanding and explanation, and the recall of Olivia's interviews, buried them in an avalanche of confusion.

Mindful of Ryall waiting at the hospice, Cristy said, 'I'll come with you, and as soon as we're done recording we must call the police.'

CHAPTER FORTY

An hour later they were at the hospice staring down at Ryall in his narrow bed, a pathetic, skeletal version of the images they'd seen of him, bony arms and concave chest connected to IV drips and computers. It was plain to see from his frailty and jaundiced pallor that he really wasn't long for this world; in fact, looking at him, it seemed a miracle he was breathing at all.

However, a weak light showed in his eyes when they opened and he saw Cristy and Connor standing over him. Cristy felt torn between revulsion for what he'd done, and pity for his deteriorating condition – after all, he was a human being and she wasn't completely without compassion. Or anger on Gaudion's behalf, and loathing for what he'd done to Rosaria and Anna, robbing them of a mother who'd clearly adored them, and for what? Cristy guessed – hoped – they were about to find out.

To her surprise his voice sounded almost strong, though gravelly, as he said dryly, 'Excuse me if I don't get up.'

'I'll fetch another chair,' a nurse said as Edmond Crouch entered the room.

Cristy and Connor greeted the lawyer quietly, then Cristy made the introductions to Ryall while Connor discreetly set up to record.

'Are you still sure about this?' Cristy asked Ryall, not entirely certain she was, given the state of him, although if he said no she might just try to choke it out of him.

'Yeah, yeah,' he coughed, using a finger to wipe the spittle from his lips.

Cristy passed him a tissue.

'I can't thank you enough,' Crouch said, looking both awkward and slightly horrified as he sat on a chair on the far side of the bed.

'Got to clear me conscience before I go,' Ryall told him, wincing as he struggled to sit up and finally not bothering. 'That's what my girl says and I know she's right.'

'You have a daughter?' Cristy said, taking a chair next to Connor to spare Ryall the effort of having to keep turning his head.

'Jessica,' he stated and grinned, showing a few hapless teeth holding out to the end. His mugshots, while not flattering, had suggested he'd been a reasonably good-looking man when he was younger, before the cancer. Other images had shown him to be tall and muscular, with a physique not unlike Gaudion's, in fact, which was what had made it easy to wonder if it was a masked Gaudion in the mirror. Now Ryall was shrunken, hairless and devastated by disease. 'Her mother never told me nothing about her until a couple of years ago,' he croaked on, 'but she lets me see her now, ever since they found out I had this.'

'How old is she?' Cristy asked, not only to be polite, but because she was genuinely interested.

'Fifteen. Knocked her mother up just before I went down.' He gave a small gasp, groaned and after a moment pushed himself on. 'She's a good kid, a bit religious, if you know what I mean, not with God or anything, well, probably with Him, but she's into all the hippy shit, you know. Same as her old lady. That's how come I've got all this healing stuff about the place; they say it's good for my soul.' Cristy had noticed all the crystals and candles, ammonites and what looked like Shamanic rattles. There were books as well, dream catchers and prayers written on Post-its. 'I'll tell you what is good for my soul,' he said, 'is seeing my girl and knowing you're going to take care of her after I'm gone.'

'We can't be seen to be paying for your confession,' Crouch advised him, 'but you have my assurance that proper arrangements will be made for your daughter at an appropriate time. Provided, of course, that what you tell us now bears out.'

448

Ryall's lashless eyes blinked slowly as he took this in, then they moved slightly away as Connor said, 'We're all set if you are, Wayne.'

'Yeah, yeah, let's get it done before I croak. I wouldn't be able to help anyone then, would I?'

A moment later Connor said, 'OK, we're rolling.'

'Feels like I'm a film star,' Ryall quipped and broke into a fit of phlegmy coughing.

When he was calm again, and his lips dabbed dry, he seemed ready to continue. 'So where do I start?' he asked.

Connor said, 'How about with what you told us on the phone earlier, that it was Olivia Caldwell who called you the morning of the killings.'

Ryall nodded, and after taking a gulp of oxygen he held the mask in one bony hand as he began to rasp out his story so far, helped occasionally by prompts from Connor, and the odd question from Crouch. Cristy sat listening, needing to be certain everything was covered before she stepped in to take the interview further, provided Ryall was up to it.

Finally, after he'd repeated his earlier claims, not verbatim, and not quite as coherently either, but coherently enough, she waited for him to take more air before asking if he had any idea why Olivia had wanted her sister dead.

RYALL: 'Not a clue. Never asked. Should have, I suppose, but there we are. I'd never done anything like it before, see, so I didn't know the protocol. I just decided it was best not to ask questions. I mean, I was just a kid really, or that's how it feels now. I suppose I was pushing thirty, but I was green behind the ears. A bad 'un, not trying to say anything else, but easily led, if you know what I mean. That's how I kept getting into trouble. Always got talked into stuff, and always ended up taking the rap. I'd just come out after a spell in Wandsworth when I got accepted for some rehab at the Caldwells' place in Gloucester. It went well, while I was there. I felt lucky, like things was finally starting to look up for me.

'It was a shock when she came looking for me, about

a year after I left. I was in me own gaff by then, a council run flat in the St Paul's part of Bristol. Proper run-down it was, bugs, damp, it had the lot going on, but I couldn't afford nothing better. They don't pay street sweepers much, in case you didn't know. I had skills, I'd learned to be an electrician while I was at the Caldwells', but it's hard finding a job as an ex-con. Anyway, I gets this call from her one day, out of the blue, didn't even know she had me number, but I s'pose they had a record of it in their files. She wants me to meet her at a caff in Bedminster, she says, she's got some project she thinks might interest me. So, there's me thinking this is the big break I've been waiting for, she's got someone who's looking for a qualified spark . . .'

He seemed to lose the thread for a moment, closed his eyes and let the mask hover near his lips as though not sure whether or not he needed it. It seemed he didn't, because his eyes opened and he continued.

RYALL: 'So I goes on the day she told me . . . Can't remember the name of the place now, but it was on North Road or Street, just down from the old tobacco factory. It's a theatre now – I think it was then, can't be sure. Anyways, proper shocked I was when she told me what she had in mind, thought I must have misunderstood at first, but I got the picture pretty fast when she told me how much she was paying.'

CRISTY: 'Can I ask how much it was?'

RYALL: 'Sure. Fifty grand, half up front, the other half when the job was done, and she'd cover all the other expense like getting me some shooter practice, hiring a car, that sort of thing.'

CRISTY: 'Why do you think she chose you?'

RYALL: 'Well, you know, I've wondered that meself since, and all I can tell you is that we had a bit of a thing going when I was at the Centre. I don't mean like sex or anything, she wouldn't have looked twice at someone like me, although I was a bit of a looker once, believe it or not. Didn't have much trouble getting the girls, it was keeping 'em I weren't so good at. Anyways, she was friendly to me and we had a laugh together sometimes, some serious chats too about the world and stuff, and when it came time for me to leave she said she was going to miss me. I thought to meself, yeah, I'm going to miss you too and I meant it. It had been a long time since anyone had been that nice to me and for it to be someone like her . . . It felt pretty special, you know what I mean?

'Anyways, I meet up with her in the Bedminster caff, and a couple of weeks later, maybe a month, can't be sure now, she sends me a phone and tells me it's what I've got to use when I'm in touch with her. Then a text turns up telling me where to go for the shooter practice. So off I toddles, and what do you know, I'm not half bad at it, even started thinking I might get meself a job as one of them armed response officers when I'd finished the business in hand.

'Then I gets another text telling me where to go for a hire car and I can keep it for a week. I figured then that she was wanting it to happen pretty soon, so I starts staking out the area, mostly the Manse, watching comings and goings, that sort of thing. Getting a lie of the land, who's about and what sort of things I need to look out for, like access to the house, where to leave the car and all that. Then I gets this call from her telling me it's the day.

'By then I weren't all that sure I could do it, to be honest, and if I'd realized it was the wife of the bloke who'd helped me with the quad bike I wouldn't have, but I didn't know that then. Didn't see him anywhere around while I was casing the place, and I didn't want to let Olivia down, or lose the rest of the pay-out, so well . . . The rest, as they say, is history. Bloody sorry I did it now though, I was right away once I found out who the sister was married to.'

His eyes were closed again, whether to try to block out the images of that day, or to continue a silent, losing battle with his conscience, or to rest a while, was impossible to say.

CRISTY: 'Didn't Olivia warn you the others would be there that day?'

RYALL: 'Oh yeah, she said they might be, and if they was, there'd be more in it for me if I took care of them too.'

Cristy looked at Connor. So Margaret and Serena hadn't been collateral damage after all. They'd been targets too. Did that mean being left out of the butterfly cult had incensed Olivia so much she'd wanted to punish them all in the worst possible way? But what about Gaudion? She'd chosen a time when she'd known he wouldn't be in the house, had used his phone to contact Ryall, had spun a web of lies to the police, and later to them, about him and his marriage . . . She couldn't have known no one would see him while he was out that day, but even if someone had spotted him, or even waved to him, the time of death would never have been precise enough to rule him out as the main suspect, or the one who'd organized it all. It might have been a random, and frankly crazy plan, with virtually no chance of success, and yet it had worked. So what the hell did she have against Gaudion to have set him up like that?

Knowing it was unlikely Ryall had the answer to that, she returned to the women and what had happened after the killings.

CRISTY: 'We know you took shots of the scene, but did you see Lexie and David Gaudion's daughter while you were there?'

RYALL: 'Yeah, kind of. I wasn't sure who it was, just got a glimpse out the corner of me eye then she was gone. I didn't know whether to go after her, or what to do, but then there she was again with a sodding gun pointing right at me. I tried to grab it, but she whacked it into me

452

nuts and scarpered. I decided it was time for me to do the same, fast as I could. Went out behind the hedges at the side of the house, same way I came in, cut through to the Hall and hopped over a couple of stiles the other side of the grounds to get to the car. I wanted to take off fast, but I knew better than to bring attention to myself, so I took it steady all the way back to my shithole in St Pauls shaking like a bloody leaf.'

Seeing how tired he was becoming, Cristy paused for a moment in case he wanted to stop – if he did, they already had his confession – but after a deep inhale of oxygen he circled a hand for them to continue.

CRISTY: 'So you went back to St Pauls. What happened then?'

RYALL: 'Nothing for about a week. I mean, the shit had properly hit the fan up at the house, police all over the place, big search for the girl. I'm completely gutted, me, because I knows by then who I've offed, but I couldn't do anything about it, could I? Unless I gave meself up and I didn't want to do that.

'So, me and Olivia, we meets up in this lay-by somewhere over the Bridge, she asks for the gun back so I gives it to her, then she hands me over a nice fat envelope and that was that.'

CRISTY: 'Do you happen to know where the gun came from?'

RYALL: 'Not a clue and I didn't ask, but her old man's a bit of a collector, I think. All I can tell you is she took it and stuffed it in a box, then she wants the phone back so she can get rid of it. No problem, I tells her and I hands it over too. I'd already deleted the shots I took, but not before I'd transferred 'em to another burner I'd got for meself. I s'pose I was thinking even then they might be a handy insurance one day. Turned out I was right, didn't it? All these years

453

later. Lucky I kept that phone safe while I was inside. Going to do a lot more for my girl now than I ever could before.'

EDMOND CROUCH: 'Why didn't you go to Olivia for money?'

RYALL: 'Oh, I thought about it, that's for sure, I even had it all worked out how I was going to do it, but then them two started up with their pod-thing and I wasn't sure which way it was gonna go. Could have left me high and dry with zilch for my trouble, so I bides me time, and next thing I knows they've gone and picked David up for it again. Well, I weren't having none of it, not this time around. Things is different for me now, I don't have anything to lose by coming out with what was what, and I owed him, didn't I, after the way he helped me when he didn't have to. Proper gentlemanly, it was of him, the way he stopped and heaved the effing quad bike out of a ditch with me. I'd "borrowed" it, see, from the Centre. I wasn't supposed to have it, and that sort of thing could have got me chucked out. So he saved my skin that day, and now the way I see it, it's my turn to save his.'

Cristy could only marvel at the way he was equating the two acts, and how one small gesture of kindness that Gaudion had probably never even thought about again, could now be having such a profound impact on his life. On Olivia's too. If it wasn't karma at work, even in this wholly disproportionate and wretchedly perverse way, she'd never know what karma was.

Deciding they had more than enough now – the rest was up to the police – she signalled for Connor to stop recording and said, 'I'm sorry if we've exhausted you, Wayne . . .'

'I'm all right,' he croaked, barely able to push the words out. 'Good to get it off me chest. Are you going to give it to the cops, save me the bother of going through it all again?'

'We can do that,' she assured him, 'but you know they'll want to talk to you anyway.'

'Course they will, cunts that they are. Tell 'em they better hurry up or that there tape is all you'll have.'

454

'It's enough,' Crouch assured him, getting to his feet. 'Thank you for coming forward with the truth at last. I could say David is indebted to you, but in the circumstances . . .'

'It's all right, I get it. He's got nothing to thank me for after what I did to his missus Just let me know when he gets out, will you? I'd like to hear that he has before I shuffle off.'

CHAPTER FORTY-ONE

After leaving the hospice, Cristy and Connor drove back to the office while Crouch went to meet with DI Thompson and his team. As Connor had made a duplicate recording alongside the original, they had the interview themselves, but more importantly for the moment, they could make another copy for Crouch to keep after he'd handed his over.

'I won't try getting word to David until after I've seen the detectives,' Crouch had said as they'd walked him to his car, 'but I'll let you know when I have and I'm sure he'll be in touch. Thank you, both of you, for all you've done to help his case.'

'All in a day's work,' Connor had quipped, while Cristy said, 'You won't forget to call his mother?' She'd have rung Cynthia herself, but knew that it was still too soon; the police had to decide first what the next steps would be.

It was a couple of hours later that Jodi waddled into the office with a bag full of Chinese takeout and a bottle of white Rioja encased in a frozen sleeve. 'Have the police been in touch with you yet?' she asked as Connor kissed her and Cristy fetched glasses.

'Not yet,' Connor replied, 'but we're expecting a call any time.'

'Can they arrest Wayne Ryall, given the condition he's in? Thanks,' she said as Cristy passed over a glass for her Vit Hit and Connor helped her to one of the sofas.

'No idea,' Cristy replied, 'but Crouch rang just now to say someone's on their way to the hospice to make sure the interview wasn't given under duress.'

'Like as if,' Connor grunted.

'And what about David Gaudion?' Jodi asked. 'Does he know anything yet?'

'Apparently Crouch has managed to have a brief call with him and Cynthia, so they both know what's happening. We haven't heard from either of them yet, but I've tried Cynthia a couple of times. I'm guessing she's either on the phone to David, or she's sharing the good news with the rest of the family.'

Sighing as she put her feet up and took out her own healthy snack, Jodi said, 'What a day this is for them all. How long do you think before he's released?'

'Not possible to say yet. Obviously, the police will want to question Olivia first, which they could be doing right now for all we know, but nothing's hit the news yet.'

'Have you tipped anyone off?'

'Sure, a couple of old colleagues we owe favours to, so they're watching the house. They'll let us know if anything happens there.'

'Like an arrest?'

'It'll be interesting to see how soon that happens,' Connor replied, sitting down next to her with his noodles and chopsticks, 'unless something spectacularly unexpected blows up in our faces to change things again.'

Putting her food down to check who was calling, Cristy immediately said, 'Cynthia,' and clicked on. 'Hey!' she cried, switching to speaker. 'I take it you've spoken to Edmond . . .'

'Oh, Cristy, Cristy,' the old lady wept. 'How are we ever going to thank you for this? What you've done, you and your podcast . . . But Olivia. Oh my goodness, Olivia.'

Understanding what a shock it must have been for the old lady to find out the truth, how hard it must be for her to process it right now, Cristy led her gently away from it for the moment and said, 'Have you spoken to David yet?'

'Yes, I have and he's . . . He's like us, can't really believe it . . . Edmond can't say yet when he'll be home, but at least we know it's going to happen. Have you spoken to him yourself?'

'Not yet, no. He might have used up all his phone time for tonight, but I'm sure he'll be in touch soon. How are the children?'

With a watery-sounding chuckle, Cynthia said, 'I've had

to come into another room because they're having a noisy celebration out there. Friends and family are turning up all the time. They didn't know Olivia, of course. They just wanted to speak to David when he rang, but really he only had time for the girls and Laurent.'

'And you?'

'Yes, me too. We didn't get much chance to talk about the ins and outs of it all, but my goodness . . . Olivia.'

Going with it, Cristy said, 'Did it ever, even once, cross your mind that she might have been behind it?'

'No, never. Nor David's either. He knew she was angry with him, he said, but she always was, one way or another, for as long as we can remember.'

'Why?'

'I don't know. It was always about silly stuff, we never took any notice of it, but she'd get so mad with him sometimes and accuse him of all sorts of things, even turning her own mother against her. There were times when he couldn't do anything right in her eyes, unless it was on the days that he could, and we never knew what it was that softened her up.' With a drawn-out sigh, she said, 'She had a lot more of Margaret in her than Lexie ever did . . . But then she met Will Caldwell and married him and she seemed more . . . *settled* at last, less . . . difficult with us all, especially David. She and Will were good together, we could all see that. She threw herself into the family business, and helped Will's father set up the rehab centre, and she was a good mother.' She paused, spoke quietly to someone who must have come into the room, then continued. 'It's only thinking about things now that I'm really seeing them . . . I mean, we all noticed at one point or another when she started changing back into her old self, becoming argumentative and resentful in ways that didn't seem to make much sense when she'd been so happy before. She started to get herself properly worked up over Lexie's issues, accusing her of being self-obsessed and a terrible wife and mother, of not being able to let the past go . . . She even told her once that David was planning to leave her and she, Olivia, didn't blame him after all Lexie had put him through. She hurt Lexie a lot with those attacks, I can tell you, and David was none too pleased about them. He had quite a falling-out with her over it and it was a while before any of them saw one another again.

'Looking back now . . . Oh dear, it's all so terrible . . . I can see how strange it was that she didn't act pleased when Lexie's treatments seemed to work. Actually, she was pretty scathing about it all, the same as her mother, especially when Lexie started going away for the odd night here and there to attend the seminars, or whatever they called them. She told David Lexie was sleeping with the leader . . . That caused more trouble between Lexie and David . . . Why didn't I see how she was always after making trouble for them? I suppose I did, but I put it down to sibling rivalry, or she was just having a bad day . . . Then something happened, I don't know what it was, but from what David said on the phone just now . . . He thinks it must have been what triggered it all for her.' She stopped and blew her nose. 'Sorry, I'm all over the place here, glad for David, shocked about her, but I should probably ring off now if you don't mind. They're shouting for me.'

'Of course. I appreciate you ringing . . .'

'Please don't think this is the last you'll hear from us. Anna wants to apologize and so she should, and Rosie's getting more panto stuff together to send you.'

Thrilled to hear that Rosaria was once again excited about the panto, Cristy promised to be in touch if there was any more news at her end and said a warm goodnight.

'Isn't that lovely,' Jodi sighed contentedly. 'There's nothing like making a difference for the good in someone's life the way you guys have for the Gaudion family with your podcast.'

'Or,' Connor added darkly, 'for the bad, if you're the Caldwell family.' He turned to Cristy. 'So are we thinking now that MacAnany and co. had nothing to do with it?'

She turned to stare at Gaudion's headshot, wondering what he was doing now, what he was thinking, and feeling. 'It's certainly looking that way,' she said, 'but I'll be interested to hear what he has to say when I get to speak to him.'

* * *

459

'Hi,' Gaudion said quietly when he rang the following evening. 'Just to let you know I've been given special dispensation to make this call from an office, considering my new status, so hopefully no untimely interruptions.'

She smiled as she took out her door keys to let herself into the flat. 'How are you?' she asked, wishing they could have this conversation in person, while having no intention of waiting until that was possible.

'Well, pretty good, is one way of putting it, I guess, but I've been trying to think all day of what to say to you that's better than thank you—'

'Please don't,' she interrupted. 'As you know, I didn't act alone, and nor did I start out with the intention of clearing your name.'

'But it's happened, or it will soon enough, and apart from thanking you, I'd like to find a way of showing my gratitude.'

Not entirely sure what he meant by that, but feeling certain his mind was working the same way as hers, she said, because it was easier, 'Maybe an interview later, once we find out what's going to happen to Olivia? How are you feeling about that?'

'Shocked, as you might expect, sad, angry . . . It's going to take a while to get my head around it.'

Understanding that, she said, 'Have you had any updates on what's happening to her?'

'I think you're better placed to get that information than I am, but I heard on the news that she's been charged.'

'She has, and taken to Eastwood Park, so she's not a million miles from her home.'

Sighing, he said, 'I keep going over it all in my head, everything I got wrong. Not just about her, but all the misunderstandings and false assumptions I leapt to about MacAnany and the others, the way I linked what they did to Lexie to what happened to her on that awful day. The timing of it, after she told O'Malley who they were . . . It made such perfect sense to me, that I couldn't see any other explanation. There simply wasn't anyone else who had a reason to harm Lexie, much less to kill her. Or not as far as I was concerned.'

'Your mother mentioned some childhood friction between you

and Olivia, and issues later when she tried to cause trouble in your marriage?'

'It's true, she did, but she'd always be sorry about it after, and Lexie always forgave her. She adored Olivia. They'd been through so much together as children with their terrible parents; they were each other's rocks even when they weren't getting along.'

'So what do you think happened to push her into doing what she did?'

With another weary-sounding sigh, he said, 'Obviously she's the only one who can really answer that. All I can come up with is an incident, the year before it happened, when we were staying in rooms next to one another at a hotel somewhere in East Anglia. We were both seriously worried about Lexie's involvement with O'Malley at the time . . . She kept saying there was an affair going on; Lexie denied it, but I was concerned about the money as well . . . Although Lexie was definitely showing signs of improvement, I couldn't deny that, there was this near obsessive following of O'Malley's instructions. Then there were the butterflies, the branding, for God's sake. Everything about it smacked of being a cult. So when Olivia suggested we start following her when she went to meetings that meant her being away for a night, I went along with it. I was probably behaving irrationally, but I wanted to make sure she was safe and not being used in some hideous way as though she was reliving the past to try to expunge it. She swore to me it was nothing like that, that she'd never put herself through anything like it and no one was asking her to. I might have listened, I think I did for a while, but then the branding happened. Olivia was as horrified by that as I was and became convinced that something terrible was being planned for Lexie. So we followed her this one time to a country house somewhere in Norfolk. It turned out to have a lot of security on the gates and . . .'

'Did Lexie know you were nearby?'

'I'd texted to say we were, and she messaged back telling us to go home. *You're a pair of fools to worry so much,* she said, or something like it, *and I love you both for it, but I promise everything's fine.*

'Obviously we had no way of knowing if she'd sent the

message or someone else had used her phone, but what could we do? There was no getting through the gates and we didn't have any other numbers to try. So we found an inn not too far away just in case she needed us. We'd stayed in hotels before, two or three times, and everything had been fine. Olivia usually travelled back with Lexie the next day, and more often than not I'd go on to London.

'I wasn't expecting anything different this time, unless we got a call from Lexie in the night, but we didn't, and I was fast asleep by the time Olivia rang to say she was experiencing a really bad vibe about Lexie and the place we'd seen her going into. She thought we should discuss it, pointing out that sisters had that sort of telepathic connection, and she was really scared. So I went to her room and—' He broke off and though Cristy could imagine the rest she was still shocked when he said, 'She wasn't wearing anything and when I tried to leave she . . . Do you know, I don't really want to go into the detail of it. I'll just say that she seemed to think I'd led her on, that I'd been doing it for years . . . She threatened to tell Lexie about all the times I'd come on to her . . . It was all nonsense, I'd never done anything to make her think I was interested in her, or certainly not in that way, but in her head I clearly had, and now I'd humiliated her in a way she said she'd never forgive.'

When he stopped Cristy quietly let go the breath she'd been holding. 'And you think that's what triggered her to search out Wayne Ryall?'

'It's all I can come up with,' he replied. 'That and perhaps a lifetime's resentment of a sister who was always a little more beautiful than her and quite a lot more liked. Even their mother had more time for Lexie than she did for Olivia, and maybe, when Lexie got Margaret interested in joining Papilio – I guess that's more likely to have been the trigger, or perhaps the final pull of it. It was just too much for Olivia. She was being shut out again, is maybe how she saw it, but as I said just now, she's really the only one who can tell us why she did it.'

'And if she pleads guilty we'll probably never know, unless she'll agree to see one of us, but I'm not expecting that to happen any time soon.'

'No, me neither.' After a beat he added, 'It's her children I feel for right now; this is a terrible time for them.'

Sharing his concern, Cristy said, 'I don't suppose the scandal will do much for the rehab centre either, which is a shame when it seems to do a lot of good.'

'It does,' he confirmed, 'and it was set up in honour of the son and brother they'd lost. This is going to hit Will and his father hard, that's for sure.'

'Not to mention what it's done to your family. Your girls being deprived of their mother, you losing your wife, and then believing you had to hide Amelia all these years to protect her from a force you didn't know how to fight . . .'

'It's going to take a lot of time for us to get our heads around it all,' he admitted, 'but thankfully our bond is strong as a family and we have a lot of people close to us who'll be there for all three children in the coming weeks and months.'

'Most importantly,' she said warmly, 'you'll be there, and I'm sure that's what really matters to them.'

With an audible smile, he said, 'I can't wait to be free of this place so I can get back there. Edmond's saying it should be sometime over the next few days, so, can I see you before I leave?'

'Of course. I'd like that. Just tell him to let me know when and where.'

'OK. And can I say that getting to know you these past weeks has been, well. . . At least one good thing has come out of this unspeakable nightmare.'

She smiled. 'I'm glad you see it that way, because I do too.' Then, after a beat, 'I guess you have to go now.'

'I do, but I'll see you very soon, which won't be soon enough as far as I'm concerned.'

As the line went dead she remained standing where she was, considering going to pour herself a glass of wine while thinking that, maybe, the next drink she had would be with him.

CHAPTER FORTY-TWO

As soon as news of Olivia's remand into custody had broken, Clover and Jackson were brought back on board, their first job being to record the stunned reactions of Berkeley Vale's residents – those who'd known the Sallis sisters for years, as well as those who hadn't. Of course everyone, not only old friends and neighbours, wanted to know why no one had suspected Olivia sooner, and many theories were aired about that. Cristy guessed they always would be, given that the horror of the Frumentarii distraction wasn't ever likely to be shared with the wider world. She understood Gaudion's reasons for not wanting to become embroiled in a legal battle with them. He couldn't prove they'd been behind his release sixteen years ago, although he was in no doubt that they had been, and without Lexie being there and able to testify – something he would never have put her through anyway – he wasn't even going to try to bring the rapists to justice.

'There's nothing at all to be gained from putting the children, Anna in particular, through any more,' he'd said during one of their brief calls while he waited not very patiently to be freed, 'so it's best that we move on with our lives and just try to forget about them.'

Although it sickened Cristy to think of those perverted monsters getting away with what they'd done, there was no way she and Connor would take action without Gaudion's backing. Nor would she tell Gaudion about the call she received from MacAnany two days after Olivia's arrest. He didn't need to know that the man had apparently felt the urge to remind her of how useful he and his contacts could be to her in the future, should she ever require access to high places. All she needed to do in return was make sure no undesirable attention was ever drawn to certain events in the past that were pure fiction anyway.

'Slimy bastard,' Harry snorted after she told him about the call. 'But it's true, someone like him, like all of those over-privileged cretins actually, can open doors we probably don't even know exist right now. On the other hand, taking them down would make a brilliant podcast if you did decide to go for it.'

'Gaudion's children matter more,' she'd responded, 'so as far as I'm concerned, they're the reason – and the only reason – we let this drop.'

Harry nodded, and they hadn't mentioned it since, while Cristy focused instead on how she and Connor were going to structure the next two episodes featuring Ryall's confession intercut with extracts from Olivia's earlier interviews. They were gathering additional material from experts to help explain Ryall's legal position and deteriorating medical condition, alongside some valuable input from the newly talkative DI Trevor Thompson. The detective's methodical approach to unsolved crimes in general would, they were certain, prove a huge bonus for the procedure-obsessives amongst their listeners, although he refused to go into specifics concerning the Kellon Manse case.

It was the evening before Gaudion's long-awaited release that Cristy received a message from Matthew letting her know that he and Marley were back from France and had decided to try to work things out.

Aiden's with us, but he wants to come to you for a while. I expect he's already told you that. I've said it's OK, hope you agree. Hayley's still in France with Hugo's parents, flying back to Edinburgh from there. I guess you know that too. Haven't listened to the latest pods, but I know from the news that big things have been happening. I'm sure you're all over it, but anything I can do let me know.

Relieved to know from him – Aiden and Hayley had already relayed their take on events via WhatsApp – that things hadn't completely fallen apart with Marley, Cristy sent a quick reply saying:

Have been in touch with Hayley and Aiden so aware of their movements. Good for Aiden to give you guys some space for a few weeks. Glad to have him here. Hope it goes well. Speak soon, C.

The following morning, while Aiden was still in bed and she was on her way out of the door, she received the call she'd been waiting for. Gaudion was on the right side of the prison walls, free to go home to his family.

'I want to get as far away from this place as I can, as fast as I can' he said, his voice thickened by emotion. 'I just hadn't expected it to happen quite so soon.'

Puzzled, she said, 'Not sure I'm following you.'

'My brother has a private plane on standby at Exeter Airport,' he explained. 'We're on our way there now. I can't tell you how sorry I am to miss you today, but please say we can stay in touch.'

'Of course,' she assured him, perhaps too warmly in an effort to disguise the crush of her disappointment. 'Apart from anything else, I'm hoping you'll consider taking part in the podcast, once you've had time to resettle at home and think things through.'

'Sure. We'll talk first about what you're hoping to get from me, but I don't see a problem. I'm afraid I need to go now, my mother's trying to get through and—'

'Don't worry. Send her my love.'

'I will, and I'll call soon.'

To her surprise he rang late that afternoon, having apparently stepped out of his welcome home party. 'I'm really sorry we didn't manage to get together before I left,' he told her, the mere tone of his voice letting her know that his disappointment had been as real as her own.

'It doesn't matter, really,' she replied, the words coming out in a swell of joy to hear from him, until she realized that wasn't quite the right thing to say and added quickly, 'I mean it does, obviously, I'd love to have seen you, but sometimes things just don't work out the way we want them to.'

'I'll make sure it's better organized next time,' he assured her. 'Not that I intend to be in prison again, you understand, and I don't imagine Richard will be chartering too many planes in the future, but whatever anyone else's plans, I'll be taking charge of my own from now on.'

Smiling, she said, 'Well, whenever it happens, I'll look forward to it . . .' She waited for the deafening hoot of a party trumpet to die down.

'Sorry, one of my cousins,' he explained. 'Yeah, yeah, I'm coming. I'm *coming*. Cristy, before I go, I want you to know I will do the podcasts . . .'

'That's fantastic!' she exclaimed. 'We can talk it through first, as you said—' She broke off again as a loud cheer erupted at the other end, and forestalling another apology she said, 'Enjoy the party. We'll talk again soon.'

Without glancing away from his computer, Connor said, 'I take it that was Mr Gaudion?'

'It was,' she confirmed, trying to tame her smile into a more dignified shape as she returned to her own screen. The earlier disappointment of not seeing him was eased immeasurably by knowing that he seemed to feel it too, and besides, they'd soon be speaking again now he'd agreed to take part in future podcasts, so all was good.

Checking the time and seeing it was already past five o'clock, she said, 'I can carry on going through Olivia's interviews if you want to get home.'

'It's fine,' Connor assured her. 'Jodi's got a friend over, and I'm almost done here anyway, so if you're up for a listen I'll play you what I've put together so far and we can decide from there how we want to link it.'

It was almost midnight by the time they'd finished structuring the next episode, and the following day, after adding their own input, together with the music and effects, opening and closing links, and spaces for breaks, they were just about ready to upload at six.

Everyone was gathered in the office, as usual, and as filled with anticipation as ever in spite of having already heard the pod. It began with Cristy giving a quick recap of the previous week's episode when she and Connor had retold Wayne Ryall's shocking story of how he'd committed the Kellon Manse Murders. (The police were unwilling at this time for them to use Ryall's actual recording, but had raised no objection to them summarizing it.)

CRISTY: 'We received news today that Ryall passed away two nights ago. Our condolences naturally go to his family, most particularly his daughter, who has asked not to be named.'

CONNOR: 'Obviously, he won't be facing justice for his actions, however, we know that Olivia Caldwell will. That will come in later episodes as events unfold.'

CRISTY: 'For now, we're going to remind you of some of the things she told us when we interviewed her a few short weeks ago about the cold-blooded killing of her sister, mother and Serena Sutton. You'll also hear Connor and me sharing some of our thoughts.'

OLIVIA: 'I expect you've heard about my "collapse" after the murders. Some people would call it a breakdown or an emotional crisis. In our family we referred to it as the "collapse". I've had a lot of therapy since it all happened, but that still doesn't mean I find it easy to talk about . . .'

CONNOR: 'If there was any such collapse, I'd say it happened because once the shock of her success set in she couldn't live with what she'd done.'

CRISTY: 'Maybe now is a good time to tell you that we're due to speak to an eminent psychologist about the probable state of Olivia's mental health, not only after the killings, but during the years she was growing up in a very difficult home.

'And in case you're wondering, we *have* tried to make contact with Olivia herself – she's currently on remand at HMP Eastwood Park – but she isn't responding to our requests for a visit. This isn't particularly surprising, but Olivia, if you happen to listen to this and you decide you would like to be heard, you and your lawyers know how to get hold of us. The same applies to any members of your family who'd like to speak out.'

CONNOR: 'We're now going to listen to what she had to say about Lexie and their mother early on in her first interview.'

OLIVIA: 'My sister meant the world to me. Our experiences as children, the lack of proper parenting, the bond we shared . . .

. . . I took her death so hard. It was like losing a part of myself, and frankly I still miss her every day.

. . . I had no idea that losing my mother would affect me so badly.'

CONNOR: 'I think it's fair to say that we were fully convinced by her that day, weren't we?'

CRISTY: 'Absolutely. I remember how moved I was by what she'd been through, how much I wanted to help her. I know the psychologist is going to talk about self-delusion – or self-deception, he preferred to call it – and the way someone can create a whole other narrative to protect themselves from a truth they can't live with. It seems Olivia has managed to do that quite successfully over the past sixteen years.'

CONNOR: 'We're going to move on now to some of the things she told us about her niece, Amelia Gaudion, and brother-in-law, David Gaudion.'

OLIVIA: 'It's very hard to think of my niece witnessing what happened to her mother and grandmother . . . I never dreamt he was capable of hurting the children, I really didn't.'

CONNOR: 'Bear in mind she's talking about David Gaudion here, the man we now know did *not* commit the murders and who she must have known somewhere in her psyche was an innocent man.

Back to Cristy and Olivia.'

CRISTY: 'Does this mean you believe he killed his daughter too?'

OLIVIA: '. . . What else are we to think when we've never seen her again?'

CRISTY: 'The fact that she was prepared to believe he'd killed his daughter makes for shocking listening now we know the truth. Actually it all does, virtually everything she said.'

CONNOR: 'These next extracts have been taken from episode four of the series where she is once again talking about David Gaudion.'

OLIVIA: '. . . He's very good at making people think things that are totally contrary to what they believe.'

CONNOR: 'Rich indeed coming from someone we now know to be an expert at this, especially in the way she turned it on herself.'

OLIVIA: '. . . Take it from me, he treated her appallingly at times, and it's only because she was afraid of losing her girls that she stayed.'

There was more, a whole lot more that filled this episode and the next, especially when the professionals began playing bigger roles and proved themselves to be as fascinating as they were insightful. *Hindsight*'s social media and phone lines became so swamped by messages for the psychologist that he agreed to record a spin-off to the series to deal with troubled souls who were struggling with their own, similar issues of denial and self-deception.

Who knew there were so many?

Over the next couple of weeks as subscriptions to the podcast increased almost exponentially and the series became the subject of many media discussions, Cristy and Gaudion spoke regularly, and not always to record his interviews via Zoom. Occasionally he called in the evenings when they were less likely to be interrupted, either by Connor or by one of the Gaudion family, or a phone call one or other of them had to take. Although they never really discussed anything beyond the detail of his interviews, or some general news about their days, she could sense that he was as pleased to be speaking to her as she was to him.

His episodes, when they began to run, turned out to resonate with listeners in a way they really hadn't expected. They'd been bracing for a ferocious pushback; however, the responses, and there was a virtual avalanche of them, were far more positive than negative, and the most interesting part of it was that he never discussed Olivia or the Kellon Manse Murders. He simply talked about Lexie and how much she'd meant to him. It had been his decision to share anecdotes from their happier times and everyone, particularly the romantics, lapped it up. He was erudite and gently spoken as he painted pictures of a lively but sometimes shy little girl who'd loved horses and who'd laughed a lot in spite of being unhappy at home; who was super-intelligent and often bossy, and who'd captured his heart from roughly the age of five. He talked about his hilarious and thwarted efforts to make her his girlfriend during their teen years, and how becoming parents had changed them both in ways they could never have foreseen.

Listening to him, watching his face on the screen as they recorded him reliving the precious times he'd shared with the love of his life, often brought a lump to Cristy's throat. He'd suffered so much injustice, so much abuse and ignorant criticism that he had never deserved, and the kind of loss a lesser man would have been unable to endure. He'd probably never been allowed to grieve properly, and so she wondered if being able to talk about Lexie now was proving a kind of therapy for him.

'Yeah, I guess it is in a way,' he admitted one evening when they talked after the latest episode of *Hindsight* had dropped. She'd made it home by then, knowing he would ring and not wanting to take the call with the others around. 'It makes me feel good to be able to say her name and not worry that people might think I don't have a right to,' he continued. 'OK, I know there are some out there who are still saying I'm guilty, that I've managed to trick the world, but the reality is, doing these podcasts seems to be reconnecting me to her in a way I could never have foreseen, much less hoped for. The girls love listening to them and, between us, Laurent said earlier that he wished Lexie had been his mum she sounds so lovely. Of course we won't tell Juliette that, and obviously he doesn't really mean it. I think he's feeling a bit left out again, so I've planned to take him sailing at the weekend, just us guys. Now, before we move on to what's happening in your world, and I want to know everything, please tell me how well – or not – you think I handled the reasons I hid Anna away for so long? Did it sound credible, or is everyone going to accuse me of a ludicrous overreaction and start turning on me now for being a controlling father who duped everyone, including the police?'

With a smile, she said, 'Well, you didn't exactly hide her away, it's just that no one thought to look over there, and going into your real fears—'

'Paranoia, as it turns out.'

'—really wasn't necessary when most parents will understand why you felt such a profound need to keep her safe. Anyone would if their child had witnessed what Anna had. What does she have to say about it?'

'More than I ever want to hear, thank you, but obviously she knows nothing about Lexie's experience at Oxford, so she's used to my shortened version of why I've been so over-bearing – her word – for a very long time. She has no reason to question it now, but that doesn't stop her getting on my case about it should I be foolish enough to try and tell her what to do now. Incidentally, has she been in touch with you since she rang to apologize?'

Cristy thought back to the hurried, emotional call when Anna had cried, 'I want to say sorry for the way I spoke to you. I shouldn't have done that. I get carried away sometimes, but thanks very much for all you've done for Dad, it means the world to all of us,' and without giving Cristy the chance to respond she'd rung off.

'No, I haven't heard from her again,' she replied. 'I wasn't expecting to, so why do you ask?'

'It was something she said in an email a couple of days ago. I'll have to dig it out to remind myself, so I'll get back to you on it. Now, that really is enough about me. Tell me about you, and I'm not talking about your life as a podcaster. What's the latest in the Matthew and Marley saga?'

With a tired groan, she switched her thoughts to a place they didn't really want to go. 'Well, you know they've been trying to work things out since they got back from France, and the children and I thought for a while that it was going well. No news is good news and all that. However, I found out today that things have taken a bit of a drastic turn. Apparently, Marley went to London to see her agent yesterday, except what she actually did was fly to Los Angeles. The first Matthew knew about it was via a text she sent just before getting on the plane.'

'Jesus,' Gaudion muttered, sounding about as impressed by that as she'd felt when Matthew had called to tell her. 'Don't tell me, he's expecting you to fix it?'

She smiled. 'He hasn't even asked to see me yet, but I'm sure it's coming. Either that or he'll ambush me somewhere, the way he does when he thinks I might refuse to see him.'

'Is she still pregnant?'

'As far as I know, unless she's had a termination she hasn't told him about. I hate to say it's the kind of thing she'd do, but she's so unpredictable.'

'Do you think he'd mind if it turns out she has?'

'I've no idea. He clearly cared about her enough to want to try harder with their marriage . . .'

'After you'd told him you weren't interested.'

'True, but I think her disappearing on him like this has actually hurt him a lot.' She sighed and closed her eyes as her head fell back against the sofa. 'It's all terribly sad really. I'm just glad Hayley's back in Edinburgh and Aiden's staying with me, because dealing with their father right now wouldn't be easy for either of them.'

'How is Aiden?'

Opening her eyes to the detritus her son had left in his wake before dashing out to the waiting Uber, she said, 'Aiden is Aiden, which you'd understand better if you knew him. He's staying over at a friend's tonight who lives much closer to the school so they can go in early in the morning for rugby training. He told me last night that he's managing a new band who are calling themselves the Airheads. He found this so hilarious when he told me that it took him at least six attempts to get the word out and it's not even that funny.'

Gaudion laughed. 'He sounds a character from all you've told me about him.'

'Oh, he's that all right.' Her voice was almost swept away by a swell of love and pride. 'But now, let me tell you who I had a call from today, out of the blue, no reaching out from me or Connor, or carefully worded little prompts on the podcast. Sorry, yes, we're back there, but you'll want to hear this, I promise.'

'Go on,' he said, clearly intrigued.

'Paolo Morelli,' she announced. 'He's insisting we call him that; apparently he hasn't been O'Malley since he was in his teens and Morelli is his maternal grandfather's name. Anyway, would you believe he wants us to record him setting the record straight about Papilio and, I quote, "the vital role it has played in the psychological and spiritual healing of so many troubled souls".'

'Well, that's a turn up,' he commented dryly. 'He's never spoken publicly about his cult, or whatever we're supposed to call it, before, so I wonder why now.'

'I asked the question and he said – again I quote, "Your podcast has misrepresented my goals in some undeservedly negative ways, so I would like to put forward the reality."'

'I see. In other words, he's either losing clients or is finding it difficult to get more.'

'Or both. So, how do *you* feel about us interviewing him?'

'As long as he doesn't get into the detail of Lexie's therapy I won't have a problem with it. I'd be interested to hear what he has to say about Olivia, though.'

'Wouldn't we all, but he's already made it clear that he intends to fully respect client confidentiality where she's concerned, so no chance of it, I'm afraid.'

'Why aren't I surprised? When are you meeting him?'

'We're doing it via Zoom tomorrow. I guess that way we won't know where he is, which seems to be how he likes it. He was interested to know about you, actually. He asked how you are.'

'So you told him to listen to the podcasts?'

'I did, and he said he'd heard them and he thinks you're only dealing with the surface of your emotions, you need to go deeper. Oh, and he's convinced you're hiding something.'

Gaudion gave a bark of laughter. 'OK, I'll bite. Did he say what he thought it was?'

'No, actually, but I'm to tell you he's completely at your disposal should you wish to be in touch.'

'Please thank him on my behalf, but I probably won't be calling any time soon, if I even knew where to call and I don't think anyone does, do they?'

'I have an email address that, history tells us, he only answers when he wants to, or senses he should. Is that Rosaria I can hear singing in the background?'

'I'm afraid so. She's on her way out to rehearsals. I don't know how they can bear it, but somehow they do. I didn't tell her I was talking to you so you can consider yourself spared for this evening.'

Having already been treated to two full-volume renditions of 'A Kiss for a Rose' via FaceTime, Cristy laughed even as her heart melted. 'It makes her so happy to do it that I honestly wouldn't mind watching her every evening.'

'The watching is OK, it's the listening that's the problem. Anyway, I'd best go and find out who's supposed to be taking her, because I have a feeling it's me. Shall we speak again tomorrow after O'Malley's interview? Morelli, sorry. I'll be interested to hear how it goes.'

'Of course, unless my ex-husband throws me some sort of curve, but even if he does I'll speak to you by the weekend.'

After ringing off she sat quietly for a few minutes staring at nothing as she pictured his face, his home, his family, the island where he lived, everything about him including the chemistry that was building between them. They spoke often now, most days, lengthy and enjoyable conversations with promises to speak again soon, yet neither of them ever suggested meeting up anywhere at any time. She wanted to see him, very much, and was sure he felt the same, but maybe, like her, he realized that once the podcast series was over there would be nothing left to keep them in each other's lives. She wasn't going to move to Guernsey and he wouldn't be coming here, so he must surely be asking himself, as was she, what was the point of trying to pretend there might be some sort of future for them when there clearly couldn't be?

CHAPTER FORTY-THREE

The following day Morelli appeared on their computer screens promptly at two looking sun-tanned, silvery-haired and a little pompous with his holier-than-thou smile and saintly head tilt.

After the initial greetings were over and the guru – apparently he didn't mind being called that – confirmed he was ready to go, Connor hit record and so began the longest, dreariest diatribe of self-promotion and *mea*-exculpation Cristy had ever heard.

They let it run, feigning fascination while knowing they wouldn't use even half of it, and trying not to laugh as, in the background, Clover affected giant yawns and Jacks fashioned himself a noose out of paperclips.

In the end, when it became blissfully clear that the man had finished his pre-prepared spiel, Connor stopped recording and Cristy said, 'That was excellent, Mr Morelli. Thank you very much for taking the time to explain your particular form of therapy.' (He hadn't told them anything they hadn't heard before; his methods were simply a little whackier, more colourful perhaps, and a whole lot costlier than most, although he hadn't seemed keen to discuss fees.) 'Before you go,' she continued, 'I wonder if you'd mind answering a few more questions, off the record, of course. Nothing serious, just a few small issues that have intrigued me since we learned about Lexie's therapy, and you're the only one who can clear them up.'

Morelli didn't appear surprised, which probably meant he'd guessed this might happen, and so was ready to assail her with yet more prepared homilies and endless monologues.

Knowing she'd cut him off if he went on too long, or tried to deviate from the point, she said, 'I'm interested to hear whether or not you warned Liam MacAnany, or any of the other men involved in Lexie's attack at Oxford, that she'd named them to you during one of your sessions?'

Morelli didn't move, kept his eyes fixed on the camera, as he gave himself a moment before assuming an expression of bafflement. 'I have no idea what you're talking about,' he replied. 'Who are these people?'

'I've heard a recording of you and Lexie discussing how much it meant to her to finally name her attackers . . .'

'How did you get such a recording?'

'Olivia Caldwell found it amongst Lexie's things.'

Clearly further perturbed, he said, 'Well, I hope you're not intending to use it for your podcast. My discussions with Lexie were – and remain – strictly confidential, and you need to respect that as much as I do.'

'Of course, and we do, but as I said, we're off the record now. So, did you contact Liam MacAnany after discovering he was—'

'I've already told you, I don't know who he is.'

'Are you sure? I mean, most people do, he's such a high-profile political player, and frankly, he told me that you two, both being from Ireland—'

'The answer to your question is no, I did not discuss Lexie's therapy with anyone apart from Serena, and that was only done with Lexie's permission.'

'OK,' Cristy said, not believing him for a moment. 'Are you a member of Frumentarii, by any chance?'

His eyes sharpened. 'I believe you're trying to trap me now . . .'

'It's a perfectly straightforward question that merely requires a yes or no answer.'

'What I know about this organization is that it achieves much for many people around the world, but no, I personally am not a member.'

She held his eyes, trying to stare him down, to push him into admitting some sort of contact with the elite group, but he was better at this than she'd expected, she realized, so accepting she wasn't going to win on this point, she said, with a friendly smile, 'Thank you for your time today. We'll be including your interview in our next episode.'

'In its entirety?'

'I'm afraid that won't be possible, but we should be able to send you the shortened version when it's ready.'

'Please do,' he replied, 'and I would ask, not for the first time, that you refrain from referring to Papilio as a cult. It most certainly is not one and you cause great offence to me, my healers and my clients by calling it so.' A moment later, after thanking them politely, he left the screen.

In the end, they edited his interview down to its most salient points.

MORELLI: 'Thank you for giving me the opportunity to set the record straight regarding Papilio. I'm afraid some people will have listened to your podcasts and gone away with a wholly inaccurate picture of our unique alliance of healers and therapists. So please let me make it clear that secrecy and concealment have no place with us; *privacy* is all we request, and respect for our choices and our methods which are never imposed on anyone against their will. I don't believe that is too much to ask, especially for those who are trying to work through some extremely challenging and in many cases life-inhibiting mental health issues. As I'm sure you're aware, and yet don't see fit to make clear, there have never been any complaints about us either to the British Psychological Society or to the police, or to any other regulatory authority. No clients, current or former, have ever found cause to regret their experiences with us, or to put an end to their counselling out of a sense of dissatisfaction or misunderstanding of our goals. To the contrary, many clients remain connected to us long after their own healing is complete in order to enjoy the confidence-building and spiritual nourishment they achieve from being in regular contact with us.'

CRISTY: 'But you will admit that the cost of membership . . .'

MORELLI: 'We're not a club, there is no need of membership, only of affiliation and discretion.'

CRISTY: 'But to be a part of Papilio is extremely costly?'

MORELLI: 'Each client is encouraged to make donations, but there is no obligation.'

CRISTY: 'Does that mean you treat some people for free?'

MORELLI: 'It means that we leave each individual to decide upon the amounts of their donations, and the frequency with which they make them.'

CRISTY: 'What about the semi-precious butterflies? Do they have to be bought from you?'

MORELLI: 'No, they are provided as gifts.'

CRISTY: 'For the benefit of our listeners, can you explain the point of them?'

MORELLI: 'They are purely symbolic and are given at the completion of each stage of personal enhancement.'

CRISTY: 'How many stages are there?'

MORELLI: 'Six, with a further six if the client requires a more prolonged and deeper form of healing.'

CRISTY: 'I know you don't want to discuss individual cases—'

MORELLI: 'Professional ethics will not allow.'

CRISTY: 'Of course, but it is safe to assume that Lexie Gaudion took part in these stages?'

MORELLI: 'This has already been established, so I'm not sure why you're asking the question.'

CRISTY: 'I'm just trying to get some clarity on your process. So would you mind talking us through the first six stages?'

MORELLI: 'I would, willingly, if you were a client.'

CRISTY: 'Then perhaps you'll tell us at what point the branding comes in?'

MORELLI: 'Your terminology completely misrepresents the meaning of the practice, which is, in fact, nothing more, or less, than a ceremony to celebrate the creation of a bond between the physical and spiritual manifestations of our journey. It is a unique process not undertaken by all, only those who feel the need to connect more fully with their improvement which is sometimes aided by experiencing a brief though intense pain that quickly blossoms into something sublime and beautiful.'

As Connor ended the playback, Meena shivered and said dryly, 'It sounds like some hideous S&M ritual to me. I don't suppose we can say that though.'

'Punters will draw their own conclusions,' Cristy assured her, 'and I don't think they'll be far from yours.'

'Do we put his email address on the website?' Jackson wanted to know.

Cristy and Connor looked at each other. 'Yeah, do it,' Connor told him. 'He can deal with his own feedback; we don't have to do it for him.'

'Off somewhere nice, Cristy?' Meena asked as Cristy began packing up to leave.

Cristy glanced at her in surprise. 'Only home,' she replied. 'Aiden's cooking us a meal this evening and I'd like to get there before he burns the place down.'

Meena laughed. 'I'll walk with you a way if you don't mind waiting for me to get my things.'

A few minutes later they left the building together to begin weaving through the two-way flow of commuters along the waterfront.

'Is everything OK?' Cristy asked when Meena didn't attempt to start a conversation.

Meena nodded. 'I owe you an apology,' she said after a while.

'I'm sorry I got on your case about Gaudion. I had no right to, but I hope you understand—'

'That you were worried. Of course I do. After what happened to Jay Wells, you were right to be concerned. I was myself for a while.'

'And now?'

Cristy sighed as she searched for a suitable reply. 'Now I'm not sure what to think.'

'But something's going on in that lovely head of yours,' Meena responded, 'so here's your opportunity to share. No pressure, no judgements, just an easy chat between friends. The way we always used to.'

Remembering those times well, Cristy realized she was actually glad to have the chance to voice her thoughts out loud, even if she wasn't entirely sure what she wanted to say. 'OK,' she began, deciding simply to let it flow, 'I know we're attracted to one another, it practically crackles down the phone line every time we speak, and if we're on video calls I can see it in his eyes as clearly as I'm sure he can in mine. And the way I think about him sometimes . . .' She laughed and swerved to avoid a cyclist.

'I've seen him,' Meena reminded her when they came together again, 'so no surprise you're having wicked thoughts. Tell me, why don't you go over there, see him in person?'

Why didn't she? She wanted to, but . . . 'He hasn't asked,' she confessed, 'and even if he did . . . What then?'

Meena laughed. 'Are you serious?'

Cristy laughed too. 'OK, I guess we could have a fling and it would be very nice, but . . .'

'But?'

Cristy shrugged. 'I don't know. I'm just not sure it's the right thing to do, is all.'

Taking her by the arm, Meena steered her out of the foot traffic to the iron railings at the water's edge. 'Look at me,' she demanded.

Cristy did.

'Tell me honestly, and remember this is me you're talking to, are you holding back because of Matthew? I know things have gone wrong again there . . .'

'It has nothing to do with him,' Cristy assured her. 'At least not in the way you're thinking, but what happened between us has made it very hard for me to trust again.'

Meena nodded, her chestnut eyes searching and gentle. 'I understand that, I really do,' she said, 'but isn't it time to start having some fun in your life? And to be loved the way you deserve?'

Smiling, Cristy said, 'I'm not sure Gaudion sees me quite that way, but it's wonderful of you to care about me. Thank you.'

'I'll always be here for you, you know that, and so will Harry. Just give a little thought to what I've said, because, my dear friend, it's high time you were happy again.'

By a strange quirk of coincidence, the morning after Morelli's interview episode was uploaded, DI Trevor Thompson contacted Cristy to let her know that a twenty-four-year-old woman had turned herself in over the Iris Newman hit-and-run case.

Jackson and Clover wasted no time getting in touch with Joe Mead, Iris's fiancé, and by the time they came off the phone they'd agreed to help him organize a vigil for the following Saturday.

The whole *Hindsight* team was there on the day, including Harry, Meena and Jodi, and because word had spread by then the crowd spilled out of the park into the streets beyond. It was a moving and joyful occasion with Iris's friends sharing anecdotes about her, making everyone laugh even as they wiped away tears. Cristy videoed some of it and sent it to Gaudion who came back with:

I know you never got to meet her, but it's wonderful of you to be there for her today. It says a lot about you and who you are.

As she wasn't quite sure how to respond to that, she dropped her phone back into her purse and joined in with the song everyone was now singing at the tops of their voices, 'Walking on Sunshine' – one of Iris's favourites.

It was almost four in the afternoon by the time she, Connor and Jodi returned to the office, tired after all the emotional outpouring, and Cristy was more than ready to call it quits for the day. The others had already taken off in their various directions and she wanted to get home to find out what Aiden was up to. However, Connor was keen to complete an edit he'd started the day before so, after texting Aiden and finding out he was at the dry ski slope with some mates, she decided to hang around for a while. There was always plenty to do, and as she still hadn't yet finalized a running order for the next episode she soon had the content up on screen, ready to start moving things around.

It had been a while, she realized as she cut and pasted various links and typed in new content, since she'd felt Gaudion's eyes on her as she worked, but for some reason she was aware of them today and it was making her keener than ever to speak to him. Actually to see him, so perhaps they could FaceTime later, if he was free, but there was a good chance he wouldn't be if he'd taken Laurent sailing again. It didn't matter; they'd had a long chat the other night after Morelli's interview, and at least twice since. It wasn't as if they had to be in touch every day, although they mostly were, and she doubted very much that he was wondering in this moment what she might be doing, or getting himself worked up over when they were going to speak again.

She wasn't worked up; she was just trying to decide whether or not she should have answered his earlier text, and if so, what should she have said?

Ridiculous, she snapped irritably to herself. He probably hadn't even noticed her failure to message back, and she wouldn't be thinking about it either if it weren't for the overriding feeling of him watching her.

'Do you think it's time we took the pictures down?' she said to Connor without looking up.

Remaining intent on his own work, he said, 'Up to you.'

Unplugging one of her AirPods, Jodi said from the sofa, 'Wouldn't it be best to do that once the series is actually over? Although I guess Olivia ought to have centre stage now.'

Agreeing, Cristy got up to start moving things around, and was surprised by the relief she felt when she put Gaudion's headshot next to Lexie's. He was no longer the focus of their attention; that place now belonged to Olivia.

'How many more episodes are you planning?' Jodi asked as Cristy sat down again.

'We'll keep going through Olivia's plea hearing and sentencing,' Cristy replied.

'Do you believe she'll plead guilty?'

Cristy shrugged. 'It's what her lawyer is telling Edmond Crouch, so I have no reason to doubt it – at this stage.'

'So when is the hearing set for?'

'It was supposed to be September the twentieth, but apparently it's been moved on to October the twentieth.'

Jodi grimaced. 'Very close to when Aurora is due,' she reminded Connor.

'Don't worry, Cristy and I have already discussed it,' he assured her. 'I'll be with you and the baby; Cristy will have the hearing covered if it happens then.'

Seeming happy with that, Jodi said, 'If she does plead guilty, will she be sentenced at the same time?'

'I doubt it,' Cristy replied. 'There'll have to be a pre-sentencing report, the lawyers will want to mitigate . . . It could be another two or three months before we know how long she'll be sent down for.'

'It'll be Christmas by then. Are you going to keep the series going that long?'

'We'll have more than enough material,' Connor said, 'and there's tons of stuff we can get more mileage out of.'

'But I thought you guys didn't go in for repetition.'

'We don't, ordinarily, but frankly, the punters seem to love it and the advertisers are fighting for spots; Harry and Meena won't be turning them down in a hurry. And nor will we.'

'I don't think I told you this,' Cristy said, sitting back in her chair, 'Harry's been approached by a couple of the tabloids about—' She broke off as two young women appeared in the doorway and, recognizing one of them, her heart flipped with shock. 'Anna,' she exclaimed. 'What on earth are you doing here?'

'We're just dropping in,' Anna explained hastily. 'Don't want to interrupt or anything. This is my cousin Becca, by the way.'

Cristy's heart skipped another beat as she realized the other young woman with an abundance of curly red hair and haunted eyes was Olivia's twenty-three-year-old daughter. And she was staring straight at the headshot that Cristy had just pinned to the centre of the whiteboards. What horrible, terrible timing.

'I know I apologized to you before,' Anna said, 'but I thought I'd come and do it in person now I'm here. I was out of order talking to you the way I did when you were at the house all those weeks ago, but there again, you didn't actually set out to clear my dad's name, did you? That just happened, so I wasn't entirely wrong.'

Cristy almost wanted to laugh at how *she'd* suddenly become the one who needed to apologize, but Anna hadn't finished.

'And now we're in the horrible position of Becca's mum being blamed for it all,' she declared. 'I mean, we know she did it, because she's told the police she did, and her lawyer, obvs, but it's terrible for Becs and Marcus, her brother. I know how they feel because I've been there with Dad, that's why I came over to get them. Marcus decided to stay with his dad, but Becs needs to get away.'

The girl's face was pale and strained, her eyes red-rimmed and ringed with shadow. She looked exhausted, ravaged by shock and grief, and must surely be terrified of the next minute, never mind the next weeks, months, even years.

'. . . so before we get our flight back to Guernsey,' Anna was saying, 'we wanted to come and ask if you'd mind not running her mum's interviews any more. It's really upsetting for the family, and they're already going through a hell of a lot, so hearing Olivia talking about my mum and dad, saying things that just aren't true, it's like twisting the knife. OK, I know she shouldn't have said it, and Will and the others don't have to listen, but they do, so if you could see your way to dropping it now, we'd be really grateful.'

It was a moment before Cristy realized she was supposed to speak, but even as she began, Anna said, 'You don't have to give us an answer right away, but if you could at least think about it . . . Oh, and if you could not tell Dad I was here, that would be great. Well, you can tell him, but not what I just said. He'll accuse me of being interfering and bossy and he'll try to ground me or something ridiculous, like I'm still a child who has to do as he says.' She checked her iWatch. 'We have to go or we'll miss the flight.'

Forgetting she didn't have her car, Cristy quickly said, 'Can I take you to the airport?'

'It's OK, we've got a taxi waiting out on the street. Thanks for listening and if you can see your way to dropping—' She broke off as Becca whispered something in her ear, then said, 'She's right, I've made the point and we need to hurry, so bye, sorry if we interrupted something important,' and they left as swiftly and quietly as they'd arrived.

Feeling a little as though they'd been hit by a small whirlwind, Cristy laughed and shook her head as she looked at the others. 'Well, that was nothing if not timely,' she remarked. 'I was starting to tell you about Harry being approached by the tabloids for a transcript of Olivia's interviews.'

'Oh,' Jodi exclaimed worriedly. 'I suppose they've offered small fortunes and Harry is already negotiating them up.'

'He probably would be if he hadn't mentioned it to me first,' Cristy replied. 'I told him that our repeats of the interviews were probably bad enough for the family; having them plastered all over the papers was only going to add to their suffering, so the answer ought to be no. Amazingly, he agreed.'

Connor looked astonished and immediately sceptical. 'Harry agreed to turn down what must have been thousands?' he declared, clearly not believing it.

Cristy grinned. 'Actually, Meena did, and we know Harry doesn't much care to argue with her.'

Laughing, Jodi said, 'So that was Gaudion's youngest daughter? She's quite something, isn't she? And looks exactly like her mother. Are you going to tell him she was here?'

Cristy gave it a moment. 'It depends on what she tells him herself,' she said, 'and my guess is he'll know everything within minutes of that plane landing in Guernsey.' Taking out her phone as it rang, half-expecting it to be him, her spirits sank when she saw it was Matthew.

'Hello, Matthew,' she said, so the others would know who it was. 'How are you?'

'I've been better,' he replied, actually sounding terrible. 'Are you at home? Is Aiden with you?'

'No and no. I'm at work and he's at the dry ski slope.'

'OK, good. Can I see you?'

In spite of wishing she could turn him down, he sounded so wretched that she simply didn't have the heart to.

CHAPTER FORTY-FOUR

THREE MONTHS LATER

'Are you absolutely sure about this?' Matthew asked, looking very much as though he couldn't believe she would be.

'I'm sure,' Cristy replied, dipping a biscotti into her coffee and taking a bite.

He watched her eat, then turned to stare down at the busy airport check-in area while she gazed past him, absently following the flow of travellers riding an escalator up to the mezzanine level where she and Matthew were sitting in a café next to the security lanes.

Turning to her, he said, 'You can always back out, you know.'

Puzzled, she said, 'Why would I want to do that? I'm very happy to be going.'

His expression remained doubtful and confused. He stirred two sugars into his coffee and waited for a flight announcement to finish before speaking again. Whatever he'd been about to say didn't make it past his intake of breath.

'It's going to be fine,' she told him, almost reaching across the table to squeeze his hand.

He didn't look at her, simply returned to his scrutiny of the queues below as if he couldn't quite figure out what they were doing there. 'The man's a killer, for God's sake,' he said.

Anger sparked in Cristy's eyes. 'Why would you, of all people, say something so stupid?' she snapped.

He glanced down at his coffee. 'Sorry,' he mumbled. 'It's just—'

'The kind of prejudice only truly ignorant people are guilty of,' she finished for him sharply. 'That's what it is.'

'OK, OK, I take it back. Everyone knows he didn't do it, but frankly I wish he had – you wouldn't be going then.'

Swallowing more impatience, she said, 'You're being childish now, so let's change the subject. It was kind of you to drive me here, you really didn't have to, and if me going is proving too difficult for you . . . Well, there's no need to hang around . . .'

'I want to. I don't know when I might see you again.'

Realizing they'd just been recognized by someone at the next table, she leaned in a little closer. 'It's when you're going to see Marley again that you should be thinking about. Have you booked a flight yet?'

He nodded. 'Christmas Eve.'

'But that's not for another three weeks.'

'I can't get away any sooner.'

Certain he could if he tried, she said, 'And you'll stay at least until after the New Year?'

'Of course.' He sipped his coffee and managed a smile as a heavyset man from the neighbouring table greeted him warmly.

'Watch you every night,' he stated proudly. 'Wife's got a bit of a crush on you, she has.'

'Oh Terry!' the plump, blonde wife protested. 'You're such an embarrassment.' To Matthew and Cristy she said, 'Lovely to see you two together. Going somewhere nice?'

'For God's sake, Mum,' a teenage girl growled from behind her iPhone.

The woman chuckled and waved an apology before ploughing on. 'Haven't missed a single episode of your podcast, Cristy. None of us have. What a turn up, eh, when we found out it was the sister. Evil bitch. What sort of person does something like that—'

'*Mum!*' the girl seethed, sliding lower in her chair.

'She deserved a lot more than ten years,' the woman ran on, undeterred. 'Should have got life. Just cos she didn't pull the trigger, makes no difference, does it? Wouldn't have happened if it weren't for her. Anyway, just wanted to say you and Connor did a brilliant job.'

'Thank you,' Cristy smiled, appreciating the feedback, while also hoping the woman was finally done.

Apparently she was, at least with them, although she continued discussing Olivia's sentence with her family in a voice that wasn't easy to tune out.

Making an effort, Cristy looked at Matthew again. 'Where were we?' she asked.

'She's right,' he told her, 'Olivia Caldwell should have gone down for longer. I bet your boyfriend was disappointed with the sentence.'

Gritting her teeth, she said, 'He's not my *boyfriend* – what decade are you in? – and he was actually more concerned about Olivia's family and what the sentence would mean to them.'

With a grunt he said, 'You have to admit she got off lightly.'

'I said as much in the pod, if you were listening, but her lawyer was a good mitigator and I think, for the record, that she genuinely regrets what she did.'

'Including framing her brother-in-law?'

Having no idea how Olivia felt about that, Cristy simply shook her head, and tried not to see Olivia's ashen face as she'd stood in the dock staring at the judge, listening, and yet hardly seeming to register his words as he delivered his summing up.

Watching from the public gallery, Cristy had felt far more moved than she'd expected to, had even for a moment seemed to connect with Olivia's anguish and fear, all the guilt and desperate sorrow she was clearly suffering. She'd had to remind herself that this woman, who'd quite probably been in love with Gaudion for most of her life, had been perfectly prepared to let him go to prison for something she knew he hadn't done. Same for Wayne Ryall – he'd have let it happen too if it weren't for the cancer. No sentence for him, of course, unless death counted, and knowing that Gaudion's lawyer was going to extreme lengths to get money to Ryall's daughter without it being traced back to him or Gaudion still made her slightly queasy.

When the judge had finally pronounced the term to be served, it had seemed to take Olivia a moment to fully understand that she wasn't going down for life. Her hands flew to her face and her narrow shoulders began to shake uncontrollably as an officer stepped in to hold her upright. Two rows in front of Cristy, Becca, her brother, father and grandfather, were weeping too. Cristy watched them, feeling deeply sorry for their bitter-sweet relief, and almost flinched when Will Caldwell turned to shoot her a look that seemed like triumph, as if she had somehow lost today and they'd won.

That had been two weeks ago, and Cristy still couldn't quite shake the feeling that look had left her with; however, what had affected her more was the way Olivia had put her hands together to thank her family for being there for her. 'I'm sorry, I love you,' she'd mouthed, and as her eyes met Cristy's she gave a brief, indecipherable nod before being led away.

'Have you been in touch with her?' Matthew asked, moving past his unanswered question.

'I've tried,' she replied. 'It was like she was saying something to me that day in court, but I've no idea what it was. Maybe she was telling me justice had been done and I should rest easy with that, even if she couldn't. Or maybe she was attempting to convey something a whole lot more sinister. I guess I won't know unless she agrees to see me, and she won't at the moment.'

'What about the family?'

'Same for them, but I can't say I blame them. There's been so much publicity surrounding the case, largely thanks to *Hindsight*, that I'm sure they'd prefer to forget we even exist.'

Nodding his understanding of that, Matthew said, 'Has *he* forgiven her?'

Suppressing her irritation, she said, 'If you mean David Gaudion, the answer is, it's not a conversation we've had, but I can tell you he's not a vindictive man. I think he's just glad the truth is out there now so that he and his family can get on with their lives.'

'And you're going to be a part of that.'

It wasn't a question, so she needn't have answered; however, she decided to remind him that she was only going to Guernsey for a few days and would be back in the middle of next week.

'Until you go again for Christmas, taking my children with you,' he stated sourly. 'To stay in his big fuck-off house in the middle of a tax haven . . .'

'Actually, we won't be staying in the house. There are cottages nearby; the children and I will be in one of them. And they had a choice, Matthew, they could be going to LA with you, but why would they want to when things are still so problematic between you and Marley? I think they had enough of that in the summer.'

His jaw tightened at the reminder. 'I don't think they like Marley very much,' he said as if they'd in some way been responsible for the disharmony in France.

Deciding not to deny it, she said, 'They blamed her for the break-up of our family, for the misery and humiliation it put them through, and for the way she seemed to matter to you more than they did.'

'That's never been true.'

'It's how they saw it, and actually it *was* true, but there's nothing to be gained from dredging it all up again now. Life has moved on and they love you too much to want to cut you out of their lives.'

'They tried—'

'But it didn't last. You're their father, for God's sake. They care about you now as much as they ever did. Granted, they might have some respect issues going on, but you only have yourself to blame for that.'

'OK, I'm a total fuck-up, let's get it out there.'

'If you want to repair things properly with them,' she pressed on, 'maybe you could try to make things work with Marley, if only for the baby's sake. Be a dad, the kind of dad you were for them.'

He took a breath, almost as if she'd winded him, and as he stared at her, his face bloodless and tired, his eyes showing his inner torment and loss of direction, she almost wanted to soothe away the sting of her words.

'You realize Marley can't come back to England with me, don't you?' he said. 'She's too far gone now, they won't let her fly.'

'But you'll go out there for the birth?'

492

'She wants me to and I guess I'm keen to see the little fella, or I will be by then.'

Cristy waved a goodbye to the annoying family as they headed off for their flight, and said, 'I know this is difficult, Matthew, and I wish I could make it easier for you—'

'If you came with me to LA you would.'

'For heaven's sake, what's wrong with you?' she cried in frustration. 'I can't do that and you know it. Marley wants *you* in the baby's life, not me . . .'

'You know she wants you too, but OK, let's not have that argument again. I get that you don't want any more children, or not mine anyway—'

'Don't go there,' she warned darkly.

'Go where?' he said, puzzled.

'You're feeling sorry for yourself and it's starting to get on my nerves. It's time to man up and face your responsibilities – you'll feel a lot better if you do.'

He was hurt, she could see it as he cast a glance to a noisy hen party who'd just taken the vacant table. 'What would make me feel better,' he growled at her, 'is you coming back to me, but OK, OK,' his hands went up, 'another discussion we're not going to have again.'

She was momentarily saved by a security announcement. When they could hear one another again, she said, 'Is Marley's father in LA?'

He nodded.

'Well, that's good, isn't it? You get on well with him. You have so much in common, being the same age and all.'

It took a while, but finally he cracked a smile and she wondered if, like her, he was remembering how she'd always had a knack for teasing him out of a morbid mood or a tearing fury over something that had ruined his day. Gone were those times, and yet, here she was, doing it again.

'He is actually a great guy,' he admitted grudgingly. 'Not sure how he ended up with such a whacky daughter, but hey, look at us, we've got Aiden and there's nothing wrong with us.'

She laughed and for a moment she felt closer to him than she had for a long time.

'What are you thinking?' he asked as though sensing it might be something he wanted to hear.

'That I should probably go through now,' she replied, knowing better than to encourage any hope in him.

His dismay showed as he watched her get up from the table.

'Are you going to stay there?' she asked when he didn't make a move.

Draining his coffee, cold by now, he stood and followed her through the café to where a short queue was forming at the fast-track security lane.

She turned to him, already dreading the goodbye, and almost resisting as he pulled her into his arms. Instead she hugged him back and realized, sadly, that they still seemed to fit. Then she was worrying about how he was going to feel when she let go and walked away.

'I'll miss you,' he murmured against her hair. 'I already do.'

Easing back to look at him, she said, softly, 'I'll always be in your life, Matthew, nothing and no one will ever change that.'

Two hours later Cristy wheeled her weekend bag into the Arrivals Hall at Guernsey airport and her heart flipped with the surprise and pleasure of finding Gaudion waiting for her. He'd said it might be his mother, or Anna, or even a taxi if he had to fetch Laurent home from the hospital. But there he was, standing watching her, tall, familiar and far too good-looking for a man his age, and clearly every bit as glad to see her.

As they approached one another she was vaguely aware of someone nearby videoing the moment, but she didn't much care as he slipped a hand under her hair, cupping her neck, and pressed a kiss gently to her mouth. The sensation of it flooded through her with such force she almost gasped.

'Hi,' he said huskily, and she realized their touch had sent a potent heat through him too. It seemed that waiting so long to see one another again had intensified the chemistry.

'Hi,' she echoed, and they continued gazing at each other, taking in the moment, adjusting to this new reality as a small crowd milled around them and a brass band began playing 'Away in a Manger'.

'Thanks for coming,' he said softly. 'It's going to mean the world to her.'

She could tell it did to him too. 'Does she know I'm coming?' she asked.

He tilted his head, a teasing light in his eyes. 'She knows it's possible, but we warned her about flight delays and how you might have to cancel if something important came up.'

'Nothing's more important than her opening night,' she smiled. 'You must know that.'

He laughed. 'We're in time,' he said, 'the car's just across the road,' and taking her bag he entwined his fingers through hers to walk them outside.

'How's Laurent?' she asked as he paid for the parking.

'You're about to see for yourself. He's in the car. I made him wait out here while I came in to get you.'

Amused by that, she said, 'Are the others already at the theatre?'

'They are. Mum will save our seats and Anna's backstage helping Rosie with her costume. My brother Richard is here with his wife, Astrid, and both their children. And if that isn't enough Gaudions for you, I'm afraid you'll probably be mobbed by the extended family at a party after the performance.'

'There's to be a party?' she said. 'I'll look forward to it.'

'OK, young man,' he said, opening the passenger door of the car, 'time to get in the back, but say hello first.'

Cristy smiled as a gangly young lad with a mop of inky dark curls and his left arm in a sling, quickly unclipped his seatbelt and stepped out to greet her. He was tall for eleven and his face was almost angelic. 'Hey,' he said cheerily, 'I'm Laurent. Nice to meet you, Cristy.'

'Nice to meet you too,' she said, shaking his free hand. 'Sorry about your injury. Broken collarbone, is that right?'

He nodded. 'At least I didn't have to have surgery, so they let me go home. Did Dad tell you, someone famous was in the hospital at the same time as me?'

'Oh?' Cristy said, flicking a quick look at Gaudion.

'Yeah, Stuart Masters,' Laurent declared. 'You might not have heard of him, but he runs the sailing club here and he's *nearly as famous as Dad.*'

Treating him to a playful cuff, Gaudion pointed to the rear door, and went to drop Cristy's bag in the boot while she lowered herself into the passenger seat.

'Rosie is going to be super-chuffed when she knows you're here,' Laurent informed her as they drove away. 'She can't wait for you to meet Judy Moore. Judy's the director, and she's really cool.'

'Why don't you message Grandma and let her know we're on our way?' Gaudion suggested.

'Oh, yeah, *bien sûr*,' and whipping out his phone he got right to it.

'As you can see,' Gaudion said as they began winding through the narrow roads of the High Parishes, frequently passing small clutches of brightly lit cottages with Santas on the roofs and reindeer in the gardens, 'we do Christmas here.'

Cristy smiled. 'Have you put a tree up at home yet?'

'Yes,' Laurent cried, 'we've got a massive one. Anna did most of the decorating, but we helped, didn't we, Dad?'

'When she allowed us. We went early,' he explained to Cristy, 'because of the party.'

'It's going to be at the house?' Cristy asked in surprise.

'Rosie invited everyone,' Laurent told her, 'so we had to do it, but we don't mind, do we Dad?'

'Not really,' Gaudion answered wryly. 'Have you sent that message yet?'

'Yes.'

'Then find someone else to message while Cristy and I try to talk.'

'No probs. I want to find out if my mates are there yet anyway.'

As he went to it, Gaudion glanced at Cristy and said quietly, 'It's really good to see you.'

'I heard that,' Laurent shouted.

Laughing, Cristy said, 'I was beginning to think this day might never come.'

He cocked her a look. 'I hope you're not blaming me for that.'

'Well, you never invited me.'

'I could say you never invited me either, but I realized you still had a lot going on with the podcast and I didn't want to put you in an awkward position.'

'You wouldn't have, but it's fine, I'm here now and that's what matters.'

He cast her another look, but it was too dark to see his expression.

'So, have you really wrapped the series up now?' he asked as they slowed to take a sharp bend.

'We have,' she confirmed, 'apart from all the press interviews we keep being asked to do about it.'

'And radio shows, and TV features, and other podcasts and town hall talks,' he said dryly. 'Which is why you have to get back next week?'

'Connor doesn't like to do the rounds on his own, and besides, he's keen to be at home with the baby as much as he can, so I need to do my bit.'

'How is she?'

'Aurora is a six-week-old night owl. Sleeps all day and wants attention all night, so poor Connor is struggling to keep his eyes open half the time. He's loving being a dad though.'

'My dad does too,' Laurent chipped in. 'Don't you, Dad?'

'Only sometimes,' Gaudion growled at him.

Enjoying their banter, Cristy said, 'They asked me to tell you – Connor and Jodi – that they'd love to take one of the other cottages over Christmas if the offer's still open.'

'Sure it is,' he responded, clearly pleased. 'It'll be great to see them. How about Jodi's mother? You said she might come too.'

'She's going to Jodi's sister instead. She doesn't like ferries, and anyway, it's Carmen's turn this year. And I guess with the baby still being so young she won't miss out too much on her first Christmas.'

'Dad said your children are coming too,' Laurent piped up. 'Hayley and Aiden.'

'That's right,' she replied, turning slightly so he could hear her better, 'although at nineteen and sixteen they're not really children any more. We'll drive over,' she told Gaudion.

As he nodded, Laurent said, 'When I'm eighteen I'll either go to uni in Paris or London, I haven't made up my mind yet. Dad says London, Mum says Paris, Anna thinks I should go to *New York*.'

'Laurent,' Gaudion said softly, 'can it now, there's a good lad.'

Laurent laughed. 'At least I don't talk as much as Rosie.'

'Don't you believe it.'

'We'll have plenty of time later,' Cristy reminded him, wondering how long it might be before the teenage silences kicked in; he was going to be lucky to get more than a grunt then.

'That's where we do rehearsals,' Laurent cried as they passed a large white building that gleamed for a moment in the darkness and was gone again. 'I was being a monster in the panto until this stupid injury happened. I got it playing rugger, but it doesn't hurt very much.'

'That's good. Can you take the sling off at night?'

'I'm not supposed to, but I think I will. Grandma's just texted back to say welcome to Guernsey. She's already saved our seats, but the numbers are here in case you don't have them.'

'Can I say something now?' Gaudion asked.

Laurent laughed as he gave the go ahead.

'I've just taken a wrong turn, so we'll have to turn around.'

'Oh, Dad! How did you do that?'

'I guess auto pilot to home,' Gaudion replied, checking the rear-view mirror as he backed into someone's driveway. 'Either that, or something distracted me.'

Less than twenty minutes later they were parked outside the island's leisure centre and heading up the ramp to go inside, with Laurent running on ahead to announce their arrival.

'Everything happens here,' Gaudion told her as they entered the main lobby straight into a cacophonous crowd with Christmas music playing over the speakers and the clink of glasses mingling with whoops of laughter and the first call to seats. The atmosphere was hectic and joyous and the heady aromas of pine scented cones and mulled wine mingled sublimely with the bleachy smell of the swimming pool.

Gaudion was immediately drawn into the crowd, taking her with him, and introducing her to so many she knew she'd never remember them all.

'What can I get you to drink?' someone offered.

Cristy turned to find a shorter, stockier version of Gaudion smiling at her, whisky glass in one hand, the other outstretched to greet her. 'Richard,' he told her, 'it's good to finally meet you.'

'You too. Did you come by private plane?'

He gave a shout of laughter. 'Not a habit,' he assured her. 'So what will you have?'

'It's time to go in,' Gaudion told him as another bell sounded around the lobby, 'but bring some wine and glasses. Are you sitting near us?'

'Right behind, apparently. Astrid's gone backstage,' he informed Cristy, 'but she should be out soon, hopefully with Mum.'

As they filed slowly towards the theatre doors, Cristy was aware of Gaudion close behind her, hand on her arm as he chatted with those he knew, which seemed to be just about everyone. The excitement for the panto's opening night was as touching as it was infectious, and Cristy could hardly believe how many had turned out all dressed up as if for a West End show. More impressive still was the size and spectacle of the auditorium when they got inside; it could easily rival, perhaps even outclass, any provincial theatre she'd ever seen. The near four hundred seats, all perfectly raked, were filling up fast, and as the orchestra tuned up in the sunken pit stage-front, the lighting and sound engineers were busy in boxes and up on gantries. The huge, blue velvet curtains were currently closed, but the width of the stage was more than evident, and on the steps leading up each side intriguing pieces of scenery were visible.

A tavern, if she remembered correctly.

As they reached their seats in the middle of the centre row, Cynthia came from the other direction, chuckling and beaming as she pulled Cristy into a welcoming embrace.

'Lovely that you came,' she whispered as the third bell rang. 'We've all been looking forward to seeing you.'

'Same here,' Cristy whispered back. 'How's Rosie?'

'Excited, nervous, looking a treat in her dress. I don't think she knows you're here yet . . . Oh, yes please,' she said as Richard pushed a glass of wine towards her.

'Cristy?' he offered, holding up the bottle.

'Lovely,' she replied, wondering if it was allowed, but why worry if they weren't?

'Are you OK?' Gaudion asked her as he took two glasses from his brother and handed one to her.

'Hi, Cristy,' a voice whispered from behind.

Cristy turned to find that a slim, pretty woman with a platinum bob and large dark eyes was now sitting next to Richard. 'I'm Astrid,' she said. 'We'll speak later, but welcome.'

Cristy saluted her with her glass and wondered if she was starting to feel a tad overwhelmed. She sipped her wine, and turned to Gaudion as he said, 'I meant to ask you . . . We've got quite a lot of people staying over at the house tonight so I wondered if you'd mind sharing?'

She blinked, not sure what to say.

'With me?' he added, his mouth very close to her ear.

A sweep of lust rushed through her.

'Yeeeees! She's here! Judy! Judy! She's here.' The voice, unmistakably Rosaria's, tore out from behind the scenes, making everyone turn to see who might have arrived.

'She knows now,' Cynthia murmured.

Cristy was so moved she almost wanted to cry, while Gaudion had lowered his head into one hand, his shoulders shaking with laughter.

Suddenly the orchestra struck up with the opening medley and gradually everyone stopped talking. The chosen songs were so lively and familiar and so rousing that Cristy felt a burst of exuberance.

Then the curtains parted and the music changed to 'Dancing in the Street', and it was all she could do not to dance too. The choreography was so joyful and energetic that she almost missed Rosaria waving and blowing kisses from the wings.

'She can't actually see us,' Gaudion said in her ear.

Nevertheless, Cristy blew kisses back, and laughed and sobbed as someone hooked Rosaria off stage.

She turned to Gaudion and seeing he was still laughing, she leaned in closer and said, 'To answer your question.'

He frowned curiously.

'About us sharing? That should be fine,' and as his eyebrows rose she matched the look before turning back to give the performance her full attention.

ACKNOWLEDGEMENTS

First and foremost, I want to thank TV news reporter and prolific crime-podcaster, Robert Murphy. Thank you so much Rob for sharing your vast experience of producing podcasts. Listening to your many and extremely varied series was not only immensely informative, but was also, and continues to be, incredibly inspirational. If any of you are interested in a highly professional and detailed approach to investigations, interviews and analysis, and you haven't already subscribed to Rob Murphy's *Behind the Crimes* podcast, then you have a lot of gripping cold cases and undercover operations to get stuck into. You can subscribe at www.robertmurphy.substack.com.

Much love and a huge thank you to Judy Moore, Rosie's great heroine and super-cool producer of amateur theatre and Christmas panto. Thank you, Judy, for sharing your invaluable insider knowledge of Guernsey, for taking us to all the locations we needed for the book and for introducing us to some of the island's best restaurants.

Thank you to John and Maggie Meller, owners of the Rocquette Cider Farm, for such generous hospitality and for the wild and unforgettable tour of the orchards. Your beautiful home provided much inspiration for *Papillon* although, of course, there are huge differences – I wouldn't want anyone to think that I was invading privacy.

Thank you to Dale Action of Boatworks in Guernsey for talking me through his company's operations and showing me around the yard.

Thank you to Randy Wallace of Jackson, Tennessee for such ready and helpful guidance regarding firearms. I was extremely touched by how swiftly and thoroughly you responded when I approached you, out of the blue, requesting information that might have set anyone else's alarm bells ringing.

Much love and thanks to everyone involved in publishing this book. Being a part of the HarperCollins family is a joy and an honour. The response to Cristy Ward and her team has been phenomenally uplifting, and thanks to all your amazing support I'm now deeply into bringing forward more cases for the *Hindsight* team to investigate.

Don't miss the next thriller from
Susan Lewis . . .

Don't Believe a Word

**They raised me. Nurtured me.
And lied about everything.**

Sadie's childhood has always been
shrouded in mystery.
But there are three things she knows.

She was raised by two aunts.
She never knew her parents.
She is convinced she was stolen.

Cristy Ward, podcast host, is gripped
by Sadie's story. It's perfect for her
next true-crime investigation.
Yet Sadie's aunt claims it's all a fantasy.

As the evidence begins to stack up, and
the lies fall apart, they all could be in a lot
more danger than they thought...